The Seamstress of Fortune

Terri O'Mahony

POOLBEG

This novel is entirely a work of fiction. The names, characters and incidents portrayed in it are the work of the author's imagination. Any resemblance to actual persons, living or dead, events or localities is entirely coincidental.

Published 2005
by Poolbeg Press Ltd
123 Grange Hill, Baldoyle
Dublin 13, Ireland
E-mail: poolbeg@poolbeg.com

1 3 5 7 9 10 8 6 4 2

A catalogue record for this book is available from the British Library.

ISBN 1-84223-201-0

Typeset by Patricia Hope in Palatino 9.6/13.5
Printed by Litografia Rosés S.A., Spain

www.poolbeg.com

About the Author

Terri O'Mahony is a native of Limerick and is a natural storyteller. She has been writing from an early age and has contributed short stories and articles published in *Woman's Way*, *The Messenger* and *Ireland's Own*. She was runner-up in the Ian St James Awards in the early 1980s and had short stories broadcast on Gay Byrne's morning radio show.

She has four daughters and one son and works full-time as a civil servant for Limerick Local Authority. Her first novel, *The Windbreaker Season,* was published by Poolbeg in 2004.

Acknowledgements

Thank you to all at Poolbeg for your support and assistance in helping me to get *Seamstress* published. A special thank-you to Paula and Lynda and Claire, to Kieran, and to all those beavering away in the background with their expert touch giving my book the finishing touches.

A big thank-you to Lucy Taylor, my editor, for all her hard work and her expertise and for calming my fears when I thought I just couldn't go that extra mile . . . thank you for your reassurance.

To Dad, who is showering me with prayers and good wishes from Heaven above, to Mam, my constant support and confidante, without her life would be so much more difficult and to my lovely children, Joy, Laura, Roseanne, Valerie and John, my love always.

Laura, thank you for all your help in getting the manuscript ready for print when my computer decided to call it a day – your help was so much appreciated.

Roseanne – thank you for deciphering P.C. language and making it easier for me to understand.

To my sisters, Eleanor and Audrey, and my brother Roger – it's good to know family are there if you need them.

To Fred – our terrier with an attitude – we wouldn't have him any other way!

To Geraldine – thank you always for your friendship.

With love to Mam, Joy, Laura, Roseanne,
Valerie and John
in loving appreciation for all your support.

Chapter 1

Hannah found it hard to sleep. It was her last night under her parents' roof in the little house in Glenmore. She looked through the window at the star-studded sky from the bed which she shared with her two younger sisters. There was just a year between them, but to Hannah she felt as though she was years older. In the last months of 1899 the world was an exciting prospect for a young girl about to embark on the greatest adventure of her lifetime.

May and Florrie were sleeping one on either side of her, May's habitual snoring, a sort of whistling sound through her nose, seemed more pronounced than ever tonight. Hannah tossed impatiently in the bed and gave her a sharp jab in the ribs.

"May! For pity's sake, turn on your side like a good girl. I can't hear myself think with the racket you're making, and I have an early start in the morning."

May grunted in her sleep and turned grudgingly

towards the wall, the bed creaking arid groaning under her weight.

Hannah stared at the ceiling, her mind in a turmoil. She didn't want to sleep just yet. She had so many things to think about, so many plans to make before morning. Tomorrow would be her eighteenth birthday and she would be leaving home, going to her aunt's house in the city of Limerick. Her mother had agreed that it was the best thing for her to get away from Glenmore, and maybe find a suitable job in the city. Her father had said nothing, but Hannah had seen the sadness in his eyes every time he looked at her lately, and she knew how he would miss her.

Of the three girls, Hannah was most like him with her quiet, determined stubbornness, her frustration with her lot, her keen awareness that she was capable of much more than her position in life allowed. Peter Benson knew that it was now too late for him to realise the dreams and ambitions he had entertained before he had married Peggy, Hannah's mother. Times had been hard, and when coachbuilding had started up in the village, he had been grateful to get a job there. Hannah had been born a year after their marriage, May and Florrie following soon after. Family commitments had been more important than idle ambitions and Peter Benson was never a man to shirk his responsibilities.

Their life had been a happy one, apart from the odd week when the coachyard had been closed, waiting for building materials to come from the city. Those had been the lean times, with Peggy and the girls working well into the night with their lacemaking, delicately patterned table-cloths, lace-edged sheets and pillowcases, and Hannah making stylish dresses for the more affluent ladies living on the outskirts of Glenmore. The money they earned for their expert handiwork was far less than the amount they would have received in the larger towns and cities, but they were never in a position to bargain with their customers. Every penny counted when Peter was out of work.

Hearing the click of her parents' bedroom door, Hannah realised that her mother was only now going to bed. She had been working late again tonight, Hannah thought, angry that her mother should have to work such long hours for so little in return. Treated like dirt, sometimes her intricate lacework was thrown back at her because she had been a day late in completing the order. Hannah's eyes narrowed bitterly in the dark room.

She was turning into a beautiful young woman, everyone said, taking after her mother in looks, with her long flame-coloured hair and startling blue eyes. "Like cornflowers", one of the lads in the village had described them when she had met him one evening on her way home. Hannah had blushed and turned away self-consciously.

It had given her a feeling of immense satisfaction to think that, no matter how humble her present circumstances were, she still had the power to turn fiery young men into fawning admirers. It was a talent, she thought calculatingly, that would serve her well when she went to the city, for there could be little difference between village boys and young city dandies.

Hannah clenched her fists now beneath the covers. If she ever married, it would be to a rich and powerful man who would treat her as she deserved. She would live in a big house with lots of servants, and if there were children, a prospect that had little appeal to Hannah, there would be a nursemaid to look after them. She had read books and studied carefully the behaviour of gentlewomen in the big cities. She knew the way they walked, the way they spoke, all the little things necessary to cultivate that finesse that seemed to come so naturally to the upper classes. In time, she would become one of them. She wasn't going to Limerick merely to work in a shop selling trifles to well-bred ladies. She had ambitions, and she would fulfil them, no matter how long it would take. Nobody would stop her.

She had seen her mother grow old before her time, dark shadows deepening beneath the once brilliant eyes. The intricate lacework had taken its toll, working late into the night with only the light from a dim candle to guide her fingers. An idea had grown in Hannah's mind, a vision of her own future, and she had thought it through, making calculations, until finally she had everything in perspective.

She did not confide in her parents as they would see her plans as wildly impossible but she had written to her Aunt Annie in Limerick with a hint at what she had in mind. Annie was a woman of the world, and used to business matters, for Uncle John had his own business in the city. She would be able to judge if Hannah's idea was a sensible one. Yes, Annie would advise her, Hannah thought drowsily, and finally closed her eyes as the pale morning light slowly filtered through the window.

There was griddle cake for breakfast, and fresh brown eggs were bubbling in the pot over the fire when the girls came into the kitchen.

"Eggs for breakfast!" May exclaimed. "It's Hannah's

birthday, and the day she's leaving home to start a new life in the city."

Peggy turned to her eldest daughter with a smile. "Come now, get a good breakfast inside you and many happy returns of the day, Hannah!" She took a small package from the mantelpiece and handed it to Hannah. "It's not very much, I'm afraid."

"Mother, you shouldn't have! I didn't want anything." Hannah opened the package and inside lay a delicate cream lace collar, its texture so fine that she hesitated before handling it. She gasped with pleasure. "You've been up half the night doing this especially for me, haven't you?" she demanded, wrapping an arm around her mother's slight shoulders. Tears of anger welled up in her eyes. "I'll repay you and Father some day for all you've done for me. Things are going to get better from now on. Just wait and see!"

Peter Benson came into the room. He was a fine-looking man, his broad, powerful build dwarfing his wife's delicate frame. He wasn't a man to display emotion, relying on his wife's sensitive nature to convey to the girls his unquestioning love for all of them. Today was different. He stood in front of Hannah, his fingers trembling as he touched her soft hair for a moment.

"My little Hannah! How the years have flown." Glancing at Peggy, who nodded, he took an envelope from his pocket and handed it solemnly to his eldest daughter. "This is for you. There's some money in there to help you over the first few months settling into the city."

Hannah opened her mouth to protest, but he ignored her.

"I don't want Annie and John to think that we would expect them to feed and look after you for nothing."

"I'll soon be earning my keep, Father. There's no need for this." She tried to force the envelope back into his hand.

"No, Hannah. You take the money and use it wisely. You know nothing of city life, and the money will make you independent."

Hannah opened the envelope slowly, pulled out the notes, and stood surveying them incredulously. "Fifty pounds, Father! I cannot take this, not when I know you need it so badly here at home!"

"Your mother and I have agreed, Hannah. The money is yours. The Bensons don't take charity from anybody, not even from their own family. John and Annie are good people, but we must be independent. Always remember that!"

Hannah kissed him gently on the forehead and nodded. "I understand, Father, and I'll accept the money gladly, for I'm not so foolish that I don't know it will be needed in the city. But, mark you, every penny will be repaid."

"Just remember all that you have been taught at home, Hannah, all the values your mother and I have tried to teach you ever since you were a little girl." His face was earnest now, his eyes holding hers with a force compelling her to listen. She knew that in his own simple way he was trying to prepare her for leaving home. "Be honest and trustworthy. Never make Annie and John ashamed of you. Make your own way in the world with as little help as possible from others. You're a strong, determined girl, Hannah, and I know you'll be able to cope with any setbacks that might come your way."

Silence hung over the kitchen now, Peter's words affecting them all deeply. It was seldom he spoke like this, and the solemnity of the occasion touched each one of them. Peggy looked at each of her daughters in turn, the look of a mother realising that for the first time her family were about to spread their wings, Hannah the first to leave her protection.

May and Florrie stood together in the corner, sobbing quietly, already feeling the emptiness of Hannah's departure. May dried her eyes on a corner of her apron and took a small package from her pocket. "We've got something for you too, Hannah," she said. Hannah unwrapped the little gift and a silver thimble fell into the palm of her hand. "It's something to make you think of us whenever you feel sad or lonely." Hannah held out her arms to her two sisters and they ran to her, their tears coming fast as they embraced.

"Come, we'll have the breakfast, and then we must be off," Peter said gruffly. He didn't want them to see that he also was grieving. His favourite daughter was going away to the big city, and in his heart he knew she would never be the same girl again, the child who used to follow him barefoot through the fields, gathering bunches of cowslips in her apron.

After breakfast, Peter harnessed the pony to the trap in the little yard in front of the cottage. Peggy stood there, flanked by her two younger daughters, as Hannah climbed into the trap, her few belongings wrapped in heavy brown paper beside her. She bent down and kissed each of them, clinging to her mother, tears stinging her cheeks.

"Take care, Mother. I'll write to you. May, Florrie, see

you do your share of the work, and that Mother takes it easy."

Peter cracked the whip smartly and they were off down the narrow road, with May and Florrie running after them. "Hannah, don't forget to write to us." Their words were lost on the wind as the trap disappeared from sight, rounding the last bend on the road to the village, and to Limerick.

They reached Limerick shortly before noon, Peter manoeuvring the trap with difficulty through the winding cobbled streets, past the busy warehouses by the dockside. The workers' dress revealed the kind of work they did. Some had whitened faces and hands.

"Flour mills," her father explained to Hannah. To her, they were like people from another world; even their accent sounded foreign. She couldn't understand what they were saying, and, as she looked about her apprehensively, doubt began to set in. Perhaps she would not fit in here with the factories and trading houses, the noise and the smoke. It was all so different from Glenmore.

"You've arrived at last!" Peter had directed the pony into the driveway of an impressive-looking house on the outskirts of the city.

Annie came running out to greet them, skirts rustling, the scent of lavender reaching Hannah's nostrils as her aunt reached up to help her from the trap. Annie was a handsome woman with a coil of thick, dark hair wound fashionably at the nape of her neck, her complexion still smooth and clear. No lines of weariness, Hannah thought, scanning her aunt's kindly face. If only her own mother's life could have been different. Peggy Benson had never possessed a bottle of lavender water in her life. Luxuries like scent were out of the question when there was barely enough to feed them.

"Come on into the house, Peter, like a good man. I have a bit of lunch ready for you."

"No, I won't be staying, Annie. I'm grateful to you just the same, but I must be back before the coachyard closes. There's a bit of work there these last few days, and I don't want to miss out on it."

Annie protested but he remained firm, so she finally gave in, leaving father and daughter tactfully alone while she scurried back into the house.

"Well, girl, this is it." Peter put a hand on Hannah's slim shoulder, his movement clumsy, unaccustomed to displays of sentiment.

"Yes, Father, and don't worry about me, I can take care of myself. Just see to it that Mother takes it easy. It will be hard for her for a while. With one pair of hands short for the lacemaking, it will be a rush to fill orders."

Her eyes were troubled as she looked up at her father, but he smiled reassuringly.

"Never mind that, Hannah. I'll see that she takes care of herself. May and Florrie are well able to cope now. Remember, Hannah, if you ever want to come back home for any reason, don't hesitate because of pride. For I know you, Hannah Benson, stubborn, like myself, you are!"

"I'll miss you all, Father, but I'll not come home until I've made something of myself." She tossed her head proudly and Peter recognised the fighting spirit in her blue eyes.

Annie emerged from the house again, rustling towards him, a package in her hands.

"Just a bite to eat on the journey home, man. Some roast beef and Molly's soda cake."

"You're a good woman, Annie, and I'm grateful to you and John for taking Hannah into your house."

"Enough of your old talk, Peter Benson! Isn't it the least I'd do for my own sister? And I'm not doing you a favour. Hannah will be company for me in that big house. John and I will see to it that she's happy in whatever she chooses to do in the city." Annie flashed a sly glance at Hannah, a secretive smile passing between them.

"I'll be off then, Hannah. Make us proud of you, girl, and remember, we're always there if you need us."

He turned the trap around and was off, disappearing from view down the long narrow drive, and through the wrought-iron gates. Hannah watched his diminishing form until she could no longer see his shoulders hunched over the pony's reins. A feeling of intense loss engulfed her suddenly, something she couldn't explain. She wanted to run after him, tell him to wait for her, she was going back with him. It was as if her heart had been torn from her, a part of her gone forever.

"Come, child, away into the house with you, and I'll see you settled into your room."

Annie put a protective arm about the girl and led her into the house. She wouldn't give Hannah much time to brood and get homesick, she thought firmly. This niece of hers was a practical young woman, and Annie knew that she would work hard to make a successful business out of her dressmaking. Since Hannah had written to her, confiding something of her secret longing, Annie had resolved to get this girl to the city as soon as possible.

Such dreams could never be realised in a little country village like Glenmore. Annie recalled Peter Benson in his youth, when he had married her sister, Peggy, and sighed. Yes, she had been right to encourage Hannah.

Hannah was standing in the hallway absorbing her surroundings dazedly. She looked at the marble floor, a mix of cool, pale greens and blues, the huge wall tapestries covering smooth cream walls in a kaleidoscope of colourful patterns. Alabaster figurines were skilfully placed at various angles in the hallway to show them off to full advantage. She followed Annie hesitantly up the broad staircase, across a landing, and into a room the door of which was ajar. Hannah gasped as she stepped across the threshold. It was the most beautiful room she had ever seen! Her feet sank into the deep pile of the red and gold carpet, and she felt a twinge of embarrassment as she looked down at her travel-worn boots and noticed that they had made a few unsightly smudges on the carpet.

The big bed in the middle of the room had blue silk sheets with matching pillowcases. An exotic-looking blue lace nightgown lay folded at the end of the bed. Who could sleep in such finery?

"Happy birthday, Hannah. Just a little gift to mark your coming of age in the city!"

Annie smiled as Hannah touched the nightgown tentatively. She held it carefully to her cheek and caressed the silky material. Perhaps I'm dreaming, Hannah thought. Soon I will wake and find myself back in the little bedroom in Glenmore with the plaster peeling from the walls, May and Florrie huddled up close to me in the creaking feather bed.

"It's beautiful, Annie, the most beautiful present."

For a moment she thought of her mother's present, the look of pride on her tired face as she handed Hannah the lace collar. The sophisticated nightgown, its elegant folds draped over the satin bedspread, could not match the intricacy of the lace collar, Hannah thought with satisfaction, casting a professional eye over it. It was an expensive, beautiful garment, to be sure, but the lacework was simple, uninteresting, with no particular design to mark its obvious exclusivity. She would show the ladies in the city what real lacework was!

Hannah stood lost in thought, ideas moving rapidly in her head, conjuring up patterns and designs. Annie watched her with interest, envying her vibrant youth, admiring her flashing eyes and luxuriant curly hair.

"I'm so grateful to you, Annie, for everything! You've given me the opportunity to realise all the dreams I've kept hidden for so long, dreams I thought would never come to anything."

"This is your home, Hannah, for as long as you want it to be – and I hope that will be for a very long time. Now, enough of this morbid carry-on. You must refresh yourself after your journey. There's water in the jug there, and as soon as you're ready, come downstairs for something to eat. You must be starving after your long morning on the road!"

Annie went downstairs, and Hannah picked up the pewter jug to pour some water into the washbowl. She washed her face and hands, drying them on soft, lavender-scented towels.

When she went downstairs and entered the parlour on the left of the hallway, a fire was burning invitingly in the oak fireplace and a table was laid nearby. Cold ham with fresh steaming potatoes, thick slices of home-made soda bread – Hannah's mouth began to water when she saw the honey-coloured fruit cake in the centre of the table.

"You shouldn't have gone to so much trouble, Annie!" she began to protest, but Annie waved her aside and went to pour tea from a slim silver teapot.

"Sit down and enjoy it, Hannah. Today is your birthday and we might as well make it a memorable one. John won't be in until after six, so we'll have a couple of hours to ourselves to discuss your plans."

Hannah sat in an armchair close to the fire, facing Annie, and as the heat began to relax her tired muscles, she opened her heart to her aunt, detailing all the dreams and hopes she had hinted at in her letter. Her doubts, too, spilled over.

"Annie, do you think I'm being foolish? I know I'm just a country girl, not used to city ways, and I wouldn't blame you if you thought me outspoken and bold."

"There's nothing wrong with your plans, girl. From what I've seen of your beautiful lacework, you have a way with the needle, and as for your dressmaking, the fashion houses in Limerick couldn't hold a candle to you! You have an eye for what is fashionable, Hannah, a great advantage in the dressmaking business."

Annie spoke thoughtfully. Hannah was taking on something the faint-hearted would have shied away from. A young girl setting up her own business was not an everyday occurrence, even in the city, and there would be no end of obstacles ahead of her. But Annie knew that Hannah was determined to get on in life, and she was not afraid of hard work. Given the opportunity to prove herself, she would not be found wanting.

"What I want to do, Annie, is to combine the two, dressmaking and lacework. The one will complement the other, and lace trimmings are so popular now with the ladies in the cities." She looked hopefully at her aunt, her face alive with enthusiasm.

She's a real beauty, Annie thought proudly. If only she and John had been fortunate enough to have a family, perhaps she would now have a daughter as ambitious and beautiful as this niece of hers.

Hannah caught a brief glimpse of the sadness in Annie's calm face and moved to her side in concern.

"Is anything the matter, Annie? Is there something about my plan that troubles you?"

Annie shook her head vigorously.

"No, girl, of course not! John and myself will give you all the help we can. Just let us know what you need, and we'll see to it."

"Oh, Annie!" Hannah put her arms about her aunt, squeezing her enthusiastically until Annie protested.

"Stop, like a good girl, or you'll kill me with gratitude! Now we must wait until John gets home before we discuss it any further. He is just as excited about all this as I am. The sewing room is almost ready for you, and when it is, you can start taking orders for dresses. John will spread the word around that Miss Hannah Benson is available for business!"

The flames danced up the chimney as Annie and Hannah sat companionably on either side of the hearth, waiting for John's return from the city. Hannah was speculating. A whole new life was opening up for her, exciting and full of promise. If her venture proved a success, she would send for May and Florrie, and together they would see to it that their mother and father were comfortably off. Her thoughts strayed to them all at home, probably preparing the evening meal, May tending the fire, Florrie laying the table. Mother would go into the small parlour at the side of the kitchen to set up the table for the lace, arranging the pieces with careful precision. They would start work immediately after they had eaten, working until the candles burnt low and their eyes ached with strain.

Annie's house was a revelation to Hannah. The splendour of the furnishings, the richness of the carpets, the paintings hung in gold frames on panelled walls. This was what she wanted, more than anything else in the world, a fine house, and people calling to see her, calling her Miss Benson, instead of 'Hannah the dressmaker'.

The front door opened with a bang, and suddenly there was John standing in the doorway with a broad smile on his face, his hands outstretched in welcome.

"Hannah, at long last! Welcome, girl!"

John was about the same height and build as her father, but there the resemblance ended. Her uncle wore an immaculate business suit, the collar of his shirt stiff and shining. His face showed none of the strain and anxiety that marked her father's, and Hannah thought wistfully of how different their lives would have been if he had pursued his youthful ambitions to come to the city. But it was too late for that kind of thinking, Hannah rebuked herself.

"You're more than welcome to our home, Hannah," John was saying. "Annie has been preparing for this day ever since she got your last letter! Your plans are sound ones, girl, and I'll give you all the advice I can. But we'll discuss all of that after dinner. First things first!"

"You can be sure, John, we have a lot of ideas to put to you."

"You women," he replied, bending down to kiss Annie playfully, "always scheming – sure the poor men haven't a chance with you!"

Hannah felt like an outsider, glimpsing for one brief moment what true happiness between two people really meant. She felt envious, and angry also, that such happiness should have escaped her own parents. She had so often seen her mother crying at home, her father standing helplessly at her side, the money counted and recounted on the kitchen table, but never enough to get them over the lean periods.

"Excuse me, ma'am, the dinner's ready now."

The woman who appeared at the door looked curiously at Hannah, and flashed a friendly, toothless grin.

"Thank you, Molly, we're ready now. By the way, this is Hannah, my niece from Glenmore. She'll be staying with us for a long time, I hope."

"From Glenmore, is it? From Daniel O'Connell's country. God be good to that saint of a man!" Molly blessed herself piously, then put out her hand and took Hannah's in a firm handshake. "You're welcome, *a chroi*, and I hope you'll be happy here, though you'll find it very different from the dacent country life." Her expression turned dark and she looked at Hannah ominously.

Molly knew all about the ways of city people. She would take this girl in hand, teach her the ways of the city. Not all the people here were like the good missus and her husband. A fine Christian couple they were, Molly reflected as she shuffled back to the kitchen. Not like some of them so-called 'gentry' who sometimes came to dinner, never giving her the time of day as she took their wraps and heard them whispering, "How does poor Annie manage with only one servant?" Upstarts, the lot of them, Molly thought grumpily as she sat down to her own supper, sighing with satisfaction as she poured herself a glass of stout, its creamy head overflowing onto the table. She was partial to the odd glass or two, and John Sullivan was a generous employer, making sure she wanted for nothing, including the few bottles of stout.

The wind moaned outside the house, not disturbing the peaceful setting inside as Hannah sat down to dinner with her aunt and uncle. A centrepiece of dried flowers and ferns graced the dining table, and Hannah wondered if she would ever be able to emulate Annie's intuitiveness, her ability to turn elaborateness into tasteful simplicity.

She had never tasted beef so succulent, or such fresh, tender vegetables, not to mention the heaps of steaming roast potatoes.

Annie watched with satisfaction as she finished her meal, laying down her knife and fork with a contented sigh.

"That was the finest meal I have ever tasted, Annie . . ."

She stopped, embarrassed, thinking how ungrateful it must sound, making little of her own mother's cooking. Roast beef wasn't part of the normal diet at home. From one end of the week to the other, they were lucky if they had a scrap of bacon with the never-ending helpings of cabbage, a vegetable which Hannah detested. But her mother had always tried her best. Hannah hurried to correct her thoughtlessness.

"I mean, Mother cooked many a good meal but beef is so expensive, and there are so many of us . . ." she finished, defensively.

"I know what you mean, Hannah love. You're a lucky girl to have such a good mother and father, and they did their best for all of you."

Annie's face was full of pity as she looked at Hannah, a look which deep down Hannah resented with all her proud heart. She lowered her eyes, avoiding Annie's kindly gaze.

"Well, what do you think, John?"

They had finished dinner and were sitting in the parlour. Hannah looked at her uncle anxiously.

"I am willing to abide by whatever you say, Uncle John. You're a businessman, you do a good trade in your shop and people respect you. Your dealings with silks and refined materials from both England and Spain make you an authority on what is selling and what will make a reasonable profit. Only you will know whether or not this business I'm thinking of starting is a sound one."

She waited expectantly while John stood up and tapped his pipe on the mantlepiece. He didn't speak until he had filled it with a sweet, exotic-smelling tobacco, and the first circle of smoke wafted towards the ceiling. His eyes closed as he savoured the precious moment.

"I believe, from what Annie says, that you're well accomplished in your lacemaking, and I think that such a talent shouldn't be neglected. But it will not be easy starting a business of your own. It will mean plenty of hard work, and there are many people who won't favour the idea of a young country girl taking over in the city. There are a number of dressmaking salons in the city, well-established houses with many prestigious customers."

"I know that, Uncle John, and I am prepared to work until I drop. I'm not frightened of competition."

Here is a girl with a bit of mettle in her, John thought, admiring her eagerness. She had a look of determination on her young face incongruous with the slender frail body. Here was somebody who wouldn't admit defeat at the first hurdle.

"We'll give you every support, Hannah," John assured her.

Annie smiled, pleased that John had been supportive of her niece's ambitions, She had known he wouldn't be otherwise. It had been the lucky day when she had married John Sullivan.

"John will be able to make contacts for you in the shop, Hannah, maybe even take some orders won't you, John?" Annie enquired.

"Of course it will mean a bit of business for me too, you know." He winked at Hannah, a mischievous twinkle in his eye. "No doubt quite a few of the ladies will be looking for lace trims for their dresses, not to mention the exotic materials my young niece will be expecting me to order for her."

Hannah was walking on clouds, each one filled with

yards and yards of silks and satins, a riot of colours floating beneath her feet. She closed her eyes trying to keep her head from spinning wildly, and suddenly felt the firm pressure of Annie's hand on her shoulder.

"That's enough excitement for one day. Tomorrow we shall start on this new business of yours, and John has a surprise for you, but you will have to wait and be patient."

"You have been so kind to me, Annie, both of you, much more than I could ever have hoped for. I will make a success of this business. I won't let you down!"

Hannah lay in bed, the light from the moon casting a muted light on the pale walls, each piece of elegant furniture clearly outlined. So much had happened since she had left Glenmore that morning. The lace nightgown still lay at the end of the bed. Hannah felt that she could never wear such a delicate item unless she was truly a lady, accustomed to such finery. There was so much for her to learn, and, if she had been discouraged when she first arrived in Limerick, her feelings had now changed to quiet resolve that her plans be fulfilled at all costs.

Annie and John would have been surprised if they could have read her thoughts just then. Hannah was ambitious, and not without that element of ruthlessness which accompanies any successful man or woman. She was grateful to them for their support, but hers was an independent spirit, and she was determined to get a place of her own in the city. With May and Florrie helping her, and perhaps some young girls who would be glad of a wage, small though it would be at the beginning, there would be no excuse for failure. She fell into a restless sleep at last, her mouth fixed in an expectant smile.

Chapter 2

The following morning Hannah woke to the sound of the curtains being swished across and Annie's voice calling her through the mists of a deep sleep. For a moment she had forgotten where she was until she looked about the bedroom and then saw Annie looking down at her, an amused expression on her face.

"Are you going to sleep the day through?"

She jumped up from the bed, horrified at the thought that her first day in Limerick had begun in such an unmannerly fashion.

"Annie, what time is it? I'm sorry I slept so late but I felt so tired . . ."

"Tired and worn out with all the travelling yesterday, and then all the talking we did last night. Sure why wouldn't you sleep late? It's only midday, after all!" Annie laughed at Hannah's shocked expression.

"In Glenmore midday is half the day's work done.

Mother would be annoyed if she knew I was lying idle in bed at this hour."

"Many of the ladies in the city sleep on long after their husbands go to their business. I'm the exception, I'm afraid," Annie added self-deprecatingly. "My country ways are still very obvious, in spite of the years spent in the city!" She poured fresh water into the basin and placed a square of perfumed soap nearby. "I like to be up to see John off to work. I just couldn't tolerate lying idle. Hurry now, there's a good girl. Molly has prepared breakfast for you downstairs, and I'm impatient to show you John's surprise!"

The excitement in Annie's voice was contagious, and within minutes Hannah was washed and dressed and hurrying downstairs.

Molly had prepared some scrambled eggs and toast with a large pot of tea in the dining-room. Hannah ate with obvious enjoyment. She sat looking dreamily into the garden, admiring the sunken pool in the centre of a cluster of furze bushes, the water sparkling with slivers of sharp ice. Annie came bustling into the room, her fashionable grey skirt rustling as she walked.

"I've already sent Molly to the sewing-room to give it an airing. Everything you may need we can see to later on!"

"You seem to be very confident that I'll make a success of this, Annie." Hannah spoke quietly, doubts rising to the surface again, the enormity of her undertaking became clear to her. Would people laugh at a simple country girl for thinking herself better than her humble origins? Would she be humiliated and forced to return to Glenmore, making lace tablecloths and fancy ball-gowns for people like the Barrys who owned the Manor House outside the village? Never!

If she had to beg, borrow or steal she would not go back to Glenmore. She was starting a new life, there was no turning back, and this was no time for self-doubt. Hannah Benson would never settle for second-best.

Annie was leading her up the staircase, speaking all the time with quiet determination. "You are my niece; I can see a little of myself in you when I was your age. I came to Limerick and made a good life for myself, married a fine man who means the world to me and who has given me so much happiness. "She gave Hannah a gentle shake, looking her directly in the eyes. "But I didn't come by all of this –" she waved a hand about her, "just by sitting comfortably and watching the world go by. I had to work for it, pushed my way into Limerick society, a task that was far from easy." Annie sighed, a distant look in her eyes. "Your mother was easy-going. She had no great ambition to become a lady and live in the city – you could be my own daughter, Hannah!" Her eyes misted with tears and she turned away quickly. "I have great faith in you, girl. Just see to it that it is justified now – we have work to do!"

In the sewing-room Annie flitted about, arranging this and that, moving furniture out on to the landing to make space for the long table which would be needed to lay out all the pattern pieces. Molly puffed heavily up the stairs and whispered something in her mistress's ear. Hannah noticed a look of disappointment cross her aunt's face.

"I'm afraid our little surprise will have to wait until tomorrow, Hannah. John has sent word from the shop that it hasn't arrived yet."

Hannah laughed, clasping her hands together with nervous anticipation. "You're both spoiling me, Annie! I think I must be dreaming, and soon I'll wake to find everything has vanished." She appraised the airy sewing-room with satisfaction, the window opening out on to a balcony overlooking Annie's rose garden below. The roses were all gone now, but already Hannah could imagine it in high summer, the scent of the flowers invading the room. It would be her very own paradise, where she would work away on the beautiful ladies' gowns that would surely be in demand for the midsummer balls.

"It's good to have a young one about the place," Molly enthused, noting with satisfaction the sparkle in Annie's eyes, the healthy glow on her cheeks. The missus needed a bit of diversion in her view. It wasn't right for a good woman like Mrs Sullivan to be wandering about the house on her own all day, waiting for the master to get home. The girl would be a tonic for her.

"You're right, Molly. A bit of excitement will do us no harm at all." Annie gave a final twitch to the curtains, then stood back examining them critically. "There! I think everything is now in order. All we have to do is wait for those ladies to find out about you, Hannah, and they'll come flocking. It's nearly Christmas, and ball-gowns will be much in demand. Now, lunch.

Annie was pouring tea in the parlour when the front doorbell sounded. "I'm not expecting anyone," she said, puzzled. "Perhaps it's somebody for Uncle John." They heard Molly's voice in the hallway, then another voice, softer, more refined. Molly appeared in the doorway, a broad grin on her flushed face. "Tis a lady, ma'am, enquiring about the dressmaker. She says the master told her about Miss Hannah, and she's interested."

Annie rose hurriedly, smoothing down the front of her skirt, brushing back an imaginary stray hair from her forehead. "Show her in, please, Molly."

Hannah suddenly wished the ground would open up and swallow her. Beside her aunt, she knew she looked like a servant girl. Annie smiled at her reassuringly. "Don't worry, Hannah. The woman will be so concerned about her own dress she won't have time to notice what the dressmaker is wearing."

"I'm Mrs O'Shea, Dr O'Shea's wife. We have just moved to Limerick from Dublin and I'm afraid I don't yet know a reliable dressmaker here." The woman was quite beautiful. Hannah thought her tall slim frame, the straight shoulders, the tilt of her slender neck, all conveyed class and breeding. Her skin was creamy, the delicate bloom of early roses on her cheeks, her eyes large and velvet brown.

"This is my niece, Hannah, Mrs O'Shea." Annie introduced them, and Hannah held out her hand warily, unsure how to handle her first potential customer. Mrs O'Shea rewarded her with a friendly handshake then smiled, a quick, brilliant smile that spread from her handsome eyes and gradually illuminated her whole face.

"I'm very pleased to meet you, Hannah. Mr Sullivan has told me quite a bit about you already and I'm sure you will do an excellent job of dressmaking for me!" Mrs O'Shea accepted Annie's offer to sit by the fire and began to explain her needs. "Dr O'Shea and I are going to a special dinner in the College of Surgeons in three weeks' time, just before Christmas. I need a new dress for the occasion – my wardrobe seems so old-fashioned lately. Look, I've brought a picture of the style I had in mind. I cut it out of a fashion magazine I had at home. She held out the cutting to Hannah, who accepted it with a certain amount of trepidation. It was all very well making altar cloths and fine pieces of lace tableware for a country parish priest and for the big houses outside the city, but a dress for a lady of this calibre, that was another matter.

"My sister lives in the United States," Mrs O'Shea was saying, "and she sends me all the latest fashion news. I'm afraid she thinks I'm terribly behind the times where my wardrobe is concerned."

Hannah studied the design carefully. The model in the cutting was dressed very fashionably in a skirt that fell in narrow pleats just above the ankle, and a tight-fitting jacket with a deep neckline. Its layers of cream lace, Hannah noted with satisfaction, were not of the quality she and her sisters had often turned out at home for the ladies of the parish. She felt a surge of confidence flowing through her.

"I think I can manage it for you, Mrs O'Shea," she smiled encouragingly at the woman.

"Excellent, Hannah! I don't mind if it doesn't exactly match the magazine cutting. After all, I'm not your typical fashionable New York lady!"

Hannah looked at her with admiration and thought she looked anything but old-fashioned in her green velvet suit with a narrow black belt to emphasise her petite waistline, and cream silk blouse with ruffled lace at the neckline. The skirt was cut fashionably to calf-length, a very modern and daring length sported only by those who felt confident enough to wear it. Without a doubt, Mrs O'Shea's wardrobe would provoke admiring glances from every fashion-conscious lady in Limerick, and Hannah resolved to prove to them all that her expertise with the needle was something to be valued.

"I really must be going now, Mrs Sullivan." Mrs O'Shea rose and held out her hand to Annie and Hannah in turn. "I shall come back, shall we say, this day next week? I can have a fitting and discuss materials. I am so excited about this! Dr O'Shea thinks I am going to wear last year's ball-gown, and I have explained to him with many sighs and woeful glances that there isn't a dressmaker in Limerick capable of running up a ball-gown at such short notice. Such a surprise when he sees my new dress," she clapped her hands excitedly, "and no expense shall be spared, my dear Hannah!" She was laughing mischievously as she closed the parlour door behind her, Molly scuttling from the kitchen to see her to the front door.

When their visitor had left, Hannah sat down again to study the design. "Very fashionable, perhaps a little daring, Hannah girl?" Annie's tone was anxious. "It's rather a big task for a first effort – do you think you'll be able for it?"

"Don't worry, Annie. There is nothing in this cutting that requires more than average skill, and since I possess a little more than the average, this gown will be the toast of Limerick!"

Annie laughed at her careless conceit, but Hannah's face remained fixed, her expression quietly confident.

"I shall begin in the morning There is so much to do – just under three weeks to perform a stylish miracle!"

"Molly, is it ready?" Annie called up the stairs, and Molly emerged from the sewing-room, her toothless grin more pronounced than ever as she nodded her head vigorously. Hannah had just finished breakfast and was planning her morning's work, cutting and altering designs to coincide with Mrs O'Shea's requirements. "Your surprise has arrived Hannah. Something John and I thought would be extremely useful."

Annie led the way upstairs to the sewing-room, flinging the door open. "There!" Hannah looked in puzzlement at the sewing-machine on the long wooden table. She had heard of them, of course, had marvelled at tales of how they could cut a dressmaker's work in half, no more tedious hand-sewing where it wasn't really necessary.

"Oh, Annie! It must have cost so much – a sewing-machine! I hadn't dreamed of having one, at least, not until I was really on my feet and making a good profit!"

"John ordered it," Annie laughed, "the minute it was decided you were coming – 'one of those modern sewing-machines,' he said, 'will be just the thing to get her off to a good start'."

"I don't know what to say, how to thank you and John . . ." Hannah bit her lip She could never have believed just a few short weeks ago back home in Glenmore, that her dreams could come to such a speedy fruition.

"You're both so good to me. I'll pay you back, every penny."

"There's no need for that kind of talk, now," Annie said sternly, taking a firm hold of Hannah's slim shoulders, forcing her to meet her eyes. "You just do the best you can and nobody can do more – and make poor Peggy and Peter proud of their fine daughter. You can rely on John and me for everything you need. The rest is in your own hands!"

Hannah sat before the sewing-machine and tentatively lifted the cover off, not even noticing Annie leave the room. The little hand wheel on her right gleamed with powerful promise, just waiting to be set to work. Annie had left a few pieces of material on the table, and Hannah inserted one of them under the needle. Her foot automatically went to the foot pedal and as the whirr of the machine began, the material glided smoothly along the polished surface, the ridge of neat, even stitches delighting her so much that she laughed aloud with pleasure.

"She's been in that room for the last six hours, John. She refused to eat lunch. All she's had is a cup of tea and a slice of griddle bread – the poor girl will starve to death!" Annie's forehead creased with worry.

John remained sitting in front of the fire in the dining-room, calmly pulling on his pipe, tobacco wafting in spirals towards the ceiling. "It's just the first flush of enthusiasm, my love. She'll settle down after a while once she learns the tricks of the trade. That girl will make a name for herself, mark my words!"

"You didn't see the determination in her face when she told Mrs O'Shea she could do the dress for her. She'll push herself to the limit to get the order finished in time, even at the expense of her health, and that's something I cannot allow! What would Peggy think of me if I didn't see to it that the girl looked after herself?"

"I declare to God, woman, you'd worry about two flies walking up a wall and then fret if one of them didn't make it to the top! "

He laughed indulgently, and Annie smiled reluctantly at the ridiculous comparison. The door burst open and Hannah stood there, her face flushed with success, her hair a tangled mass as she swept it out of her eyes impatiently.

"Oh Annie! Uncle John! I just don't know where the time went to! There's so much to do, and the new machine . . . I don't know what I would have done without it! The work isn't half as tedious and I can really concentrate on the delicate lacework." She strode across the room and stood in front of John. He looked up at her face, at the brilliant eyes, the pale cheeks now glowing and he thought what a magnificent woman she would make in a few short years. Men would be beating a path to her doorway.

"Uncle John, there is no way I can thank you for everything! But I promise you sincerely, that you won't regret any of it. I'll make you proud of me, and when all the rich ladies travel from every corner of Ireland to have their ball-gowns made by Limerick's 'most exclusive dressmaker' I'll tell them my success is due to the kindness of my dear aunt and uncle, Annie and John Sullivan!" She bent down and gave John a shy kiss on the forehead, then turned to Annie, and fell into her arms, her face streaked with tears.

By the end of the month, Hannah had put the finishing

touches to Mrs O'Shea's gown. She could have finished it sooner, but she took special care with it, knowing that her first order would bring many more prestigious customers. Mrs O'Shea was a popular lady in elitist circles, and Hannah, with her innate business acumen, knew that people would be impressed by whatever fashion that lady chose to wear.

"Why, Hannah! It's just what I wanted! It's an exact reproduction of the magazine cutting!" Mrs O'Shea's delighted expression as she fingered the delicate fabric told Hannah that here was one customer who would be coming back to her again.

"Uncle John ordered the fabrics from London. I hope you're pleased with my choice. Please, you must try it on, and I can make whatever alterations that are necessary."

As Mrs O'Shea slipped the shimmering ivory-coloured gown over her head, Hannah closed her eyes and said a silent prayer that the dress would need no further improvements, if it should be too tight, or pucker at the front.

"There! What do you think, Hannah?"

When Hannah opened her eyes, Mrs O'Shea was standing before the long mirror near the window, pirouetting gracefully as she studied herself with satisfaction. Hannah thought she had never seen anybody so exquisite in all her life. The folds of the gown clung fetchingly to the slim curves of her graceful figure, not a pucker, an uneven seam visible. Hannah's intricate lacework hung fashionably about the low-cut neckline, winding its way decoratively down the front of the dress. The overall picture was stunning.

"You look wonderful, Mrs O'Shea!" Annie gasped from the doorway. She hadn't meant to intrude on the fitting but the door had been ajar as she passed. She couldn't resist taking a look at the finished garment.

"It's not me, Annie. It's Hannah's excellent handiwork." Mrs O'Shea turned once more in front of the mirror. "I shall be the most fashionable lady at the Surgeons' Ball – all the ladies will be so envious." She laughed girlishly and embraced Hannah. "I shall make sure you get many more orders, Hannah, although it grieves me to think that I can't keep you all to myself. I know that I shall be the very first to wear New York fashions in Limerick thanks to my talented young dressmaker!"

Hannah was kept busy up to Christmas Eve with orders from ladies clamouring for new ball-gowns. Mrs O'Shea had spread the word and they were all anxious not to be outdone by Limerick's most elegant follower of style and chic. Hannah couldn't help thinking about her mother and sisters during that time. How they would marvel at such extravagance! Some ladies ordering two or three gowns at a time. She felt excited by the idea of going home for Christmas, of telling them all about life in the big city, of her great prospects now that her little business was becoming established.

Uncle John had ordered a large bottle of expensive lavender water from his supplier and Hannah had already wrapped it carefully, visualising her mother's puzzled face when she opened it. She imagined the tired eyes lighting up with pleasure, the half-hearted admonishment that Hannah should not have purchased such an extravagance. Her mother deserved nice things now, and it was time her father took things easy for a change. Hannah was going to set things finally right. She owed it to herself and to May and Florrie to make a new life for them.

Early on Christmas Eve, just before Uncle John came home from the city, she decided that now was the time to urge her sisters to come back with her to Limerick. There was nothing for them in Glenmore and soon she would no longer be dependent on John and Annie's hospitality.

John had hinted at leasing her one of his storehouses near the flour mills for a paltry sum of money. "I know how proud you are, Hannah Benson, so I'll be business-like and take a shilling a month from you!"

"A shilling a month then, until I can afford to pay you a proper rent!" Hannah had agreed, and they had sealed the bargain with a glass of Spanish sherry which John kept for very special occasions. Annie had smiled at Hannah' s intense expression as she bargained with John. The girl would have many fine suitors clamouring for her attentions, but it would be as a businesswoman that Hannah's would excel. Annie couldn't see any handsome young man getting in the way of her ambitions!

Chapter 3

A light falling of snow trickled persistently on to the streets of Limerick on Christmas Eve, the last Christmas of the century.

John finished work early so that he could get started on the journey to Glenmore before dark. He had thanked all his assistants for their hard work during the year, and had fattened their pay packets with a handsome bonus. John was well-known for his generosity towards his workers. Any time a vacancy arose in his shop, there was a line of hopeful would-be employees waiting outside the shop door. His reputation as a bountiful employer had travelled well outside the city. The name of John Sullivan was synonymous with wealth and opportunity.

"Come, Hannah. We'll go then. We should be there before dark if the mares hurry themselves!" John rose swiftly from the dining table, wiping his mouth with a linen napkin.

"One moment, Hannah," said Annie.

Hannah followed her aunt into the hall, where her few precious gifts lay on the polished hall table, wrapped in coloured paper. "I have some things for your mother, and Peter and the girls. Wish them all a very happy Christmas for me. Perhaps in the New Year I'll take a trip to Glenmore myself. I'd love to have a good long gossip with Peggy. I'm so ashamed that I have postponed the visit for such a long time."

Only John knew Annie's reason for not visiting her sister. He knew the heartache she endured each time she saw Peggy and Peter with their three girls, the loving bond between them so obvious, as only a bond between a mother and father and their children can be. Annie felt a failure at not having produced a child for him, a fine son who would one day have taken over the business in Limerick, with the sign John Sullivan & Son hung in large, bold lettering over the shop.

John himself had entertained such dreams at one time, when they had first been married. He had visualised a little girl with dark curls, like Annie, and a little boy, with a roguish smile who would fill the house with laughter and mischief. Their plans had come to nothing, for Annie had found out that she couldn't have children, and since that revelation, the matter had never been discussed again. The passing years had made their disappointment easier to bear, for their deep love for one another had sustained them, blending them together in one impenetrable unit, the envy of many of their friends who had borne six or more small ones.

"And this package is for you, Hannah. I wouldn't be offended if you opened it now and, if it is to your liking, perhaps you would like to wear it as your travelling outfit." Annie smiled as Hannah took the package with eager hands.

"Have we got time, Uncle John?"

He stood in the dining-room doorway, a broad smile on his handsome face. "Go ahead, girl. There's all the time in the world for a young woman so beautiful herself!"

Hannah ran up the stairs, hearing Annie's pleased laughter behind her. She fumbled with the string of the box as she sat on the bed, oblivious to the inviting picture she made in her dressing-table mirror, the flushed cheeks, the sparkling eyes, the attractively arched eyebrows. Her luxuriant hair hung in loose curls on the nape of her smooth, delicate neck. Anybody who should gaze on Hannah then would say that she was a lady of breeding, of finesse, as good as any of the ladies who came to order their ball-gowns.

At last the final layer of tissue paper lay on the floor and Hannah gasped in delight as the contents of the box lay revealed before her. A travelling suit of the finest cut, wine-coloured, trimmed with black braiding, falling in soft folds to the fashionable length, just above the ankles. There was a blouse also, deepest pink with unusual wine-coloured stripes. She undressed rapidly, throwing her beige, nondescript day dress on the bed, stepping carefully into the skirt of the suit. When she had finished dressing, she stood before the mirror, staring at her reflection, wondering if this could really be the unsophisticated country girl who only a short time ago had come to the city. She saw before her a tall, elegant young woman, haughty and confident. The suit fitted her perfectly, emphasising the curves of her youthful figure, and as she stood there admiring the unexpected vision, she felt momentarily triumphant. She was not a lady yet, but the prospects looked very pleasing.

"Well, what do you think of Miss Hannah Benson?" She swept down the stairs, holding her head proudly erect. John clapped his hands appreciatively.

"You're as fine a picture as I ever did see, Miss Hannah," Molly cried, coming from the kitchen just then. "None of those so-called ladies could hold a candle to you, and that's for sure!"

"You look very elegant, Hannah girl." Annie kissed her cheek, a tell-tale hint of tears in her eyes. The girl was growing up, looking more self-possessed and at ease with herself. The fine clothes only emphasised the fact.

"Thank you, Annie. I've put your present beneath the Christmas tree in the parlour, and something for you, Uncle John. Nothing as extravagant as this," she looked down and indicated the richly-coloured travelling suit, "but I chose them carefully, and I think you'll like them."

She had gone to great lengths to find out what sort of tobacco John smoked, not wanting to ask Annie, because that would have ruined the surprise. Molly had enthusiastically volunteered the information, and also the sort of pipe the master preferred. Hannah had ordered them secretly, giving John's supplier an order for two pipes of his liking, and two pouches of his favourite tobacco. Hannah had looked at the man coyly behind long, silky eyelashes, tossing her gleaming curls as she pledged him to secrecy, and he had nodded his head, completely mesmerised by her vibrant beauty.

A gift for Annie had been more difficult. Hannah knew

she could not possibly get her anything to wear, for all Annie's clothes were far more expensive than anything Hannah could afford. Nor were perfumes necessary, as John purchased all Annie's perfumery from a prestigious house in Dublin. Finally, Hannah had decided to make Annie a silk blouse, one she had admired greatly in a fashion magazine Mrs O'Shea had left with her. It had several pieces of intricate lacework worked into the material, and Hannah had spent many long evenings in the sewing-room in order to get the blouse finished in time for Christmas. The completed garment had been a remarkable success, and Hannah had felt proud of her work as she looked at it critically on the tailor's stand.

She would have liked to stay to see Annie's look of disbelief on Christmas morning, but she knew that she must be at home for Christmas. It was a journey home with a special mission to be carried out, one which would have its difficulties, she had no doubt. She would not come back to the city until May and Florrie had promised to fall in with her plans.

"So on with you, now." Annie pushed them towards the hall door. "You'll never be there before dark at this rate, and I hate to think of John driving through the night." They went outside into the cold, December afternoon, a mist already beginning to form on the bare branches of the laburnum trees lining the driveway. The horses were harnessed and waiting, stamping their feet impatiently.

This carriage was so different from the one in which she had travelled to Limerick with her father all those weeks ago. Was it only weeks? Hannah felt she had been in the city now years instead of weeks. The splendour of the ladies she came into contact with each day seemed to have rubbed off a little on her gauche, rural ways, making her more sophisticated in outlook. She had become more impatient with herself, more self-critical, as she endeavoured to "better herself", as Molly put it sarcastically, one evening when Hannah had tried to mimic the refined accent of one of her customers. Improvements had to be made, Hannah told herself determinedly, ignoring Molly's sarcasm. If she wanted to become a lady, she would have to sacrifice a good deal, maybe even genuine friendships. But she would overcome those problems. Better to be a lady of breeding than an ignorant ladies' dressmaker.

"It's a splendid carriage, Uncle John, so swift and yet so light. I can hardly feel the bumps on the road as we travel!"

"It's not so bad," John replied modestly, but Hannah could sense the pride in his voice. "The motor cars are going to come in fairly soon now. All the gentry will want one, but I say you can't beat the feel of a horse's power beneath you."

They sped through the darkening countryside, leaving the lights of the city behind them, the horses gathering speed as John coaxed them onwards. A grey fog began to form, and Hannah relaxed against the leather upholstery, letting her thoughts drift pleasantly as she thought of all she had to tell her sisters about life in the city.

"Not long more now, Hannah. I suppose you're longing to see everybody again. Partings are painful, but reunions more than compensate for the sad farewells!"

"I'm so looking forward to seeing them all again, Uncle John. It seems such a long time."

It was dark as they neared the tiny cluster of cottages that formed little knots of flickering lights on the outskirts of the village of Glenmore. Hannah grew apprehensive as John steered the horses down the narrow road leading to her home. Her unease was something she could not explain. She felt some unnamable premonition, and she had always dreaded facing the unknown.

"Whoa there, boys, whoa!" John commanded, and the horses halted outside the gate of the little cottage. One candle burned brightly in the window and the front door was wide open, a streak of faint light flickering its way down the narrow pathway. Hannah stepped down from the carriage. It was unusual that nobody had come to greet her, for they must have heard the clatter of the carriage wheels.

"Things don't appear as they should be, Hannah," John said quietly. He took her arm and led her up the path, knocking politely on the front door, then stepping inside when there was no answer. The murmur of voices could be heard coming from the little room at the back of the cottage, and Hannah slowly opened the kitchen door. She had never seen the kitchen so full of people, all quietly praying, some with rosary beads clasped in their hands. She looked about the room, frantically searching for her mother. Where were the girls? Surely they had been expecting her, for she had written to them about her plans. Then she saw her – her mother, sitting by the window, her face waxen in the flickering glow of the candle. Her fingers were nervously fingering the rosary beads she held tightly in her hands, and behind her, their heads bowed, shoulders heaving with uncontrollable grief, were May and Florrie.

"It's a wake, Hannah," John whispered in her ear. "From the looks of it, some relation of your poor mother, and at such a time too, on Christmas Eve."

Hannah quietly made her way across the room to her mother's side. She looked down at her, placing a hand on the thin shoulder.

"Mother, what's happened? Where's Father?"

"Hannah! You're here at last. Oh, girl, I thought you'd never come!" Peggy clutched Hannah's hand, squeezing until the girl winced with pain. "Something terrible has happened. It's your father – he's gone, Hannah – dead!" She looked up at her daughter with despairing eyes.

"It was one of the carriages he was working on," May said tearfully. "He was trying to get the work finished for Christmas so that we'd have a bit extra. He wasn't too careful, the carriage slipped and fell on top of him! He was lying there for ages before anyone found him." May stretched out a hand to touch Hannah, trying to find some comfort in her sister's presence. Hannah was home now, everything would surely be all right, now that Hannah was here.

"Where is he, Mother?" Her voice was controlled, unemotional. Her mother pointed towards the kitchen door, to the small bedroom at the other side of the narrow hallway. Hannah walked slowly, each step dragging, as she thought of what awaited her. It must be a bad dream, she thought desperately. She clenched her fists tightly, her knuckles stretching the pale skin almost to breaking point. She acknowledged some of the people in the room with an automatic nod of her head, and they looked at her sympathetically.

The coffin lay open on the bed in her parents' bedroom. She shivered suddenly as she approached the long narrow box, then felt a hand on her shoulder and John was standing there, his presence steadying her as she looked down at the face of her father. Rosary beads were entwined in his fingers, his hands clasped piously on his chest, a peaceful look on the still face. His hair had been combed neatly to one side. Hannah smiled, for he had never liked his hair to look "settled" as he called it. She remembered him in her childhood, holding her hand as they ran through fields, his hair wild and blowing across his eyes as he bent to pick her up in his arms.

Her face felt wet, but she didn't know why. It couldn't be tears, for she felt no desire to cry, just an uncomfortable knot in her throat. John offered her a handkerchief and she accepted it, wiping her face absently. "It has been a shock, Hannah, a terrible shock. Cry as much as you want, girl. Let it all out – you'll feel the better for it."

"But I'm not crying, Uncle John. I can't." A loud gasp came from her throat, a choking, gurgling sound, and she threw herself into his arms, her grief mingling with sudden anger. "Why, Uncle John? Why now, just when I could have made things easier for him, repaid him for everything he has done for me?"

She knew John could not possibly understand. Her anger was towards the unjust and cruel ways of the world, where hard work was rewarded by a lonely death under the wheels of a carriage, a carriage being built, probably, for a rich, fat gentleman who knew nothing of poverty or of scraping a living for a family by working seven days a week.

"I'll see you get retribution, Father, for all the lost years and for Mother's tears when there wasn't enough to feed us. You know me, Father, you know what I'm capable of. I won't disappoint you."

John listened to her whispered tirade, felt the frustration welling up inside her as she lay against him, her heart thumping wildly. He felt frightened for the girl. There was something inside her, something not altogether good and healthy driving her, forcing her past the point where reason and common sense tempered blind ambition.

Father O'Brien came out of the kitchen with her mother, his voice softly comforting. "It's a hard cross to bear, Peggy. The loss of a good man is never easy to explain, for God's ways are, indeed, not our ways."

"John, I'm so sorry, John. I had no way of letting you know. The accident only happened yesterday." Peggy Benson lifted her face to her brother-in-law, the misery etched deep into the tired circles beneath her eyes.

"Don't fret yourself, Peggy. Everything will be taken care of; just leave it to me. After the funeral, we will all travel back to Limerick. Annie will take care of you all." John put a consoling arm around her, thinking how different she was from his own Annie, how frail and vulnerable she appeared, as though all the troubles she had endured up to now were suddenly confronting her at once, leaving her defenceless in the face of her husband's death.

They had finished saying the rosary in the kitchen, and the little group of mourners came shuffling into the hallway, their heads bowed, shaking hands with Peggy first, then with the girls. Many of the young men there looked at Hannah a second time as they left the cottage, for she had altered a great deal in the short time she had been gone from the village. She was a young woman of means now, of growing respectability, her head held proudly as she stood there, her defiant eyes glistening with tears.

James McCarthy noticed her. He saw a young woman who was going places, a valuable asset to a man who chose to make his fortune through the hard work of others. He would keep an eye on Hannah Benson's progress, he thought calculatingly, as he smiled at her, his handsome face appraising her with practised guile.

"Take care of your poor mother, Hannah," Father O'Brien whispered to her as he climbed into the trap outside the front gate. "She's been through a lot and she needs somebody strong, like yourself, to lean on now." He looked across at May and Florrie, huddled together in the doorway. "They're good girls, in their own way, but not strong like you, Hannah. You look after your mother. It's strength she needs now, not pity."

"Don't worry, Father, that's what I'm here for – to take care of her." Hannah looked about her with cold contempt. "She'll never have to lift a finger again in this place, or anywhere else. I'm going to take over the running of this family now." The priest saw the naked determination on her face, and knew that his advice had been unnecessary.

"We'll leave on Stephen's Day, Peggy, after the funeral. I'll send word to Annie tonight to expect us around midday," said John.

They went back inside and Peggy stood uncertainly in the kitchen, her pale face bewildered. "I think perhaps we should have a cup of tea, or maybe a drop of whiskey. John, you'd prefer that, surely?"

"Sit down, Mother," Hannah ordered, pushing her mother gently into the chair by the fire. "Let the girls and I see to things. Uncle John, sit down by the fire there with Mother. I'll see to the tea. May, go and see to Uncle John's horses, see that they're fed and dry for the night in the shed. Florrie, you put the kettle on the fire, and I'll get John a glass of whiskey." Hannah bustled about the kitchen, taking control of the situation, while her mother sat back gratefully in her seat and closed her eyes. Things were better now that Hannah was here. She was so like Peter.

Hannah set the table with some of the Christmas treats Annie had given her, some cold ham, pickled onions, a fine, tender goose that Molly had taken extra care in preparing, and now looked very tempting as it rested on the blue enamel platter in the centre of the table. There were two griddle cakes and a large fruit brack, glistening with luscious pieces of fruit.

"Come now, Mother. Uncle John, sit up to the table and eat some of this fine display Annie has sent."

May and Florrie stared wide-eyed at the table. Never before had they seen such an assortment of delicious food. Ham was a rarity, because it was so expensive. A goose had been an annual treat at Christmas time, a gift from the coachyard to all its employees, but this Christmas there had been no such token of benevolence. Peter Benson was already forgotten, for there were many more willing and eager to fill his place.

There was just a small gathering at the church the

following morning. Peggy Benson, her head bent in silent defeat, followed the narrow wooden coffin into the church. Hannah reached out and supported her arm as she stumbled on the slippery steps. Afterwards, in the overcrowded graveyard, a light fall of snow descended on the coffin as it was lowered into the ground. Father O'Brien said a final blessing, then the mourners filed away quickly to the warmth of their own homes to enjoy the rest of Christmas, casting pitying glances at Peggy and the girls as they knelt on the frozen ground. A crude, black cross over the grave read simply, PETER JOHN BENSON, RIP 1849-1899.

Hannah thought how her father would have loved to see the beginning of a new century, to see the promise of a more prosperous future. "It's a fine time to be alive, Hannah girl," he had said only a few days before she had left for Limerick. "Just think, this Christmas heralds the beginning of a new century. Changes are happening all over the world, especially here in our own country. The Fenians are strengthening, the Home Rule Party are finally gaining a strong voice in England. Mark my words, Hannah, this is the beginning of an eventful time in this little land of ours."

Hannah felt the biting north-east wind penetrating her bones as she knelt there and she got up stiffly, helping her mother as she struggled to stand, her body shaking with sobs. "Oh, Peter, Peter, what are we to do without you?"

John was standing a little apart from them, not wanting to intrude on their private moment of grief, and he hurried now to her side.

"It's all right, Uncle John," Hannah stood between

them, her heavy winter coat flapping about her as the wind grew stronger. "Mother, I shall take care of you now. Father is gone and you must look to the future."

Peggy looked at her, not recognising this daughter of hers who had matured so much in the past few months.

"You are a good girl, Hannah, but so young. How can we possibly manage without your father's wage?"

"I've told you, Peggy, anything you need, myself and Annie will see to it that you don't go without," said John.

Hannah looked at her uncle, and he saw in her face a little of what he had seen the previous night when she had gazed upon the lifeless body of her father. He felt uneasy. This young girl before him had plans which, she seemed convinced, only she could carry through, plans which could alter the course of all their lives.

"We are very grateful to you, Uncle John, and glad of your hospitality in taking us to live with you and Annie in Limerick, but soon I will be in a position to take care of Mother and the girls independently, without troubling anybody."

John opened his mouth to protest. They were family, after all, but the words died on his lips when he saw Hannah's expression.

"I want Mother to know that, Uncle John. I want her to have the confidence of knowing that I am capable of earning a living – without the fear that perhaps I shall take a fall and land us all in the workhouse!"

The last was spoken with wry amusement, but the look of horror on Peggy's face made John assert with conviction, "There's no fear of that happening, not while I'm around. So take heed, Hannah, you'll be under my wing until such time as I can be certain you're able to fulfill your high ambitions."

"We should be at home, in out of this biting wind." Peggy shivered and pulled her thick shawl tightly about her. "Come, girls, or you'll be sickening for something if you stay out much longer in this weather. Your father, God rest him, doesn't feel the cold any more . . ." She blessed herself and touched the little wooden cross with pinched, blue fingers. "Goodbye, Peter, my love."

"Come, Mother. There's no point in standing here in the cold." Hannah hurried her from the churchyard to where John's carriage was waiting. They journeyed back to the cottage in silence, the snow now blanketing the countryside, leaving it silent and pure.

"Father would not have wished us to be sad on Christmas Day, so I would like you all to sit in front of the fire, while I distribute some gifts." Hannah spoke firmly, an undertone of annoyance in her voice as she looked first at her mother, then at Florrie and May, their faces streaked with tears.

"Hannah, I think perhaps we can leave the gifts until we get to Limerick tomorrow," John said gently, noticing the weariness in Peggy's face. Some people needed to grieve, it helped them come to terms with their loss, and Peggy was such a person.

"No, Uncle John. Mother, I cannot allow you to sit muttering prayers for Father's soul when, if there is a God in heaven, his soul has been saved a thousand times over!"

"Hannah!" Peggy looked at her daughter in disbelief.

"I'm sorry, Mother, but I am doing only what Father

would have wished. The sooner we throw off these shrouds of mourning the better for all of us!"

John said nothing. He was seeing a side of Hannah he did not really care for, cold and uncompromising, a blatant insensitivity towards the grief of those who most cared for her.

"There, Mother! Open it. Uncle John helped me to select it, and I must insist that you wear it, for there are many more bottles to follow!"

Peggy took the parcel reluctantly. She thought surely it was a sacrilege to accept presents only hours after Peter's funeral, but she didn't want to annoy Hannah any further. Maybe this was the girl's way of hiding her grief. She opened the parcel, revealing a large casket of finest lavender water its contents sparkling heather-coloured in the dancing flames of the fire.

"Oh Hannah! However could you afford such a luxury?" She unscrewed the glass top and carefully tipped a few drops of perfume into the palm of her hand. Hesitating, she bent down and inhaled the light, flowery scent, its delicate perfume filling the small room.

"And for you, Florrie . . ." Florrie accepted the parcel eagerly. She gasped as a silk embroidered shawl tumbled onto her lap, the colours bright and bold, incongruous in the dull, grey kitchen, where the aftermath of death was still painfully present. "It's from Spain," Hannah explained. "Uncle John ordered it for me. Only the finest silk went into the making of it."

Florrie fingered the shawl apprehensively, afraid that it would disintegrate beneath her touch. "It's so beautiful, Hannah, the finest I ever did see," she whispered. She held the soft material close to her cheek. Silk shawls were things to be dreamed of but never possessed by people such as herself.

"May, your turn now!" Hannah smiled at May's bemused expression. Her sister stared at the parcel Hannah had thrust into her hands, then quickly tore at the gold string and the wrapping paper, until finally the contents were revealed. Boots made of the softest black shiny leather, just like the ones she had seen on some of the fine ladies from the big houses outside Glenmore. There were two rows of shiny black buttons on each one, and a tiny, narrow heel. They gathered around May as she lifted the boots out of their packaging, admiring their fine workmanship. "They were made in Limerick, only the very best, worn by all the gentry in the city," Hannah said proudly.

She sat back in her chair, watching Florrie as she draped the shawl about her shoulders, her eyes bright with excitement. She saw her mother's face, the lines of misery a little less prominent as she smiled for the first time, Hannah thought, since she had come from Limerick. John looked across the room at her, and their eyes met, Hannah nodding her head, satisfied. This was only the beginning.

John could understand her motives, but he had begun to see enough of her character lately to make him feel uneasy. She had the makings of a good businesswoman, of that he had no doubt, but her feelings were concealed beneath a shroud of driving ambition. He felt a chill run down his spine. His imagination was running away with him, he cautioned himself. After all, what was she but a young girl determined to see that her family were well looked after for the future.

"I'm going to open my own shop, Mother," Hannah turned to Peggy. "May and Florrie can help me with the lacemaking and I'll make up the garments. Uncle John has promised me all the help I need."

"Hannah, do you think you are in a position to take on such a responsibility? It's such a big step for a young girl, a girl in your position."

"That's why I'm so determined to succeed!" She looked at the doubtful faces about her, and began to feel irritated again. "Don't you see? This is an opportunity to better ourselves. Father would have agreed with me. He would have left this place long ago, but he had us to think about. We owe it to him, to ourselves, for God's sake!" She continued on, a stubborn glint in her eyes. "We'll be respected in the city. People will be clamouring to have expensive dresses made for them by the Bensons. We won't have to go begging for the money like we used to do, to the big houses in Glenmore!"

"But, Hannah, we don't know how to act like ladies. We have no refinements. We're just plain country people." Peggy was frightened now. This was a different Hannah to the one she thought she had known all her life, proud, imperious, her powers of persuasion manifesting themselves in her exaggerated gestures.

John remained silent. This was a matter between Hannah and her family. It wasn't his place to interfere.

"Look at your lives here, Mother. May and Florrie, what can you possibly look forward to? Annie and John have been good to me, setting me up in their own home, putting their trust in me. If they can have faith in me, why will you not follow suit?" She stopped then, looked at her mother's doubtful face, at the anxious looks of May and Florrie. If they didn't want to go, she would have to persuade them. She would get her way – and she would never come back to live in Glenmore!

"We'll give it a try, girl," Peggy said quietly, rising slowly to put another block of wood on the fire. "You've worked hard in the city. It's only right that your family should be with you now. We'll help you all we can." Hannah jumped up and threw her arms about her mother. John sighed with relief. Hannah's anger and frustration were qualities not to be reckoned with.

"There's no need to be frightened," Hannah said, seeing the worried faces of May and Florrie. "I'll make up the garments. All you have to do is to continue making the finest lacework that will be the talk of Limerick, with all the ladies competing to have a dress trimmed with only the best of Limerick lace!"

Hannah was satisfied now that her plans were finally accepted. She had thought that her mother's feelings for the cottage and the village of Glenmore would prove too strong an adversary for her own intention of removing the family to Limerick. But all the spirit seemed to have gone out of Peggy now that Peter was dead. She had no wish to stay in a place where memories were not so much happy ones as bittersweet. Peter had worked hard all his life, and had received nothing in return. Hannah's plan had been voiced at a time when Peggy was most vulnerable, and she accepted it almost as a blessed release from the past.

Hannah could hardly wait to be out of the cottage and

back to Limerick. Uncle John had slept on the settle-bed in the corner of the kitchen the previous night, and it had humiliated her to think how different circumstances were here to those in the beautiful house in Limerick, which boasted three guest bedrooms. Living in the cottage, she now saw, had been only a few steps away from the most abject poverty, and Hannah had no wish to prolong their stay.

"When shall we start for Limerick, Uncle John?" Hannah turned to him as he sat by the fire, soft swirls of tobacco smoke curling from his pipe.

"I think the sooner the better, Hannah girl. I've sent word to Annie to expect us at noon tomorrow, so we'll leave after breakfast." He smiled at Peggy reassuringly. "It's the best thing, Peggy, for all of you. Peter wouldn't have wished it any other way."

The next morning was bright and bitterly cold, the windows frosted over with thick sheets of ice, the pathway leading up to the cottage frozen like sparkling glass. John was worried as he looked through the kitchen window. They would have to leave soon, for it showed no sign of thawing, and if they journeyed any later the ice would be at its worst. The horses were not accustomed to travelling long distances in such weather. One stumble and he could lose one of them, or worse still, the carriage might overturn.

He did not voice his concern to the others, but after breakfast, he smiled brightly and rubbed his hands together saying, "That was a grand breakfast, Peggy, just the thing to set us up for the journey! I think it best that we leave now. We can take it slowly because of the ice. Those horses of mine are lazy devils – they don't care to travel in rough weather!"

An hour later, the girls were settled in the carriage, May and Florrie sitting erect on the soft leather seats, half afraid to relax in such comfort. John gave Peggy a little time to herself as she went about the cottage, needlessly checking windows and doors, her eyes bright with tears.

"Mother, it's time to go!" Hannah called impatiently. The cottage would be sold, and any money they would get for it, hardly very much as it was badly in need of repairs, would be used for their business in Limerick. Peggy seated herself in the carriage and looked straight ahead as the carriage moved away down the narrow winding road.

She didn't look back. Hannah had told her they were starting a new life now, and there was no room for regrets, for thinking of what might have been. John drove the horses calmly, but speedily, over the treacherous black ice, through the rapidly diminishing countryside, towards the bright lights of Limerick.

John watched them as they sat in the carriage, each one lost in her own thoughts. He pitied them all, but most especially Hannah. She was the strong one, and so, bore all the responsibility. They were so different from her. Like lost sheep, John thought, incapable of standing on their own without some support. Annie would do her best to make them feel at ease in their new environment, and John vowed silently to help them in every possible way.

It was quite dark when they reached Limerick, the streets deserted and unfriendly, a heavy mist falling on the dark cobbles. It was late evening on Stephen's Day, and everybody was indoors enjoying the holiday festivities.

Nobody looked through their windows to notice a solitary carriage pass by, the occupants' faces pale and anxious as they peered through the darkness to catch a glimpse of their new surroundings.

When the carriage finally pulled up at the house, May and Florrie were weeping silently, overcome with tiredness and fearful of what awaited them. Peggy sat motionless but for the slight tremor in her hands as she tried to pull on her old brown knitted gloves. Hannah put a hand under her arm, and guided her from the coach, helping her up the long driveway. Annie was waiting, her figure silhouetted in the bright light streaming from the hallway. As the little party approached, she ran to meet them, hands outstretched.

"Welcome Peggy, dear Peggy!" She threw her arms about her sister, the tears flowing down her cheeks. Annie's eyes met her husband's, and a silent message passed between them. "John, you put the carriage away. Peggy and the girls must be half-frozen. Come along, all of you! I have a fine dinner waiting for you and a blazing fire to warm you. Come along, girls!" She hurried them into the house. John smiled to himself. Annie would sort everything out in her own matter-of-fact way. She would see to it that they put the past behind them.

Chapter 4

It had been a wretched Christmas. Jonathan Mayhew thought despairingly. His sister Christine trying to persuade him to attend tedious parties and afternoon tea sessions with her boring friends who looked at him with such sympathy that he felt like slapping their smug faces. In the end he had flatly refused to leave the house, keeping to his room most evenings.

He paced back and forth in front of the blazing log fire in his sister's parlour. He was feeling particularly restless tonight and could feel a tightness in the back of his leg. It was beginning to act up again, and his incessant movements only aggravated the condition. If only he hadn't been discharged so soon, he thought angrily, dragging his leg across the green Persian carpet. The Boer War had been his saviour. He had relished every bloody moment of it, the excitement when his commander had called, "Charge!", the cries of the men standing side by side as they surged forward. It was all over now. He had nothing to show for it but a worthless leg, its frequently excruciating pain a mocking reminder of the war.

The door opened and his sister appeared. Christine O'Shea stopped on the threshold and looked anxiously at her brother. She was worried about him lately. She didn't like his strange moods, sometimes brimming over with gaiety, then suddenly engulfed in terrible moments of despair. Jonathan smiled now and extended his arms towards her.

"Come, dear sweet sister. Don't frown so much. It will give you wrinkles too soon, and your face is much too pretty to endure such a disfigurement!"

Christine went to him, her face still a mask of concern. They sat together on the couch in front of the fire, silently watching the flames as they shot up the chimney, casting their shadows on the polished oak-panelled walls.

"I'm worried about you, Jonathan." Christine spoke slowly. She was never sure these days how her brother would react to kindly concern. The war had a lot to answer for, lost lives, lost limbs, young men grown old before they even had a chance to live.

"You mustn't worry. I'm fine." He rested his strong, suntanned hand on her delicate white one. "Didn't Robert tell you it would take time for me to settle down again? And with such a skilled doctor to take care of me, this old leg will soon be dancing waltzes with the fairest of Limerick's women!"

He spoke lightly, but she could see the glitter of desperation in his eyes, could sense his frustration with his unaccustomed inactivity. He rose, wincing at the pain that shot through his leg.

"I think I'll go down to Fitzgeralds' before bed."

"You spend far too much time in that place," Christine said disdainfully. "Gamblers and drinkers of cheap wines, and gaudily-dressed women enticing young men such as yourself!"

She heard the front door bang behind him, and stamped her foot in frustration. Moving to the window, she saw him walking awkwardly out through the front gate, the halting stride not quite befitting the tall, handsome figure with the mop of curling coal-black hair.

It was past midnight when Robert O'Shea turned the key in the front door and quietly entered the hallway. He tiptoed up the stairs and stopped when he saw the shaft of light from under the bedroom door. Christine was still awake, then. She had always stayed awake for him, listened for his weary footsteps on the stairs, her anxious enquiries about his patients like a balm to his exhausted limbs.

She was sitting up in bed now, her long fair hair a gleaming mass on the white pillowcase. She saw the tiredness in his face, the weary stoop of his shoulders. He sat down heavily on the bed.

"I told you, my love, I'm quite capable of putting myself to bed and sleeping the sleep of the dead!" He smiled tenderly at her, cupping her delicate chin in his hands.

"I like to wait up for you," she reminded him. "I don't like the idea of you coming home to a dark, sleeping house."

He lay back beside her on the bed, closing his eyes momentarily. "It's been a tough one tonight, Christine." His voice came hoarsely.

"Mrs Flannery and the baby . . . they're all right?" Christine enquired concernedly, looking down at his pale, drawn face.

"Yes, just about. The baby was a breach, all twelve pounds of him. Can you imagine the poor woman's struggle to bring that size of an infant into the world?"

Christine remembered her own struggle to bring baby Emma into the world just twelve months ago. She panicked each time she remembered it; the pain, the moaning and animal-like cries that seemed to come from some other wretched woman, and not from her own parched lips. Secretly she vowed that it would be a long while before she would repeat that ordeal.

"I'll go and visit her tomorrow, and take some things for the baby, some nourishing food for the other children."

"God, Christine! How those people survive is beyond my comprehension! Open sewers running outside the houses, tiny rooms overcrowded, some dying of consumption in damp, filthy corners!" He spread his arms wide with despair, and she felt so helpless and cut off from the realities of his profession. "They're trying to inspire those wretched people with paltry dreams of an independent Ireland, a Gaelic Ireland, when all they want is enough food on the table and a decent place to bring up their hordes of children!"

She saw the fire in his eyes now and knew that his tiredness and frustration had nurtured a deeper emotion, one which could not be readily appeased by sleep. She spoke sympathetically, stroking his forehead with her soft hand.

"Hush now, darling. You're just overtired. Things will appear so much different after a good night's rest."

He relaxed under the gentle pressure of her hand, and

soon she heard him breathing deeply, his face alabaster white in the light of the half-moon outside the bedroom window. She covered him lightly with a blanket and then lay back against the pillows, listening to his gentle snores. She would go to see Mrs Flannery tomorrow, she decided. Maybe Jonathan would go with her. It might take his mind off his own troubles to see the plight of some of Robert's patients. Her decision made, she closed her eyes and relaxed as sleep overcame her.

"Jonathan, I want you to go somewhere with me this afternoon."

They were sitting at the breakfast table, Robert immersed in a medical book, Jonathan toying with the slice of bacon on his plate.

"It isn't going to kill you, Jonathan, to eat that tiny slice of bacon! Honestly, it's worse than coaxing baby Emma to eat!" Christine's voice was sharp, unlike her usual pleasant manner, and both her husband and brother looked up suddenly. Robert cautioned her with a warning glance, but this seemed to incense her more. "I know what you have endured, Jonathan, and I am doing my utmost to understand and be patient, but . . ." She looked at her brother helplessly. There was so much more to Jonathan's moods than she could understand, things that could not even be explained medically.

"I am sorry, sister. I know I'm tiresome and you would be better off without me. Indeed I'm grateful to you both for suffering such a monster in your household!"

Christine smiled, her anger dissolving. She promised herself to be more understanding in the future.

"And just where are you two off to this afternoon?" Robert O'Shea asked, closing his book and concentrating on his bacon and fried kidneys.

"I thought Jonathan might accompany me to visit Mrs Flannery. The walk may do his leg some good."

"Walk, Christine?" Her husband looked at her worriedly. "Surely you will take a carriage? I don't like the idea of you walking in that particular part of the city."

"We shall take the carriage to the dock, where Seamus can wait until we return from Mrs Flannery's. It will be particularly bracing to walk along the quay – the afternoons are not too cold, and there is a fine fresh breeze from the Shannon.

Inwardly, Robert O'Shea praised his wife's resourcefulness. She was determined to bring Jonathan out of the nightmare which had tormented him ever since his discharge. Maybe if she could help him to come to terms with his injury, then the healing process, both physical and emotional, would materialise in a shorter time than the medical experts had predicted.

"It is an excellent idea, Christine! It will do you good, Jonathan, shake off the lethargy of over-indulgence during the Christmas period!"

"I can see I'm outnumbered, two to one." Jonathan sighed deeply with mock resignation. "Very well, sister, you may now restrain your powers of persuasion – I am to be your escort into the bowels of this fair city this afternoon!"

Robert studied his face professionally. Christine had a hard task before her. This brother of hers would need much time and infinite patience. If anyone could make him well again, Christine was certainly the right person for the task. Robert looked at her regal face as she sat at the table, her hair piled high in a becoming twist of curls on top of her head, her neck, white, arched and graceful. He was a lucky man to have found such a treasure. He loved her with every breath in his body, and knew that his love was genuinely reciprocated.

Christine had not only beauty, but also integrity and strength of character. She had promised her mother, a lady very much like herself, who had borne sickness bravely for two long years before her eventual death, that she would take care of Jonathan. When war started between the Boers and the Commonwealth, Jonathan was one of the first to enlist, his eyes blazing with youthful enthusiasm. He went for the fun, for the thrill of the battle, and he came back a brooding, restless man with a damaged leg which would probably give him bouts of agony for the rest of his life.

"We must do something to celebrate little Emma's birthday tomorrow, sister," Jonathan remarked as they strolled along the quay that afternoon. Seamus, a delighted look on his face, stood dutifully by the horses until their figures disappeared from view, licking his lips at the prospect of a ball of malt in the Dockside Inn before the mistress and her brother returned.

"We must have jellies and some sugared fruits, and a big chocolate cake for my favourite niece," Jonathan enthused, grinning down at his sister, his innocent talk of childish pleasures making her laugh aloud.

"You can be such a little boy at times, Jonathan! Of

course, we'll have all those treats, and you shall play a happy birthday song on the piano, for little Emma likes nothing better than to hear her favourite uncle sing to her."

It was a pleasant afternoon for walking along the dockside, the cries of the seagulls echoing behind them as they entered the bustle of the city streets. Jonathan tried to keep pace with his sister, but his leg was beginning to throb, and Christine could see the lines of pain on his face.

"It's not far now. I was stupid to leave the carriage behind. It is too soon for you to walk such a distance!" Christine looked at him anxiously.

"It is not your fault, sister. It's this damned leg!" He mouthed the adjective so as not to offend her, and she hid a secret smile. If only he knew, she had heard men swearing many times before, in the privacy of her husband's surgery. Grown men had been known to yell and swear with such abandon that Mrs Tansey, the cook, had raised her eyes to heaven and said that if the men were the ones to have children, there would never be a second one!

They had left the busy streets behind them now, and Christine threaded her way carefully through a maze of narrow, filthy lanes, the smell of urine and human excrement heavy and sickening to those unaccustomed to it. Jonathan held her arm protectively, annoyed at the heaving feeling in the pit of his stomach. He thought the war had knocked all that sensitivity out of him. Christine held a handkerchief lightly to her nostrils, but showed no signs of being overly dismayed.

"Before we go in, Jonathan . . ." She stopped outside a tiny two-windowed hovel at the end of a dirty laneway.

Her brother looked at her expectantly. Christine lowered her voice. "Mrs Flannery does her best to keep the place as clean as is humanly possible in these conditions." She looked down at the narrow stream of human waste running past the front door. "She would be so embarrassed if you were to show any signs of disdain, the smell – you understand?"

Jonathan nodded. "Never fear, I will be my usual discreet self, sister. My God, do people really survive in places such as this?"

Christine knocked gently on the front door. A young boy of about nine years opened it cautiously. He was pitifully thin, his patched trousers hanging at half-mast on his bony legs. His shoulder blades protruded skeleton-like through the thin wool of his jumper. "Me Mam is lyin' inside, missus." He motioned her inside, and Christine smiled at him.

"Thank you, Sean. This is my brother, Jonathan, and we've come to see your new baby brother!" They went inside to the kitchen.

No light entered from the tiny slit of a window near the back door, only the dark shadow of the equally squalid house behind. The air was damp, and everywhere there was the foul smell of urine and sickness. Mrs Flannery lay on a makeshift bed in the corner, near the open fire. The baby was cradled in her arms, his sprinkling of light-coloured hair barely visible above the woollen blanket. She smiled at Christine shyly, and tried to sit up, her pale face showing all the signs of a difficult labour. Christine went to her and gently pushed her back on the pillow.

"Lie still now, Ellen, there's a good woman. I've brought a few things for the baby, and the other children."

"You're very good to us, missus, and the good doctor too. I don't know what I'd have done without him last night." She looked down at the sleeping baby, her tired eyes emotionless. "I just don't know how we're going to manage – six small children now, and Tommy has only the promise of a job in the docks."

The floodgates had opened, and Mrs Flannery's voice rose anxiously, all her fears tumbling out. Christine held her hand and murmured comfortingly, while the woman sobbed quiet, heart-rending sobs.

Jonathan stood in the background, not knowing quite what he was doing there. Christine should never have asked him to come here. He was angry with her. She had taken up too much of his time, he argued with himself at first, bringing him along like a quiescent lap dog on her errands of mercy. But something else began to trouble him. For the first time since he had come home from Africa, he had ceased to regard his own troubles. A paltry inconvenience it seemed now, to endure the pain of a shattered leg, compared to the misery this woman and her family had to tolerate each day of their lives. For the first time in his life, something akin to conscience was eating away inside him.

Christine was introducing him to the woman. "This is my little brother, Ellen. Not so little, I think," she laughed softly, and the woman gave a watery smile.

"A fine young man, Mrs O'Shea, not like yourself, he being so dark and you so prettily fair."

"We are as different as two peas in a pod, Mrs

Flannery," Jonathan said, looking with affection at his sister. "She is my protector, keeping me on the right path, for I am a bit of a devil, I'm afraid!"

The other children crawled from their hiding places now, anxious to meet the two visitors, their eyes wide with curiosity. Christine distributed the sweets and pieces of fruit, horror-struck by the signs of consumption already visible on the faces of at least two of them; the bright spots of red on the sunken cheeks, the rasping cough as they struggled for breath.

The baby woke just as they were about to leave, his lusty cries summoning the other children to him. They fussed over him, holding his tiny hands, singing softly as they tried to comfort him. Mrs Flannery looked over their heads at Christine and Jonathan, a look of such helplessness that Jonathan had to turn away, not wanting her to see the truth in his eyes. He could have told her that she would be lucky if any of her children survived another year and the baby lived beyond another month in the unsanitary conditions they had to exist in.

They left quietly, hearing the hungry cries of the infant as they walked briskly through the now darkening streets. Christine was quiet. She wondered if she had been right in bringing Jonathan with her today. Perhaps the visit had made him feel even more morose, more troubled.

His voice broke through her thoughts, startling her momentarily. "Those wretched people! Nobody really cares if they live or die! I thought I had seen enough despair and poverty to last me the rest of my life, but that . . ." He waved his arm helplessly in the direction of the narrow laneways. "That is what misery is really like."

"Don't upset yourself, Jonathan," Christine said soothingly, noticing his tense face.

"Don't worry, Christine. It did me the world of good to accompany you there today. It just puzzles me why in God's name isn't there some voice for people like the Flannerys?"

Christine struggled to keep pace with him, his angry outburst giving him renewed strength as he walked faster, his leg dragging along the pavement. She should have taken the carriage as far as the Flannerys', she thought. It was a mistake to walk that distance with him today. They were walking along the quayside now, where Seamus was waiting with the carriage, his face flushed with good malt whiskey.

Christine sank thankfully into the carriage, while Jonathan sat upright, his face rigid, eyes staring unseeingly through the gathering gloom at the twinkling lights in the harbour. They would soon be home, Christine thought with relief. Perhaps Robert could give him a light sedative, something to calm him down. It was not good for him to get so agitated over something he was powerless to remedy.

Chapter 5

There had been a particularly cold spell in the first days of the new century. Lakes and ponds were frozen solid as workers made their way to work through the narrow Limerick streets, their mouths covered with woollen scarves keeping throats and chests safe from the ice-laden treacherous weather.

Annie sat in front of the blazing fire in the parlour, her book open in front of her, a shawl wrapped tightly about her shoulders, her eyes scanning the page indifferently. She was worried. Peggy and the girls had settled into their new surroundings with little difficulty. Gradually, over the weeks, they had relaxed and grown more confident, a little overawed at times by the graciousness and obvious wealth of the ladies who came to see Hannah about "something to make my friends green with envy!". But it was their dependence on Hannah that Annie worried about, their constant reference to her about simple things like the stitching on a particular pattern, work they had been well accustomed to back home in Glenmore.

"When will you be back, Hannah?' Peggy would enquire worriedly when her daughter went out to buy materials. "If a customer should call, however can I deal with them? What shall I say to such fine ladies?" The panic in her voice would make Hannah flinch with annoyance, and Annie knew the situation could not continue.

There was only one thing to do. Annie had always believed that a person should not get involved with another's affairs, but this time she would have to make an exception. She stood up purposefully, throwing the book on the table, and went upstairs to Peggy's room. She found her sister sitting by the window, a delicate piece of lacework in her hand, her eyes squinting as she deftly wove the needle backwards and forwards.

"Peggy, for Heaven's sake, why can you not use the lamp? You'll go blind working like that!" She quickly turned up the oil lamp on the little table near the door, and immediately a soft glow of light flooded the room.

"It's just habit, I suppose, Annie. I'm so used to working in the half-light."

"Well, things are different here, Peggy. You have no need to spare the lamps. Use them at your will. You must learn to live with changes – which is why I've come to speak to you now." Annie sat on the bed and faced her sister. "Peggy, you have a fine family, each one a credit to you and poor Peter, God rest him, but Hannah . . ." she paused, looking at Peggy's puzzled face. "Hannah is different, exceptional, a good business head, honest and trustworthy, as her customers have quickly discovered."

Peggy listened mutely, wondering where the conversation was leading. She was grateful to Annie and John for taking them in. If they had done anything to offend them . . .

"Peggy girl, you will have to give Hannah space to breathe! She is torn in two trying to set up a business and mollycoddling the rest of you at the same time!" Annie finished the sentence breathlessly, waiting apprehensively for Peggy's response. Peggy rose from her seat by the window and looked at the moon shining through the bare trees.

"I know what you mean, Annie, and you're right. It's time to put the past behind us and stand on our own feet, without leaning on Hannah all the time."

Annie felt a sense of relief. She had not been wrong in her estimation of her sister. "I'll have a talk with the girls, Annie, and thank you for reminding me what a weak fool I am. The girl must be feeling so frustrated, with the business going so well, and the three of us hanging on to her like three suckling ewes!"

"She is ambitious, Peggy, something that shouldn't go to waste."

"She has always been so, ever since she was a little girl." Peggy sighed and looked at Annie, her gaze questioning. "Where did I get her from at all, Annie? Such determination she never got from her mother, and that's for sure. From her father, maybe, but even Peter was without that restless streak in him."

Annie remained silent. She remembered her own restlessness as a young girl, the impulsive desire to see as much of life as she could fit into her own small domain in the west of Ireland. She could have never endured a life like Peggy's. She thought of her own courting days with John Sullivan and thought she would burst with the love she still felt for the man. Even then, in that small country parish west of Cahirciveen where they had grown up together, he had that streak of business-like acumen. She had got a position as a ladies' maid in one of the big houses in Castleconnell outside Limerick when she had finished school, and John had become apprenticed to a merchant in the city. Within a year he had made a name for himself, taking over the ordering of goods in the tailoring shop in Patrick Street, earning him a handsome bonus from his grateful employer. One day he had taken her by the arm on her afternoon off and told her he had a surprise for her. He had led her through the streets of the city, to a little run-down shop at the back of a row of tenement houses by the quay, and proudly pointed to it.

"Our future, my love. Now we can get married and I'll look after you for the rest of your life!"

Annie looked up, the smile still on her face, to see Peggy looking at her curiously. "Sorry. Peggy. I was lost in my own thoughts there."

Hannah was something like herself, she thought, and if she had anything to do with it the girl's ambitions would be realised. If only she'd had a daughter like Hannah, she thought wistfully, then gave herself a mental telling-off. She had a lot to be thankful for with a husband who would give her the moon, if she asked him for it! She smiled at Peggy, rising from the bed and smoothing down her skirts. "Leave that work until the morning and come downstairs with me. We'll have a nice cup of tea and a slice of Molly's griddle bread before John comes back from his meeting!"

Jonathan sat at the piano, his voice rising and falling affectedly as he thumped out, "Happy birthday, dear Emma", making the child clap with delight. Christine lifted the little girl from her tiny stool and watched with affection as she toddled across to the piano.

"Come, my little one, sit on Uncle Jonathan's lap and we shall play a duet!" He lifted her up, and her tiny fingers moved eagerly towards the ivory keys. "I think you have the makings of a great pianist in this little one, Robert," he said, as he guided Emma's hands across the keyboard. "Very definitely so."

Robert smiled with pleasure at his daughter. She was such a joy, always smiling and dancing, even at such an early age, trying to piece sentences together, her interpretations altogether enchanting. In a year or two, maybe, they could have another little one, a companion for Emma. He looked across the room at Christine, who was filling out glasses of sweet sherry. She didn't seem too enamoured at the prospect of another pregnancy. He had tentatively approached the subject only a few nights ago, and she had laughed gaily and dismissed the subject with "poor little Emma needs our undivided attention for another while, dear Robert. There is no great hurry. I am still quite young, am I not?" She had looked at him then, a look of such promise, her hair like a cloud of sunshine about her shoulders – and he had forgotten all thoughts of another child. After all, they were so lucky to have little Emma, and they were such a happy family together, watching the child grow more beautiful each day.

"Come now, some sherry, gentlemen, and some iced lemon drink for my precious one!" Christine held the tiny cup to the baby's lips and she gulped thirstily.

"A toast," Jonathan cried, holding up his glass, "to Emma!"

Robert and Christine held up their glasses and smiled at each other. Jonathan saw the look which passed between them and, for a brief moment, envied them their happiness. He knew he could never make such a devoted husband as Robert, could never find a woman such as Christine. He knew too well his own weaknesses, his selfishness, his impatience with life's many injustices.

There was a knock on the door of the parlour and the maid appeared, a small parcel in her hands. "This has just arrived, ma'am, a present for the child."

"Why, how lovely! Who has sent it?" Christine took the parcel, and read the little note attached. "It's from Hannah, my little dressmaker. How kind of her!" She untied the string of the parcel. Inside lay a miniature child's cloak, made from the most beautiful lilac velvet, trimmed with delicate lace roses, a garment which had obviously taken much time and many hours of fine needlework. Christine gasped with appreciation and held the cloak up for inspection. The two men nodded their approval.

"That girl is skilled, there's no doubt about it!" Robert said.

The baby's golden curls glowed next to the soft lavender shade, and when Christine fastened it around the plump little shoulders, she twirled clumsily, awaiting their approval. "Oh, do look, Robert! Such a little charmer! Already she knows what a beautiful outfit does for a woman!" Christine laughed, and holding her daughter in her arms, waltzed about the room, Emma screaming with delight. "I really must go and thank her for such a beautiful present."

"You certainly found a treasure, my dear. She'll make some man a fine wife, talented and beautiful also, or so I believe!"

"This girl, is she from these parts?" Jonathan asked, his curiosity aroused.

"Some part of Kerry, I believe. Her father is dead, an unfortunate accident just before Christmas. The family are staying with an aunt, Mrs Sullivan, and Hannah has already made a name for herself in Limerick society. All the ladies are enchanted by her wonderful designs."

Emma started to fidget restlessly, and Christine rang the bell over the fireplace. "Mary, would you take Emma for her bath? I shall be up shortly to put her to bed." She handed the baby carefully to the maid.

"Of course, ma'am. The little mite must be worn out from all the excitement!"

Robert planted a kiss on the baby's forehead. "Your very first birthday, little one, and many more to follow!"

They sat by the fire companionably, the remains of the birthday cake on the silver cake stand, Jonathan's glass half slipping from his hand as he dozed in the heat of the cosy room. If only life could be always so he thought sleepily. His head dropped onto his chest, the empty glass falling from his hand onto the soft carpet. Christine rose and quietly placed the glass on the table.

"He seems more relaxed tonight," Robert observed in a whisper.

"I hope so, truly I do," Christine replied, not altogether convinced.

Her brother was still far from being a whole person. His reaction to the visit to Flannerys' had unnerved her. The old Jonathan would merely have pitied the poor people's plight, and would then have thought no more of it. The Jonathan she had seen that afternoon had been inflamed with the injustice of their situation. While she knew in her heart that he had been right, she felt that at the present time he was more vulnerable than he would otherwise be to the harshness of the life these people endured. He needed time to come to terms with life after the hell of a war he had been through. He was ripe fodder for any militant group that might attract him. Christine had no time for militancy. She believed in the right for Home Rule, for an independence which would give Ireland a self-governing status. But she detested violence. The Irish Republican Brotherhood was a breeding camp for Fenians, and their policy was well-known – independence at any cost.

She resolved to watch him carefully from now on. Maybe she would arrange an evening at home with some friends. She knew many eligible young ladies who would be only too pleased to keep him occupied for a time. He would be able to laugh with pleasure at their vanities and rid himself, perhaps, of the dark depression that was proving such a burden to him.

Hannah had been working constantly for almost five hours. Her back ached with tiredness, but she had to get the dress finished before Friday. It was now late Wednesday evening and the lace had yet to be attached, the seams of the garment finished, and many other troublesome details to be taken care of. Mrs Deery was not an easy customer to please. She was going overseas with her daughter, a visit to friends in New York. She was bringing "dear Madeline" with her so that she might have the opportunity of meeting a "nice young gentleman" who might prove an acceptable husband for the girl.

Hannah had seen Madeline when she had come for some fittings, and had pitied her. Her clothes were over-fussy, and did nothing for her petite figure. Madeline had the narrowest waist Hannah had ever seen, a valuable asset, particularly when her hips blossomed round and opulent.

Hannah held up the dress and examined it critically. She had altered the chosen style considerably, changing the colour from an uninteresting grey to brilliant sapphire, matching Madeline's eyes. Mrs Deery would, perhaps, not be pleased with her audacity, but the damage was done now, Hannah thought mischievously. If Mrs Deery did not like the finished dress, then Hannah's reputation as a dressmaker might well be finished in Limerick. She had taken a gamble, and there was no going back now.

She remembered Madeline's face, the look of complete lack of interest when she had seen the style her mother had chosen for her. Madeline's only real asset, her slender waist, would be completely lost in such a design. Hannah had altered the pattern to such a degree that it was now completely unrecognisable from the original. The bodice of the dress was closely fitting, the high neckline trimmed with rich, cream lace. The skirt fell in straight folds, a row of tiny buttons, covered in the same material as the skirt, running up each side, and an alluring slit to show Madeline's pretty turn of ankle underneath.

She had just completed the pressing when she heard the doorbell downstairs, then voices in the hallway, one soft and feminine, the other a deep, friendly male laugh. When Hannah heard somebody coming up the stairs, she hurried to the little mirror on the sewing table and pinched her cheeks, checked her hair, pinning an untidy stray curl into place.

There was a soft knock on the door and a feminine voice called, "Hannah, may I come in, my dear?" Hannah immediately recognised the dulcet tones of Mrs O'Shea. She opened the door, her look of genuine pleasure in seeing her favourite customer suddenly overshadowed by a diffidence which, to the onlookers, appeared charming. The source of her embarrassment appeared from behind Christine O'Shea. Out of the shadows stepped a tall, elegantly dressed man, his smile teasing as he looked at Hannah.

"Hannah, forgive me for calling at such a time! Annie has told me you are very busy, but I just had to come and thank you for your wonderful present to baby Emma. This . . ." she indicated her companion with a desultory flourish, "is my brother, Jonathan Mayhew. He was quite adamant that he should accompany me this evening in order to see, as he said himself, the amazing little dressmaker who has transformed his sister from a mundane doctor's wife into a breathtaking vision!" Christine O'Shea laughed, the pride in her voice obvious as she looked up at her brother teasingly. "There, Jonathan! Behold my little treasure, the girl who has every woman in Limerick rushing to buy silks and laces so that they may also be transformed!"

Jonathan gave Hannah an appraising look, his eyes resting on her gleaming curls, some of which had escaped from their hairpins, resting attractively on her slender neck. But it was her eyes that hypnotised him, the most bewitching shade of blue he had ever seen in a woman, their brilliance seeming to penetrate his very being as her unflinching gaze met his.

"I am happy to meet you, Hannah, if I may call you Hannah?" His question held a hint of merriment, as though he was ridiculing her gaucheness, her evident inexperience in dealing with male frivolity.

"Certainly, Mr Mayhew, that is, Lieutenant Mayhew, for Mrs O'Shea has told me of your recent discharge. I am very pleased to make your acquaintance. Please, won't you both sit down? I shall have some tea sent up. I'm sure Molly has just this afternoon baked one of her delicious barm bracks – you must sample some."

Christine sat down on the velvet-covered chaise longue which Hannah indicated, while Jonathan stood staring idly through the window. Hannah had seen his face darken for just a flicker of a moment when she had mentioned his discharge, and she regretted her insensitivity. She had observed him as he crossed the room, the dragging leg causing his face to crumple with obvious pain. She forgot her shyness as she hurried to offer him a seat. He waved his hand dismissively.

"No, no, Hannah. I'm quite all right standing. This old leg of mine needs a bit of exercise." And, as if to bear out his statement, he began to pace restlessly up and down in front of the window.

Hannah felt that here was a man who was trying hard to come to terms with a physical injury that was eating away at his very soul. She had known him for just a few short minutes, but already she could identify with his restlessness, his feelings of isolation and frustration. His strength was trapped inside a body that no longer enabled him to act like a man.

Hannah became conscious of an unfamiliar feeling inside her as she looked at his powerful build, his shadow seeming to engulf the whole room. She moistened her trembling lips with her tongue and wondered why she should feel so warm, for the room was not overheated. Just then he turned his face to her, their eyes meeting in silent, mutual appraisal. Hannah had never felt like this before.

Jonathan Mayhew was a man who could instinctively sense a woman's unawakened desires, and Hannah was no exception. He smiled with sudden relief. Perhaps all was not lost. He would enjoy getting to know Miss Hannah Benson for she was quite the most interesting girl he had ever encountered – a girl not to be trifled with.

Molly brought them tea and dainty slices of barm brack. It was her own recipe handed down from her mother, and her mother before, a delicious concoction of fruit and brown sugar soaked overnight in strong, cold tea, then mixed with flour and butter and baked until risen to a golden brown.

"How delicious!" Christine O'Shea delicately sampled a slice, while Jonathan helped himself to a second slice, licking his lips with obvious enjoyment. "I must get the recipe and slip it into Mrs Tansey's cookbook. She would never forgive me if I suggested that she try a different recipe to her own which, though perfectly wholesome, lacks that certain something that Molly's has!" Christine finished her tea and sat back comfortably in her chair. "I really came to thank you for the lovely birthday present which you sent to Emma. Such an adorable gift, and it must have taken quite an amount of your precious time to complete!" She looked at Hannah with genuine admiration. "You have magic in those hands of yours, Hannah Benson! One day you will be rich and famous, and I shall be proud to tell everyone that I had the privilege of being your very first customer!"

Hannah smiled self-consciously. "You are very kind, Mrs O'Shea. The gift for your daughter was a pleasure to make. I hope it fitted properly?"

"Of course, Hannah! Jonathan will agree with me when I say that it looked quite charming on little Emma!"

"A credit to your expert hands, Hannah," Jonathan confirmed, his compliment causing her cheeks to redden once more. Hannah was not so unworldly that she did not recognise the faint stirring of male interest as he looked at her appreciatively. He would be accustomed to complimenting ladies, Hannah thought wryly. A man like that would scatter compliments and trite phrases as she and her sisters used to scatter corn to the chickens at home in Glenmore. It meant nothing to him.

Christine O'Shea watched her brother's eyes light up with interest as he spoke to Hannah. It was good to see him take an interest in a pretty girl once more, to hear him flirt lightly with Hannah, to see the girl's blushes, so becoming in her preoccupied young face. Impulsively, she voiced her thoughts. "Jonathan is just recently returned from Africa, Hannah. He hasn't been feeling too well of late, and Dr O'Shea and I thought a little get-together would do him the world of good." She looked directly at Hannah. "Perhaps you might like to come, my dear. Nothing very elaborate, just a small gathering."

A look of doubt crossed Hannah's face and Mrs O'Shea added, "Of course, the invitation extends to your mother and sisters also, and your dear aunt and uncle."

Hannah's worried expression cleared and she smiled unreservedly.

"How very nice of you, Mrs O'Shea! I will speak to Annie, of course, but I'm sure we'll be very happy to accept your invitation."

"Splendid! I shall send some formal invitations within the next few days. And now, I think it is time we were leaving." She looked at Jonathan, noting with pleasure his relaxed features as he sat on the window ledge. "Come, brother, or Dr O'Shea will think I have deserted him!"

"Never!" he asserted, rolling his eyes as he followed her to the door.

"You are tired, Hannah, and I am sure we have overstayed our welcome!" Hannah protested genuinely, but Mrs O'Shea was already outside the door.

In the hallway they met Annie, just on her way out of the parlour, her face creased in anxiety. She managed a friendly smile as she said goodnight to Mrs O'Shea and her brother. "I've just invited Hannah to a little musical evening at our house, Annie, and your good self and John also, if that's possible?"

"Why, of course, Christine!" Annie thanked her warmly. "Hannah has not seen much of Limerick society since she came here. It will do her good to meet some new people, get to know a little bit about the city which, up to now, hasn't extended beyond the four walls of that sewing-room of hers!"

"Goodnight, Mrs Sullivan," Jonathan bowed politely as he escorted his sister outside the hall door. Annie stood at the open door, watching them thoughtfully as they got into the carriage, Jonathan's tall figure towering above Mrs O'Shea's petite one. Annie had a feeling about this man – with his mop of dark curls and brooding eyes he could capture the heart of any woman. She would have to warn Hannah about city men and their smooth ways. She would talk to her in the morning. Right now she had other things on her mind.

Chapter 6

A chill January breeze whistled about the house as Annie stood at the front door of the house, looking anxiously down the driveway. John was late this evening. He usually sent word if a meeting was running late or if something unexpected had happened. It was the unexpected she feared most of all. It was now dark outside, and he had said he would be home by nine o'clock. She looked again at the clock in the hallway. It was past ten.

She knew he had been keeping something from her lately. Every time she had asked him if something was wrong, he had laughed and said, "Just business matters, Annie. Nothing for you to be concerned about." But she was concerned. Everyone knew that the conflict between the city traders and the union supporters had reached boiling point. More and more poorly-paid employees were putting pressure on their employers to allow them to join a labour union, to give them some measure of security in their work.

John was totally in favour of their demands. "You can't stop progress," he had argued at many a heated meeting. "Give the workers what they're entitled to." He was known to be a good employer, always generous with bonuses and with time off, but others were not so lenient. There was growing resentment among workers, talk of strikes, and of walkouts on the job.

Annie heard the carriage coming up the driveway and saw John looking tired and worn, his steps heavy as he approached the house. His expression was apologetic as he looked up at her. "I'm sorry, my love. There was no way I could get word to you tonight. The hall was packed with union agitators, and the doors were locked to keep out the trouble-makers."

She took his hat and coat and hung them on the hallstand, then ushered him into the parlour.

"Sit down next to the fire and heat yourself, like a good man."

When she was satisfied that he was sitting comfortably, she went to the oak cabinet by the window and poured a generous measure of whiskey into a glass.

"Here, drink this," she ordered.

She didn't like the blue-tinged cheeks, the too-bright eyes, as he lay back mopping his brow. When he had finished his drink he looked up at her, his troubled eyes confirming her fears. "Jameson wants a lockout. Imagine, Annie, to close the doors on all those misfortunates whose families are depending on their wages just to keep them fed! Myself and a few others voted against, but we were outnumbered." He spread his arms helplessly. "If the workers want a union, which they are entitled to, then the employers will see to it that they lose their jobs. 'If we unionise them, sure they'll be striking every hour of the day for petty grievances,' Jameson said with his bully-boy roar. 'It's as simple as that!"'

"Good God, man, I had no idea it was that serious!" Annie was appalled. "What does it mean for us, John? We can't keep those men from earning a living – and what will happen to the business?"

John's face was a mask of defeat and she felt angry, angry with those who had put his business in jeopardy, who had rewarded his kindnesses with treachery. He reached for her hand and smiled suddenly.

"Don't trouble yourself, girl. It's nobody's fault, you know, just changing times and all the upheaval that goes with it." He stared unseeingly into the flames of the fire. "It was inevitable. I've said it many a time that we should be prepared for the day when the workers will be looking for more than just a little bit extra in their wage packets at Christmas time. Mind you," his face lit up with pride as he continued, "none of my workers caused any trouble. They stood up there, in front of the employers, and they said that John Sullivan was a fair-minded man, and if they were never unionised it would make no difference to them because they were always treated with respect."

"There now!" Annie cried with pleasure, gripping his hand firmly. "Didn't I say you had no need to worry about your workers? A good and loyal bunch of young men and women who would stand by you no matter what!"

"You're right, Annie love," John smiled at her and inwardly thanked God, for the umpteenth time, for giving him such a good and caring woman. Whatever troubles were to come, he felt secure knowing that she would be beside him, supporting him whenever he needed her.

Trouble was brewing, that was a certainty. Michael Jameson was a brute of a man, both at home and in business. He had his poor wife and children living in fear of his heavy hand and malicious tongue. He was known to ill-treat his workers, docking their pay for trifling offences which were, in the main, purely conjecture on his own part. John had occasionally tried to reason with him, tried to convey the workers' point of view. Jameson had laughed in his face.

"An eejit of the highest calibre, that's what you are, John Sullivan!" he had mocked, his large body shaking with coarse laughter.

Hannah sat up in bed suddenly. She had heard something, a loud, crashing noise. It seemed to have come from downstairs, in the front parlour. It was still dark outside, just the faint light of a half-moon shone through the bedroom window, casting eerie shadows on the walls and ceiling. She got out of bed and put on her dressing-gown, pulling it tightly about her, for the night was chilly. Tiptoeing to the bedroom door, she opened it cautiously. May and Florrie's room was directly opposite, and she smiled wryly in the darkness as she heard May's comfortable snoring.

There was no sound from downstairs now, and she was about to turn back into her own bedroom when John appeared out of the shadows.

"Did you hear it too, Uncle John?" she whispered.

He nodded silently, putting a finger to his lips. He

pointed in the direction of the stairs and she followed him, their feet making no sound as they padded softly downwards. Only when they reached the hallway did John speak to her.

"You stay here, like a good girl. I'll just check the parlour."

"What could it be? An intruder? Please be careful, Uncle John." Hannah's voice trembled slightly, and she stared up at him, her eyes wide with fear. John squeezed her arm comfortingly, at the same time taking a small revolver from the pocket of his dressing-gown. He opened the door cautiously.

Hannah cried out in dismay as she looked at the scene before her eyes. Annie's beautiful tapestries, which had hung so elegantly on the cream walls, had been slashed to pieces and thrown onto the floor. The expensive glassware, rare china ornaments, boxes of silver tableware had been scattered about, the glass stamped into the expensive carpet. The furniture had been daubed with red paint. John looked about him silently, his eyes resting on a crude, hand-painted message written on the carved mirror over the fireplace, SULLIVAN – UNION PIG. The red lettering stood out garishly, the vindictive message causing Hannah an involuntary shiver.

There was a movement in the doorway, and Annie stood there, her face full of bewilderment. Hannah put an arm about her, feeling Annie's shoulders twitch nervously, hearing the stifled gasp as she absorbed the scene of destruction before her.

"John, what has happened?" she whispered hoarsely.

"I knew there would be trouble, Annie. I sensed it last

night at the meeting. I'm afraid I'm a bit too outspoken for my own good." He stood by her, stroking her hair gently as she rested her head on his shoulder, Hannah withdrawing a little, feeling herself to be an intruder. "God knows, I don't like to point the finger at any man, but this . . ." he waved his arm about the room despairingly, "has all the appearance of retaliation. Jameson gave me a sly hint last night that if I was to champion the workers' cause, then I would be asking for trouble. I didn't think he'd go this far though."

There was a loud banging at the front door persisting until finally Molly could be heard shuffling slowly from her bedroom beside the kitchen. John went into the hall, meeting Molly's startled gaze as he motioned her to stay where she was, at the same time calling out in an authoritative voice, "Who's there? What do you want?" The voice that answered him was half-fearful, half-apologetic.

"Mr Sullivan, come quickly. It's the shop!" John recognised the voice immediately. It was young Sean O'Neill, the boy who helped him with the supplies, checking that all orders had been filled correctly. Sean was a good, conscientious worker, and John had come to rely on him, putting him in charge of locking up the supply store at the back of the shop at the end of the working day. He opened the door hastily and Sean staggered inside, his face red and streaked with dirt.

"Mr Sullivan, you must come quickly. 'Tis the store, sir . . . and the shop! They're on fire!" John's face remained expressionless. He turned to Annie, standing in the hallway, her small figure pale and ghost-like as she swayed a little.

Recovering herself, she said quietly, "You must go,

John. See if there is anything that can be done. The fire may spread to the cottages behind the stores – the women and children . . ." Her voice trailed off in the sudden stillness. They stood there like statues, waiting for somebody to make the first move, afraid that any action would plunge them into a worse nightmare.

Hannah spoke first, her voice calm and reassuring. "Come, Annie, Molly will make us a nice cup of tea. Perhaps a pot of tea would be in order, as the whole house seems to be awake now." She gestured up the stairs to the landing where her mother and May and Florrie stood, their faces frightened and questioning. "You go, Uncle John, and see what has happened. I'll take care of everything here." John looked at her gratefully. She was a strong girl. Annie would be safe in her hands. He followed Sean from the house and soon the carriage was speeding swiftly through the night. His heart sank as they neared the city and saw the orange flames spiralling viciously towards the pitch-black sky.

"There!" Sean O'Neill pointed excitedly in the direction of the shop. Large crowds were gathering, watching the spectacle with bemused eyes. As John drew nearer, he could see some of his workers dragging buckets of water to quench the flames. Tears of angry frustration burnt his eyes. He felt their despair; they were fighting not only for their employer's business, but for their own survival also. He hurried towards them, the line of helpers now growing in numbers as buckets of water were thrown on the ever-kindling flames.

A cold, fearful touch circled his heart, and he found it hard to breathe as he realised the terrible thing he had done, the oversight which would cost him his livelihood, and disrupt his life forever. The consequences of a fire in a business like his were dire. His whole stock was wiped out. To make it worse, he had let the insurance cover slide, putting the money into bricks and mortar instead, intent on expanding the shop. He had ignored the renewal of the premium, and he would get no sympathy from anyone for his foolishness.

Mad thoughts ran through his head as he bucketed water from nearby houses, his face drenched with sweat. His shop was destroyed. All that would remain would be his good name – that should be worth something. Even in these times, surely an honest fool was better than a conniving one, such as Jameson.

But this fire would be the making of Jameson, he thought bitterly. Customers wouldn't wait for John Sullivan to be back on his feet again. He felt weary, his eyes smarting from the hot smuts blowing in the night air. Perhaps it was an accident, John mused hopefully as he stood with the others, all their frantic efforts in vain as the fire consumed the last remaining wall of the shop. But in his heart he knew better. Jameson had had some part in the mischief. He would get the best part of his customers, that was certain. He could hire and fire as he pleased, because all the other shop workers would be frightened now to mention the dreaded word union.

After breakfast the following morning, John called everybody together in the parlour. Annie had done her best to put the room back into some semblance of order, but the tapestries were completely destroyed. Peggy sat quietly, her eyes wandering about in disbelief. Poor Annie, she thought, looking at her sister's pale face. She didn't deserve this trouble. Peggy wondered if they had done right in coming to Limerick. Maybe they had brought bad luck with them, depositing it on the doorstep of these two kindly people who had taken them into their beautiful home and made them feel that life was worth living again.

"I've called you all together because I want to talk to you about our future, what's going to happen now that the shop is gone." John's voice faltered and Annie took his hand comfortingly. "Whatever happens, I want you to know that this house is your home, for as long as you want it. It will take some time for me to get back on my feet again, but that's for me to worry about."

"What about the bank, Uncle John?" Hannah asked. "Won't the bank help you to get started again?"

John swallowed hard. He found it hard to look at Annie, his darling Annie who had put so much trust in him. He had failed her, failed all of them. He sat down suddenly, his head in his hands, and his shoulders shook with silent sobs. Concern was written all over Annie's face.

"What is it my love? Tell us – surely nothing can be so bad . . ."

"Yes, Uncle John. Please tell us – let us help you." Hannah looked down at him anxiously. She had never seen her uncle so vulnerable, the misery on his face uncharacteristic.

"You have a lot to learn about the business world, Hannah. I doubt if the bank will look favourably on these unfortunate circumstances. You see, I have committed the most terrible crime in business."

"Whatever do you mean, John?" Annie gripped his arm, forcing him to look into her face.

"I have no insurance, Annie. The premium was due for renewal and I put the money into starting the extension for the new shop." He looked at the small group now listening intently to him, Annie kneeling by his side, stroking his arm, her fingers trembling as he tried to steady them with his hand. "They need to see some concrete proof that I can surface again with my good name intact, and I don't think I exactly inspire them with confidence right now."

He went to the window and looked out at the garden, the wintry sunshine playing on the emerald-coloured water of the pond. "I think I can make a go of it again, Annie. I have a solution to this whole sorry mess – but the money I need can't be made here in Ireland." They were all staring at him now, trying to understand the magnitude of his predicament.

"You'll have to leave Ireland – go across to America?" Annie spoke quietly, her eyes pleading with him to deny the obvious. She had often thought that with John's ambitious streak, he might look one day farther afield, just like his brother Vincent had to the New World. But she hadn't imagined it would be under circumstances such as these. She bent and kissed his forehead, taking his hand in hers. "How long, John. How long will it take before you can come home?" Her voice shook and there were tears in her eyes.

John replied sadly. "Six months, maybe a year. I just don't know. I want you to stay here, Annie, all of you." His voice took on a new strength and he spoke insistently now. "I'll have an easier mind over there knowing that you are all together here. Hannah can continue with her dressmaking, with May and Florrie helping her, and I'll rely on you Peggy to see that Annie doesn't fret too much while I'm away."

"Don't worry, John. We'll be fine. You just take care of yourself and hurry back to us." Peggy went and put an arm about her sister. "It's our turn now to repay all your kindness to us. I'm only sorry we can't do more financially. Sure, we're more of a burden than a help to you."

"None of that talk, Peggy Benson!" Annie spoke sharply. "It's a pleasure having you here with us. John has said many times since you came that the house is all the better for your company. It's a lonely place with just the two of us, and now, with John going away."

"When will you go, John?" Peggy asked.

"As soon as possible. There's a steamer sailing from Cobh next Wednesday."

"So soon!" Annie exclaimed, her voice trembling.

"I won't stay there any longer than need be," he promised, scanning the anxious sea of faces around him. He didn't know if he was doing the right thing, but what else was there to do? He felt comforted when he looked at Hannah. She was the strong one. She wouldn't let him down. There was no rebuke in her gaze, no disappointment with him for his terrible error of judgement. Just a look of sympathy which cut through to his very heart.

"Oh, John, I almost forgot." Annie went to the mantlepiece and took a small white envelope from it. "It's an invitation from Mrs O'Shea." She was crying now, trying to appear as though she was reconciled to John's leaving them, the envelope fluttering from her grasp on to the floor. "She's having a musical evening next Thursday – but you will be gone then!" The tears started to course down her pale cheeks, and John put his arms about her.

"There, there now, no more tears! Anybody would think I was dead, the way you're carrying on!"

"Don't say things like that, John, not even in jest. The other side of the world is as good as being dead." She buried her head in his chest and wept.

"You must all go to Mrs O'Shea's evening," he said, putting his hand under Annie's chin, and fixing his eyes on hers. "You shall go and explain to them that I am away on business, and will be back as soon as I have made my fortune!"

May and Florrie smiled at him, at the absurd explanation, and Hannah nodded solemnly. She was glad that he had approved of their attending Mrs O'Shea's musical evening. It would help take Annie's mind off his departure. She would make her aunt wear the flattering grey silk dress she had made for her after Christmas, and her grey leather boots with the little silver buttons, and her mother would look equally elegant in that cream linen skirt and lace blouse with the fashionable ruffles circling her neck.

"We shall go, Uncle John, and we shall make you proud of all your womenfolk. Limerick society will talk about Mrs O'Shea's musical evening for a long time afterwards, because it will have been graced by the attendance of Mrs Annie Sullivan and Mrs Peggy Benson and daughters!" Hannah gave a mock curtsy, and John clapped his hands in approval.

"That's my girl! You're a tonic, Hannah Benson. You'll have all the men in the room fighting for your attentions before the night is out!"

May looked at Hannah enviously. "She was always the one for seeing the bright side of things, Uncle John. Don't worry about a thing – you see to your business and bring back lots of money to start afresh here in Limerick!" May smiled and Florrie spoke up now, a dream-like quality in her voice.

"Everything will turn out right, Uncle John. There's always a happy-ever-after even with the saddest of events – everything happens for a particular purpose." She blushed then when she saw several pairs of eyes focused on her. It had been the longest speech she had ever made to anyone, but the situation had seemed to call for some response and she had been sorry for Uncle John in spite of his mistake in not paying the insurance premium.

"Well said, Florrie my girl. We'll look on the bright side and wish for a happy-ever-after." Annie looked at her encouragingly and Florrie smiled, relieved. They didn't think she was silly. She knew she would never equal Hannah in looks or character, but she was quite happy to stand in the shadows. Already her youthful days back in the small village in Kerry were beginning to fade from her mind like some disagreeable memory she was only too glad to relinquish.

The next few days were spent in getting John ready for his journey. His best suits had to be cleaned and pressed, his shirts starched, his shoes polished. Molly could not resign herself to the master leaving home, "leavin' a houseful of women to fend for themselves, sure the poor man will be distracted with thinkin' about his wife left on her own, God help us, and with the deepest of oceans separatin' them!"

"You'll go to Vincent, John?" Annie enquired, two days before his departure. They were walking in the garden, Annie wrapped warmly in her soft lambswool shawl, John with his arm protectively around her. Peggy had discreetly warned the girls to let them have some time to themselves, so everybody had melted into the background, letting Annie and John savour their last few days together.

"Yes, I've already written, letting him know the time of my arrival in New York. I shall stay with Maura and Vincent until I find my bearings, make a few contacts maybe."

Annie felt relieved. At least with his brother and sister-in-law John would have the security of a family, people he could trust and confide in. Vincent had a lumber business, importing wood from the northern territories of Canada. He had been in America for almost ten years now, and had made a name for himself in the building industry, setting up his business in regions where lumber was in constant demand and prices at a premium.

"I'll have to round up a few bottles of his favourite weakness and pack them carefully." John's eyes twinkled in amusement as he recalled his brother's regular request each year, about a month before Christmas.

"Go into the hills around Limerick, John, like a good man, and send me the finest Christmas gift a man could ask for."

John would willingly comply, so that on Christmas

Day a bottle of poteen would be proudly displayed on Vincent's dinner table and two or three more carefully locked away in the cellar "for private consumption," as he explained in mock solemnity to his wife.

The night before John's departure, there was a loud knock on the front door and Molly, answering it, stepped back in surprise when she was confronted by three male figures, their faces hidden under dark-coloured scarves, only their eyes visible in the gloom.

"We'd like to speak with Mr Sullivan." The speaker's voice was gruff, his tone urgent.

"Wait here," Molly ordered sharply, her voice inferring that she would tolerate nonsense from no man. "I'll see if the master will see you." She peered closer at the three of them, her eyes cautiously scrutinising. "I know you, Mathew Hogan!" she cried triumphantly, and poked him in the chest with a long, bony finger. "I don't know what ye're playin' at, comin' here at night, all dressed up like *amadans*, as if the master hasn't enough to trouble him without you lot tormentin' him, and he bound for foreign parts in the mornin'."

"All right, all right, Molly!" Mathew Hogan drew the scarf from his face. "Like a good woman, fetch Mr Sullivan. We only want to wish him well and give him a little something to start him off right, so to speak."

Molly eyed them suspiciously before she turned and knocked on the door of the parlour. "If you'll pardon me, Mr Sullivan, there's a few . . . gentlemen here to see you."

John hid a smile as he answered her. "Show them in, Molly."

She nodded her head at the three men standing

awkwardly in the hallway, motioning them into the parlour.

Mathew Hogan led the way, twisting his cap nervously, while the other two followed him like great, bungling shadows. "We're sorry for intrudin' on you tonight," Mathew apologised, looking at Annie, but she smiled welcomingly.

"Not at all, Mathew. It's good of you to call, and on the night before John sets off for America."

"That's why we've come, sir." Mathew looked at the other two men with him, and they removed the scarves from about their faces. John recognised them as two of Jameson's employees, fear plainly visible in their faces as they looked at him, a silent plea not to divulge their identity, which they tried so hard to disguise.

"It's like this, Mr Sullivan." Mathew spoke up, self-ordained spokesman for the group. "None of us liked the way your business was burnt down. We all know it was no accident, and we know you were the one who stood up that night at the meeting and declared to everyone that unions for employees were necessary to protect men like myself, and these two here, who live in dread of Jameson every day of their lives." His eyes burned brightly, his articulation momentarily choked by anger. Pulling a long brown envelope, dirty with handling, from his coat pocket, he handed it to John.

"Take this, and don't refuse it, Mr Sullivan, for we've sacrificed a lot to put that package together, not allowin' for the brunt of Jameson's wrath if he were to find out that we had done this thing."

John stood silently, the envelope clutched in his hand.

The clock on the mantelpiece ticked deafeningly in the silence of the room, until Annie rose suddenly and, in a quiet voice, said, "Open the envelope, John. These men obviously went to great pains to deliver it tonight. I think a drop of whiskey wouldn't go astray for any of you?"

The faces of the three brightened, becoming more relaxed, as she moved to the sideboard and poured out three good-sized measures of whiskey. She handed the glasses to each of them while John opened the envelope with clumsy fingers.

Inside was a bundle of soiled, well-handled notes. "There's a hundred pounds there, sir," Mathew said proudly, as he eagerly gulped the glass of whiskey. "We had a collection in all the shops in Oakland Street. All the workers on the counters and in the stores, even the delivery boys. They all put their hands in their pockets and gave something, and glad to do it, they were, Mr Sullivan. We all wish you well, and hope you won't have to stay over for long."

Annie looked at John's face as he gazed unblinkingly at the bundle of precious notes in his hand. There was medicine here, and food for the table, and the little bit put by for emergencies, like getting the sack from Jameson's. John's thoughts ran wildly through his head. He thought of the men who had come here tonight, hiding their identities with woollen scarves, because fraternising with a union supporter would mean instant dismissal. He looked up, his eyes wet with tears. The three men lowered their eyes to the floor. It wasn't right to watch a man cry, especially a respected, strong-minded man like John Sullivan.

"I'll be glad to accept your very generous gift!" He

spoke loudly, his voice filling the room. Annie knew he was trying his best to pull himself together in front of the men, and she joined with him, thanking them for their kindness. They relaxed once more, the sensitive moment having now passed. They had performed their task, and it had been acknowledged with obvious appreciation.

"That's all we came for, Mr Sullivan." Mathew put down his glass on the polished surface of the coffee table and turned to go. The others followed him, pulling their scarves once more tightly about their faces. Mathew paused at the front door, then turned slowly to John. "You're a good man, a decent man, John Sullivan. I wish you the very best of Irish luck across the water, and another thing . . ." He pointed a finger at John, "The times are changin', and we'll get our union yet, in spite of Jameson and his likes!"

Through the window, John watched them hurry down the drive, their heads bent, their coats and scarves pulled closely about them. He turned to Annie, the envelope still in his hand, and spread his arms helplessly. "Annie, what was I to do? If I had refused it, they would have been insulted, but the fact that I accepted it doesn't make me any happier. There are women and children who'll feel the loss of this money! For many of them it will be a matter of life and death!"

Annie nodded sadly. "You did the right thing. Those men thought highly of you, John. You had no choice but to accept their offer of help. They have gone home feeling twice the men they were, knowing that they have helped in some small way to get John Sullivan started in business once more."

The morning started early with everybody up and

breakfasted by nine o'clock, Molly serving hearty helpings of fried bacon and eggs and wedges of griddle bread, "to fortify the master for his long journey. He'll not taste the likes of my griddle bread for many the day to come!".

John agreed wholeheartedly and did justice to her cooking, clearing his plate and drinking the last cup of strong black tea. Hannah just picked at her breakfast, and Annie pushed her plate to one side after a half-hearted attempt to eat something.

"I have an idea!" John exclaimed, observing the gloomy faces around the breakfast table. "Why don't we all go for a little drive in the carriage this morning? May and Florrie haven't seen much of Limerick since they arrived, and I don't have to leave until lunch-time."

"Yes, what a good idea, Uncle John!" Hannah rose quickly, glad to be doing something, secretly dreading the time of departure. "Get on your warm coats, girls! You'll have your first sightseeing trip around Limerick! Hurry now, and maybe we'll have time for a nice hot cup of chocolate and some currant scones in Murphy's Hotel."

May and Florrie dressed excitedly, forgetting for a moment the significance of the trip, Uncle John's last trip with them for many months to come.

Hannah sat silently in the carriage, her face a mixture of sadness and curiosity as she looked at the young girls and boys on their way to work in the flour mills, their heads covered with white scarves, unusual wooden boots on their feet.

"They're called clogs," John explained when she enquired. "They couldn't wear ordinary boots to work;

the flour would ruin them after a while. The wooden clogs are more durable."

"They're so young, Uncle John! Some of them look as though they could do with a good breakfast to start them on their day."

"Those are the times we live in, Hannah, long hours and low wages. And no employer asks what age you are when he knows he can exploit you by holding the threat of dismissal over your head." John saw both pity and indignation in her dark eyes. "There's nothing you or I can do about it. Those people are glad to be earning a wage to keep their families fed, and a roof over their heads. They know no better, and that's the pity of it."

The carriage made its way slowly through the streets, already crowded with shoppers and workers alike, mingling together, their breath rising in little puffs of frosted smoke in the chill air of the morning. The sirens sounded from the factories, summoning the workers to their jobs, and from the dockland, heralding the arrival of some cargo of merchandise in the quays. Hannah felt the faint stirring of excitement inside her. Her eagerness to be part of this great mass of liveliness and industry rose up and enveloped her whole being, until she felt she could no longer bear to remain just a spectator, waiting for her opportunity to prove herself.

'One day,' she thought, as the carriage stopped outside Murphy's Hotel, 'one day I'll have the finest carriage in the whole of Limerick, and the girls and boys I'll have working for me won't have to trudge their way to work with nothing to look forward to but long, hard hours and the sharp tongue of an unscrupulous employer.' Her business would be the start of a whole new era in industry.

She smiled to herself as she followed John and Annie through the glass door of the hotel, the porter bowing politely as he closed it behind them. May and Florrie blushed self-consciously. Nobody had ever opened a door for them in their lives, and they wondered if they should give the man something for his consideration.

"I don't feel very comfortable – that man holding the door for the likes of us," May hissed to Florrie. She fumbled in her purse but Hannah put a detaining hand on her arm. "No, May – it's not done. Expensive hotels like this have porters all the time opening the door for their patrons.'

"Sure, what harm can it do to give the poor man something for his trouble?" Florrie asked, while Hannah led them away quickly, the man lowering his head and smiling at them as they passed him, Florrie blushing uncomfortably.

Hannah urged them forward into the dining-room where the smell of hot chocolate and strong coffee floated in the air, the atmosphere friendly as the occupants sat about on easy chairs, sipping their steaming cups, their conversation low and discreet.

"Look as though you are accustomed to such mornings," Hannah whispered furiously. "We have no need to be intimidated by such people. We are as good as anyone here in this room, otherwise why would Uncle John and Annie bring us here?" She looked impatiently at her sisters who were sheepishly following Peggy to a little booth in the corner. "Good God! I thought you were actually going to genuflect in front of that porter. That's his job, and he likes it. He doesn't expect to be paid by everyone who comes through the door of the hotel!"

May gave a small smile and took Florrie's hand comfortingly. "My, hasn't our sister got such great notions of herself since she came to the city." She thought Hannah was so hard to understand at times.

A few eyes were turned in their direction as they sat down, for they made a very pleasing picture in the dining-room that morning, particularly the tall, elegant young girl with the striking cascade of burnished hair rolled simply at the nape of her neck, her brilliant blue eyes lustrous in a finely sculpted face, her cheeks pink with excitement. Hannah had become quite expert at copying the most fashionable styles from the many dress catalogues John had delivered regularly to the shop, and many of the women in the room that morning glanced enviously at her sophisticated outfit.

May and Florrie, although not quite equalling their sister's striking good looks, nevertheless received many an admiring glance. Hannah had painstakingly shown them how to dress their hair, and had advised them what colours suited them best for their darker features and curling black hair. They were dressed this morning in coats of similar design, one plum-coloured, the other a striking shade of green, both designed and made up with Hannah's help. Peggy, looking at them sitting there talking animatedly amongst themselves, felt proud of her daughters, especially of Hannah, who had turned almost overnight into a young woman, capable of running a business single-handed, elegant and self-assured.

Peggy could see some of the young men in the room eyeing Hannah admiringly, and a sudden fear clutched at her heart. These young men were of a class that differed greatly from their own, whose fathers owned wealthy businesses and traded in exotic goods from faraway countries. They could only cause heartbreak for her daughters. Trifle with their affections they might, but no young gentleman would think to associate himself by marriage with a girl whose background proved to be so lacking both in wealth and social standing.

"Peggy, you're in a world of your own, girl!" John's voice broke through her thoughts. "It's time we were getting a move on. I have to be in Cobh by late afternoon; the boat sails at six. Just as the Angelus bell is ringing out, you'll all think of me, then say a little prayer that the journey across won't be too hazardous." He spoke jokingly, clutching his stomach in mock agony. "I've heard that seasickness is the worst fate that could befall a body, with the tossing and turning of the boat, rising and falling on the gigantic waves."

"John! I don't want to hear any more of that kind of talk!" Annie spoke sharply. "I just want you to reach Vincent as soon as possible, and make enough money in New York so that you can return safely to us. Not a fortune, mind you, John Sullivan! You know yourself I was never one for pushing a man too far, making him take on more than he was capable of, just to keep me in luxuries."

John leaned across and whispered something in her ear, and Peggy and the girls saw her blush to the roots of her still luxuriant hair. "John Sullivan! Shame on you! I don't know if I should be letting you go away at all – a devil of a man let loose on the promiscuous streets of New York." Hannah knew that whatever Uncle John had said to Annie, it had not been an insult, but something private, something shared by two people who loved each other uncompromisingly.

For a moment Hannah experienced something not unlike envy, as she looked at the happy, flushed face of her aunt, and the admiring gaze of her uncle as he gently teased her. She saw her mother turn away, as if the sight of John and Annie together brought bittersweet memories of Peter to the surface.

"Right then, ladies. Time to be going." John led the way through the now crowded dining-room, out into the busy street filled with trains and carriages, the patient dray horses pulling great loads of merchandise, coal and piles of tanned leather. Hannah wrinkled her nose in disgust as the powerful stench of the raw hides on their way to the tannery reached her nostrils.

"You'll get used to the smell when you've been in Limerick another little while," Annie smiled at the grimace on her face. "It's a good industry, you know, employing many a poor man for casual work who otherwise would remain idle – and I'm sure you wouldn't turn up your nose at the finished product." Annie nodded towards a well-dressed woman just entering the hotel, her feet proudly displaying a pair of the finest boots Hannah had ever seen, dark brown patent leather, with smart leather tassels at each side.

"They were made in Limerick?" Hannah asked in disbelief.

"Every lady who possesses a pair of such boots can boast proudly that they were made in her own home city of Limerick!" John said, and Hannah could hear the note of pride in his voice, see the wistful look in his eyes as he stood there in the street, gazing hungrily about him for the last time before his departure for America.

Annie was adamant that she should travel to Cobh with him to see him off. "I don't care what you say, John. I'm not letting you leave the country without a soul to wave goodbye to you. My mind would be tormented thinking of you." Her voice broke miserably, the tears shining in her eyes, and John nodded. It was for her own sake that he had wanted her to stay in Limerick, to say goodbye in familiar surroundings with Peggy and the girls to comfort her after he had left. But he should have known she would want to be with him until the very last moment. They had never been separated in all the years of their marriage.

The girls were tearful as they said their goodbyes, and Peggy squeezed his hand comfortingly. "Don't worry about a thing," she whispered softly to him as he settled himself into the seat of the carriage next to Annie. "We're used to looking after ourselves, and Annie will be in good hands. We won't let her sit around the house, growing pale and thin with thinking about you!"

Annie smiled and patted her ample hips. "Sure, maybe it would do me no harm to get a bit on the thin side. There's too much of me there already!"

"Don't you do any such thing!" John warned. "I want you to be just as you are now when I come home, not some rake of a woman with a pale, sorrowful face."

They were still teasing each other as the carriage made its way down the drive of the house and out through the front gate. Peggy and the girls stood there waving until they were out of sight, then turned back into the house. "May God go with him," Peggy prayed quietly, and Hannah closed her eyes, silently echoing her mother's prayer. She was going to make sure that her business was a success, do everything in her power while Uncle John was away to make it grow into a profitable enterprise, something he would be proud of when he returned. She owed it to him, and much more.

They turned and went into the house, the parlour bright and cheerful with the log fire burning in the grate, a tray laid for tea with one of Molly's fruit cakes cut into dainty slices and buttered generously.

"We have been very fortunate, girls. I'm sure you all realise that." Peggy sank tiredly into one of the armchairs, and looked up at the three girls standing before her, her face serious. "We will all say a prayer that John will reach America safely, and that it won't be long before he is home with us again."

Molly entered the room just as they were all on their knees, their heads bowed as they prayed silently, and she went down on her knees and prayed with them. They had finished their tea and were sitting around the fire, sewing and putting the finishing touches on a day dress for Madeline Deery when the Angelus bell rang clearly from St Clement's church, its sonorous tones penetrating the cosy room, filling the occupants with a profound feeling of loneliness.

"He's gone – may God speed him," Peggy said quietly, blessing herself, her hand trembling.

Hannah went to the window and looked out at the garden, its winter nakedness making the big house seem strangely vulnerable. Annie's journey home from Cobh would be a lonely one, her thoughts full of John, the emptiness in her heart like a sharp knife, merciless in its cold indifference. Hannah turned quickly from the window, shivering involuntarily.

"We must do everything we can to help Annie just now," she spoke decisively, pacing up and down the room, her expression thoughtful. "We will all go to Mrs O'Shea's night. We will dress up and smile at everybody and be gay, for Uncle John's sake."

Her enthusiasm was infectious, and soon they were all discussing the dresses they would wear, how they would arrange their hair, the people they would meet. May and Florrie worried about their lack of social graces. What if they should make a show of themselves, they asked Hannah, two pairs of eyes looking up at her anxiously.

"Hold your heads high. We mightn't be very far up the social ladder, but we're not beggars either. We must do Annie proud and act as though we're accustomed to such social events." Hannah glanced at her mother questioningly, and Peggy nodded.

"Hannah's right. We will go to Mrs O'Shea's and make it a night to remember."

"In the nicest possible way!" Hannah amended, and they all laughed.

Molly heard the laughter from the kitchen and smiled. Thank God the missus had such a gay bunch to return to. She would make a good meal for all of them tonight. The missus would surely be famished after the journey back from Cobh. A good, wholesome Irish stew, Molly decided, that would take the chill out of her bones. Maybe some apple cake and fresh cream to follow. She bustled about the kitchen, humming tunelessly as she prepared the meal.

It was ten o'clock when the sound of a carriage was heard pulling up outside the front door. Peggy and her daughters waited anxiously, peering out into the night. Annie got down from the carriage, Molly's nephew, Sean Og, helping her as she swayed a little, putting her hand on his arm for support. She walked slowly up the steps to the front door. Hannah saw the circles beneath the dull eyes, the pale face filled with quiet resignation. In that moment she admired her aunt. This woman who had taken them unquestioningly into her home without asking for any return for her kindness, and now to have her husband taken from her, his livelihood a pile of burnt-out ashes.

"Come in out of the cold, Annie, like a good woman." Peggy helped her into the hall, supporting her as she led her into the warm parlour. "Sit down by the fire and drink this, all of it!" She handed Annie a glass of whiskey, and Annie accepted it reluctantly. "Go on," Peggy insisted, "every drop of it!"

Annie put the glass to her mouth and drank slowly, until finally she relaxed against the soft, velvet cushions, her eyes half closed. Peggy took the glass from her hand and placed it on the mantlepiece.

"I'm exhausted! The journey was very tiring, and after John left I just . . ." Her voice trembled and she put her hand up to her eyes. "Thank God for Sean Og, that he was there to bring me home. I don't think I could have managed on my own."

"We'll have something to eat now. You'll feel better after you have something solid inside you." Peggy went out into the kitchen, and presently Molly appeared. The meal was all ready to be served. "You're all right, ma'am?" she asked now, examining Annie's face with concern.

"I'm fine, Molly, and John was in good form when he was leaving. So we'll have some of your wholesome stew now, for I can smell it even from here, and to tell you the truth, I'm half-starved!"

They sat down together, John's seat at the top of the table empty. Annie chattered lightly throughout the meal, and Hannah could see that she was making a valiant attempt to bring some normality back to their routine, her quick smile not quite reaching her eyes as she looked repeatedly at John's vacant seat.

"When do you think we'll hear from him?" Peggy asked as they sat in front of the blazing fire, the hot meal giving Annie back some colour to her cheeks.

"God only knows. He'll send me a cable as soon as he gets there, but it will be a long journey. I only hope the elements will be good to him and he'll arrive safely." She blessed herself and they all sat in silence, praying silently with her.

"I'm sure of one thing anyway, Annie," Hannah said, putting a reassuring hand on her shoulder. "Uncle John won't delay in writing to you. He knows how worried you'll be."

"He's the most considerate of men, right enough," Annie said, her voice catching a little, the glisten of tears in her eyes. "I promised myself on the way back from Cobh that I wouldn't sit around the house crying like a lost banshee." She lifted her head determinedly. "I have work to do here, and you, Hannah, have a thriving business to run, the finest lacemaking in the country!"

"Can we go to Mrs O'Shea's do, Aunt Annie?" Florrie asked, hopefully.

"We most certainly can!" Annie smiled up at her. "It was the last thing John said to me before he sailed, 'make sure all of you go to Mrs O'Shea's evening, and make me proud of you!'" Annie stood up and beckoned to Hannah. "Come, Hannah! Suddenly I'm not tired at all! We'll go upstairs and choose what we shall wear to this social gathering. There are ladies who'll be dressed in the very latest designs from Paris and America, gowns to make you sit up and take notice – but we'll show them all!" She winked at Hannah, her old cheerfulness restored. "All our dresses will be exclusive, from the small but esteemed dressmaking business of Miss Hannah Benson!"

Chapter 7

The advent of springtime heralded a flurry of preparations for the aristocracy of Limerick as ladies vied with each other to make their party the talk of the town, the extensive preparations relieving the boredom of days not bright enough or warm enough to spend outdoors.

One such gathering which had been anticipated with great delight by ladies and gentlemen alike was that of Dr and Mrs O'Shea's Valentine's Eve ball. The company would be a mixture of military and businessmen alike, some debonair and handsome and unattached, much to the delight of the single ladies intent on netting themselves a man before the start of the summer boating trips on the Shannon. Carriages were lined in twos outside Dr O'Shea's residence when Sean Og halted the horses outside the front gate. He alighted eagerly, the importance of the moment making him stick out his chest proudly as he helped his female charges from the carriage and onto the busy pavement. The front door of the house was thrown open, the cheerful buzz of conversation reaching the street from the brightly-lit hallway. The scent of expensive perfume and the rustle of silk almost made them turn back again to the safety of the carriage.

"May! Florrie!" Peggy whispered sharply. "Remember what I told you – act like decent young women, and you have nothing to be ashamed of."

"Mrs Sullivan! And dear Hannah! How nice to see all of you!"

Mrs O'Shea greeted them effusively as they entered the drawing-room. She was dressed in the most magnificent black silk dress, trimmed with delicate lace patterns of roses and spidery heathers. Hannah looked with satisfaction at her own handiwork on the beautiful woman.

"Everyone here tonight has admired my gown," Mrs O'Shea whispered in Hannah's ear. "They are just dying to meet my elusive young dressmaker, and what a surprise they'll get, my dear, for you look absolutely radiant tonight!"

Hannah blushed and a few men turned their heads to look admiringly at the lovely girl with hair like spun gold piled high on top of her head in a mass of rich curls, her gown complementing the slender lines of her young figure.

Hannah had sat up most of the night putting the finishing touches to her dress, and she was more than pleased with the result. It was a deep shade of midnight blue with shimmering threads of gold running through the material. The length was most fashionable, half way between calf and ankle, showing to advantage shoes that were trimmed with pearl-studded buckles.

Peggy looked admiringly at her daughters. May and

Florrie were both very stylishly turned out, thanks to Hannah's creativity. One was in sea-green taffeta, the other in pale lemon. Both wore wide silk sashes of silver about their waists, and Hannah had arranged their hair most becomingly in chignons at the napes of their necks, secured simply with lace snoods. But it was Hannah who was the most striking, her head held high as Mrs O'Shea escorted her about to meet her guests, smiling graciously, eyes sparkling with pleasure as she revelled in her surroundings.

Peggy looked at her, vaguely troubled. Where did she ever get a daughter such as this? May and Florrie she could identify with; they were like her, a trifle embarrassed and uncomfortable in the midst of such opulence. Hannah seemed to fit in as though she belonged, as though she had never known any other life than that which she was now clinging to so tenaciously, as though she was afraid that some trick of fate would deprive her of such splendour. A shiver ran down Peggy's spine. She could no longer protect this daughter of hers, because suddenly she seemed like a stranger, a girl who was filled with a frightening determination to relinquish all the ties of her past. Peggy wondered fearfully if that included her own mother and sisters.

Suddenly Hannah turned and looked straight into her mother's eyes. She smiled then, and it was as though a great shadow had passed over and the sun had once more shone through. She could see Hannah excusing herself from the lady she had been in conversation with, her gaze never faltering until she reached her mother's side.

"You are the most beautiful woman in this room tonight, with Aunt Annie a very close second!" Hannah put an arm around each of the two women and ushered them further into the gathering. "There will be some supper first, and then a famous singer from the London Opera House will sing some of your favourites, Mother. Some of Moore's melodies, and some arias from the great operas. Oh, Aunt Annie, was there ever such a night?" She turned to her aunt excitedly, and Annie thought she had never seen the girl look so alive.

"Perhaps, since we have already been introduced, it would be fitting if I were to ask you to sit with me at supper?" The deep male voice from behind her shoulder startled Hannah and she looked about quickly. She could feel a deep blush envelop her face as she looked up at the handsome figure of Jonathan Mayhew.

Annie nudged her sister discreetly. "They make a handsome couple, Peggy. Such a fine young man! Look how he listens so attentively to Hannah – and the bold lassie herself is talking to him as though she has known him all her life!"

"I feel so frightened for her sometimes, Annie. She is so independent, so sure of herself. If anything should happen to sour her happiness, I don't think I would be the right person to console her." She broke off, despair plainly visible on her face. "You would have been a fitting mother to Hannah, Annie." Annie started to protest, but Peggy went on, "No, Annie, I mean it. I'm only a countrywoman, not used to city ways."

"But you will get used to the city, Peggy! Already the girls are settling in, and they have a nice little business at the back of them."

"Hannah is different," Peggy went on, as though Annie had never spoken. "She was born to live a life far removed from the one she was born to. Just look at her!" She nodded in the direction of the dining-room, where Jonathan Mayhew, his hand held lightly under Hannah's elbow, was guiding her towards her seat. Her face was turned up to his, serene and smiling, occasionally blushing at some compliment. "She is thriving on city life, and is never awkward in company. She seems to seek such gatherings rather than avoid them."

Annie followed Peggy's wistful gaze, and had to admit to herself that her sister was right. She felt a little ashamed of another feeling that had gradually surfaced as Peggy spoke, a feeling almost of triumph, that the likeness between Hannah's character and her own had been sensed by Peggy. She spoke earnestly to Peggy as they took their seats at the dining-table, May and Florrie seated one at either side of them.

"Listen, Peggy, if there's anything I can do for Hannah, at any time, you know that I won't hesitate for one moment to help her. I know she has changed a great deal since she came to Limerick. She has grown into a beautiful young woman, a woman any man would be proud to marry, and she shall marry – but not just yet. Hannah is a sensible girl. She knows what she wants and is determined to get it. She won't act foolishly, never fear!"

Peggy heaved a sigh of relief. "I don't know what I'd do without you, Annie. You make everything sound so simple. There I was, not ten minutes ago, seeing my daughter's life in ruins, married to the first handsome man who made eyes at her. Now I just feel so silly, for imagining so much trouble!"

"There's a good woman!" Annie squeezed her hand

affectionately. "Now, let's enjoy ourselves, and forget our troubles for one evening!"

Jonathan looked at Hannah, his gaze slightly puzzled, a teasing smile in his eyes. "You intrigue me, Hannah. Sometimes you seem like a shy child, with that lovely becoming blush on your cheeks . . ."

Hannah lowered her eyes, suddenly very interested in the pattern of wild flowers on her dinner plate.

"And then at other times, you seem to be the most sophisticated young woman, full of dreams and ambitions, so determined to make a success of your life!"

"Maybe it's best that you should not analyse me too earnestly. I find it hard to understand myself sometimes." Hannah looked up at him, her brilliant eyes bewitching him. "I wish I could be more like May or Florrie sometimes. They have no real ambition, apart from finding happiness by settling down with a couple of reliable, hardworking men. But I need so much more from life!" She smiled at him then, almost apologetically. "I'm sure all this talk from me doesn't interest you in the least."

"On the contrary – I find everything about you most entertaining." He looked at her, the wealth of meaning in his eyes making her heart pound almost intolerably. Jonathan covered one slender hand with his own, tanned, masculine one. Hannah did not pull away. It felt good, his touch sympathetic, and her heart fluttered like a trapped butterfly, longing to escape into the raptures of sweet, unreserved love. He was not a philanderer, Hannah knew instinctively. His eyes were kind, the pain he had endured during his service overseas still obvious, but his gaze met hers, genuinely concerned.

"I like you, Mr Mayhew," Hannah said suddenly, looking up at him, her eyes sparkling with just a hint of girlish flirtation.

"And I like you, Miss Benson," he returned, the touch of laughter in his voice.

Annie, watching them discreetly, hoped that she had not spoken too soon to Peggy, reassuring her of Hannah's sound common sense. Jonathan Mayhew was a decent young man, no harm would come to Hannah with him. But he was recovering from one of the worst ordeals a man can go through, a war with such disastrous consequences that he had returned, disillusioned and in constant pain, an enduring reminder of man's inhumanity to his fellow man.

He would need time to recover, for all the scars to heal so that he could face the world again without the haunting memories which must be, at present, his constant companions. Hannah deserved a better chance in life than to be burdened with a young man who had yet a long way to go to find true peace of mind.

The supper was superb, the gleaming silver plates topped with elaborate displays of cold meats and chutneys, sweetbreads and various delicacies which Hannah politely refused because she was afraid of appearing ignorant of the manner in which such food should be eaten.

"Oh, come now!" Jonathan coaxed her, holding up the most appetising roast pigeon. "Just a little then, and if you don't like it, I shall personally make a tour of the entire table to find something which shall prove pleasing to your discerning palate!"

Hannah laughed and nodded her head consentingly.

Jonathan served her a large portion, ignoring her protests, and as the tempting smell of the meat reached her nostrils, she picked up her knife and fork, tasting tentatively at first, then discovering that the meat had the most delightful flavour of spices finished her portion just as Jonathan was extending his hand to pour her some more wine.

"Oh no, please, Jonathan. I mean . . ." she blushed as she continued self-consciously, "Mr Mayhew. I'm sorry, I didn't mean to be so familiar. It must be the wine. I'm not accustomed to it. I feel quite lightheaded."

"You shall call me Jonathan, and I shall call you Hannah," he said, his dark eyes glinting with amusement. He filled her glass and she protested half-heartedly. She knew there was no point in refusing. He was a man used to getting his own way in everything, and Hannah felt a pleasurable tingle run down her spine as she became aware of his strong, masculine presence so close to her. He must have experienced a similar sensation, for suddenly he took her hand and placed it against his cheek, a swift, impulsive movement that caught her completely unawares.

Christine O'Shea, seated at the far end of the table, spotted the gesture and felt an enormous sense of relief. Her brother must be on the road to recovery when he could respond like this to an attractive young woman. However, a frown clouded her features as she studied the young couple. Hannah was a dear girl, and she was very fond of her, but as a candidate for marriage to Jonathan, she could never be considered. Robert O'Shea followed his wife's perturbed gaze and smiled with satisfaction.

"Now there's a happy couple tonight, my love," he whispered in his wife's ear. "You have done more than any doctor could have done for Jonathan by inviting that young girl here. She is just the tonic he needs!"

"Yes, Robert, but only short-term, I think?" She looked at her husband questioningly and he was surprised by the tenseness in her usually placid tone. "Jonathan is so vulnerable right now, and Hannah is such an attractive young woman, but this friendship must go no further, Robert. Hannah would not be a suitable partner for Jonathan. He must find a wife of social standing, somebody both cultured and refined, who will be an asset to him socially. Hannah is not that person." She looked at her husband with an expression of mingled shame and defiance. "I know I sound very much the shrew, but it is nonetheless the truth."

Robert looked about the room at the assortment of people eating, drinking and laughing together, expensive jewels adorning the ladies' necks and slender fingers, the men with their gold cigarette cases and diamond-studded collars, distinguished colleagues and members of the various elitist clubs in Limerick. Such a gathering would laugh derisively at a match between a lieutenant in the Queen's regiment and an obscure little seamstress.

"I think you may be right, my dear," he said slowly, looking at his wife as though he were seeing her for the first time. He had not known that Christine could show such calculating astuteness. She had spoken the indelicate truth as only a true member of Limerick's upper class could, and he had agreed with her, much to his own disgust. "Let them be happy for tonight; it is a night for the young, Valentine's Eve, Christine. They are still so misty-eyed with the elixir of unshattered dreams." He bent forward and kissed her tenderly on the cheek, smiling at her indulgently. "Who knows what the future will hold for each of them?"

He lifted his wineglass to his lips and drank long and deep. He could feel himself becoming morbid, the memory of Mrs Flannery's dead baby still with him. He had gone to see the infant only that morning, and found the mother staring into the makeshift cot with wide, confused eyes. She had awoken late, she had told him, for once not disturbed by the hungry cries of the baby, to find him cold and lifeless in his cot. The other children had stood around him, not crying, showing no hint of emotion at all, only that quiet resignation of theirs. They had not expected the tiny being to live, and he had not.

Robert had cried silently on the way home, for poor wretched Mrs Flannery and her swarm of unhealthy children, for her despairing husband who searched in vain for some kind of employment which would keep them from starving, and lastly, he cried in mingled anger and relief for his own good fortune in having a healthy young daughter who would never know the stench of poverty and deprivation. He sat now, the effects of the wine dulling his senses, obliterating the memories of the day.

The tables were cleared and the opera singer took his place at the piano, his expansive frame commanding attention from the buzzing audience. Soon, there was complete silence. The lamps were dimmed by the servants, and the powerful voice filled the still room.

Hannah listened enraptured. Jonathan relaxed in his seat, feeling for the first time since he had returned home, a quiet contentment. Hannah was good for him. She was so different from the other girls with whom he had flirted so capriciously in the past. He realised now how artificial they had been, with their incessant twittering and feigned coquettishness. Hannah was real, a pearl in the midst of countless imitations.

Annie and Peggy sat directly behind the young couple, saw the two heads come close together. Both women's thoughts were in unison. Such happiness could only be short-lived. They would teach each other many things, one of which would be the painful lesson in how to say goodbye. Two young people from different backgrounds – the most they could hope for was a few hours' happiness, such as they had this evening. Annie could have wept for Hannah, that she should be so disillusioned at such an early stage.

The dream of the New World lurched precariously on the raging seas, ploughing through the tumultuous waters as it sped away from the shores of Ireland on its way to the New World and another chapter in John Sullivan's life, one which he was finding hard to accept with a glad heart. Just a few passengers were brave enough to face the sea-sprayed decks, their feet sliding along the dangerously wet surface. John looked out over the vast, angry expanse of heaving black waters, and felt an overwhelming sensation of loneliness. His thoughts were full of Annie with her ready smile and words of comfort whenever he was feeling particularly depressed – how he needed her comforting presence just now! He had never been on a long sea voyage before, and the constant rolling of the ship on the stormy seas made his stomach churn.

"'Tis a night for sittin' at the fire in the comfort of your own home!" A voice sounded behind him and he turned, startled. He saw a short, portly man with twinkling brown eyes in a small, round face, one hand firmly holding a bowler hat on his head, his other hand extended in greeting. "Murphy's the name, Michael Murphy, from the green plains of the Golden Vale in Tipperary on my way to fame and fortune in the great land of America!" John smiled at the man's jovial enthusiasm and accepted the outstretched hand.

"John Sullivan is my name, from Limerick, and you could say I'm on the same mission as yourself, to make my fortune and return safely to Ireland!"

"Hold on to my hand, and we'll take a clumsy stroll along the deck, exchange a few stories and maybe get to know a little bit more about each other!"

John clung gratefully to his companion as they made their way gingerly towards the stern, both gasping for breath as the sheets of salty spray lashed their faces relentlessly.

"Yours is a sad tale, and that's for sure," Michael Murphy looked at John solemnly, noticing the lines of worry, the grey pallor on his pinched face. Here was a man who needed a friend, a man who was missing the company of a fine woman back home, his eyes betraying all the misery of a bitter twist of fate. "I'm in the building trade myself."

Modesty prevented him from telling John that just before his recent trip back to Ireland, he had completed the new Astor Hotel in the heart of New York. Never blow your own trumpet to a man when he's down, that was Michael Murphy's philosophy. Better to give him a bit of encouragement. He'd need it if he was to survive in New York. Ellis Island was full of would-be millionaires, dreamers who all too soon faced the grim realities of life in prosperous America.

"My brother is well set up over there." John stopped for a moment, trying to catch his breath, his voice breaking with weariness. "Vincent has promised to help me as much as he can." He hesitated for a moment. He had only met the man, but already John knew that Michael was a man of integrity, one who could be trusted with a man's confidences. "I had a business in Limerick city – a modest living as a shopkeeper dealing in a variety of goods, silks, satins and cotton. I also dealt in importing dried foods, teas, sweetmeats and ham from our own bacon factory, Shaws, in Limerick." He took a deep breath, tears coming to his eyes, Michael's attention and silence an encouraging incentive to continue. As John related the whole story of the fire, his depression seemed to lift as though a terrible burden had been released from his shoulders.

"You get in touch with me when you're settled." Michael said when he had finished, putting a hand in his pocket, momentarily leaving his hat to the mercy of the harsh wind. "Here's my card with my address. A shopkeeper and a bricks-and-mortar man may not have a lot in common, but you're a sound, decent man, lookin' to make an honest livin', and if nothin' else maybe we'll become the best of friends, am I right?" He looked questioningly at John, a roguish twinkle in his eye.

"I'll be happy to look you up, Michael, as soon as I find

my bearings. You've lightened my troubles this evening."

"No more of that, now. There'll be no more feelin' sorry for yourself. God knows what that good woman Annie would think of her brave John if she could see him now, staggering along the deck of the finest ship that ever sailed between the Emerald Isle and America, his eyes filled with salty tears and his heart full of despair."

John straightened himself up determinedly, trying to ignore the sick feeling in the pit of his stomach. "You're an honest man, Michael, and I thank you for your frankness. You've brought me to my senses and given me new courage to face whatever lies in store at the end of the journey." The two men looked at each other as they stood there, alone now on the deck, and they clasped each other's hands in a silent pact, the roaring sea a lone witness to their new-found friendship.

Chapter 8

New York harbour bustled with activity on a cold, sunny morning in March 1900 as Vincent searched the sea of tired, apprehensive faces as they alighted from the passenger ferry.

There had been a three-hour wait at Ellis Island that morning, and many of the passengers were close to weeping as they finally set foot on American soil, their few ragged belongings clutched close to them, children crying with cold and hunger, their mothers' eyes bewildered, their fathers' filled with a mixture of despair and anticipation.

John was standing on the quayside. The bustling throngs and the shouts from the dockworkers as they loaded luggage and various items of treasured household furniture onto wooden trolleys made him think of Limerick harbour, and his heart felt like a cold block of stone inside him.

"John, man, is it you?" He heard the shout coming from the direction of a small group of people waiting eagerly, their eyes scanning the passengers. Suddenly, a tall figure emerged, his broad frame dwarfing the crowd on the quayside, one big brown hand thrust forward in welcome. "I thought you had got lost out there on the ocean waves, you were so long coming in to harbour!" John shook hands with his brother, the firm clasp warming him to his very soul.

Vincent was just the same as he remembered him, a little fatter maybe, and looking a lot more prosperous. A gold watch and chain hung from the lapel of his stylish overcoat, and he stood there, a commanding figure planted amidst the scurrying mob, beaming at John.

"Vincent, I'm so pleased to see you at long last, even though the circumstances are not what I would have wished." John's voice faltered, and Vincent, seeing the hopeless look on his brother's worn face, put his arm about him reassuringly.

"Come now. Maura and the boys are waiting with a good hot stew, not as good as the Irish stew, mind you, but a fair substitute. We'll have you back on your feet in no time." Vincent led him through the dense crowds towards a carriage waiting outside the busy harbour.

"John! John Sullivan!" They both turned and saw a small man, his face red with exertion, running towards them.

"Michael Murphy! Sure didn't I nearly forget to say goodbye to you in the excitement of meeting with Vincent here again!" John introduced the two men and they chatted easily, their knowledge of New York's business life a common chord of conversation between them.

"You keep in touch now, John Sullivan. And remember, if there's anything at all I can do for you, you need only ask and I'll do what I can." They shook hands warmly, and the last John saw of Michael Murphy was the top of his bowler hat bobbing its way briskly through the crowds.

"Now listen to me, John. Ever since you wrote telling me about your circumstances, I've been setting the ball rolling, so to speak." Vincent spoke rapidly, his sentences evidently well-rehearsed, as he outlined his plans. John sat looking through the carriage window, amazement written all over his face as he watched the teeming throngs of people, some dark, some fair, their voices rising and falling in a babel of foreign languages.

"There's a warehouse I haven't been using for some time now – a comfortable size, in need of a little bit of renovation, but it's a start. You can take out a loan from me – I know you're too proud to accept something for nothing, even from your own brother – and buy a few of the essentials. The lumber men are always clamouring for goods when they come to the city delivering the timber. Women's things mostly, as well as sugar and spices, flour, beans, dress materials and children's boots."

"Wait a minute, Vincent!" John was looking at his brother in astonishment. Memories came flooding back to him, and once more he was a young boy of ten, playing in the school-yard, two other boys tripping him, laughing loudly as they heard him stumble and fall, banging his head against the rough ground. The blood had streamed from his forehead into his eyes, great rivulets of warm red blood blinding him as he brushed his hand across his face. Suddenly, Vincent was there. He had towered above the two offenders, a glint in his eye that made them lower their heads and cower obsequiously before him. Vincent had lashed out at them then, leaving each one with a matching swollen eye and a dark warning, "Leave my brother alone! Go fight someone your own size."

John looked at his brother now. So many years had passed since that encounter in the school-yard, but he knew now, as he had known then, that Vincent was his unquestionable ally, his prop in any emergency that presented itself.

"I'm only a few minutes in this land of opportunity, and already you have my future planned for me." He spoke quietly, the tension which had made him feel dull and despairing since he had said goodbye to Annie at Cobh beginning to lift a little.

"You have yet to find out what a determined man I am, John. No brother of mine is going to find himself without security at this stage of his life!"

The carriage sped through the busy streets and avenues, the sounds alien to John, and yet bearing a comforting similarity to those in the streets of Limerick; young girls on their way to work in the factories, loaded carts, their drivers shouting with irritation when someone got in their way.

"This is it! We're here, at the residence of Vincent Sullivan Esq and there's Maura waiting at the gate, I'll be bound, for the last hour or so."

Maura Sullivan was a woman who was no stranger to the many twists of unpredictable fate. Born in the oblique heartland of Kerry, her parents constantly striving to keep their children's bellies filled, she had determined at an early age that there was no greater purpose in life than the mere art of survival. The day her father had shepherded them along the narrow country road to the door of the workhouse had been a day that would constantly torment her. Her mother had died in the workhouse, her father had put a rope around his neck one night and hung himself from one of the beams in the kitchen storeroom. She had stayed in the workhouse until she was old enough to earn a living. She had been sent to Donoughmore House on the outskirts of Limerick city, and had remained there for three years as parlour maid. Vincent Sullivan had been the most handsome man she had ever laid eyes on, the cheeky look in his bold dark eyes, the way he would put his arm around her waist, sending the blood rushing to her cheeks. He had been a carpenter then, calling on all the big houses, boldly enquiring if there was any work that needed to be done by a man who wouldn't charge "more than what he is worth – and Vincent Sullivan is worth his weight in gold!". Even then he had a way with the ladies, and many times Maura had envied the way he would tease the other two parlour-maids, making them blush and hang their heads shyly, wishing with all her heart that it was she who was the object of his mild advances. And then it happened. She had been alone in the kitchen one evening stoking the remaining ashes in the fire, her head bent earnestly as she tried to coax the dull glow into some sort of flame before the cook came back from Holy Hour at the church.

"And what's a pretty girl like you talking to herself on such a beautiful night? Wouldn't it be nicer if you'd keep a lonely man like myself company instead of making love to a pile of ashes?"

She looked up, startled to find Vincent Sullivan towering over her. She had felt her heart fluttering wildly as he reached down and gently pulled her to her feet, putting his mouth on hers, so gently at first that she thought she must be dreaming, then more urgently as she felt his desire grow more persistent.

"Cook will be back any minute. I'll be dismissed, Vincent – and what would I do then, with no home to go to?"

He had ignored her pleas. Afterwards they had both lain on the settle-bed next to the now spent fire, Maura's head lolling sleepily against his shoulder. She had to admit he hadn't to do much persuading. Ever since she had first seen Vincent she had wanted him, with all her heart, and now she had him and nobody could take him away from her.

"By God, but that's the best news yet!" Vincent had beamed at her, his handsome face animated and his hands grasping her shoulders excitedly. "A child. I'll not take anything less than a fine son mind you, to give me a hand with the business when we go to America."

"America, Vincent. What are you talking about?" Maura had looked at him anxiously. She was three months pregnant, and there had been uproar in the household when she had informed the mistress. She would have to go at once, of course, there was no question of her remaining. She had been so frightened when she had confronted Vincent with the news, fearful that he would reject her, deny that the child was his. And then he had been so good about everything, had bought her ticket to America, telling her firmly that she wasn't to worry about anything, he would stand by her and they'd be married in New York. Maura had thought she was the luckiest woman alive. She would have followed him to the ends of the earth.

The day they left for America, the blonde, blue-eyed daughter at Donoughmore House informed her father matter-of-factly that she was pregnant.

"Who is he? Give me a name and I'll have him hanged, drawn and quartered for this!" her father had thundered, his eyes blazing as he confronted the girl.

"Daddy, don't upset yourself. After all, I'm already promised to Andrew, Sir Dalton's son. We'll just bring the wedding forward a little, and nobody will be any the wiser."

"I still want a name. I'm entitled to that much, Rachel."

"It's the carpenter, Daddy – and you won't lay your hands on him now because I'd say he's well on his way to making a new life for himself and his little serving girl in America!"

They had married in New York. Shortly after Paul had been born, Vincent's absences from the house became more prolonged, sometimes he stayed away overnight, not arriving home until the early hours of the following morning. Maura had busied herself with looking after the baby, trying to convince herself that Vincent was the type of man who was making his way up in the world, probably forging some valuable contacts at these meetings he attended most evenings in Elizabeth Street. Then the little notes had started coming, folded and pushed under the door of their apartment in South Brooklyn.

"You should go to those meetings in Elizabeth Street, Mrs Sullivan. Perhaps you will learn a little more of your husband's activities." She had been almost hysterical when the first note came. She had hidden it in her dressing-table, not showing it to Vincent, afraid that if she did so her whole life would collapse around her, everything she held so dear swept away on a vague cloud of insinuation and spitefulness. The first note had been succeeded by a spate of similar ones, and in the end she could no longer ignore them.

She had gone to Elizabeth Street, leaving the baby with Martha, a young Italian immigrant living on the floor above them. She had hurried through the Jewish district, past men with beards down to their waists, babbling in several Yiddish dialects. And she had found him. As the evening sunlight set on the huddled sprawl of tenement buildings in the shadow of Brooklyn Bridge, Maura had stood in one of the most notorious crime-ridden streets in the Lower East Side.

She pushed open the door of number 4. She could hear voices from upstairs, then laughter, and the sound of something rolling across the floor. She went up the stairs, her knees trembling, her feet making no sound. She tapped lightly on the door. There was silence for a moment, then a female voice called out, "Who's there?"

Maura hesitated, then without answering turned the handle on the door. It opened easily, and she pushed it in further with the toe of her shoe.

"Maura, what the hell –" Vincent was undressed to the waist, lying on a bed of pink silk sheets, the woman next to him wearing a revealing lace night-gown. All Maura could see was a haze of pink and white satin and pink ribbons on the woman's hair, on her nightgown, even the bedspread was patterned with tiny pink roses.

"I always wanted to know just what went on at these meetings, Vincent," she said. If she'd had a gun in her hand she knew, with a frightening certainty, that she would have killed them both. But she hadn't, and so she had turned and walked back out on the landing, down the stairs, and didn't stop until she had reached their apartment, turning the key in the lock with an amazing calmness. She sat by the window overlooking the river. Later she would go up and collect her baby. Right now she had to be on her own. Some time to think. She had married a man who would be unfaithful to her for the rest of her life, and the only question she had to ask herself now was could she bear the humiliation? She closed her eyes wearily and knew at once what the answer would have to be. She would stay with Vincent, because there was nothing else she could do. She had followed him to New York, she had borne his son – wasn't she committed to him for better or for worse? She had a roof over her head, a husband who was going places, a man earmarked for politics. He would be a success, and he would take her with him.

Vincent came home early that evening. There was no mention of the woman, or of Maura's trip to Elizabeth Street, and she had remained silent while Vincent had played with his son on the floor of the bedroom. In bed that night, he had turned to her with an earnest look on his face, his eyes searching hers for some flicker of understanding or forgiveness. Maura didn't know which.

"You are my beautiful wife, the woman I'll love forever." He covered her body with his and she stiffened involuntarily.

"And you are my handsome husband, Vincent, but tonight I just want to sleep. This hasn't been one of my good days. Goodnight." She turned over on her side, and he lifted himself from her, reluctantly.

She'd come round. She had no alternative. Anyway, it was about time she learned some of the ways of the world. He closed his eyes and slept while Maura remained wide-eyed, tears soaking her pillow, watching the first pale streak of dawn invade the small bedroom.

And now here they were, John and Vincent, as different in character as in looks, coming up the driveway. For a moment Maura felt a sudden fear overwhelm her. Her husband's touch poisoned everything and everyone he came in contact with. She would have to see to it that John didn't get bitten by Vincent Sullivan's unscrupulous tongue. She would help him, for Annie's sake.

Vincent led John towards the house, which was situated in a quarter of the city that was obviously prosperous, for children's nannies, dressed in crisp blue and white uniforms, were chatting amiably to each other as they brought their tiny charges for their customary morning stroll. The avenue was lined with uniform trees bearing the promising buds of an early spring, their bareness in stark contrast to the dazzling white facade of each house.

"John, it's so good to see you after all this time!" John looked down at the smiling face of his sister-in-law. She had tears in her eyes as she took his hand, squeezing it gently.

Vincent Sullivan's two sons sat in their bedroom, a worried look on Paul's face. He was a handsome young man, his blond hair falling untidily over one eye, his hand pushing it back from his forehead irritatingly. Steven flicked the pages of a book he was reading, his lethargy dispelled for a moment as he read aloud a paragraph for his brother's benefit.

"Listen to this, Paul, 'Every member of the family, from the oldest to the youngest, works incessantly, pinning and stitching, cutting and concealing loose threads on the garments which will adorn the over-fed bodies of those who exploit them.'" He looked up at his brother, anger burning in his eyes. "A dozen people at a time, crammed into those tiny rooms, virtual sweat shops, working non-stop for a miserly couple of dollars a month – and that's how our good father earns his money in order to send us to Harvard!"

Paul turned to his brother, his fists clenched tightly, a hard look on his face. "Don't you start. I've already had a dressing-down about Dad's little 'business ventures' from David Goldman. We had a right good set-to about it – I gave him a shiner of a black eye, but my heart wasn't in it. I knew he was right, Dad's tenement blocks should be condemned."

Steven got up and went to the window, looking out thoughtfully, his gaze taking in the spectacular vista of the Hudson River lined on either side by sinewy snakes of cargo boats and passenger ferries. "Dad shouldn't have chosen law for us, Paul. It makes us delve too much into the social injustices we see every day of our lives walking through the ghettos. Most of them caused by our dear

Dad, hard-working Vincent Sullivan – the man of the people!" He finished his angry tirade mockingly then turned to Paul. "And here comes Uncle John from the homeland, another unwitting victim to be initiated into the corruption of Tammany!"

"Paul! Steven! Your uncle is here!" Their mother's voice drifted urgently up the stairs. They both exchanged glances, the look in their eyes almost like a silent pact of solidarity between them.

"Uncle John is here," Steven repeated his mother's words slowly. He closed the textbook and shoved it back on the shelf. Together they descended the stairs to greet John Sullivan.

"Meet your incorrigible nephews, John," Maura said proudly, her minute figure dwarfed by the boys, one on either side of her. "Paul, Steven, meet your Uncle John. What do you think of your fine nephews, John?"

Vincent thumped the boys on the back good-naturedly and John could see a cold look in their eyes as they moved away from him. "They both can pack a fine punch into the bargain – two strapping lads, would you ever think they were only seventeen and eighteen years, John? Look at the muscles on them arms!" Vincent's mouth twisted in a gratified smile. "Take after their father. Nobody gets on the wrong side of Paul and Steven Sullivan!"

The two boys grimaced good-naturedly and held up their fists playfully to John. "Don't worry, Uncle John. We'll protect you. New York is a sweat shop of unscrupulous employers and dirty politicians. You'll need us to see you don't get into trouble!"

Vincent Sullivan looked at his sons sharply. If he didn't

know better, he'd swear they were having a go at him, young upstarts. They had no objections to taking his money when they were invited to a Long Island bash in one of their fancy friends' houses for a weekend. The two boys returned his gaze.

John liked the look of the boys. Their faces were open and honest, their affection for Maura obvious as each of them put an arm about her waist, teasing her gently. Something unsettled him as he felt the tension between Vincent and the boys. Surely a father and his sons should be more at ease with one another. Maura plucked nervously at the lace bodice on her dress, her eyes pleading with Paul and Steven to leave well enough alone. It wouldn't do to get their father angry. Not now, when they had a guest in the house.

"I'm afraid you have a lot to get used to, John. This house is like bedlam at times, the way those boys go on, my own Vincent included!" Maura's face betrayed some unspoken question which John sensed had been bothering her ever since they had met. "John," she turned quickly and looked at him with frank, worried eyes, "it's Annie I feel for, dear Annie. I know how she must be feeling right now, and my heart aches for her." She grasped his arm anxiously. "Will she be all right, John? Is there somebody looking after her? I know Molly will see to it that she doesn't fret too much, but she needs someone she can talk to when she starts thinking too much about things."

"I was worried myself, Maura. Up to the very day before I left I was sick with the thought of her pining away and me not there to console her, but Hannah has been a godsend to us."

"Hannah?" Maura looked puzzled. "Isn't that the little niece in the country? But isn't she just a young one?"

"She's growing up now, Maura, into a fine sensible young lady. Her father is dead since before Christmas and Peggy and the girls have come to Limerick to live with us."

"Well, now!" Maura sat on the bed, the worry lines dissipating, her face once more breaking into a smile.

"Hannah has started her own little dressmaking business. The Bensons' lacemaking is becoming famous the length and breadth of Ireland, and she seems to be well on the road to making a worthwhile future for herself and the rest of her family."

"Little Hannah, a businesswoman!"

"There'll be no stopping her in a few years' time," John replied, sitting down wearily on the window-seat overlooking New York harbour. "She'll do well, for she has learnt from bitter experience. She understands what it is to be short, to be a casual worker exploited by the wealthy and powerful. No employee of Hannah Benson will have cause to strike!"

"Annie, she has enough money to get by?" Vincent looked at John sharply. He knew that John was a proud man; he wouldn't divulge his true circumstances even to his own brother if he could help it. "You need only ask, man. I'm here to help you, so don't act the gombeen now by keeping things from me." They were sitting in the drawing-room after dinner, Maura leaving them discreetly while the two boys went to their rooms to study. Maura and Vincent had plans for their sons' futures, their memories of a hard upbringing in Ireland still fresh in their minds. Paul and

Steven were being educated, perhaps to fulfil their own dreams, but most of all because, in Vincent's firm opinion, education was the best legacy he could give to his sons.

John stared into the glass of rich red liquid in his hand, pausing for a moment before he answered Vincent's question. "I had a bit put by, though not much, because I didn't know such a disaster could ruin my livelihood so suddenly, and in such a terrible way." His hand trembled and suddenly Vincent was at his side, taking the glass from him, putting a firm hand on his shoulder. Taking two fresh glasses from the cabinet he poured a measure of clear liquid into each.

"By God, man – there's nothing like it. The elixir of life – no finer present could you have brought me from the old country!"

Vincent took a quick mouthful, and John followed suit, but he sipped his glass of poteen slowly, letting the liquid settle in his throat for a moment before swallowing the fiery substance.

"When this is gone I have some good brandy kept for special occasions, like the arrival of my brother from Ireland. What occasion could be more worthy?" He winked at John and the ghost of a smile formed on John's pale blue lips, the eyes momentarily glinting with amusement.

"You're a good brother to me, Vincent Sullivan, and you'll not regret taking me under your roof – temporary, mind, for I won't be a burden to you."

Vincent regarded his brother thoughtfully, started to say something, then changed his mind. Perhaps it was too soon. The ways of the New World would have to be taught to this innocent brother of his slowly. In time, he would initiate him into the system. Politics was the power of the people and, Vincent had discovered to his advantage, the gateway to prosperity and social standing. Workers desperate for employment and unskilled immigrants flocked to Vincent Sullivan, the Democratic hopeful for the East Side. As a member of the Tammany Hall organisation, a group of powerful businessmen within the Democratic party, he was in a position to "fix" things for them, with letters of recommendation to employers, and addresses of clean places to live in a teeming city of overcrowding and disease. In return, he was becoming an established name.

People on the East Side had jaundiced views of Tammany, calling it "corruption" and "exploitation of the unskilled". But what would they know about exploitation? Vincent was a man of the people, an immigrant himself, not a man to associate himself with any politics that were less than honourable. Tammany was, after all, a political platform for the vulnerable immigrant, an organisation instigated by fair-minded men like himself. "Survival of the fittest," he had argued with Maura when she had expressed doubts about his political ideology. "Don't trouble yourself, woman, with things that are of no concern to you." So she had remained silent.

The drink had relaxed John, the warm liquid coursing through his tense body, making him feel that all was not as desperate as it seemed. Vincent was talking about going to the lumber yard in the morning, having a look at the vacant warehouses facing onto the harbour. "I have a few worthwhile contacts. A man like you, accustomed to trading in raw materials and food imports, will be a godsend to the lumbermen."

"Your own business, Vin – it's going well for you?" asked John. "Not that I doubt it for a minute. Sure I need only look around me here to see you're a prosperous man!"

He looked about at the magnificent chandeliers hanging from the carved ceiling, the luxurious Persian carpet, the cream silk drapes on the long latticed windows extending from ceiling to floor, the breathtaking view of New York harbour. To the left of the bustling mecca of merchant ships a large, bold sign on a billboard was plainly visible, VINCENT SULLIVAN, TIMBER IMPORTERS.

"It's taken me a while to get where I am today, John. I've worked hard for it." Vincent took a quick gulp from his glass and the expression on his face became serious. "This is a town of favours and back-handers, John." He stretched his long legs out in front of the blazing log fire, his eyes thoughtful.

"There's a saying here: 'You scratch my back and I'll scratch yours.' It has many advantages, and I want the best for my boys. I'm going to see they become the most influential lawyers in this country – they have the brains, if they use them." A look of irritation crossed his face for a moment, and John detected that relations might not be all that they should be between Vincent and his sons. "Lazy at times, not putting their heart into getting their exams. But they'll learn – if I threaten to cut off their allowances . . ." Vincent gave a short, sharp laugh, downing his glass with one gulp.

"Things are bad in Limerick right now, Vin," John spoke slowly, visions of the burning shop, the leaping flames rising hungrily to consume every vestige of his hard-earned business made him sweat and shiver simultaneously.

"The workers are calling for Trade Unions. They've already started them in England and Connolly is trying to organise the workers in Dublin."

"They're trying the same here. Carnegie had trouble with his men only last month, an all-out strike they had organised! His right-hand man put a stop to it!"

The look of harsh vindictiveness on Vincent's face surprised John. Having always been a man to look after his workers, to see to it that they were given a fair wage and good working conditions, he assumed that Vincent thought the same, had the same principles.

"This man, his right-hand man – what did he do, Vin?" John asked quietly, a strange feeling of unease creeping over him.

"He brought in the Hungarians, organised a few hundred immigrants to take over the steel works. That soon had the rest of them running back to their jobs. It's the only way to deal with militants."

"They're surely not militants, Vin. Just a few honest men looking for their rights. What harm is there in a workers' democracy?"

"What harm is there?!"

Vincent shouted so loudly, that Maura heard him in the sewing-room downstairs. She pricked her finger with the tip of the needle, her lace tapestry suddenly stained with blood. She reached into her pocket, and with trembling fingers, pulled out the note she had received through the letter-box that morning. They had started again. Angry, spiteful words, venom running along the pink notepaper, saying terrible things about Vincent and Helena Curley. She had thought those times were safely tucked away in the past, before they had improved their lot and moved into more fashionable New York circles.

Maura wasn't a fool. She knew Vincent hadn't stopped seeing his little immigrant actress with the voice of a nightingale who could charm a packed audience in the theatre as capably as she could charm her husband in bed. Alice, the little kitchen maid, had avoided looking at Maura as she handed her mistress the note.

"It's for you, ma'am. Not posted, just dropped through the letter-box."

Maura had nodded, her face pale and strained. Everybody knew about Vincent Sullivan's indiscretions. Helena Curley wasn't the only one, just the prima donna of all the pretty little immigrants who arrived unceasingly off the ferry in New York Harbour.

"Mrs Sullivan? You want to know what your husband does on Saturday evenings? You think maybe he is visiting Dimitri, the young Russian who cannot find work since he came to New York? Or perhaps he is asking Giovanni, the fish-shop owner if he has a place in his shop for Orlando, the son of the poor widow on Rivington Street who cannot keep body and soul together unless her son gets work? Don't fool yourself, Mrs Sullivan. Go see for yourself."

Maura had read the crudely-written address at the end of the page, her eyes swimming with tears. She wouldn't go. She couldn't go. It would kill her to discover Vincent with another woman – once was enough. What the eye didn't see, the heart couldn't grieve over, and she had firmly stood by that philosophy since her trip to Elizabeth Street all those years ago. She crumpled the note in her hand, then impulsively spread it out again on the writing table in front of her, noting the address.

She had been to the immigrant aid shelter that morning, and what she had encountered there had been disturbing. Vincent's name had been mentioned there in stilted Hungarian, Russian, and Italian accents. They had looked at her out of dark, hopeless eyes. Maura had turned away in shame, running from the reproaches. Perhaps one of those had written the letter, somebody who hated Vincent Sullivan so much, that they wanted to hurt his family.

She knew what she had to do. She would have to see for herself, go to the address on the note. Otherwise, she would go on wondering, and tormenting herself with thoughts of Vincent humiliating her even further by parading in public yet another of his women. If only she had someone to talk to, someone she could confide in. She couldn't tell the boys. Things were bad enough already between Vincent and his sons. She would never confide in John. Another face came into her head slowly, so tangibly reliable. A face with dark, honest eyes, a man whose outspoken candour enlightened the pages of his newspaper, *The Jewish Parable*. A frequent visitor to the immigrant aid shelter, Samuel Blum had established a friendship with Maura which was frequently remarked on by the other voluntary workers.

"What they have to talk about, I just don't know." Sal Klinger, a German immigrant remarked to Father Androtti, the Italian priest who was trying desperately to stem the tide of Italian immigrants leaving the trappings of their faith on the quayside when they disembarked from the ferry. "They are both working in the service of God. Maura Sullivan is a good God-fearing woman with a good husband who has done a lot for the immigrant population of New York," Father Androtti said severely. "Do not read any more into it, Sal – and do not listen to gossip. Without people like Maura Sullivan and Samuel Blum our work would not be able to continue."

"I received this note yesterday, Samuel. I thought I was finished with that sort of thing years ago." Maura handed him the note, its crumpled appearance making Samuel Blum look up at her pityingly.

She had gone to see him that morning, in his newspaper office in Hester Street. The street outside was filled with the cries of street vendors, the noise from the printing presses at the back of his office adding to the dizzy buzz of industry. Samuel surveyed the note thoughtfully, leaning back in his chair. The woman in front of him had become a good friend. She had passed on to him the obscure messages of the Jewish immigrants, begging him to print them in his newspaper, seeking wives, husbands, sometimes even looking for justification of their unforgivable act in not keeping kosher.

She was a devout Catholic woman, but her faith encompassed all the misery of those other immigrants who looked for a comforting hand to guide them in the new country.

He knew about Vincent Sullivan. A few times he could have even destroyed the man by printing some of his 'double-account' dealings with unwitting shopkeepers on the Lower East Side. But he knew any move like that would only hurt Maura, and his respect and concern for the woman far outweighed his dislike of her husband.

"What can I do, Samuel?" Maura asked, her eyes bright with tears. "I don't want the boys to know about their father, but if these notes start coming again they'll find out for certain."

Samuel stood up, putting the note into his breast pocket. He came round the desk and stood in front of Maura, putting a gentle hand under her chin, wiping away the tears with the back of his finger. "Don't trouble yourself any further, Maura. I'll see to this, and when I get to the bottom of it, you'll have no more notes to bother you. Now go home like a good woman. I have work to do."

Maura turned slowly and went to the door, then paused, her hand resting on the handle. Without turning, she spoke quietly. "You know who it is, don't you Samuel? You know who is sending this terrible filth about Vincent?" He didn't answer. She acknowledged his silence with a nod of her head, then she was gone, leaving behind her the faint smell of lavender.

Samuel Blum waited until he saw her leave the office, staring through the dirt-streaked window until she rounded the corner of Hester Street. He took the note from his pocket and read it once more. Then he thumped his fist on the desk, sending a shower of papers scattering to the floor. A young reporter in the outer office looked up with surprise at the sound. Samuel threw open the door of his office, two bright sparks of anger burning on his cheeks. "Eli – I'll be away from the office for the rest of the morning. Take over for me."

"Where can I contact you, Mr Blum – in case there's an emergency?"

"*This* is an emergency, boy." The door opened and shut, and he was gone, striding purposefully past the carts of fresh fish and vegetables, a man fully aware of where he was going, and what he was going to do there when he arrived.

Samuel climbed the stairs of the tenement building in Washington Place, a child with big eyes and legs crooked with rickets surveyed him curiously on the top stair.

"Golda, your Mama, is she inside?" he asked gently, patting the little girl on the head, delving into his pocket and extracting a cinnamon stick. She grabbed it eagerly her expression ecstatic as she chewed.

"Yes, Mr Blum. She is inside, but she is crying. She cries a lot sometimes."

He knocked on the door, there was the sound of footsteps padding across the floor, then the door was opened cautiously.

"What do you want? I don't want to talk to nobody. Go away, Mr Blum." She spoke vehemently through a narrow slit in the doorway, and he could see that her eyes were red and swollen from crying.

"There are things that must be said, Ella. I must speak with you."

He pushed in the door with a firm hand, and she stood back, all the fight leaving her. She threw herself into a chair by the enamel sink filled with dirty laundry. He took her raw, red hands in his and held them tightly, forcing her to look at him.

"The '5' gave you away, Ella. Your reading and writing has been coming on well since you came to America, but you still cannot master the correct shape of the '5'." He traced the letter in the air and she turned away from him.

She was a disgrace to her religion, to everything her people stood for over the years, and Mr Blum knew the terrible thing she had done. He would be angry, say terrible things to her, and it was no more than she deserved.

"It was because of Ruth. That was why you wrote that note to Mrs Sullivan. Tell me, Ella. Tell me everything."

She looked at him now. He wasn't angry. His eyes told her there was compassion there, even understanding of why she had written the terrible note to Vincent Sullivan's wife.

"What could I do, Mr Blum?" she cried aloud, wringing her hands in agitation. "She was such a good girl, never an ounce of trouble from her. And then that terrible man met her outside the theatre one evening. He told her she was beautiful, that she should be on the stage." She paused, her eyes bright with anger. "Mr Blum – I want my Ruth to have an education, to attend the cheder, to educate herself against the ways of men like this one. And now she is out nearly every night, not coming home until the daylight breaks the sky. What was I to do, Mr Blum? He will ruin my girl's life!" She cast a hand wildly about the damp room, the pile of washing stacked against the far corner. "I work until my fingers are raw from the soap, washing the dirty linen from the homes of people like Vincent Sullivan and his wife. I work, Mr Blum, so that my children can be educated. It was what my husband, God rest him, would have wished. And now this man has violated my beautiful girl, and I don't know what to do!"

she cried agonisingly, her moans filling the tenement room.

"He won't bother her any more," Samuel Blum rose quietly, his voice betraying none of the anger he felt would suddenly rise up and choke him. The woman looked at him hopefully.

"You will not tell Mrs Sullivan I wrote this note, no? You are a good man, Mr Blum."

"I will not tell Mrs Sullivan, Ella. And I want you to promise me that you will write no more notes to her. It is not her fault that her husband is the man he is." He opened the door and looked back at her, sitting quietly now, her shoulders hunched in defeat.

"Where is Ruth, now?" he asked.

"She dressed herself in her best Sabbath dress, and ribbons in her hair, Mr Blum. She is meeting him – I know she is!" She was beginning to get agitated again, her thin face turned to him, a mask of despair.

"I'll bring her home to you." He almost tripped over the child still sitting on the stairs, her ears straining to hear what Mama and Mr Blum were shouting about. Mr Blum had said that he would bring Ruth home. That was good. Maybe Mama wouldn't cry any more. She missed Ruth. Ruth sang songs to her about the old country. Not so much lately, though. She never seemed to come home lately.

"Watch the coin, my lovely. If it stands on its side when I roll it across the floor, then I have lost my chance to kiss you. If it falls, then . . ."

Ruth laughed nervously. Every time she saw him her

heart melted inside, so much so that she would have done anything for him. Such a handsome man, and he was interested in her Ruth Wasserman, a little Jewish immigrant, when he could have the pick of New York. The very thought overwhelmed her. She watched as he rolled the coin across the floor, watched it sway for a moment, then fall face upwards on the floor.

"I've won, little Ruth! Now for my reward!" He held her gently, stroking her shoulders, pulling her close to him until she could feel him trembling, his lips moist as he bent to kiss her.

"Mr Sullivan, I do not think . . ." She began to struggle against him, but he held her tightly. The more she tried to pull away from him, the more he held on to her, and then she heard the sound of something tearing, her best dress being ripped apart by his strong hands. She was frightened now. It wasn't a game any more. A picture of Mama's face came into her head. She could hear her pleading with her.

"Ruth, this man is not for you. Stay away from him. He is a bad man."

"Mama!" she cried out, faintly, as Vincent Sullivan threw her on to the bed in the ugly, dark room, filled with the sound of the organ-man turning the handle of the organ vigorously on the street below.

"I must go home – my Mama will be worried." The music from outside invaded her brain, grating on her nerves until she thought her head would burst open. He was lying on top of her now, and she closed her eyes, her lips working feverishly in prayer. "Jaweh . . . please help me . . . I want to go home."

The heavy weight of the man was suddenly lifted from

her, and she saw the look of surprise in his eyes as he was hurled across the room, the power in Samuel Blum's hands strengthened by the cold fury he felt inside him, as he watched the helpless girl struggle beneath the bulky figure of Vincent Sullivan.

"Come, Ruth. I'm taking you home, and that's where you'll stay and look after your Mama, if you know what's good for you!" He spoke gently, but she could see the grim look on his face, his eyes cold as steel. She nodded acquiescently. She had been so frightened. She should have listened to those who warned her about Mr Sullivan. Gelda, the girl who worked in the fish-stall in Hester Street, one day she had been big with child, people whispering that Vincent Sullivan had gotten her into 'trouble'. The next week, she was back at the stall, pale as a corpse, her body no longer big and bloated. They had said she had done a terrible thing. She had gone to the old woman who lived at the back of Fell Street in the Italian ghetto. The woman had done something to Gelda, and now the baby was gone.

She shivered when she thought that she could have been in the same trouble as Gelda, only for Mr Blum. She looked at him gratefully, as he pulled his coat about her shoulders, hiding the torn dress beneath.

"Come, Ruth. Time to go home."

Vincent Sullivan lay half-conscious against the wall, his eyes focusing on the small, stockily-built man. "She wasn't worth it, anyway," he muttered. "None of them are worth it, except Helena. There's a real woman for you."

Samuel went to the immigrant aid centre the following morning. He saw Maura, her face tense as he approached her. "I want to speak to you – in private."

He indicated the small office at the back of the reception area, and she followed him, closing the door behind her.

"You'll get no more notes, no more addresses to torment you. That I can assure you. As for your husband's ways . . ." He shrugged his shoulders dismissively. "You are a fool, Maura. You know a man like that cannot change his ways. A man like him doesn't deserve a good woman like you!" His speech delivered in one breath, Samuel sat back in his chair, the pulse at the side of his neck quivering in anger.

Maura felt the colour rush to her cheeks. The friendship between her and this man had grown to such an extent over the months that she could hear whisperings all about her every day. She would never think of another man the way she thought of Vincent, and yet Vincent had betrayed her so many times. And there was only so much a wife could take.

Samuel reached for her hand and held it for a moment. "You don't have to live the rest of your life in misery, you know, joined to a man who doesn't respect you. If you ever need me, Maura, I will be here for you. Remember that."

"Samuel, you're a good man, and a Jew . . ."

"So? I'm a Jew? And you're a Catholic, and we harm nobody." He smiled at her then, and it was as if a light had been suddenly switched on inside her, brightening all the good parts of her life, leaving the ugly, sinister parts firmly entrapped in the shadows. "I have shaved my ear-locks and beard, and visit the synagogue when I can, not when I must. This would be a sacrilege back in the old country, but in America it is different, Maura. It is better to adjust to new situations than to hold on foolishly to the past." He looked at her earnestly. "Do you know what I am saying to you, Maura? You must change too. You have a life of your own. Make the most of it."

They stood together in the narrow room, their eyes searching each other for confirmation of what they felt in their hearts. "You're a good man, Samuel Blum," Maura whispered softly.

He kissed her gently on the forehead. "Remember, Maura Sullivan, remember I am here, whenever you think your time has come to make a new start."

Three months had passed since John's departure. At first, Annie had been nervy and irritable, Peggy and the girls diplomatically keeping their distance when they felt she needed to be alone with her thoughts. Gradually she adjusted to coping without John, for Annie Sullivan was a woman who had no time for self-pity.

"John is well. He seems to be getting on fine with Vincent, and he has told me not to worry, and that's what I intend to do," she told Peggy philosophically one afternoon at the end of May. It was a beautiful day, the rose garden already touched with the warm kiss of sunshine. They sat in the little arbour beneath the sewing-room, listening to the soothing whirring sound of Hannah's sewing-machine.

Since Christine O'Shea's musical evening, there had been many orders for dresses. Hannah felt she had never been happier. May and Florrie sat in the corner of the sewing-room, their heads bent industriously over the lace collar they were completing between them, for it was a complicated piece needing much concentration. Mrs Deery had been pleased with her rebellious dressmaker. She would never admit it to the girl, but Madeline's appearance had been transformed by the various adjustments Hannah had made to the original pattern. Hannah had the gift of seeing beyond the drab exterior of her client, coaxing to the surface features more pleasing to the eye, especially to the male eye.

Mrs Deery and her daughter had spent a month in New York and Madeline's success had been gratifying. Each evening had been a social whirl of parties and dances, and liaisons with fine young men, sons of wealthy businessmen and ambitious politicians. She had been practically engaged to be married before they had left for home, to a handsome young New Yorker whose father was involved in the steel industry. They had arranged for him to visit Madeline in Limerick during the summer months.

On their return, Mrs Deery had wasted no time. "I want at least six day-dresses, Miss Benson, and four ball-gowns," she commanded Hannah. She never called Hannah by her first name, as so many of the other lady customers did. Mrs Deery believed that class barriers had to be maintained if the lower classes were to be kept in their place. She had found a treasure in Hannah Benson, but she would be the last person to admit it.

Hannah had now reached a stage where she was beginning to think of hiring a few casual girls for piece-work. Her savings were rapidly accumulating, and thanks to the foresight of Annie, she was on good terms with

Edwin Carstairs, the bank manager on Lombardy Street. Each order was duly logged in her 'fortune diary', as Hannah had named the little leather-bound black book which she kept hidden under her mattress. The name of the customer and the amount paid, or the amount owing, was entered accurately in Hannah's precise handwriting. The money was deposited in the bank each month, and the familiar, hurrying figure of Hannah Benson could be seen on the first Friday of each month leaving the bank with a satisfied smile on her flushed face.

May looked up from her work and brushed a weary hand across her forehead. "Finished, at last!"

"And I'm finished, thank God!" Florrie joined in, setting the lace collar aside carefully.

"Good!" Hannah smiled at them both. Something else besides her success in the business was making her feel unusually light-headed today. A note had been delivered two days previously, handed to Molly by a young boy who worked in the kitchen of Dr O'Shea's residence.

"For Miss Hannah from Lieutenant Mayhew," he had announced in an insolent tone.

"That'll be enough of your cheek, lad," Molly had reprimanded him and he had lowered his head and blushed, his brazenness deserting him under Molly's stem gaze. Molly had handed the letter to Hannah, had seen the girl's eyes light up with pleasure, before turning and hastening to her bedroom, where she waited until she was seated at the little writing table by the window before opening it.

He wondered if perhaps she might meet with him at Murphy's Tea Rooms on Friday afternoon? They could take a stroll by the pier afterwards, and watch the St Fintan's boats prepare for the regatta at the weekend. No reply was necessary if her answer was affirmative, which he hoped would be the case. He would call for her after lunch, if that was convenient? If she declined the invitation, then perhaps she would send a note round to the house, but he hoped with all his heart that she would accompany him on what he thought might prove to be a most enjoyable outing, especially in such attractive company.

"What a way with flattery this man has," Hannah spoke softly to herself. She would, of course, accept. A small flicker of doubt kindled at the back of her mind, but she chose to ignore it. It was her first outing with a handsome young man, an officer in the Queen's regiment, no less. He was a man looking for some female company for an afternoon by the river, no more. She tried to convince herself that the meeting meant no more to her either, just a brief reprieve form the workload that had been so demanding lately.

She looked at her sisters now, and felt a little guilty. She hadn't told anybody about Jonathan's invitation. Something had prevented her from telling her mother, instinctively sensing disapproval. No, it was better to keep this to herself. After all, it was perfectly innocent. The poor man needed a bit of cheering up after what he had been through.

"Annie, I want to ask your advice." Hannah came out into the garden, taking a seat next to her aunt, her mother dozing restfully in the seat opposite. "I need some more workers, and I need a bigger place to work – not that my present situation is unsatisfactory!" she continued hurriedly, noticing the startled look on her aunt's face. "I have imposed long enough on your goodwill and generosity, Annie. I feel I'm ready now to stand on my own two feet."

"But Hannah, you're not thinking of moving out of the house?"

"Of course not, Annie!" She saw the look in Annie's eyes, frightened, uncertain. "Uncle John would never forgive me if I walked out on you while he was away. I could never forgive myself!" Hannah put her hand on the other woman's shoulder. "We will continue to live here, if you'll have us. But I've been discussing things with Mr Carstairs, and he knows of a place that would be adequate for what I have in mind."

Hannah clasped her hands together, her face alive with enthusiasm. "It's an old grain storehouse left vacant at the back of the flour mill. It hasn't been used for a while, and it probably needs a good going over before I can move in. He's going to see to it that I get more machines also – importing them from London!" Her eagerness was contagious.

Annie stood up and hugged Hannah impulsively, a delighted expression on her face. "I'm proud of you, girl! To think that after only such a short time you're getting a place of your own, with girls working for you, and machines imported from England! I must write to John this very day and tell him the news, though it won't come as any surprise to him, I can tell you. He knew you had something special in those hands of yours the very first day you arrived in Limerick!"

"There's something else, Annie," Hannah said

thoughtfully. "The piece-workers I need. I'd like to visit the convent, talk to some of the girls there. I have seen some of their work, and they are so talented with the needle!"

Annie hesitated. Behind the grey imposing walls of the convent on the edge of the city was a life far removed from the bustling industry of the outside world. Girls, some not more than thirteen years of age, handed tiny infants in at the little side door of the convent chapel, to be looked after by the nuns. The babies were taken care of inside the convent until they were old enough to work in the large linen laundries that catered for the aristocracy in Limerick and its outskirts. Sometimes the girls, with swollen bellies, the birth of a child imminent, would be taken in by the nuns and given food and shelter until the baby was born. There was no sympathy; words of comfort were never forthcoming. The fleeting shadows of the nuns with their high-winged headdresses would be seen on the bare, clinical walls as the girls knelt, scrubbing away at the already clean floors, a penance for their great sin. No kindness was given, and none expected.

People passing by the convent would peer through the iron grilling curiously, and see small groups of young women walking slowly about the courtyard, their heads bent in silent prayer. The more charitable of the onlookers would bless themselves and whisper a silent prayer for the tiny innocents born inside that fortress of mortification and guilt.

Over the years, a few of the girls showed talent in making lace altar cloths and priests' vestments. Soon it became fashionable for ladies to order their lace tableware and dress adornments from the "girls in the convent". The lack of personal contact between the silent lace weavers and the ladies of the town was an added advantage. All business was transacted through the nuns, and this made it all much more tasteful.

It was there that Hannah decided she would get the girls for the dressmaking. They could work in the warehouse from morning until evening, returning to sleep in the convent at night. Annie looked doubtful.

"I don't know, girl. The nuns are very strict. Never before have the girls been taken into employment in the city. It was the disgrace, you see, of having a child out of wedlock."

"Then it's about time for things to change." Hannah tossed her head obstinately.

Peggy Benson moved suddenly in her chair and opened her eyes. "Glory be to God! Was I sleeping at this time of the day, like an old woman? Why didn't you wake me, Annie, and me with a hundred things to do before the dinner tonight!"

Hannah looked after her as she bustled into the house and soon they heard her voice in the sewing-room, scolding May and Florrie for a flaw in some important order for the schoolmistress.

"She's a changed woman since she came to the city, and it's thanks to you, girl!" said Annie. "I thought she'd fall apart once your father passed on, God rest him, but you've given her something to hang on to. She hasn't the time to sit and brood over her misfortunes."

"Things will be easier from now on, I can feel it in my bones, Annie. Ever since Father died, I feel a hand guiding me, showing me what to do." She glanced up at the window of the sewing-room, then lowered her voice as she spoke again of her plan. "You'll come with me to the convent, Annie? I have to deliver an order to Father Brosnan at the presbytery, then we can go straight on to see the nuns. Mother need not know about it until everything is arranged."

Annie nodded resignedly. Hannah was going too fast for her, some inscrutable force driving the girl on, leaving the rest of them watching from the sidelines. But as she had said, things had turned out well for her so far.

"Get your coat and bonnet, like a good girl, and we'll go before I change my mind. And if the nuns throw us out, mark you, remember I warned you!"

The small, plump sister padded silently ahead of them through the marble corridor, the smell of beeswax and disinfectant mingling potently, the very walls exuding a powerful stench of cleanliness. They were shown into a small sitting-room, bereft of any ornamentation except for a large, black crucifix on the wall. A small square tablet of wood inscribed with the words Servus Servorum Dei was nailed to the wall beneath the crucifix.

The nun closed the door quietly behind her and they waited, the silence in the room oppressive. Annie went to the narrow window and looked out at the magnificent array of pink and yellow roses in the garden. Hannah remained seated, her hands folded neatly in her lap, her face expressionless. The door opened suddenly and another nun appeared; this one was tall and thin, her face stiff and unfriendly.

"I understand you wish to see me, Mrs Sullivan?"

"Yes, Reverend Mother. My niece here, let me introduce

her, Hannah Benson." The nun nodded curtly in Hannah's direction, refusing the hand she offered in greeting.

Hannah remained silent. She didn't like this woman with cold grey eyes, but her feelings didn't matter. She had come on business here, and she was determined not to leave until the next part of her plan was in order.

"So this is the girl yourself and poor Mr Sullivan took in when she needed a roof over her head. Aren't you the great woman, God only knows what would have happened if the girl had been left to fend for herself after her father died. Terrible things are happening to young women in the city."

Her sharp eyes held Hannah's, a distasteful expression on her thin face. Hannah felt a tremor of anger race through her body. Annie saw the flush of temper on her face and hurriedly intervened.

"Oh, but it's been the other way round, Mother! Ever since Hannah came to live here I have had such peace of mind, especially since John went away. She is a great support to us all, and a great businesswoman. That's why we've come here today, to make a suggestion."

"We've come to offer you a proposition," Hannah said, her voice rising in the silent room. "I am expanding my dressmaking business in the city. I have found some premises where I can employ at least four more casual workers – piece-workers, girls who are able to work with little supervision, and who have an eye for delicacy and fine detail in lacework."

The nun waited, her expression puzzled now. She had to acknowledge that the girl had character, her first impression of a forward, outspoken young woman modified by the steady, honest gaze of the dazzlingly blue eyes.

"How can I help you? We do some lacework here in the convent, but the girls are not employable. They are in the service of God, endeavouring to atone for their past sins."

"And could they not atone for them equally well in my sewing establishment?" Hannah's directness was like a blow in the face to the Reverend Mother. Her lips twitched in anger, two blotches of livid red appearing on the pale cheeks.

"I hope you're not being disrespectful, Miss Benson?"

Hannah smiled, her eyes wide with benign incredulity. "No, Reverend Mother, but I prefer to speak truthfully, and I want you to understand that I've come here today to employ some of your girls in the sewing business. I can teach them so much more than they can possibly learn here. They'll learn a trade which will stand them well when they eventually find themselves back in the real world again."

She emphasised the word "real" and Annie closed her eyes and prayed that Hannah wouldn't provoke the nun any further.

"There will be payment, of course. No worker of mine will ever be paid anything less than what is fair."

The nun's eyes lit up with interest. The convent chapel was badly in need of repair. The roof wouldn't last another winter, and windows needed to be replaced.

"I can offer them employment during the day, and they can return to the convent in the evening."

That sounded like a more pleasing arrangement to the Reverend Mother. In that way, she could keep a watchful eye on the girls, and have the bonus of the extra income for convent funds.

"I will have to discuss your proposition with the other

Sisters, and we will have to see which of our girls are suitable for such a responsibility."

"If I may make a suggestion?" Annie intervened tentatively. "Perhaps Hannah could see the girls' work and then she could assess which of them would show most aptitude for the work?" suggested Annie.

"Yes, would that be possible?" Hannah turned to the nun eagerly.

"You have seen our pledge, Servus Servorum Dei?" The Reverend Mother finally spoke, looking at Hannah with cold superiority.

"Yes, 'a servant of the servants of God'."

The nun was taken aback, her aloof facade crumbling.

"I have not attended school officially," continued Hannah. "Mother needed us at home, helping her with the needlework, rather than studying books in class, but I have read many books."

"Then you know that we serve only our Creator. We do not work for financial reward, and God would not wish any of us to be exploited by people whose practice it is to pay as little as possible for a day's work."

But Hannah was not to be roused; she answered with calm confidence. "I will pay the girls what they are entitled to. I am sure the money will be put to good use in the convent, and perhaps a little can be put aside each week for the girls' own needs? It will be an incentive for them, a little bit of independence when they need it most."

The Reverend Mother nodded. "I will arrange a meeting as soon as possible, and Father Brosnan must be contacted. He is the chaplain of the convent. If they agree that the girls may go to work for you, Miss Benson, I will send for you, and you may choose whichever girls are satisfactory to your needs." She rang a little bell on the mantlepiece, and the same sister who had shown them in returned. "Sister Margaret, you may show Mrs Sullivan and Miss Benson to the convent gate."

This time, the Reverend Mother proferred a hand to Hannah and she accepted it, the cold flesh like a lump of ice against her warm palm. She shuddered involuntarily as they left the convent behind them, the warmth and brightness of the early summer's day more than welcome after the silent, unfriendly atmosphere of the nuns' domain.

"Well, Hannah, are you satisfied now? For a while there I thought the good Sister was going to call down fire and brimstone on the two of us. The look on her face would have frightened a banshee!" Annie linked her arm through Hannah's, and they strolled, laughing, through the throngs in the marketplace, the smells of fresh fish and boiling cockles suddenly making them feel hungry. "A nice piece of boiled haddock with plenty of onions wouldn't go astray, Hannah. If we hurry we'll be home before Molly has the pot off the range!"

A face in the crowd watched them as they hurried through the busy square, his eyes fixed firmly on Hannah, craning his neck whenever she disappeared from view. He would bide his time. There were plenty of houses outside the city where he would be put up for as long as need be. They were still looking for him back in Glenmore, for the name of James McCarthy had been the first on their list when the army barracks had been blown up.

Chapter 9

The early summer morning sounds of birdsong and the refreshing feel of the gentle breeze on his skin filled James McCarthy with a feeling of wellbeing as he sat astride the cart of vegetables commandeered by him from a reluctant farmer from Glenmore who knew better than to argue with a rebel the likes of James. Sacks of potatoes and onions were thrown in on top of him to conceal him from the sporadic checks by soldiers on his journey to Limerick. An ally had given him the address of a house, then been shot as he tried to escape through one of the barrack windows. James had clambered over his body, evading the shots whizzing above his head, his commandant's victory cry ringing in his ears, "IRB! *Guth na Saoirse!*" The voice of freedom.

They had failed, this time, but they would have another day. There were men hiding in the hills at Ballingarry, just waiting for the command. More arms were needed, and they would have to contact a few of their comrades overseas to help them out there. He would lie low until then. He would have plenty of time to get acquainted with Hannah Benson.

James McCarthy had a score to settle. It was Peter Benson who had seen to it that James would never work in the coachyard at Glenmore again. He had sullied his name among the bosses, and even the workers had boycotted him. Peter Benson had told them he was a troublemaker, one of the new breed of Fenian "rabble-rousers". That harsh denunciation rang loudly in his ears, even now, almost six months after Benson's death.

"There'll come a day when you'll be tripping over yourselves to fight for the cause, a country free from British rule forever," he had said to Peter Benson.

"Get out of here, boyo, and don't come back here recruiting young fellows to join your organisation." Benson had gripped his shoulder, and pushed him roughly towards the gates of the coachyard, while the others jeered and taunted him. James could recall the angry glint in Benson's eyes, the flush of raw contempt on his face. He watched until Hannah and Annie disappeared from sight. There would be plenty of time for revenge.

On Friday morning, three days after her visit to the convent, a letter arrived addressed to Hannah. It was from the Reverend Mother, "Mother Mary of the Angels," she signed herself. Hannah smiled at the incongruity of the name. Maybe at one time, many years ago, before she had become cold and judgmental, Mother Mary of the Angels might have done justice to the beautiful name. The letter read:

Dear Miss Benson

If you could possibly call to the convent at 2.30 this afternoon, Friday, we can discuss our business arrangement in greater detail.

Yours in Jesus Christ,

Mother Mary of the Angels.

A carriage drew up outside the house after lunch. The driver enquired if Miss Hannah Benson was ready for her trip to town. Lieutenant Mayhew, he confided, thought that, as the afternoon was so fine, a carriage ride in the country, after some refreshment in Murphy's Tea Rooms, might be a pleasant addition to their outing.

Peggy was disapproving. "They're not of our class, Hannah. Sure, what must Mrs O'Shea be thinking? Her brother, a Lieutenant in the Queen's army, keeping company with a young seamstress?"

"Everything is already arranged, Mother," Hannah said calmly. "Lieutenant Mayhew is looking for a little diversion, nothing more. I have no illusions about his intentions, which I am sure are strictly honourable. He is a gentleman, and I have no intention of getting married for at least another five or six years. So rest easy, Mother!" She winked at Annie behind her mother's agitated figure.

"Get along with you, you shameful girl!" Annie pushed her playfully towards the front door.

The driver opened the carriage door for her, and with all the grace of a young woman accustomed to such attention, Hannah stepped up into the carriage and sat on the polished leather seat. Her outward appearance showed nothing of the fluttering anxiety of her heart, her head a whirl of doubt and apprehension. She was trying her best to make herself a worthy companion for men like Jonathan Mayhew.

This afternoon's meeting probably meant only a few hours in the company of a pretty girl to him, but to Hannah, having reflected on little else for the last few days, it had by now taken on much greater proportions. It was to be her initiation into Limerick society, where people would notice her. Hannah was roused from wistful reflections as the carriage came to a halt outside Murphy's Tea Rooms.

Jonathan Mayhew watched Hannah alight from the carriage, and noticed in spite of the excruciating pain in his leg the slender ankles beneath the bright yellow day dress, the pretty arch of her neck as she looked about her expectantly.

He came down the steps of the tea rooms to meet her, and took her hand, holding it lingeringly for a few moments. Then he took her arm with an impatient movement and led her towards a seat in a secluded alcove near the window. "I'm afraid my leg is acting up today, and the carriage seemed the safest means of transport. Walking is only for the young and able, not for bitter, worn-out soldiers like myself!"

Hannah sat down uneasily. His movements, his sharp criticism of himself, the restless look in his dark eyes, all signified a hopelessness which she sensed couldn't easily be appeased, especially by a girl whose experience with male companions was sadly lacking.

"I'm sorry you're not feeling well, and now I'm afraid I must irritate you still further, Lieutenant."

"Jonathan," he corrected her, his face softening for a moment.

"Jonathan, then. I have an important meeting this afternoon, at the convent. I hope to employ some of the girls there in my sewing business, so I'm afraid our outing must be curtailed."

"Nonsense! I have been looking forward to this all week and nothing must interfere with our enjoyment. We shall have some tea and currant scones, then Michael shall take us in the carriage to the convent."

His eyes were like two dark pools of turbulent water, eagerly scanning every feature of her face, every movement she made as she seated herself with her back to the window, the bright rays of sunlight shining directly on the halo of burnished curls wound elegantly about her head. He had never seen a woman as perfect as the one now sitting opposite him. Hannah lowered her eyes before his admiring gaze. He smiled then, and with one swift movement, reached across the table, took her hand and pressed it to his lips. Hannah closed her eyes, savouring the moment. No man had ever kissed her like that before; no man had ever, with the eloquence of his eyes alone, told her how beautiful he thought she was. They sat in silence, each communicating to the other a precious feeling known only to those on the threshold of intimacy.

Mother Mary of the Angels motioned silently to Jonathan to remain seated in the small room at the back of the laundry.

"Men are never allowed within the confines of the convent, Miss Benson. The girls are here to repent and ask God's forgiveness for their wrongdoings. Men are a source of temptation at all times to these misfortunate creatures."

The nun spoke with cold contempt and Hannah shivered at the venom in her words.

Inside the laundry were four rows of washbasins, a woman standing in front of each one, their hands raw and red from the scalding water. They worked silently, white aprons covering their drab dresses, their hair held severely with starched white kerchiefs. The smell of carbolic and disinfectant nauseated Hannah, and she felt little beads of sweat forming on her forehead.

"I have made out a list of girls I think should be satisfactory." The nun went along the rows, calling out names as she went, tapping each named girl on the shoulder as she called her name – Mary Fitzgerald, Sarah O'Dwyer, Eileen Rourke. The girls looked up indifferently, their faces pale and without any glimmer of interest. "The rest of you, go on with your work. You," she nodded to the small group of women now standing awkwardly, waiting for direction, "come with me to the office. Miss Benson here wants to speak with you." The women were not much older than Hannah; many, in fact, looked younger. One of them, Hannah noticed with dismay, looked about twelve, her thin body twitching nervously under the Reverend Mother's scrutiny.

The women listened while Hannah, tentatively at first, then with growing confidence, outlined her plans for the warehouse. "I need reliable workers. You must be neat and clean: hands must be washed before handing each piece of work, especially the lace, but you know about the work involved in lacemaking already." She surveyed their silent faces, their eyes now showing some signs of growing interest.

"There will be some payment, of course." Hannah hesitated, calculating an amount in her brain. It had to be a figure pleasing to the Reverend Mother, something to sweeten her reluctant acquiescence to Hannah's proposition. "It will not be a great amount at first. Shall we say, two shillings a month? Perhaps a little more," she went on hurriedly, registering the unimpressed expression on the Reverend Mother's face. "It depends on how many orders we can get through in the first month. Then I will be able to calculate more accurately the wage I can afford to offer."

Nobody spoke in the room for several moments. Then the small, thin girl approached Hannah shyly, her voice almost a whisper. "We're very grateful to you, miss, and if the Reverend Mother thinks it's all right, then we'd be happy and willing to have the chance to work for you."

Hannah heaved a sigh of relief. At least the girls seemed to be friendly enough. After a while when they got to know each other better, she would be able to judge their abilities, find out who was more suited to miniature frames of delicate lacework and who had the better eye for pattern-cutting and machine-stitching.

"I think there should be a trial period, Miss Benson. We will have one month's testing time, and after that I will review the arrangement," said the Reverend Mother.

Hannah nodded, pleased that there would be no further disagreement with the nun. The girls' faces wore uniform expressions of surprised bemusement as Hannah left the office, the little fat nun again shepherding her to the front door of the convent.

Jonathan was waiting for her in the carriage, his eyes

closed as he lay back against the seat. "I got bored listening to the endless chants and prayers echoing from the chapel, and besides, I don't think I was very welcome in that hallowed place this afternoon." He noticed Hannah's preoccupation as he ordered the driver to take them to the pier, and refrained from speaking further until they reached the metal bridge under which the boats were lined up, ready for the race.

The river bank was thronged with people enjoying the holiday atmosphere. Young women were dressed in bright summer dresses and gay flowered bonnets. Young men, some in Her Majesty's uniform, some in navy and white striped boating blazers, teased the girls, and watched their blushes with wicked delight. Green and white bunting stretching from one end of the bridge to the other stirred lethargically in the slight breeze blowing across the Shannon. The drone of bees flitting from cluster to cluster of wild woodbine and hawthorn branches was a hypnotic intrusion on the perfect summer's day.

Jonathan took off his jacket and spread it on the grassy bank of the river. Hannah sat down gratefully, her new button boots beginning to pinch her toes. 'Vanity is a terrible curse,' she thought ruefully, trying to ease her bruised toes discreetly from the confines of the boots.

Jonathan sat beside her, his nearness making her tremble with a mixture of emotions, arousing in her an impulsive desire to reach out and touch the powerful arm suddenly resting against hers. He turned then, a puzzled look on his face, and leaned closer, his forehead touching the brim of her bonnet. He did not ask permission, nor did she protest, as his lips lightly brushed hers.

Hannah, her eyes closed, heard the explosive cheer of the crowd on the bridge, heralding the arrival of the first boat at the finishing point. The sudden clamour broke the intimacy of the moment and she pulled away self-consciously. "Oh look, Jonathan! The boats are all in. Let's go to the pier and see who has come in first!" She rose hurriedly, then froze in shame as she tripped over her boots, having forgotten that she had kicked them off under cover of her skirts.

"Some lucky twist of fate always seems to favour me when I'm in your company, Miss Benson," he said teasingly. She had hitched up her skirts as she struggled to put on the boots and his eyes rested with pleasure on her slim ankles.

Hannah's face was bright red as Jonathan led her, laughing, towards the dais where a tall, distinguished-looking man with a grey beard was presenting trophies to the crew members of the winning boat. "Three cheers for St Fintan's! We'll beat them blind on Sunday, lads!" The roar of victory went up all round the pier and the bearded man smiled indulgently.

"Do you know who that man is?" Hannah asked Jonathan.

He shook his head, puzzled, for the face seemed strangely familiar, somebody he had seen before in a similar situation. "It's Tom Clarke! He's one of the old Fenians. They gave him the Freedom of the City, after he came back from America."

Jonathan looked at the man with renewed interest and then remembered something. He had been in London, just before his posting to Africa. There had been uproar in the city at the time, for the country houses of several members of parliament had been devastated by bombs planted by the IRB. Tom Clarke's face had been on the front page of every London newspaper, his gaze unflinching, his eyes bright with the fire of Republicanism. He had been sent to jail.

Jonathan looked at the man now with renewed interest, the stoop of the angular shoulders seeming to belie any spark of militancy.

"Father didn't hold with violence. He was always frightened that something would happen to close the coachyard. 'Take the bread out of children's mouths, them Fenians,' he used to say to Mother," said Hannah.

But Jonathan's thoughts were far away. He was thinking of Mrs Flannery, living in a dirty hovel with swarms of children, no healthy sunshine or clean air penetrating those walls steaming with rot and mildew. Who was there to speak up for these people? Hadn't they pledged their faith and given their precious vote to the Nationalists, begging Redmond and his followers to get them a decent way of life? But what was the good in having an Irish party in Westminster who depended on the power of the Liberals to give them a voice in the government? Maybe Tom Clarke and his like had method in their mad idealism? Maybe it was time for some force to be used to make the government sit up and take notice of people like Mrs Flannery.

"He lives here, in the city?" Hannah's voice roused Jonathan from his reverie.

"Yes, at the back of the barracks. They say he's due to go to America again soon, to get some support from Clann na Gael. He's getting old, but he has a great way with him."

"So I've heard. Even Mother was impressed when she

heard his speech at the Freeman's ceremony last year. My father and herself travelled from Glenmore to see him. Mother said she never saw a finer figure of a man, and such eloquent words!" Hannah suddenly smiled, remembering her father's look of horror as her mother's face took on a trance-like appearance, reliving Tom Clarke's "fightin' words".

The crowds had dispersed and Jonathan, his leg well rested by now, suggested to Hannah that perhaps it would be nice to walk back to town. "Christine will be delighted to see you. We can have some dinner, and then, I promise you, I shall take you home to Mrs Sullivan!"

Hannah looked doubtful. A pleasant afternoon by the river was one thing, but dinner at Dr O'Shea's was quite another. Whether he didn't realise the obvious, or simply chose to ignore it, restrictions in fraternising with members of a lower class seemed to go unnoticed by the unwary lieutenant. Hannah, for all her youth and inexperience, was a sensible young woman, and knew where to tread carefully. She was Mrs O'Shea's seamstress, nothing more. Not until she made a name for herself in Limerick society would she grace the dinner table of the doctor's wife.

Jonathan tried to persuade her, but she stood firm. A chill breeze stirred the rippling waters of the river, and she shivered in her thin summer dress.

"I can see there will be no more arguing with you, so I shall do the next best thing and get you home out of this evening chill." He helped her into the carriage and they journeyed once more through the wooded Kilburn glen, then the deserted streets of the city, and past the cathedral striking the hour of seven, the sound echoing through the streets with their stench of bacon and cabbage, pigs' heads and boiled potatoes. Those who lived near the bacon factory were more fortunate than their fellows, emerging from their gloomy hovels at the end of the day to wait at the factory gate for any stray bits of salty bacon unsuitable for the breakfast tables of the city's gentry.

James McCarthy sat on the front step of one such hovel. He ate from a plate balanced on his knees, a glass of stout by his side. There was to be a meeting tonight in the Merchants' Hall. Tom Clarke would be there, making his final speech before he went to America. He would appoint members to the Supreme Council, members who had distinguished themselves in the line of duty. James sat up, straightening his shoulders. Then, when he saw that nobody was about, he saluted, military-style, to a non-existent officer. Tonight will be the night, he thought to himself, shovelling the pile of buttered potatoes into his mouth. James McCarthy will be recognised at last, a man who's not afraid to stand up for his country!

A girl came out of the house behind him, her grease-stained skirt brushing against his shoulder provocatively. "Are you goin' tonight, Jem?"

"I am. Not that it's any business of yours, Eily Mitchell."

"Sure why wouldn't it be my business? Aren't you stayin' in my father's house, and only for us you'd be picked up by the police as sure as they'd look at you!"

James dropped the plate on the step angrily and stood up, towering above the brazen-faced girl. "Keep your voice down, you witch of a woman! Your father will be in as much trouble as myself if it's found out he's sheltering one of Tom Clarke's men!" A look of terror appeared in her brown eyes and she clasped her hand to her mouth, turning quickly and retreating into the house.

The women were a scourge. Maud Gonne had a lot to answer for, setting up her women's organisation, trying to put herself on a level with John O'Leary. *"Inghinidhe na hEireann,"* they called themselves. The brazenness of it! Women only got in the way in politics. They were good for other things, though. His thoughts lingered a while on the soft flesh of Eily Mitchell lying beside him at night after her father had gone to his bed. Her face looking up at his, sweat glistening on her brow as she responded eagerly to his restless lovemaking.

Sometimes he would lie there listening to her gentle snoring close to his ear, and think of Hannah Benson teasing him with her haughty look. He would cry aloud then, and Eily would jump up in bed, alarmed, putting a finger to his lips, urging him to keep silent. He lived his life in a feverish cycle of frustration. Hiding, like an animal, in stinking houses and isolated mountain hide-outs, awaiting the Brotherhood's call to arms. Waiting, also, for his chance to avenge Peter Benson's public denunciation of his sacred loyalties back in Glenmore.

He had got a job with the Board of Works, draining the land on the southside of the city where they were planning to erect a fever hospital. The pay was adequate for his means, and he thought that he would soon have enough saved to move out of Mitchell's house, stand on his own for a while. Eily Mitchell was becoming a nuisance. She had a way of wheedling information out of a man when he was in a responsive mood, especially after a few glasses of her father's whiskey which she kept topped up with water, "in case the oul fella suspects anything". She would wink knowingly at James then. He didn't trust women like Eily Mitchell. Better to be out of her clutches all together.

"Well, girl, how did you get on with the good Reverend Mother?"

Peggy Benson sat sewing by the lamp in Annie's parlour. Annie was reading a letter from John, her eyes greedily savouring every word in John's flowing handwriting.

"A month's trial, Mother. Three girls, God help them, not much older than May and Florrie, younger maybe, but their poor pale faces could be those of women of thirty. They seemed so resigned, as if all they ever expected from life was misery and hard work."

Annie looked up from her letter, her face full of pity. "Sure, they know nothing else, Hannah, born and reared in a prison with bars on the windows shutting out the daylight. You must have been like an angel sent from Heaven to rescue them. Please God, things will go well for you! 'Tis a good turn you're doing for those girls, and you'll be rewarded for it, Hannah."

"I'm no angel, Annie. There's work to be done, and there are girls willing to do it. If they have talent, then it's no thanks to me."

"But you've given them a start, girl. That's all Annie is saying."

"Don't speak too soon, Mother. There is so much to do yet: I must organise the warehouse, arrange financial matters with the bank. Sometimes I wonder if I'm being foolish, thinking I can start up a business here in the city with no experience of the trade except what I know in my heart and with my hands." She looked across at Annie, desperately seeking some reassurance. "Please Annie, you must know what I'm trying to say. Look at Uncle John! He had a prosperous business, everything going so well for him, then overnight his shop burned to the ground and nothing was left but a heap of ashes. Will the same thing happen to me? Will people like Jameson turn against me?" She spoke tiredly now, her back to them as she looked out onto the garden. "My views are not so different from Uncle John's. I want to have an honest day's work for an honest day's pay, and if any of the girls want to join a union to protect their rights, then I have no intention of stopping them. I want people to say that Hannah Benson treats her employees fairly."

"You're talking like your poor father, God be good to him." Peggy had tears in her eyes. "He was a man with great vision. He used to read bits out of the paper about the workers in Dublin fighting each other for a job on the docks for a miserable twelve shillings a week. Twelve shillings to keep themselves and their families, Annie, can you imagine? We had it hard in the country, but those misfortunates had no chance at all. Any notion of looking for better wages and the "troublemakers" were left without any work at all. God, but we live in terrible times!"

"It won't happen to my workers, Mother." Hannah felt so tired. It had been an eventful day, the meeting at the convent, her afternoon with Jonathan, the dawning realisation that he meant more to her than perhaps she had known. "I'm going to bed. Have May and Florrie finished Madeline's ball dress? Mrs Deery was most insistent that it should be ready for tomorrow night. It seems that the Mayor's Ball is one of the most extravagant events of the year, and Madeline is once more on parade for all those eligible, handsome young dandies!"

May had excelled herself this time, Hannah thought, holding the dress out in front of her, examining it critically. The green silk folds had been complemented with insets of cream linen, no seam visible in the numerous rows of alternate materials, the delicate lace collar dotted with swirls of gold-coloured lace rosebuds.

Madeline Deery would be the talk of Limerick after the Mayor's Ball. Hannah's spirits lifted a little, her confidence restored. She opened May and Florrie's door quietly, and listened. Silence. She saw Florrie huddled beneath the blankets in the bed by the window. May's bed was empty, the covers folded back neatly.

The atmosphere in the Merchants' Hall was charged with pent-up emotions as Tom Clarke took his place on the platform. A few of the younger men, their faces shining with perspiration and Republican fervour shouted, "Down with Redmond and his yes men! Long live the IRB!" There was a thunderous din of hand-clapping and feet-stomping. Tom Clarke put up his hand for silence, and immediately an expectant hush came over the crowd. James McCarthy noticed the dark-haired girl seated just inside the doorway, her pale face half-frightened, half-exhilarated, the dark eyes staring mesmerised at Tom Clarke as he began his speech.

James smiled in gratification. The old man had a way with him, his words and gestures an incitement to even the most reluctant of those who had doubts about the tactics of the IRB. He couldn't take his eyes away from the girl's face, something about her touching a chord in his memory. She turned slightly, the light momentarily catching the dark sheen of her hair, and when he caught her eye, a blush spread from the top of her ruffled, lace blouse to the roots of her dark hair. He winked at her insolently, and she cast her eyes downwards. That one would be worth getting to know, he thought, eyeing the soft line of the girl's body as she sat demurely, her hands clasped on her lap.

"Redmond and his party are at a standstill. The Conservatives won't give us an inch in Westminster, and the Liberals are not going to burn their hands with Home Rule politics – if they ever get back in office!" Tom Clarke waved his fist in frustration at the crowd and they murmured in agreement. "We need young blood, new ideas, a revival of the spirit that led our forefathers into rebellion, the spirit of freedom for our nation!"

The crowd roared and pushed forward towards the platform, the smell of human sweat and stale smoke making May feel light-headed, her stomach heaving as she was shoved aside roughly. She felt something cool against her cheek and realised that she was lying, face downwards, on the concrete floor. Her shoulder was hurting her, a shooting, intense pain like a knife pushing its way mercilessly through her flesh. She closed her eyes thankfully as darkness descended, blotting out the milling crowd and the deafening noise of voices raised in feverish hysteria.

"Are you all right there, *a chailin*?" The man's voice sounded close to her ear and May opened her eyes slowly. She was lying on a wooden box in a small, dimly-lit room, a sackcloth beneath her and a pillow cushioning her injured shoulder. The man's face seemed very close to her, a row of white, even teeth smiling at her, a hint of arrogance in the handsome face as he tossed a lock of brown, wavy hair out of his eyes impatiently. "Aren't you the great one now all the same to disrupt one of the great Tom Clarke's speeches, and just as he was about to give me the credit for my fine work for the cause!" James McCarthy's voice was menacingly soft.

May felt the tears prick her eyes and she wished she had never come to the meeting. It was Molly who had put the idea into her head the other evening when she had been sitting by the range in the kitchen with her. Molly had been telling her stories about her childhood in Kerry, and May had listened wide-eyed to her tales of the great Fenians.

"John O'Mahony himself, the great man, a devil of a fella, and a powerful way with the women he had. God help us! Sure it's easy to turn our heads with a look from a fine broath of a fella like himself, a cross between that saint of a man, Daniel O'Connell, and the great Parnell!" Molly had sat by the range, her eyes misting over as memories took hold, and May had eagerly waited for her to continue. "They were stirring times, *a chroi*, men hiding in the hills. We could see them signalling to each other from our bedroom window, and the police banging down the door, wantin' to know did we know anything about the rebels. But even if we knew, our lips were sealed. Ah sure, they were only dreamers, all of them."

"I hear tell they're recruiting again," May said. Sean Og had been telling her about the meetings held in Jack Heuston's house in Barrington Street. "Only for young fellas, no women," he had told May importantly. "Sure women only get in the way, most of the time."

"That woman in Dublin," May confided in Molly, "the one the poet is mad about, she's after starting up a group of young women, just like the men. Maud Gonne is her name. They have uniforms and all, and they parade up and down in the park, just like real soldiers." She saw the spark of interest in Molly's face, the glimmer of hope in the old woman's eyes. "Well now, maybe things are moving again. It's about time that Redmond fella had something to shake him up over there in England. Home Rule, how are you! And people starving and fighting each other for a pig's head outside the bacon factory on a Saturday night! What good is Home Rule to a man who has to watch his children starve for want of a dacent day's wage?"

May had decided that night that she would go to the meeting at the Merchants' Hall. She hadn't told Molly, and she hadn't told her mother. Nobody knew of May's sudden interest in the Republican movement that was to take such a fateful turn that night.

May lay back on the hard pillow and looked about the room with interest. It was very small, one slit of a narrow window allowing a tiny slant of light through. The man was boiling water on top of a small range in the corner. May felt a surge of excitement as she looked at the broad back with its powerful muscles contracting beneath the rough working shirt. James McCarthy had never looked so handsome to her. She knew he hadn't recognised her, for she had been only a slip of a girl back in Glenmore, delivering pieces of lace tableware to the gentry. She had often passed him on the narrow road leading up to the priest's house on the outskirts of the village, and she had lowered her head, blushing self-consciously, for he had the eye of a rover.

He had laughed at her blushes, and May had been angry. Hannah was, of course, the beauty in the family, but it wasn't fair that men like James McCarthy should think so little of May, not even a cursory "good day to you, girl," because she hadn't the way with her to tease their arrogant presumption. She had seen him looking at Hannah, had seen the way he tried to catch her eye after Mass on a Sunday.

Hannah would have no time for the bold James McCarthy. But May was different. She had lain in bed at night, praying that he would notice her some day. Tonight her dream had come true. He hadn't kissed her, but he had been close enough to, his wavy dark hair against her cheek as he bent over her.

She winced suddenly, the pain in her shoulder a reminder of the night's mishap.

"I'll make you a drop of hot whiskey. That'll help the pain. Then I'll have to get you home, somehow." He was beginning to get irritated. He hated having to act the nursemaid to a silly young one who shouldn't have been at the meeting in the first place. Tom Clarke had made him go to the back of the hall when had seen her slip sideways.

"Get that young one out of here, James, like a good man. She'll be trampled to death. And I'll contact you later in the week," he had added meaningfully.

James had been disappointed. Tonight he had thought he would get his place on the Council. It had been half-promised to him by the commandant in Glenmore, just before the barracks operation. Wasn't it he, James McCarthy, who had set the dynamite and dragged boxes of ammunition to safety out the back door over the dead bodies of British soldiers? Wasn't it he who had helped to round up all the young men in Glenmore, disillusioned with the Irish Party's lack of progress in Westminster, and urged them to join the IRB at a time when leadership in the organisation was sadly lacking? And now he had to wait even longer for his moment of glory.

The meeting had passed without any honours being given, and the fool of a girl had caused the greatest sensation by collapsing. Clarke had insisted that she be brought into the records room at the back of the hall until she had recovered, and now here he was, making her punch and promising her to take her home! He stole a look at the girl again and had to admit she wasn't a bad-looking sort. May's hair had escaped from its pins and was tumbling around her shoulders in a shining mass of dark curls. Her eyes were closed again, the pain tearing at her shoulder. He noticed the long, black eyelashes brushing the pale surface of her cheeks and for one mad moment he wanted to stroke them with his hand, feel the softness of her hair against his hand.

"Here, drink this." He spoke gruffly and she opened her eyes, startled, smiling up at him uncertainly as she took the cracked mug from him.

"You don't remember me, James McCarthy?" May asked him shyly. She looked straight at him, and then he remembered. The small shy one he had seen with her beautiful sister outside the church at Glenmore, three girls standing together, laughing and clutching their bonnets with dainty hands. The eldest one would stand proud and aloof, the other two smiling shyly, blushing, whenever a young man stopped to speak with them.

"You're May, May Benson."

"You must remember Hannah, my sister, and then there's Florrie. After my father died we came to Limerick to stay with our aunt Annie."

"Hannah Benson's sister," James spoke slowly, his mind working rapidly as he digested the information. Talk about a stroke of luck! It wouldn't be long now before he'd have his own back on that scourge of a man, Peter Benson. He'd be able to manage this one, a few soft words, a smile and a promise, and she'd think he was the Angel Gabriel himself. The effort would be no hardship to him. Her admiring gaze had not escaped him, the look bordering on adulation in her inexperienced eyes. James McCarthy smiled, his whole face lighting up as he thought of the prospects awaiting him.

Hannah had stayed up late, sitting by the window in her bedroom. She heard the clock in the hallway strike the hour of midnight and wrung her hands in agitation. She hadn't told Annie or her mother about May's disappearance. She half suspected that Sean Og had something to do with it, because she had found May and himself whispering together in the kitchen that morning. Sean had said something about a meeting. "Maybe it's best you don't go, miss. I'll only get into trouble if anything happens to you." Hannah had heard May argue with him, then Sean saying resignedly, "All right so, but don't tell them I had anything to do with your goin' tonight!"

Hannah had heard about the meetings. A man called

Jack Heuston was rounding up young boys to train for the IRB. There was another group who were organising the girls to follow in the footsteps of Maud Gonne, getting them ready for the rebellion. Hannah didn't hold with the likes of women who wore men's uniforms and carried brushes over their shoulders as dummy weapons, drilling like men.

A few of them had been in the People's Park the previous Sunday after twelve o'clock Mass, marching up and down, a stern-faced woman shouting out orders to them. "Will you look at the get-up of them!" she had heard a woman whisper to her companion. Then the jeering had started, and people had whistled rudely and thrown stones at the girls. They had turned and run, the older woman shouting at the crowd to join with them and help their men to rid the country of British rule.

"Fight, good women of Limerick! A day will come when you will march in glory beside your men! Now is the time to prepare for our greatest confrontation, the climax of our struggle against the oppressor." A trickle of blood had run down her forehead as a flying stone glanced against her brow. She had turned then and walked away slowly, her head held defiantly, blind to the jeers and ribald taunts of the crowd.

May was easily led. If she got in with that crowd, it wouldn't be easy to persuade her to break loose. Since she had come to the city she had become more aware of the young men and women brought up in poverty and struggling to earn a living, and their infatuation with the Republican cause. Sean Og had, no doubt, been putting ideas into her head; and Molly was no better, Hannah thought crossly.

She brushed her hair abstractedly, hearing a sound in the hallway, the click of the front door, then a subdued padding of stockinged feet across the hall and up the stairs. Hannah opened her bedroom door and looked outside. She saw May walking across the landing slowly, her breath coming in short, painful gasps. "May! For pity's sake, where were you until this hour?" Hannah hissed angrily, grabbing May's arm and pushing her into the bedroom. May cried out and it was then that Hannah noticed the limp shoulder, and her pinched, pale face.

"I was at a meeting, Hannah. Tom Clarke himself was making a grand speech, and the people went mad for him! There was a bit of a commotion and I got thrown to the ground. Somebody stepped on my shoulder." She was hardly able to speak now, the pain coming in short agonising darts, the noise in her head like thunder as she struggled to remain conscious.

"Aren't you the fool of a girl! And how did you get home, and you in such a condition?"

May's eyes lit up for a moment in spite of the pain. "Hannah, wait till I tell you! Didn't I meet up with James McCarthy. You remember him – Father had words with him on account of his Fenian ways."

Her voice softened as she spoke, and Hannah looked at her sharply.

"James McCarthy brought me home, Hannah. He made me some hot punch and Tom Clarke made him bring me home in a carriage from Jameson's coachyard. Oh Hannah, it was a grand night, in spite of everything!" She closed her eyes. Hannah loosened the buttons of her coat and lifted her feet onto the bed.

Looking down at the pale face of her sister, an uneasy feeling crept into Hannah's heart. There was no need to disturb Dr O'Shea tonight, but she'd have to call him in the morning. May's shoulder needed seeing to. Her mother and Annie would have to know where the girl had been, but she'd cross that bridge in the morning. Hannah pulled the blankets up over May and then climbed into the bed beside her. Soon the sound of gentle snoring invaded the room as May fell into a deep sleep, her head lolling against Hannah's shoulder. Hannah lay awake until the first light of dawn broke through the darkness when, weary from trying to unravel troubled thoughts of May and James McCarthy, and what she would tell her mother about the night's events, she finally fell into a restless sleep.

"Aren't you the *amadan* of a boy to be bringing that young one to them meetings, and then for you to run away and leave her, and her lyin' on the ground in mortal danger of her life!" Molly raised her hand and gave Sean Og a sharp clip on the ear, her eyes wild with anger. "The doctor is upstairs with her now, and I wouldn't be a bit surprised if the mistress sends you packing. 'Tis trouble enough she has in this house besides you bringin' more on top of the poor woman!"

"I didn't want her to come! She made me bring her, and she ruined the whole meeting. Tom Clarke made McCarthy take her home out of it, and sure that was the end of it, and he about to elect men to the Council."

"Well, thanks be to God there was one gentleman among ye last night, that's all I can say," Molly said, her fury subsiding a little. "Ye could learn a lot from the old brigade, and no mistake. There were real gentlemen in that lot, not like the young crowd tearing around the countryside today. If Ireland has to depend on them gombeens, then it's a sad look-out for the likes of us!"

Sean Og remained silent. What did old women like Molly know about the cause? Jack Heuston had said that exciting things were about to happen. The Americans were sending them more money now, because they were growing tired of Redmond's bootlicking in Westminster. They wanted action, Jack Heuston had said. "We must be ready, boys, when the time comes, ready to fight for our country!" What did old ones like Molly know about stirring talk, the likes of what came out of Jack Heuston's mouth, the likes of Tom Clarke's speech at the meeting last night?

"You'll have to stay in bed, I'm afraid, until that shoulder is properly set. I've strapped it up tightly, but there will be no more sewing until I say so. Is that understood?" Dr O'Shea looked at May sternly. She blushed and turned away self-consciously.

"Don't worry, doctor. I'll see to it that she rests herself, even though she deserves every ounce of this trouble for all the upset she's caused." Peggy looked at her daughter grimly. Only now was she beginning to calm down. Hannah had explained what had happened the night before, for the time being leaving out the bit about James McCarthy. She didn't want to worry her mother unnecessarily.

Peggy Benson knew about James McCarthy and his wild ways. The very mention of his name could drive her into a frenzy since he had threatened her husband after the row at the coachyard. Hannah thought it was best only to reveal the cause of May's accident. McCarthy's involvement was of no consequence, for the present. She would have to keep a watchful eye on May, though. Just when she thought things were going so well for them, this had to happen.

Dr O'Shea had left and Peggy confronted May, sitting in the bed, her face pale and an obstinate look in her dark eyes. "There was no harm in it, Mother, and a lot of what that old man said made good sense. The country needs to be shaken up a bit. There were people there last night who thought the IRB's way was the only way." She looked at her mother hesitantly at first, then, gathering her courage, announced, "I'm going to join the women's branch of the *Slua*, Mother. I've made up my mind. There's a woman that Sean Og knows who drills young women in fighting ways. Mrs Rice is her name. As soon as I'm up and around again I'm going to join them."

Peggy started to protest angrily, but when she looked at the stubborn expression on May's face she judged it best to leave well enough alone. The girl would soon get tired of the constant drilling and the discipline that went with membership of such a group. If she refused to allow her to join them, she would probably disobey her and do it anyway. May was growing up, and she would have to learn things the hard way.

"If that's what you want, girl. But remember your poor father's words, 'no good ever came out of violence and bloodshed; the pen is mightier than the sword'. They were your father's very words – and I never found that good man wrong in any of his thinking!"

Chapter 10

The summer days passed quickly in Limerick, the heat and the sunshine enticing people out onto the river, young couples lazily drifting in hired paddle-boats down the length of the Shannon as far as the tea houses in Killaloe. Hannah Benson's name was frequently mentioned in such places. Over the clink of teacups, the young women enthused over the very modern fashion designs pioneered by the seamstress from "someplace in Kerry, I do believe."

The warehouse on the dock had been equipped with sewing-machines imported from England. A small section at the rear was set aside for the laceworkers, for the work was so intricate, and required so much concentration, that Hannah insisted only two girls at a time should work at a piece. In that way, she could oversee each stage as it progressed, and any mistakes could be rectified with the minimum of delay. She soon got to know the girls from the convent, came to understand their frequent periods of silence, their obedience to the Angelus bell as it struck the hour of midday, when they would discard all work and go on their knees to recite their prayers in unison.

Hannah discovered that the very small thin girl, Mary Fitzgerald, was as good, if not better, than her own sister Florrie at making the delicate lace gloves so much in demand that summer. When the gloves were finished, the fine-spun lace would be folded and fitted easily into the centre of walnut shells, much to the delight of the customers. By the end of the summer, every fashionable lady in Limerick had a pair of Hannah Benson's "cobweb gloves" in her wardrobe.

Hannah was now able to pay the girls two shillings and fourpence a month, a sum she regarded as well-deserved, for the girls had proved willing and able workers. The Reverend Mother appeared well satisfied with the arrangement and congratulated herself for having made such a wise decision. The money the girls earned was beginning to realise itself in the new roof on the chapel and, true to her word, a little of the girls' wages was set aside each month for when they would eventually leave the confines of the convent.

Two of the girls, Sarah O'Dwyer and Eileen Rourke, had been there since birth, Sarah's mother dying in childbirth, Eileen's sneaking through the convent gate in the darkness of night, leaving behind the infant girl to be cared for by the nuns.

"And you, Mary, have you been with the nuns for long?" Hannah had asked Mary Fitzgerald one evening as they were finishing their work. "Just over a year, Miss. I had some trouble. The nuns took me in and took care of myself and the child." She looked at Hannah then, her tired eyes blank and indifferent.

"You have a child?" Hannah asked incredulously. The girl could be no more than fourteen, surely.

"There wasn't much money in the house. Me father was a carter in the docks, more often out of work than in, Miss. Somebody had to do something, and the sailors on the boats are very generous." Something in her face had pleaded with Hannah not to enquire further, a look of shame burning deep into the skeletal face. "As soon as I have enough money together I'm going to America, with the baby. 'Tis a fine life they have over there, Miss, plenty of work for those willing to do their share." Her face brightened for a moment as a spark of hope surfaced, then as quickly faded again. "But that's a long way away, Miss. I pray to God that you'll do well in your business, for you've given us all something to hold on to."

In the autumn a small parcel was delivered to the warehouse. "Oh look, everyone! Something that I should have ordered long ago, but I was too afraid to even think of such a move, and now dear Annie has taken the task into her own hands!" Hannah startled the girls from their work as she cried out with pleasure. They gathered round and looked in admiration at the brass plaque with the words, *Hannah Benson, Seamstress of Quality*, engraved in bold lettering.

By midday, Sean Og had been sent for from the house, and the plaque erected on the door of the warehouse. "This is only the beginning, girls," Hannah promised them, a look of satisfaction on her flushed face. "I've just received a letter from Belfast. Mrs O'Shea has been in contact with some friends of hers who order large amounts of linen from the linen works up there – these people have factories in the south of England." Hannah paused for breath, looking at the girls' expectant faces. "They want us to work for them, making gentlemen's shirts. Sub-contracting is what they call it. The amount I will be paid is very generous, and it would mean an increase in your wages, of course." Hannah looked about her hopefully. "I couldn't take on the work without first consulting my workers, so I'm asking you, do you think we can do it?"

The girls stood there bemused. Mary Fitzgerald turned a questioning glance at the others and they nodded. "Whatever you decide to do, it's all right with us, Miss. It's glad we are to have the work, and we'll do our best for you."

Hannah had arranged with the Reverend Mother to send her four more girls from the convent. She had been finishing up in the warehouse late one evening, and was just about to set off for home, when a dark-haired, insolent-looking girl had called.

"I hear you're hirin' girls to work in your factory?" She spoke commandingly, a hand on either side of her voluptuous hips, and Hannah had taken an instant dislike to her.

"Only girls who have an interest in sewing, who are willing to learn the trade," Hannah answered quietly.

"A friend of mine – he says he knows you from a long time ago. He told me to come here if I wanted work." The girl's eyes were suddenly cold, a sullen twist to her mouth. "James, James McCarthy. He said you might be able to give me some work. Times are hard for young girls like me."

The sneering tone in her voice was unmistakable. Hannah stiffened at the mention of James McCarthy. She wanted to have nothing to do with him. Ever since May's escapade, she had tried to put him out of her mind, but her sister's reluctance to talk about the meetings she attended only made Hannah more suspicious. She knew May was seeing him. She could see the sparkle in her eyes when she came home from the meeting hall in Barrington Street every Thursday night. Only a man could put that look in her eyes, Hannah thought, frightened for her sister. And James McCarthy was the only man May had dealings with since she came to the city. The thought of the two of them together was a sinister prospect.

This girl standing before her in a dress too tight for her, every curve of her body emphasised by the gaudy red sheen of the material – she was James McCarthy's type all right. Hannah didn't want to have anything to do with her.

Something told her the girl was not to be trusted; a dangerous gleam of malice was evident in the slanted dark eyes. If James McCarthy had sent the girl to her looking for work, it had been for some special purpose of his own. He was no friend of Hannah's, but if he had any dealings with May, then she wanted to keep a watchful eye on him. Maybe through this girl she could do just that, even though it was against her better judgment. Her hair was dirty and matted, strands falling over her face, and one fleshy thigh was visible through a tear in her dress.

"If I employ you here, cleanliness is essential," Hannah told her, eyeing the girl's long, grimy fingernails. "The sewing needs a lot of handling, therefore hands must be washed regularly so that the delicate lace-work doesn't get soiled." The girl smiled placidly, knowing the mention of James McCarthy's name had given her a foothold in the place. "What's your name?" Hannah asked, annoyed at the girl's insolence.

"Eily, Eily Mitchell, miss, and I can start whenever you like."

"The day after tomorrow, then. There are a lot of orders in at the moment, ladies requesting dresses for the autumn balls. Perhaps you might be able to do some pressing, but you must be careful." Hannah was doubtful the girl could do anything as delicate as pressing lace collars and cuffs, but she'd keep an eye on her. Maybe she just needed a little encouragement; perhaps she was wrong about her motives for seeking employment. In any case, she'd keep her on until she found out more about McCarthy's interest in her business.

It was no secret among the upper circles in Limerick society that Lieutenant Jonathan Mayhew had taken an inordinate interest in the beautiful seamstress. Wherever Jonathan was seen at the various musical evenings in the merchants' houses on the outskirts of the city, boating down the Shannon on sultry afternoons in late summer, shopping in George's Street, Hannah had been always by his side, her arm linked through his. This did not escape the notice of Mrs Deery, whose eyes were constantly seeking out scandal.

Mrs Deery had not enjoyed a satisfactory summer. The family had closed their house in the city and gone to their summer residence, a little seaside village on the west coast. Madeline's gentleman friend from New York had arrived, according to plan, his intention being to woo Miss Deery with due speed, so as to be in a position to propose to her before autumn.

Things weren't going too well for his father's business in New York, and they needed some working capital fast. Madeline's father was a wealthy businessman, his merchant ships supplying vast quantities of beef and pork to the British navy. Once Madeline was his, there would be no more financial worries for Bulman & Son Steel Refinery.

Mrs Deery had been completely won over by Frederick Bulman's attentions to her daughter, but Mr Deery, with the astute eyes of a keen businessman, had seen through the young man's ardour for his comparatively dull daughter. He had confronted him the evening before Frederick's intended proposal to Madeline, and had delivered his ultimatum.

"You leave my daughter be, young man. I'm not so desperate to see her married that I'd choose a fortune-hunter as a husband for her. Never mind what that fool of a wife of mine thinks, Madeline shall marry somebody I choose, and that will be an end to it!"

He had even given Frederick two hundred pounds to console his bruised pride, and Madeline had woken the following morning to discover that her young admirer had left for America.

"A summons from his father, girl," Mr Deery had explained calmly, and without further comment had buried his head in the trading pages of *The Limerick Echo*.

Mrs Deery had also been presented with proof of

Jonathan's interest in Hannah. As her carriage drove down George's Street one rainy afternoon, through the damp mist on the carriage window she had seen Lieutenant Mayhew and the young seamstress sitting in the window of Murphy's Tea Rooms. Her face had reddened with sudden anger as she thought of her own worthy Madeline sitting silently opposite her, a fortune at her hands and no suitor willing to accept her.

She had wasted no time in paying Mrs O'Shea a visit, subtly bringing the conversation round to poor Lieutenant Mayhew, and how he must be feeling so lonely, away from his military friends in London. "But I suppose Miss Benson provides some light diversion for him. I hear he has been most attentive to her, but surely not a suitable match, Mrs O'Shea?" Christine O'Shea had felt annoyed with her. She knew what the woman was saying was true, and she felt angry with her brother for making himself a target for idle gossip.

As the months passed, Christine thought it time to take the matter into her own hands. Jonathan would be much better off in their house in London, among his own friends, where his attentions might be better directed at young ladies of his own class. Hannah was a fine young woman, respectable and well-mannered, but it was time now for him to settle down and find himself a suitable wife.

Christine O'Shea had already sent out her invitations to a social evening at her home. An invitation addressed to Mrs Sullivan and friends had been discreetly pulled from the bundle and torn to shreds, Christine watching them disintegrate in the drawing-room fire with some misgivings. Harsh measures were required in such circumstances, she reassured herself. Hannah would no doubt be disappointed, but she was a pretty girl and very much in demand at social gatherings about the city. Some other invitation would surely be forthcoming. Meanwhile, Mrs Deery and her husband would attend with Madeline whom, she suspected, had little of Hannah's success with male companions. She would seat the girl next to Jonathan, and perhaps she might arouse some spark of interest in him.

The atmosphere at Annie's house had been subdued ever since John's departure for New York. Each of them had poignant memories of the death of Peter Benson and the events culminating in John's departure for America. A parcel had arrived from New York on a steamer bearing timber for the building of the Fever Hospital behind St John's Cathedral. Inside the parcel were gifts from John, and a long letter to Annie telling her not to worry, that his business was doing very well, thanks to the lumbermen from Toronto in Canada who welcomed his friendly banter with his customers, his willingness to order any goods that they found difficult to get.

'They're a grand bunch of men, Annie,' he wrote, *'something like the carters in the docks in Limerick, and I feel so much at home when I see their barges docking in the harbour every month. The homesickness doesn't feel so intolerable then.'*

He had stopped mentioning Vincent in recent letters,

just bits about Maura and the boys, and how big and strong they had grown.

'How the time flies! Soon I hope I'll be with you once more, please God. You'll be well looked after, for I have written to Carstairs at the bank and I'm sending him money to deposit in your account. So anything you might need, Annie my love, go to him, for he's a decent sort, and he'll see you right.'

John had good reason for not mentioning Vincent in his letters. He didn't agree with his brother's politics, and found it hard to identify with this man who exploited the immigrant workers under cover of the Democratic banner. They came to Vincent Sullivan reluctantly, having explored all other means of getting employment. New York had enough of its own unemployed, besides helping the boatloads of hopefuls from Italy and Russia, starved and persecuted out of their homelands.

Over the months, John had seen how Vincent operated, getting a job for an immigrant Jew in a garment factory behind Park Avenue, a "factory" comprising one narrow room into which twelve frightened immigrants were crammed. The Contract Labour Law had forbidden the employment of unskilled labour, yet such garment factories were in abundance, employing men and women for the paltry wage of four cents an hour. John had reluctantly come to the conclusion that his brother was one of those unscrupulous politicians roaming the docklands of New York in search of immigrant votes. He had never openly confronted Vincent with his suspicions, and would never speak to Maura about his brother's activities, but he had seen enough to have his fears confirmed.

In spite of Vincent's less than honest politics, he had taken John under his able wing, providing him with a storehouse to store his consignments of merchandise, and a premises situated in the sprawling Lower East Side. Vincent had spread the word that "honest John Sullivan" was his brother from the old country, and soon he had a healthy influx of lumbermen from the North, and housewives speaking in a variety of foreign idioms, their shyness giving way to growing confidence as they came to rely on the honesty of "the big man from Ireland".

He had just asked Maura to parcel the Christmas gifts for home one evening when Vincent came in from the lumber yard with an excited look on his broad jovial face.

"John, man, will you come into the front room? I have something I want to put to you!"

Maura looked at her husband's face and her heart missed a beat. She had seen that expression before, when that Tammany crowd had asked him to stand as one of their Democratic representatives. That had been the last time she had felt she really knew her husband, for he had changed, the greed of the organisation eating into his heart until his only ambition was to make his fortune from the sweat of poorly-paid workers. The women in the immigrant shelter had been right. Her husband had no desire to see the unions taking over in the sweat shops and the factories, because it would mean the end of what was known as the "exploitation vote". She was ashamed of him, and of what he stood for, and she hoped with all her heart that Paul and Steven wouldn't follow in his footsteps.

"Like I've said to you, John, steel is becoming big business over here. Anybody who hasn't a bit of money invested in it is a fool." Vincent put his hands on his brother's shoulders, looking solemnly into John's puzzled face. "I'm thinking of getting out of lumber, John. I've put a bit of money aside, and I hear one of Carnegie's steel works is up for sale. Now, I'm going to put something to you, and I don't want to hear no for an answer." He straightened up suddenly and reached for the cigar box on the table. He took out a cigar, biting off the end and lighting it from the open fire.

"I'm going to hand over the business to you, John – not as a present, mind, for I know that's not your way. As security for Maura and myself in case anything should go wrong with the steel business. You can work the lumber yard, employ who you like, extract your own profit at the end of the month, and your name will be over the main gate in New York harbour."

John stared at him, his eyes wide with incredulity. "But I can't buy the business from you, Vin! Sure, whatever money I have is the working capital you gave me, and I haven't that paid back yet. Sure, what would a shopkeeper do with a lumber yard?"

"But, didn't I explain to you," Vincent spoke slowly, emphasising each word. John was an awful innocent of a man. "You'll have no money to invest, because all that'll be changed will be the name. I'll still be behind you, advising you. I'll keep an eye on the workers, see that they don't try to pull the wool over your eyes by shifting half-consignments of timber overnight for their own sidelines!"

He saw the hesitation in John's face and felt his muscles twitch with irritation. He couldn't afford to lose out on this offer. If John didn't go along with him, then he'd find somebody else. Tammany had files of businessmen just waiting for an opportunity to have a hand in Vincent Sullivan's timber business.

But John was his brother, and blood was thicker than water. Besides, with John in charge, the business would stay in the family, for there were the two boys to think about. A finger in every pie, that was Vincent Sullivan's motto.

John thought about Vincent's offer as he lay in bed that night, tossing and turning. He wondered what Annie would think of her husband, about to become one of New York's prosperous businessmen? He smiled to himself in the dark.

He could hear her now, half laughing, half mocking. "Aren't you the great fellow, John Sullivan! Not twelve months in America and already you think you can run the place!"

He knew Vincent wouldn't propose anything that wasn't for his good. Vincent might be unscrupulous in dealing with strangers, but blood was different. Besides, if Vincent wanted to try his hand at the steel industry, then who was he to stand in his way? John made up his mind to accept Vincent's proposal. He wouldn't tell Annie yet, not until everything was settled. Maybe this time next year he'd have her sleeping next to him in bed, her soft roundness pressed up against him.

Instinctively, he put out his hand in the bed, touching

the emptiness beside him. His heart ached with loneliness. If only Annie were here, he would feel more easy in himself. He could confide all his troubles in her, and in her own sensible way she would guide him and tell him what was best to do.

He remembered Michael Murphy, the man he had met on the boat coming over. Maybe now would be a good to make contact with the man. John felt he was at a turning point in his life, a time when he needed a friend to share his thoughts. Vincent was a strong man, he would have no patience with John's apprehension in taking on this new venture. Michael Murphy would understand, though. He felt in his bones that the man was a friend you could rely on. Yes, he would try to contact him after the New Year. It would be a good start to his new venture. His mind now clear of any troublesome thoughts, he turned into his pillow and slept soundly.

In the fashionable district of Newtown Perry, the coaches were lined up outside Dr O'Shea's residence. Stylish women and distinguished men were laughing and wishing each other well as they went up the front steps and into the elegant hallway. Music floated through the doorway of the parlour, the musicians for the evening playing to a packed room. The table in the dining-room was set with an assortment of cold plates and trifles, fresh salmon, strawberry syllabub and jugs of fresh cream, porter cakes and apple fritters.

Christine O'Shea flitted anxiously around the table, hoping there would be sufficient to last the evening. She had decided on a buffet supper at the last minute, because two of the servants had become suddenly ill and there would not be enough serving girls to cater for the vast crowd.

That had put paid to her idea of seating Jonathan beside Madeline. But that was just a minor setback. There would be other opportunities in the course of the evening to bring them together. She looked across the room and noted with satisfaction how elegant Madeline appeared this evening, her dark hair pinned high on top of her head, a jewelled tiara framing her pale face. She flushed self-consciously as Jonathan came across to her, bending slightly to say something, the polite incline of his head not going unnoticed by Mrs Deery.

If only somebody like that would show some interest in her daughter. She had grown tired of parading her in all the social circles of young, eligible men. Madeline wasn't getting any younger. All her friends were already married, some with a couple of children to their credit. Her eyes lit up as she saw Jonathan take Madeline's elbow and guide her towards the table. In that moment, she saw Christine O'Shea also regarding the young couple intently. Mrs Deery felt a flicker of hope. Perhaps all was not lost. Hannah Benson might have the looks to charm a man, but at the end of the day it was money that mattered. Madeline's dowry would be a generous one, an attraction to any man who might wish to live comfortably for the rest of his life.

Christine could see Jonathan looking anxiously towards the front door, his brow furrowed with impatience. She felt a twinge of conscience, but immediately dismissed it from her mind. After all, she only wanted what was best for her brother. And Hannah was not the girl for him.

"If you will excuse me, Miss Deery, I must speak with my sister."

"Of course, Lieutenant Mayhew, and thank you for helping me choose from such a fine selection of delicacies. Mrs O'Shea has excelled herself this evening!"

Jonathan watched with amusement as Madeline started on her second helping of strawberry syllabub, adding a generous dash of cream.

"Christine, has Hannah been invited here tonight?" He came across to her, a puzzled look in his eyes.

"I'm sure there was an invitation written," Christine replied without a qualm, "but maybe it is a busy time for Hannah and her family. Seamstresses are in such demand, you know. And I would think her order book is bursting at the seams, she has become so well known by now."

Jonathan shook his head. "I don't know. Why, I met her only last evening in the Crescent Square and she said nothing about being busy . . ."

"Jonathan, my dear brother, Hannah is a beautiful young woman, and I am sure she is not short of admirers. Perhaps she has another engagement this evening."

"But she would surely have sent me a note."

Christine O'Shea began to feel uneasy. Little white lies had a habit of getting one into trouble, and she was already floundering in her own deception. "Oh look, Jonathan, there is Miss Deery! Doesn't she look charming this evening?"

Jonathan turned without interest. He was disappointed in Hannah. Why had he misinterpreted that look which had passed from her beautiful eyes to his on those summer evenings when they had walked by Plassey bank, her fingers touching his, such a delicate touch, such promise in them?

He had even given her a gift, "a little token, Hannah, of our friendship", but his eyes had insinuated more than just friendship as he put the silver locket about her slender neck.

"It's beautiful, Jonathan, quite the most beautiful gift I have ever received!" She had blushed then and looked up at him with troubled eyes. "But I have nothing for you."

He had taken her hands in his then, holding them to his lips, his gentle kiss sending shivers of delight through her body. "Your gift to me is your love, Hannah – that is all I will ever need!"

She hadn't protested, her eyes shining like the most precious of jewels. No, Hannah was not the sort of girl to trifle with a man.

Christine was whispering in his ear. "Jonathan, is that not your military friend, Duncan Fitzroy? Don't his parents have a house in Belgrave Square in London? He seems to be paying Madeline Deery an inordinate amount of attention!"

Jonathan looked to the window seat in the corner where Madeline sat, a tall fair-haired young officer by her side. Her blushes seemed to suggest that the young man was paying her a compliment, and she put a hand to her throat, self-consciously fingering the sparking diamond necklace.

"It's probably Miss Deery's jewellery he's admiring," Jonathan replied cynically.

Christine smiled with relief. At least she had taken his mind off Hannah for the present. "Go and speak with him, Jonathan," she suggested persuasively. "It's such a long time since you have had any male companionship of your own age. You may get news of the war, of what is happening in the Transvaal. There is no greater stimulation than a congenial conversation with a friend."

Jonathan smiled wryly. He had no wish to have a friendly conversation with Duncan Fitzroy, a man he especially despised. During Kitchener's command, Duncan had been one of those who attacked farms and smallholdings with fanatical savagery. Women and children outside Pretoria were rounded up like animals, their husbands and fathers shot without mercy in front of their horrified eyes. It was that part of the war which Jonathan found repulsive. He awoke most nights, bathed in sweat, the nightmares so real that he thought if he reached out in the darkness he could feel the sharp blade of the sword piercing through his flesh, the pain causing him to cry out. It was this aspect of the war that had caused him to doubt the morality of his profession.

He could see Fitzroy coming across the room to him, and he turned away quickly, having no wish to speak to him.

"Jonathan, old man! How good it is to see you! Come, we must have a long talk. I have much to tell you!" He thumped Jonathan on the back enthusiastically, his flirtation with Madeline put to one side for the moment. He led the reluctant Jonathan out on to the terrace, overlooking the sweeping magnificence of the hanging gardens at the back of the O'Shea's house. "It's not by chance I'm here tonight, you know." Fitzroy's expression became serious as he stared at his former comrade. He was behaving with the exaggerated camaraderie of one who felt uneasy.

"I have a message for you, from the War Office. Because of your injury, you can't return to your original command, of course, but as a war correspondent you would be invaluable." Duncan watched, gratified, as a flicker of interest appeared on Jonathan's hitherto impassive face.

"War correspondent? But what do I know of the politics of war? I have no experience of that type of work." His mind was racing wildly. The possibility that his career was not yet finished filled him with a new optimism. The cloud was lifting finally, revealing a whole new aspect of his life that might not be altogether unappealing. "When am I required to give my answer?" There was a tremor of anticipation in his voice.

"I'll be taking the morning train to Dublin, and I should be in London by the following day. Can I give them your answer then, Jonathan? Are you agreeable to such a posting?" Duncan had no doubt as to what Jonathan's answer would be. Within the month, he was confident, Lieutenant Jonathan Mayhew would be on his way back to the Transvaal.

The church bells in the cathedral sounded the Angelus for six o'clock. Ellen Flannery heard them as she sat by the fire in the kitchen waiting for her husband to come home. There was no food in the house, the children had gone to bed hungry – she had gathered them all close to her and had sung to them until they had finally closed their eyes. Kevin was due home, and she was frightened. It was pay night, and the foreman at the docks had promised to meet them at Scanlon's public house on the quay. She knew what that meant.

'It's the women who should get the money into their own hands,' she thought wearily. There would be the usual grand gesture from the foreman as he waved the pay packets in front of the workers' faces. Then Kevin and another couple of eejits would buy him a whiskey, their eyes fawning gratitude for the few days' work in the harbour. There would be more rounds, and Kevin, as good as any of them, would drink his fill, until he staggered home with empty pockets. Then the rows, and the bitter words, and the children woken from their sleep at the sound of their father's heavy hand across her cheek.

Ellen sat in the darkness, visualising her husband sitting amongst his cronies in the bar in the docklands, doing the great fellow, she thought bitterly, handing out pints of stout to all and sundry. She heard the dull thud of something heavy against the door outside.

"Ellen! Ellen! Let me in, like a good woman, before I'm petrified with the bloody cold!" His voice sounded cantankerous, the words running into each other as he struggled to speak through the stupor of whiskey. She sighed and rose slowly, drawing the bolt back from the door.

"Come in, Kevin," she greeted him quietly, as he fell into the kitchen.

There had been a letter from John. Annie had read it with trepidation, sensing some conflict in his words, the tone of his few references to Vincent a worrying factor.

'There are great things happening over here at the minute, Annie, my love. Vincent has decided to pull out of the lumber

business for a while, and leave me in charge. Imagine, Annie, me a timber exporter! A little shopkeeper from Limerick! I was only thinking the other day of my friend, Michael Murphy, the man I met coming over. I was thinking I'd contact him after settling in, and then the other day, didn't he walk into the shop, as large as life, a beaming smile on his face! Oh, Annie, it felt so good to hear his roguish voice again!'

Annie smiled at the reference to Michael Murphy. She was grateful to the man for being such a good friend to John. She looked anxiously at the next part of the letter.

'Vincent is going into the steel business, Annie. He says that's where the money is for the future. They're making fortunes over here building railroads and making bridges. Even Michael Murphy himself is ordering the stuff for his new hotel in New Jersey, installing lifts to take people up to the top of the building, if you don't mind, and no puffing and panting up flights of stairs!'

Annie laid the letter aside, her expression thoughtful.

"Annie, are you coming into the parlour? Will we have a glass of sherry to cheer you up?" Peggy looked anxiously at her sister's pale, pinched face. She was looking more middle-aged lately, even walking with a distinct stoop in her shoulders as if she was burdened with the weight of the world.

"I'm just coming now, Peggy." She stood up and Peggy saw the letter on the writing desk.

"From John, Annie? Is there any news, any sign of him coming home?"

"Sure I don't know, Peggy. It's hard to judge a person's

feelings in the few lines of a letter. If only I could be over there with him!"

Peggy squeezed her arm comfortingly as they went downstairs. "Don't let it get you down, girl. He's well, and he's doing fine in his business, with Vincent looking after him. One of these days you'll hear from him, telling you he's coming home, his pockets lined with gold from the streets of New York!"

They were laughing as they went into the parlour. May had been reading a small, leather-bound book which she promptly hid behind her back as her mother entered the room. Peggy looked at her sharply, and May returned her gaze unflinching.

"Is there something wrong, Mother?" she asked innocently.

"What book was that you were reading?" Peggy asked quietly.

"It's the book that woman Maud Gonne sent her from Dublin!" Florrie volunteered peevishly.

Since May had started taking an interest in *Cumann na nBan*, she had no time for Florrie. All their walks along the bank as far as the butter factory had been curtailed, for May showed no further interest in meeting the young men who winked at them from behind the factory gates, slipping them some of the creamy butter-toffee sweets in exchange for a promise to meet them on the bank wall after their shift was over.

"Didn't I tell you to keep away from all those goings on, and after what happened to you at the meeting last year – To think that you still haven't learnt your lesson! But you're a terrible stubborn miss!" Peggy snapped at May angrily.

She knew the girl had been going to the meetings in Mrs Rice's house in Pimlico Street. She had asked Sean Og to follow her one evening, which he did, reluctantly. His own involvement with the Fianna in the city was frowned upon by Annie, and he didn't want to lose his job in the Sullivan household. Word soon got round where a fellow's loyalties lay, and there weren't many employers who wanted to take on a Fenian sympathiser.

Sean Og felt sorry for May, their allegiance to the cause a bond between them. He had given Peggy only the minimum information about what went on at the meeting, leaving out the part about James McCarthy meeting her beside Jameson's coachyard, his arm carelessly thrown about her waist. The look that had passed between them was more than the look of mere friendship between a girl and a man.

"Will you ever make your sister see sense, Hannah?" Peggy turned to Hannah pleadingly. Since Peter had died she had leaned on Hannah, perhaps too much, as Annie had rightly reprimanded her, but then, who could a widowed mother turn to when she was sick with worry, thinking about May and her *Cumann* meetings? And then there was Florrie, making eyes at the boys from the butter factory.

Hannah sat silently in the corner, the light from the lamp on the small table illuminating her work as her fingers deftly wielded the needle to and fro across the wooden lathe of fine lacework. She didn't want to know about May and her problems tonight. She had enough of her own, God knows, to make her feel despondent.

"Leave her be, Mother. Sure there's no harm in what

she's doing, and she works hard enough at the sewing all day. Aren't those meetings only a bit of diversion for her!" Hannah spoke indifferently, her tone weary.

Mrs O'Shea had visited her that morning at the warehouse. She had smiled her usual charming smile at Hannah. "The waist is just that little bit too loose, Hannah," she had announced, and had proceeded to indicate where her dress should be altered. The conversation had turned to Jonathan, Christine skilfully reticent about the evening's entertainment at her house. "Just an opportunity for Jonathan to meet with some friends from his regiment, Hannah," she had said casually, turning this way and that in front of the long mirror, surveying her dress critically. "It has been such a long time since he has had some company of his own kind!"

The meaning behind her words did not escape Hannah. Mrs O'Shea thought that she was obviously not the type who should spend time in the company of an officer in the Queen's regiment. That was why no invitation had been sent.

Hannah's mind cleared, the shroud of happiness which had enveloped her since her first meeting with Jonathan suddenly dissipated, and she saw herself as Mrs O'Shea, and others of her class, saw her. She was a humble seamstress, and Christine O'Shea's voice with its condescending tone irritated her.

"He has been feeling too lethargic for his own good, lately," Christine went on, observing Hannah from the corner of her eye as she smoothed the folds of her dress. "It will be good to see him more cheerful, as I am sure he will be, tonight!"

She saw the girl turn pale, a look of such pain in her brilliant eyes that for a moment she felt the urge to put her arms about her, and tell her that Jonathan had eyes for no other woman but herself. She recovered herself in time. Her brother's romantic involvement with Hannah had been a nagging worry, for Christine was a woman very conscious of breeding and class. While Hannah was undoubtedly a charming young woman, a woman any working man would be proud to call his wife, she was not the one for her brother. Madeline Deery was a far better proposition. Her father traded in most European countries, also in the Eastern states of America, a man held in high regard by the wealthy merchants of the city. Madeline Deery and Jonathan, the idea was one to be cultivated.

Hannah, her heart like a cold lump of ice, had watched Mrs O'Shea leave, the carriage disappearing from sight behind the flour mill. So Jonathan had grown tired of her, had been longing for more sophisticated company during their long walks by the river, their quiet interludes sitting on the grassy bank in Arthur's Quay listening to the military band. How she had looked forward to those meetings, her heart thumping wildly as he sat so close to her. But now he was ashamed of her. So ashamed that he couldn't bear to have her meet his friends from London, to sit with them in Mrs O'Shea's parlour, make conversation as though she was one of them, accustomed to such gatherings.

And that was the most bitter truth of all. Hannah was not one of them, never could be, as long as there were ladies like Christine O'Shea who regarded her as a working girl, a commonplace ladies' seamstress. She fingered the locket at her throat, tears in her eyes. Should she discard this trinket which obviously had not meant as much to Jonathan as it had to her? No! She told herself desperately. While she wore it, she had some of his presence with her always, and perhaps a miracle might happen that would indicate which path their lives would eventually take. She had great faith in Divine Providence, and if something was to be, then fate would decree it so. She straightened herself up defiantly. She had forgotten her true purpose for one unguarded interval. It would not happen again. She would make a name for herself, not only among Limerick society, but maybe even further afield. By the time she was finished, men would be tripping over themselves to touch the back of her hand with their lips. But behind all her brave thoughts, there was only one man she would wish to brush the back of her hand with his sweet lips.

They sat in Annie's parlour, listening to the ships' horns in the harbour blowing an arrival or a retreat from Limerick's port. Molly brought in a plate of sweet cherry cake and Annie opened a bottle of sherry, pouring a little into each glass, presenting one to each of them.

"Stay with us, Molly. You are one of the family, and today our thoughts are with John – may God protect him so far away from home." Molly put the glass to her lips reverently, blessing herself and saying a silent prayer.

Hannah's hand trembled as she brought her glass to her lips. There must be no looking back. Only the future was important now. Her sewing business was thriving, and she had more orders coming in from England through her contacts with the linen mills in Belfast. A shop had become vacant in Portobello Street, not far from the warehouse, and touching on the genteel Newtown Perry portion of the city. The bank was not adverse to lending her capital to buy it and the repayments being well within her capabilities. A shop in Portobello Street would place her in a position where she would be much more accessible to the city ladies. She would have two girls in charge of the shop, with a display of garments in the window, some of the latest designs from New York and London.

Hannah sipped her sherry. She vowed she would make no further contact with Jonathan. She resolved to dismiss all thoughts of the warm feel of his arm about her waist as they strolled in Capanti woods by the mill stream. She would try to block out the memories of those long, hot days which now seemed so distant. Hot tears pricked her eyelids. If Jonathan had truly cared for her, then he would not have sent his sister to do his humiliating work. She should have known better than to let herself fall in love with a man whose indifference to her was like a sharp needle burning through her flesh.

Jonathan decided to take the position in the Transvaal. Hannah's non-appearance at his sister's ball had disappointed him, but Christine's words had opened his eyes to the obvious, that Hannah was a beautiful woman with possibly many admirers clamouring for her attentions. What could she ever see in him, a man whose frequent bouts of depression encouraged long silences, the injury to his leg making him poor company for a young woman? She had spent some time with him during the long summer months out of sympathy, perhaps, or friendship for Christine, or maybe simply boredom. He blushed when he thought of the locket he had given her, an impulsive gift, but he had been so sure that it had been the right thing to do, their friendship blossoming so promisingly. There was nothing to keep him in this city. He lived in a world apart from Limerick society, his regiment the only real life he knew. He would go and visit Hannah just one more time before he left to take up duty.

Hannah greeted him politely, but the easy compatibility which had existed previously between them had disappeared, her body stiff and erect as she sat on the divan in Annie's parlour. Neither of them mentioned the ball, and unasked questions lay heavy in the quiet atmosphere.

"I am going back to the front, as a war correspondent, Hannah." Jonathan spoke at last, angry with her for her seemingly calm indifference. "I think it is the only course open to me now. There is nothing to keep me in Limerick, after all, and I am impatient to be doing something useful with my life."

Hannah turned her gaze from him, afraid that he would see the desperation in her eyes. More than anything, she wanted him to stay, but Mrs O'Shea had shattered her fairytale illusions. He was a gentleman and she was a country girl, her father a coachmaker. She wished now he would go away and she might never set eyes on him again. Then maybe she could get on with her life, and her dream of becoming a wealthy, respected lady could surface once more without risk of compromise.

The determination on her face was misconstrued as coldness, and Jonathan admitted defeat. She didn't care if he went, had probably never cared, he admitted to himself reluctantly. A man with the awkward, stumbling gait of a cripple would not be a worthy partner on the dance floor for somebody so desiring of perfection as Miss Hannah Benson, he reflected bitterly.

So he left. Annie watched him walk down the driveway from behind the curtains in her bedroom, and her heart went out to Hannah. Annie was an astute woman, and could see only too well the conniving measures of Christine O'Shea's plan. She could have told Hannah long ago, when she had first seen the sparkle of love in the girl's eyes, that nothing could come of it. Jonathan Mayhew was his sister's protégé, no matter how suited the couple seemed to be. "He'll rue the day," Annie murmured to herself, watching his carriage disappear down the long avenue. "He'll rue the day he walked away from the finest girl in the whole of Limerick!"

Jonathan was packed and ready to leave in the morning. Before he went to bed, he tiptoed into little Emma's bedroom to kiss her goodbye. The little girl lay restless in her cot, tossing and turning feverishly, her forehead moist with sweat. The servants had developed a strange fever over the Christmas, taking to their beds one by one, and now it seemed she had caught the same illness. She put out her little arms to him as he bent to kiss her, her eyes bright with the fever.

"Mama! Papa!" she called plaintively.

"Hush now little one, you must rest. Papa will be home shortly and he'll give you something to help you breathe a little better."

Emma's breathing came in short, painful gasps, tears

running down her cheeks with the effort of trying to inhale through her swollen lungs.

Jonathan stroked her forehead, whispering soothingly to her, until she finally closed her eyes, her breathing loud and ominously laboured.

Christine came into the room, her face pale and tired-looking. She had sat with Emma for two nights now, and still there was no improvement in her condition.

"Robert has promised to be home early from the hospital tonight," she whispered. "I'm worried about Emma. I've sent word to him that she's no better, even though I do hate troubling him just now. The hospital is already overcrowded with people suffering from the same symptoms as Emma."

They both sat in silence, Jonathan's face clouded by a deep frown. He didn't want to alarm his sister, but he had seen the same form of sickness before; it had been rampant among the prisoners in the camps at Johannesburg. There had been no cure for it, and he had watched as hundreds of children, some of them younger than Emma, had died painful, agonising deaths.

There was a sound of heavy footsteps on the stairs, then Robert O'Shea appeared, his face drawn, his shoulders stooped and limp.

"Christine, my love, two of Mrs Flannery's children have just died at the hospital. It's the diphtheria – our little Emma has diphtheria!"

Christine grasped Emma's cot, the skin of her knuckles stretched tightly. She turned then to Jonathan, a look of such pain, such hopelessness, that he put his arms out to her and she went to him, burying her face in his chest.

Robert O'Shea stood by helplessly. He was losing Emma, his own precious little daughter, and all his experience as a medical man could not cure her. He buried his face in his hands and wept quietly.

The notice on *The Limerick Echo* stated "house private", as Dr and Mrs O'Shea, their grief intolerable, buried their daughter in the shadow of a chestnut tree in Mount Lawrence cemetery. Jonathan prolonged his stay with them by two weeks, until word from London eventually came, officially requesting him to report to the War Office for a briefing on his duties in Africa.

"I hate leaving you like this."

"It is for the best, Jonathan. You cannot let this chance slip by. Write to me, dear brother." Christine's eyes shone with tears as she clung to him.

He felt her body painfully thin against him, and wished with all his heart he could do more to help her, especially now when she most needed him.

Madeline Deery stood in the doorway self-consciously, a maid announcing her as Jonathan and Christine looked up in surprise. "Madeline, my dear girl! What a pleasure it is to see you!"

Christine held out her hands to Madeline and she stepped further into the room, blushing when she bade Jonathan a good morning.

"I'm sorry, I didn't mean to intrude, Mrs O'Shea, but Mother sent me to ask if there was anything you needed. Please don't hesitate to call upon us if there is anything at all." Her timid voice trailed off and Christine motioned her to sit down.

"You are so kind, and please tell your mother that I am very grateful to her for her concern."

The happenings of the last few weeks had put all thought of matchmaking from Christine's head, intrigues and deceptions no longer of any consequence as she tried to pick up the pieces of her shattered life. A match between Jonathan and Madeline was no longer of any great urgency, as his departure for the Transvaal made any further strategies to separate him from Hannah's affections unnecessary. Nevertheless, in a detached way, she watched them now as they sat looking out onto the garden, and she could almost sense a comfortable empathy between them, and her own heart ceased to beat so restlessly as though she was taking solace from the relaxed cameo they presented.

Christine liked Madeline. She had a soothing influence. Unlike her mother, she had regard for people's feelings, knew when it was time to offer sympathy and understanding and when it was necessary to melt into the background. Since Emma's death, she had called regularly, never staying more than the time necessary to offer assistance, promising to call again, "Only if I am not intruding, Mrs O'Shea." Jonathan had witnessed her concern for his sister, and had been impressed by her genuine wish to be of assistance.

Hannah sent a letter and a wreath of dried summer flowers, interlaced with pink satin ribbons. She would have liked to visit Mrs O'Shea, offer her some words of comfort at such a time, but her recent encounter with the lady had strengthened her resolve to maintain the barrier of formality, and so she sent a letter expressing her sympathy.

Madeline Deery was talking to Jonathan, her soft voice

reaching Christine as she sat apart from them on the divan, her book open in front of her, her eyes hardly taking in the words as she scanned the page indifferently. "Perhaps, Lieutenant Mayhew, you would not think it too bold if I wrote to you from time to time. I could keep you informed of your sister's welfare," she said in hushed undertones, "then perhaps you wouldn't be unduly worried about her." Her solemn expression brought a half-smile to his lips. "Mother says my letters have often caused her to laugh aloud, when she had been abroad on business trips with my father." Madeline hesitated self-consciously. She didn't know why she had said such a thing! There had been a lull in the conversation and, in case he should think her too dull, she had blurted out her ridiculous suggestion about writing. The man must surely think her a fool. She blushed with embarrassment, and then Jonathan smiled his slow teasing smile, sending her blood coursing through her veins. There was no doubt about it, but Lieutenant Mayhew was a very attractive man.

The day Hannah moved into the shop on Portobello Street, Jonathan Mayhew left for his assignment in Africa. No communication had passed between them since that fateful meeting when Jonathan had given up all hope of a more than friendly relationship between them, and Hannah now felt that part of her life was over. Lieutenant Mayhew had set his sights on far more challenging exercises, dedicating his strength of purpose to reporting on the deadlocked confrontation between the Boer Commander Kruger and Britain's Lord Kitchener.

Chapter 11

During the early months of 1901 Jonathan's reports from the war zone were read with avid interest in all the British newspapers, his incisive comments a little too frank for the Conservative government. He questioned the tactics of their 'civilising mission', and his accounts found their way to the breakfast table of many an outraged Tory supporter. The war office had asked him to 'tone down' his briefs from Johannesburg. 'Nobody cares to read paragraphs of self-indulgence. Please confine yourself to the rudiments of British tactical involvement,' they had written, and Jonathan smiled wryly at the threatening insinuation. He would have to toe the line, if he was to keep his job.

It was not only the English newspapers that were intrigued with Jonathan Mayhew's reports from Africa. In the offices of the recently-established newspaper, *The Limerick Lamp,* sat a rotund red-haired little man by the name of Senan O'Looney. He had a copy of Jonathan's latest report in front of him, which he studied carefully from beneath bushy red eyebrows. He smiled as he read, admitting grudgingly that for an Anglo-Irish reporter, the man was doing a damn good job.

'I have sat with my fellow countrymen in dug-outs filled with crawling insects, the likes of which an Irishman has never seen before, and hopes he will never have to endure again. I have done battle under the relentless blue skies of Johnannesburg with Irishmen who are serving the cause of freedom of those who struggle against the dominion of the British overseer. Was there ever such a hopeless and utterly futile conflict?'

By God, there was hope for those West Brits yet, with a man of such insight among them, O'Looney reflected. He wouldn't mind having a word with this young fellow, if he ever got back in one piece. He might be able to put an interesting proposition to him.

'Your accounts of the war, your theories and observations are relayed here to me in Ireland with interesting candour. Your glowing references to the Limerick men, some fighting on one side, some on the other, have opened our eyes to the stupidity of a nation that allows its countrymen to be sawn in two for nothing other than the pompous supremacy of an empire which has held the whip for too long. I should like to meet you when you eventually return to Limerick, as I understand you are a brother of Mrs O'Shea, the good doctor's wife? Perhaps you might call to my offices at Ellen Street, if it wouldn't be too inconvenient?'

The signature was scrawled illegibly, as if the writer was unaccustomed to such polite observances, and wished to be done with the odious task as soon as possible.

Jonathan read the letter sitting in a Jeep halfway between Johannesburg and Pretoria. The man sounded intriguing. He would be interested in meeting with him, to see what sort of a fellow the editor of the new Limerick newspaper, *The Limerick Lamp*, was really like. If nothing else, his stint as war correspondent had proven to him that he had a flair for journalistic work. Perhaps when he got home, he would be in need of a job, for he had decided that he would resign his commission. Something Madeline had said in one of her letters had confirmed his doubts about his future with the army.

'There was such a fracas in Dublin! Queen Victoria herself came over to recruit men for the war, but the Republicans held a great protest. That fascinating woman, Maud Gonne, was at the head of the protestors shouting "Up the Boers! Up the Republic!" Are they right, Jonathan? Is there any sense at all in keeping a race of God-fearing people down, when all they want is to farm their own land, and make an independent life for their children?'

Madeline had more insight than he had given her credit for.

Jonathan was present at the signing of the peace treaty at Vereeniging, the culmination of the Boer War, the treaty ending the bitter hostility which had taken so many lives, and left so many shattered beyond hope. All his illusions about a just war, the need to prove one nation's supremacy above another, were finally resolved. He had seen enough death and needless destruction to last him a lifetime. His reports back to London were not received favourably. In a note from the War Office, it was implied that if he wished to resign his commission, no obstacle would be put in his way. Jonathan smiled ruefully – it seemed his career had come to an abrupt end.

In the summer of 1904 Mother Mary of the Angels sat facing Hannah in the small room next to the laundry. Three years had passed since her first encounter with the girl, and as she looked at her now, the nun drew in her breath sharply, her habitual disdain for youth and beauty momentarily suspended. Hannah Benson had turned into a remarkably beautiful young woman with all the manner and breeding of a gentlewoman. Her face, devoid of any touch of rouge or tinted powder, had a porcelain quality about it, with the creamy sheen of her skin, and the faint blush of natural colour on her cheeks. The eyes were hypnotising, two pools of startling blue, like sapphires, the Reverend Mother thought, lost in unaccustomed admiration.

Hannah, unaware of the impact she was achieving, started to speak, her voice troubled. "I want to speak to you about Eily Mitchell, Mother. Her father works in the docks. He gets work on and off, lately none at all."

"I know the girl," the nun sniffed in distaste. She had seen the girl and her like encouraging the young men from the mills on their way home from work. They pinned their skirts up high above their ankles, their faces painted with rouge. Eily Mitchell in particular stood out from the rest with her loud, ribald laughter, and her coarse tongue.

"She's in trouble, Mother," Hannah said quietly. The noise from the laundry was deafening, the rhythmic scrubbing on the washboards, the clanging of the buckets of boiling water as the girls poured the contents into the large vats of washing.

"You mean a child?" Mother Mary of the Angels asked, unperturbed.

It was becoming more prevalent than ever lately, girls desperate for money, waiting for the ships to dock, eagerly anticipating the sailors' shillings in return for their favours. The convent had four such girls staying at the minute, and now it seemed there would be another.

"She's a good worker. I admit I had my reservations about her when I first took her on. But she has proved herself and now she is as fine a lacemaker as my sisters, May and Florrie." Hannah hesitated. She would never admit to the Reverend Mother that she knew who the father was, a member of the Supreme Council of the IRB. She would deal with him in her own way. He was also courting her own sister, May, at the same time he had been bedding Eily.

Hannah had tried reasoning with May, had told her that James McCarthy would only bring her misery.

"You're only jealous, Hannah, because you have no one to snuggle up to on a cold night!" May had retorted. That was the cruellest blow of all.

Never, from the time they had been young girls back in Glenmore, had there been a cross word between them. Now James McCarthy had ruined their friendship, driven a barrier between them. Even Florrie was on May's side, covering up for her when she was late home, leaving the latch on the front door undone so that she could slip in easily without waking Annie or her mother.

"When is the child due?"

"She is about four months gone. I would say late October. She can continue to work for me until she no longer finds it comfortable. Then maybe if she could come to you for the last couple of months? As soon as her father finds out, he'll throw her out of the house."

"And wouldn't the man be right?" Mother Mary of the Angels interrupted, her voice scathing. "A daughter like that is no advantage to a man. She has made her own bed; now she has to lie in it."

"Will you take her in?" Hannah asked, irritated by the nun's attitude. Even a girl as wild as Eily Mitchell deserved some degree of compassion.

"Yes. After all, that is our duty. God is forgiving."

But not his servers, Hannah thought to herself cynically. Elly Mitchell would get no mercy from the unyielding heart of Mother Mary of the Angels.

"Why didn't you tell me before now?" James McCarthy glared at her, his eyes burning with anger. "For Jesus's sake, girl, I can't support myself, not to mind a woman with a child!"

Eily looked at him, a flush of anger spreading over her plump face. "Oh yeah, Jem McCarthy! But if it was the Benson one who was in trouble, you'd see her right, I dare say!"

"None of your lip, or I'll tell your Da. I'll deny

everything, and he'll believe me; he'll have to, me over him on the Council!" He grinned at her triumphantly, knowing he had got his point across. Eily was terrified of her Da, had often felt the sting of a blow across her face from him. She'd have to keep quiet about this, for her own sake. "Maybe you could get rid of it?" he asked hopefully. "I know a few ould wans behind the market who know what to do. Nobody need ever know."

Eily looked at him horrified. "Jem McCarthy! Get rid of the little thing? And me never again able to face the priest in confession, or receive Holy Communion? Besides, I'm too far gone for that kind of thing. This is a real baby inside me, James – there'll be no murder done on my part!"

"All right, all right, so you'll have it – but expect nothing from me, mind. I have my own affairs to attend to."

"And wasn't I one of your affairs until you put your eyes on May Benson? You're a waster, Jem McCarthy, and one of these nights you'll be blown up by one of your own bombs, and maybe me father will go with you, and that'd be a double blessing for me!"

He advanced towards her, his hand raised to strike out, but she moved swiftly out of reach and ran out into the laneway, her heart pounding with fear as she hurried through the narrow, dirty lanes, reaching the quay as the Angelus bell rang out from the cathedral. There was a high tide tonight. The quay was deserted; everybody gone home to have their supper. A few swans swam idly by, lifting their heads unconcernedly as they drifted past Eily, standing close to the water's edge. It would only take a second. One quick movement, and she'd be in the water. She could close her eyes and pretend she was a swan, floating down river, lifting her head to the sky with its clouds, pink and white, scurrying across the evening sky.

No, she couldn't do it. Maybe if it was just herself, she would have chanced it, but now she had the baby to consider. She put her hand to her stomach, already swollen beneath the tight waistband of her skirt. For the first time in her life, she had something that was all hers. Not even Jem McCarthy could take it away from her. Let him have the Benson girl. What did she care? May Benson would sooner or later fall into the same trap as she herself had, then she'd see what a great rebel the bold Jem McCarthy was.

James hurried to the Merchants' Hall for the meeting. He had forgotten all about Eily and the baby; the girl's dilemma meant nothing to him. She had known what she was doing when she got involved with him. Now it was up to her to sort herself out. He felt excited tonight, his pulse racing as he thought of the preparations they were going to make for the demonstration in Dublin. Things were moving finally. He had grown tired of playing games. It was time the people stood up for themselves and forced the British to give them their independence. The King was coming to Dublin. The streets would be lined with people trying to catch a glimpse of him as he waved from the Lord Mayor's carriage, and in the crowd there would be some of the Brotherhood ready to start trouble.

The smile on James's face was enigmatic as he entered

the hall and took his place on the rostrum. He could see May looking up at him from her seat on the women's side and he winked knowingly in her direction. She blushed, feeling the sweat on her forehead, the trickle of dampness running between her breasts as the room grew warmer with the swell of the crowd and the heat of the evening. The women would be with them this time. They were all going up on the train Saturday morning and returning that night, having left their mark on the streets of Dublin. The officer in charge of the women's *Cumann* frowned at May disparagingly, but the girl ignored her, her eyes glued to James McCarthy as he outlined their plan of action.

He was making good money now, for the work on the Fever Hospital had been completed the previous summer, and he had been glad of the employment from the Board of Works as a casual labourer, plastering and laying the stonework for one of the wards called after Dr O'Shea's little girl, The Emma O'Shea Fever Ward. Casual work suited him, for he could be attending to his 'militant' duties between times when he was laid off. And he was managing to put a bit of money by, but he wouldn't tell May that. Never tell a woman what one hand held and what the other was doing had always been his motto and he stuck by it. Once, when he had been laid off the job, James had begun to feel restless again, no orders for him from headquarters, afraid all the time that he would be picked up for questioning by the police. May had been afraid then. She had thought she would lose him forever if he didn't get some work, for he had been talking of leaving Limerick and going down the country "where there was some real action".

But his agitation abated after he had gone to see Michael Jameson at the back of Leamy's bar on the quays. As well as owning half the town, Jameson had a coachyard at Lower George's Street, just touching the fashionable district of Newtown Perry. Jameson had a reputation for employing young boys, unskilled in the trade, most of them orphans left at the convent gates with nobody to care what happened to them. He had them working in the coachyard from dawn to dusk for half the regular wage, and anybody who rebelled against the injustice of their employment was told to get out. The dockers had come together and become members of the National Union of Dock Labourers. The men in the coachyard wanted to do the same, with big Jim Larkin coming down from Dublin to urge them to join the Irish Congress of Trade Unions. "Not an hour on the day, not a penny off the pay, men!" Larkin had roared at them, his bulky frame towering over them from the steps of one of the coaches.

Jameson had come out then, had raised his fist and threatened the union men. "You join a union, and I'll bring in more men and sack the lot of you! There's many a man would be glad of a wage to bring home tonight. I won't be short of labour!"

James McCarthy had no time for unions. They only got in the way of the real business of the day – Ireland, a free nation. He had no time for theorists either, or their high fallutin' ideals. It was time to fight, for fighting was the only means of winning freedom for the Irish people. Jameson and himself had something in common. They were both anti-union, and both ruthless in their methods. When Michael Jameson offered McCarthy a job in his coachyard as "general overseer, you know what I mean?"

James accepted readily. He knew what Jameson meant, all right. He was to see to it that none of the men stepped out of line, or went behind Jameson's back, looking to join the union. He was to become Jameson's informer.

"I'm going, Hannah, and that's all there is to it!" May looked at her sister stubbornly, two blotches of red glowing angrily on her cheeks.

"What'll Mother say? She has little enough regard for *Cumann na mBan* – you heard her, 'women dressed up as men!' How am I going to tell her you want to go to Dublin to demonstrate against the King's visit?" Hannah tried to reason with May, coaxingly at first, then threatening her. "I'll take you out of the shop on Portobello Street, and put you back into the factory! You won't be able to see the young dandies passing on the quay."

"I don't care!" May retorted, tossing her head arrogantly. "Put me back in the warehouse if you want! As long as I have James I have no interest in the Limerick dandies passing up and down Portobello Street!"

"What am I going to do with her, Annie?" Hannah asked in despair.

They were sitting in the parlour on the evening before May's departure for Dublin.

"I can't tell Mother. She'd be worried to death about her. I'll have to pretend that she's working on an order that has to be got out by the weekend, pretend that she'll be in the factory tomorrow, instead of up there in Dublin with all the rabble of the streets, throwing cans and stones, and God knows what else might happen!"

"You can't be looking after her forever, child. She's a young woman now, and she knows her own mind. Let McCarthy take responsibility for her, if that's what she wants."

"I don't think she knows what she wants," Hannah murmured worriedly.

She had confided in Annie about Eily Mitchell, because the responsibility of keeping it to herself was too great, especially when May was involved with the very same man who had gotten Eily into trouble. "You know the kind of man he is, Annie. If anything should happen to her . . ."

"Let things be for the time being, Hannah. Let her go to Dublin. Maybe it will knock some sense into her when she sees the savagery that goes on at one of those demonstrations."

Hannah nodded slowly. Maybe Annie was right. She'd leave May go to Dublin, and not let on a word to her mother. There was no use upsetting her needlessly. Besides, it was only one day. May would be home by tomorrow evening.

"You can have the day off for your Republican duties," Jameson winked at James McCarthy, "but I want you to do me a little favour before you go. Hannah Benson's place in the docks – I hear she's doing very well lately, employing men she is now, carting orders of linen from the Belfast ship." James saw the look of venom on the man's ruddy face. "She's payin' them union wages, if you don't mind, organising the girls on shift work, payin' them extra for every batch of shirts that's finished by the delivery date. She's puttin' ideas into their heads, and then they go home to their Das and tell them what wages they should be earnin'. A union agitator, that's what she is, one of Larkin's lackeys!"

He leaned closer to James as they sat in Coonerty's public house, the smell of stale porter on his breath. James turned away slightly. The man was a bully, but then that was none of his business. He didn't have to like the man to work for him. Besides, he was about the only employee who was well paid. "You know about dynamite and such things, lad?"

James nodded, intrigued. "'Tis my business to know. What about it?"

"I have a little job for you. Miss Hannah Benson is just after getting in a load of linen from Belfast. It's stored at the back of the warehouse. Now if something was to happen to that consignment, it would set her back a bit, eh? Take her mind off matters that don't concern her. A sort of a warning, if you know what I mean?"

James looked at the man sitting in front of him, saw the sneer on his fat, bloated face, the malicious twinkle in his eyes. It was something he should have thought of himself. He had put his revenge against Peter Benson to one side since he had been elected to the Supreme Council of the Brotherhood. He hadn't forgotten though. It remained in the background, festering, taking root in his mind every time he held May in his arms.

May was his for the taking, every look from her dark eyes told him she would follow him to the ends of the earth, if need be. It was a pity that he had it in for the Bensons – he had grown fond of May, with her earnest face looking up into his as he spoke of the day when all the Fenian Brotherhood would rise up in revolt against the British crown.

"Are you on, lad?" Jameson asked impatiently. The boy was a dreamer. Something in the way he looked at you made you feel uncomfortable. Unstable, Jameson thought, but then they were the best sort for the kind of work he had in mind.

"I'll do it, but it'll have to be tonight, for after the rally in Dublin the police will be out in force in the cities rounding up the organisers. My name will be all over the newspapers by tomorrow night."

Jameson heard the note of pride in his voice. There was nothing this boy wouldn't do for the cause. Blowing up Hannah Benson's factory would be no trouble for a fella like him.

"You have a key?" James confronted Eily as she laid the table for the supper. Her father was due back from the public house any minute. She looked at the clock on the wall anxiously. If his supper wasn't on the table when he came through the door, there'd be hell to pay.

"What if I have? What business is it of yours?" She looked at him and saw the dangerous glint in his eyes. "What do you want the key of the warehouse for, Jem?" she asked him, her voice more subdued.

"I have business there tonight. There's nothing you need to know, nor your father either."

She eyed him sharply. "Look, Hannah Benson is a dacent sort. She gave me a job when the whole town regarded me as a . . . "

"Whore?" James taunted her. "Sure everybody knows that's what you are, Eily, and who's going to believe the child you're carryin' is mine, eh? More likely the bastard of one of them sailor fellows from the ships. And that's what I'll tell your father if you don't hand over the key to me, now!" He held out his hand threateningly.

Eily felt in the pocket of her apron and took out the key, handing it over to him reluctantly. "I suppose May Benson is going to Dublin with you in the morning?"

"She might be," he answered her evasively. Eily Mitchell had no interest in the movement, and he had no wish to involve her. She was a troublemaker, challenging him every time she opened her mouth. May was easier to get along with. She did what she was told, no questions asked. God, but they'd have a great day in Dublin tomorrow!

Jonathan had remained in London for several months after his return from Africa, waiting for his discharge papers to come through. Christine had written to him, pleading with him to go to the War Office, to ask that he be reinstated with the regiment.

"What would Father say if he were alive today, Jonathan, to see his only son stripped of his commission all because of a few misguided ideals?"

Jonathan had sighed resignedly, tearing up his sister's letter and depositing it in the waste bin. Christine would never understand. He was done with the army, had developed a new interest, an exciting perspective in his life.

The letter he had received from the editor of *The Limerick Lamp* had intrigued him. He was at a crossroads in his life, some exciting challenges presenting themselves to him. The memory of Ellen Flannery, lying on the damp mattress in that miserable dark hovel still haunted him. He wanted to make things better for people like her, to be close to their way of thinking, to see what steps could be taken to rectify some of the many injustices wrought on them. Then he had met a most eloquent man at a gentleman's club in Eton Square, shortly after his arrival in London. Sir Cedric Humphries owned a large estate in Wexford. He and a few of his friends, all literary enthusiasts, for Sir Cedric contributed pieces of poetry and prose to the various literary periodicals in London, had decided to set up a National Literary Society in Ireland strictly for the preservation of Irish history and culture.

Sir Cedric had greatly admired Jonathan's writing talents as a journalist during the Boer War, and asked him directly if he would be interested in joining their literary circle. "I understand you have connections in Limerick, Mr Mayhew? It is quite an interesting coincidence that one of our members, who has recently set up his own newspaper, is also resident in that beautiful city by the Shannon, a man by the name of Senan O'Looney."

"I received a letter from him while I was in Africa," Jonathan revealed, instantly excited by the prospect of a new venture into an area hitherto unknown to him. Wild ideas ran through his head, a vista of challenging possibilities opening up before his eyes. He was impatient to be back in Limerick once more. He would go to see this fellow O'Looney; maybe there would be a job for him with his newspaper.

He told Sir Cedric that he would be pleased to join the National Literary Society. Two weeks later he left for Limerick.

The explosion lit up the night sky, several ships in the dock sounding distress signals as, one after another, thunderous blasts rent the air. James McCarthy ran past the flour mills, along the dock road and up O'Curry Avenue, his heart racing with wild trepidation. That would give Miss Hannah Benson something to think about. He laughed, a loud, exhilarated laugh, his face red with exertion as he made one final sprint, reaching the safety of Cornmarket Row where he had taken rooms in a tenement building.

Since Eily had told him she was pregnant, he thought it wise not to dally under Mitchell's roof. The man had a savage temper. If he ever got wind of who had been Eily's downfall, James didn't think much of his chances if it came to blows. He ran up the stairs of the tenement building. A couple of children, half-naked, their bones luminously visible in the semi-light of the narrow hallway, watched him curiously. When he got to his room, he went hurriedly inside, throwing himself on the narrow trestle bed in the corner. He closed his eyes then and savoured his moment of triumph. It had been a good night's work, and there was still tomorrow, the rally in Dublin, May Benson's soft body leaning against him suggestively as they shouted their defiance against the King's visit. He closed his eyes and slept until the first light penetrated the dirty window.

Hannah stood at the foot of May's bed, looking at the

neatly folded-back sheets, the nightgown thrown across the counterpane. So she had gone already.

Her mother would spend the day worrying, and praying that nothing would happen to her poor, misled daughter – and Hannah knew she would get no peace until May was safely back in Limerick. She had decided, after all, to confide in Peggy, late last night after May had gone to bed. Though she hated to distress her mother, she had judged it better to let her know the facts than to be drawn, herself, into May's intrigue. The possible consequences of deception could be, she reasoned, ultimately more distressing. Her mother had gone to her own room, grim-faced, and Hannah herself had spent a restless night, dreaming of Uncle John, his face sorrowful, flames from the burnt-out shop in the background. Then flashes of Jonathan, his handsome face so close to hers, his gentle fingers tracing the line of her neck until she wanted to cry out, to tell him stop, that it was Madeline he had married, it was Madeline he loved.

"I'm sorry, Miss Hannah, but you'd better come quick!" Sean Og hopped from one leg to the other in agitation. "Last night, Miss, in the dock – an explosion."

Hannah grabbed him by the shoulders, her fingers digging into his flesh until he winced in pain. "What explosion, where? Is it the warehouse? The machines?" Her mouth felt dry; she found it difficult to swallow. Thoughts of John's misfortune made her legs feel weak. She had to sit down. Surely not twice. Dear God – not when she was getting on so well.

"I think the machine-room is all right, Miss. Just the

storeroom, where the materials are kept," he soothed her, his voice full of pity. "The night watchman heard the first explosion and ran to get help. The second one went off at the back of the grain store, well away from the machines, thank God." Hannah uttered a silent prayer of thanksgiving. If the sewing-machines were intact, then things weren't too bad. They could always move into the shop in Portobello Street until the warehouse was fixed up again.

"Oh Peter, Peter! What are we going to do at all, with all this misfortune on top of us?" Peggy Benson wailed, wringing her hands in distress.

Annie spoke up sharply. "Come on, there's a good woman. Can't you see Hannah has enough troubles not to be listening to your lamentations on top of them? Have you been to the warehouse, child? What's the damage?"

"The storeroom at the back is gone. All the materials are ruined, but the machines are fine," Hannah answered tiredly, taking off her coat and placing her hat on the hall stand. The police had been questioning her, asking her if she knew anybody who had it in for her. She had her suspicions, and they tormented her.

When she had gone to the quay that morning to see the destruction, Eily Mitchell had been there, her eyes avoiding Hannah's. She had grown to like the girl, in spite of her rough ways and sharp tongue. If Eily had anything to do with it, then James McCarthy was at the back of it. And if James McCarthy had set the explosives, then May was in more trouble than she realised. The man was dangerous. The men in Michael Jameson's coachyard in Limerick were afraid of him, and with good reason. Three of them had been fired in the last month because they had written to Larkin asking his advice about pay. James McCarthy had found out, and had denounced them. Three more men had been hired in their places the following day.

"Annie, I must talk to you," Hannah beckoned to her aunt as she came out of the kitchen. They went into the parlour and Hannah closed the door quietly behind her. "I'm worried, Annie. May was due back hours ago, and it's past ten now. I've sent Mother to bed, for she's tired out from worrying. When May gets back I'll give her the sharp edge of my tongue; I'm tired of her headstrong ways. You'd think she'd know better than to worry Mother so."

"That girl is well able to look after herself, Hannah. James McCarthy is a wild fellow, but surely he'd have the sense to look after the girl, and it her first visit to the big city."

"He's a good-for-nothing, Annie," Hannah said suddenly, the look of hatred in her face surprising Annie. Her niece wasn't one to speak ill of anybody, even the bold James.

Hannah fell silent, the clock on the mantlepiece ticking loudly in the room as the hands moved slowly towards the hour of eleven. Eily Mitchell had come to her in the warehouse as she was sifting through the tattered remains of the bales of linen.

"'Tis truly sorry I am, miss," she blurted out to Hannah. Her eyes were fixed firmly on the ground as she admitted her part in the night's events. "'Twas Jem, you see. He made me give him the key to the warehouse. He'd have told me father, about the baby, you see. I had to, miss!" Eily looked up at Hannah, her eyes pleading.

"It's just what I suspected myself, Eily, and I'm glad you told me, for I know I can rely on you from now on. Don't ever let the likes of James McCarthy frighten you again. He'll get what's coming to him, never fear!"

"He's gone to Dublin for the demonstration, miss."

"But he'll be back, and then I'll have something to say to him – and I'll make May see some sense, too." Hannah spoke with conviction.

But Eily was troubled. She knew something that maybe Miss Benson should know, something that involved May. She spoke up, her voice trembling a little. "I think he's gone for good, miss. He's taken his clothes, for I went round to his room this morning to tell him that I was going to tell you about the key, and he was gone. Taken all his clothes, not a trace of him left!"

A line of policemen stood in front of the gathering crowd as they surged forward, trying to catch a glimpse of King Edward the Seventh. May stood on top of the parapet surrounding Nelson's Pillar, a banner crudely attached to a narrow length of stick in her hand, stating in bold, black lettering 'Up the Republic!' James was standing at the front of the crowd, his face filled with hatred as he watched the Lord Mayor's coach pass by, ashamed of his countrymen as they shouted, "Long Live the King!"

"Long live the Republic! Death to British tyranny!" James shouted, his eyes bright with revolutionary fervour. There was a scuffle behind him. He felt a fist in the small of his back and he turned angrily.

"Bloody Republicans, making trouble for us! Where's the sense in shouting for a free Ireland when all you can do is traipse around the country blowin' up barracks and puttin' the fear of God in people?" The man shook his fist at James, then suddenly he was on the ground, James towering over him, hands reaching for his throat.

"James, James! Come away, like a good man. Don't let him rouse you." May's cry went unheard.

By the time the police had intervened, two men had cracked ribs and James, his eye swollen and bloodshot, limped away from the fracas. May, sobbing bitterly, was supporting him. "We'll stay the night here. I know a man who'll take us in, for there's no goin' back to Limerick for me. I saw that policeman take a good look at me. We're in this together, girl. Will you stay with me?" He had already made up his mind, coming up on the train, that Dublin was the place to be, for the time being. Limerick was a small place, with everybody knowing everybody else, no place to hide, to make plans. Even Jameson wasn't to be trusted. James suspected that he had already given his name to the police in Limerick. Everywhere he went he was watched, and Eily Mitchell was a scourge, following him around, her belly swollen with the child she was carrying, her dirty, tear-stained face accusing.

He was well rid of them all, until the call came. And it would come soon. He was sure of that. The Fianna were swelling their ranks in Dublin, ever since Hobson and the Countess joined forces. He wanted May with him, though. He wanted to see the look on the Bensons' faces when he brought her down, broke her spirit until she no longer cared what happened to her. Then he would throw her aside, send her back to Limerick, the innocent sparkle in her eyes dulled. He leaned heavily on her now, his body teasing hers as he swayed against her, brushing her hips seductively.

May wasn't going to let James McCarthy out of her sight. She wanted to be with him always, to look after him. Neither her mother nor Hannah could prevent her from feeling the way she did. She knew about Eily Mitchell. Nobody had told her, but she had seen the early signs of pregnancy in the bloated stomach and the noisy retching as Eily bent over the enamel bucket in the back of the warehouse. She had heard rumours that James had done the mischief, but May knew Eily Mitchell. Probably some sailor from the boats; didn't everybody know the sort she was?

"I'll stay with you tonight, James, and every other night if you want me?" Her meaning was clear to James; it had been easier than he expected. He pulled her towards him, his lips rough against her trembling ones.

"We'll have a fine time, *a chroi*, you and me, working together side by side for the cause!"

May smiled uncertainly, struggling with fear and doubt. But it was her life, after all. She could do what she pleased with it.

May married James McCarthy in the sacristy of a little church in Rathbone Street in Dublin one late August morning in 1904. She wrote to her mother, telling her not to worry, and that she was very happy.

'I know what you think of him, Mother, but he is a good man, at the back of his wild ways. He has brought me to the theatre twice, and I saw Maud Gonne, and she so beautiful, Mother, in a play written especially for her by the poet, Will

Yeats, and everybody stood up and cheered at the end, and James clasped me to him, and said there was only one other woman as beautiful as the one on the stage, and that was me. Oh Mother, forgive me for running away the way I did, but I could burst with the happiness my own dear James has given me!'

Hannah watched with amusement as Florrie, her face serious, outlined the pattern she required for a ladies' riding suit. It was coming into the autumn and the orders were in already for the riding meets in the country mansions which would continue until Christmas. The young man listened, a half-smile on his face as he winked at Hannah over the top of Florrie's head.

"Well now, ma'am, that's a tall order, and I don't know even after seven years at the tailoring trade that I'll be able to meet your requirements, so to speak!"

Florrie began to say something, then blushed as she realised he was only poking fun at her.

"Martin Manley! I could kill you, so I could, and you letting on you didn't know a thing about ladies' patterns!"

He looked at the sketch in Florrie's hand and considered it for a moment. "That's an easy one. Once you've done tailoring for the men, it's no problem to suit the ladies as well, for it's only a skirt instead of a trousers that's wantin'."

"There'll be two needed for the hunt at the end of January. Lady Ballantyne and her daughter ordered one in grey and the other in dark brown velvet. They're very particular, Martin – I just want them to be perfect." Florrie looked up at him anxiously, his tall figure dwarfing her minute one.

"With you giving me the odd hand, *a chroi,* I could finish off a hundred suits, all in different colours, by the end of the month!"

Hannah saw the way he looked at her sister, a look she thought she had seen a long time ago in Jonathan Mayhew's eyes. It hurt her as much as ever now, and she envied Florrie. She saw her sister's flushed, shy face, Martin's bold, teasing banter as he playfully took Florrie's hand in his, delighting in the blushes she was trying so unsuccessfully to hide. She didn't pull her hand away from his either, Hannah noted with amusement, and wondered if her little shy sister was finally coming out of her shell, the attentions of a young man making her blossom as no other could. Florrie had always been the timid one, the shy one, her head immersed in books. Florrie had always been sitting in a corner, when they had some spare time away from the lacemaking, making up little pieces of poetry and short stories. And now here was Martin Manley, recognising the timidness masking a heart of solid gold. Martin had come to Limerick shortly after the explosion at the warehouse. He had been sent by the great man Larkin himself, he said, to see if she needed anything done, for Hannah's views on a fair day's work for a fair day's pay had reached the listening ear of the Labour movement in Dublin. A tailor by trade, Manley had been impressed with Hannah's contented workforce, her insistence that they take one hour's break at noon so that they'd return refreshed for the afternoon's work.

Hannah had liked him from the beginning, and before he was due to go back to Dublin, she had tentatively offered him work in the warehouse. "Tailoring is becoming part of ladies' dressmaking now – Uncle John has written to me telling me about the factories in New Jersey that are making the same style of suit for both men and women." Hannah had eagerly outlined her ideas to him. "He has sent me some very elegant patterns, and I've shown them to some of my customers, who were very impressed indeed. Now, with a qualified tailor on hand to suit the ladies, Hannah Benson's dress designs would be expanded even further!"

Martin Manley didn't need time to think. He had nothing to go back to in Dublin, and his work with the union men could still remain active in Limerick. And then there was Florrie Benson and the way she'd looked at him.

Eily Mitchell groaned in the bed, turning on her side, the pain in her back forcing her to cry out loud. The room was small, with just a crucifix above the bed, and a jug of water for washing on the wooden table in the corner. She heard the baby stir in the crib, then a loud, hungry wail and she buried her head beneath the bedclothes, wishing that the piercing, demanding cries would stop. She was tired. The work at the warehouse hadn't slackened since well before Christmas, and she had been feeling unwell since the child had been born in October.

She had gone to the nuns in the convent at the end of August, after her father had found out about her. She could still recall the sting of the blow across her face, his fury as he shoved her out the door.

"Get out of it, you slut! Just like your mother before you! She couldn't keep away from the boats either, and the sailor men with their foreign money and plenty of drink!"

She had come to the convent then, and had regretted her decision ever since. It would have been better to die on the streets than to endure the humiliation she felt here.

A week before the baby arrived she had been scrubbing the convent floors, carrying buckets of water upstairs from the kitchens beneath, her back breaking as the baby kicked inside her in protest. She had complained to the Reverend Mother but the eyes turned on her had been cold as ice.

"You must atone for your sins, Eily Mitchell. That is the punishment God has sent you. You must work until your mind is empty of wicked thoughts, your past life put behind you for ever!"

The baby, a boy, had been born the first week in October. She had writhed in the bed, cursing Jem McCarthy aloud, the pains tearing her body apart until she felt she could bear it no longer. "Dear Jesus, what did I do to deserve this?" she had screamed in the empty convent room. The two nuns attending her had moved in and out silently, ignoring her protests as they turned her roughly on her back, the birth of the child imminent. They were praying to the Mother of Sorrows as the child came into the world and Eily had vowed to herself then that she would never again let herself be caught in such a predicament.

She had stayed in the convent afterwards, because there was no place else to go. Her father had told her not to come home, and she hadn't enough money to rent a room for herself and Matthew, the name she had given the baby. The baby stopped crying and Eily lay back in the bed again, sighing with relief. Her back was killing her. She had hurt it carrying those buckets of water to wash the floors before the baby was born, and now the pain remained. She couldn't stay with the nuns much longer. She had heard Mother Superior talking to one of the nuns in the corridor the night before.

"She'll see sense before the baby is much older. I have discussed it with Dr O'Shea and he is very much taken with the idea; his poor wife hasn't been the same woman since her own poor child was taken from her. This would be a blessing for such a fine couple."

The threat had been there, and it haunted Eily, for she knew they were planning to take her baby from her. She had nobody to stand up for her. Jem McCarthy was married to May Benson and living in Dublin with never a care for Eily or her child. If Matthew was taken from her, she would prefer to throw herself into the river than to go on alone.

She tossed and turned all night, and in the morning, Mother Mary of the Angels called her into her office. "You know, Eily, that it is almost impossible to bring up a child on your own without any support." The nun's voice was placating, uncharacteristically gentle.

"I have work with Hannah Benson, and more to come, for she's doin' well since the warehouse was fixed up. I could manage."

"Manage, my girl, but is that enough? Your son needs a father, a strong hand to guide him, and a mother who will teach him to be an honest, upstanding young man." Eily heard the reproach in her voice, the insinuation that his mother wasn't a suitable model to imitate.

She stuck out her chin defensively. "I can get a room in the town, get some young one in to look after him while I'm at work. Maybe I can even take some piece-work to do at home," she reasoned wildly, the thought that Matthew might be taken from her filling her with desperation.

"I have a couple in mind who would look after the child like their own," the nun continued, ignoring Eily's pathetic pleas. "I cannot tell you who they are – we are forbidden to do so, for reasons which I think are obvious. But if you do not wish to be thrown out on the streets with your child then I suggest you follow my advice."

Eily turned then and ran from the room, her eyes blinded with angry tears. There was no hope for her. In her heart she knew she could not provide for the baby on her own. Hannah Benson had been good to her, even after Jem McCarthy had run off with her sister. But she couldn't help her in this situation.

Mary, another girl who had her child in the convent, had been forced to give her up for adoption, just like Eily was being made to do. Mary's child had been a year old, and she had cried on Eily's shoulder the day the Mother Superior had taken the child away in a carriage to the adoptive parents. And now the same thing was happening to her. There was no way she could prevent it from happening. The aching loneliness in her heart as she looked down at the sleeping baby in his cradle – that was her real penance.

"I don't want another child, Robert. I don't think I could face it." Robert O'Shea looked at his wife and drummed his fingers distractedly on the table. Her beautiful hair had lost its former lustre, her body grown gaunt, a dull film of inertia across her vacant, staring eyes. He knew they would never have any more children of their own. Since Emma's death Christine had taken to sleeping apart from him in the guest-room at the end of the landing. The only intimacy she now allowed her husband was a kiss on waking in the morning, and before going to their separate bedrooms at night.

Mother Mary of the Angels had spoken with him at the hospital where she attended children in the fever ward. "A little boy, Dr O'Shea. Discuss the matter with your wife, and then come and see me at the convent."

"There is a child, Christine, at the convent, a little baby boy in need of a good home." He looked at her pleadingly, taking her small, cold hand in his. "Please Christine, this is our last chance of regaining the happiness we once had."

"A happiness resulting from the birth of our darling Emma, Robert. Since she died, my life has been no longer worthwhile!" Christine lowered her eyes and wept silently. But she didn't relinquish her hold on his hand, and he felt a flicker of hope in his heart. This baby had surely been sent to them from heaven, an answer to his unceasing prayers for Christine's recovery.

"I shall have the baby brought to you, and then, if everything is satisfactory for you, we shall make the adoption arrangements." Mother Mary of the Angels smiled graciously at Mrs O'Shea. She noticed how pale the woman appeared, the stylish grey suit cut close to an extraordinarily thin body. Dr O'Shea should look to his own wife, and forget the women in the slums, she speculated privately. The woman was a walking ghost. The door opened behind them and a nun appeared, carrying the baby in her arms.

Christine O'Shea stood up slowly, extending her arms to take the child. "What is his name?" she almost whispered. She looked down at the baby in her arms, saw his smile, a sweet baby smile of innocent pleasure. Emma used to smile like that when she had held her in her arms, singing to her, watching her smile as Christine blew kisses to her through her fingertips. "What is his name?" she repeated. The Reverend Mother looked at Dr O'Shea questioningly and he nodded in relief.

"His name is Matthew. His mother's name you need not know."

"Matthew," Christine whispered softly. "That is too sophisticated a name for such a little fellow. I shall call him Mat."

For the first time in such a long time, Robert O'Shea saw his wife's smile reach her eyes, transforming her face into the one he had first fallen in love with so many years ago.

On his return Jonathan was delighted to see his sister in such good spirits, the old sparkle back in her eyes once more. "You must stay with us, Jonathan, for as long as you wish. I may not be entirely in agreement with your decision to leave the regiment, but I can see I am not the only one who has improved in spirits since our last meeting. Your newfound interest suits you, brother, for I have never seen you look so fit and healthy!"

It was true. Jonathan's face was now bright and alert-looking, the knowledge that he could wield a pen just as mightily as a sword filling him with confidence in his ability to make something useful of his life.

He visited Senan O'Looney shortly after his return to Limerick. The offices of *The Limerick Lamp* in Ellen Street were small and cramped, a tiny desk stuck in one corner, mounds of untidy files strewn about the floor and on top of dusty shelves. The printing room was at the back of the building, almost as small as the office through which Jonathan had walked, skirting bundles of papers and long-forgotten demand notes and invoices.

Senan O'Looney kicked them aside indifferently. "It's only a small newspaper starting out, boy! What do the creditors expect? I'll pay them when I'm good and ready!"

Two men were at the printing machine, and a young boy was busily sorting the ink-wet papers, placing the sheets in sequence.

"You see, I have nothing against you personally, but it's your kind who are destroying the culture of our land, aping the English, trying to proselytise the poor ignorant Irish with your own writings and traditions!" He banged his fist down on the printing machine emphatically. "That's why I've started this newspaper, to stir the people into thinking about their own Irishness, make them proud of their roots!"

Jonathan listened, fascinated by the red-haired bullet of a man who spat out fiery arguments with all the fanaticism of a man unwaveringly dedicated to his purpose.

He agreed with most of O'Looney's theories. What

good was independence without the necessary fervour of nationalism? If a people wanted to be independent, then they had to be protected from outside influences, cultivating their own self-sufficiency, speaking their own language, manufacturing their own goods, buying only items manufactured in their own country.

"Mind you, Jonathan lad, 'tis Gaelic nationalism I'm thinkin' of, not the Republican kind. I have no time for revolutionaries! Where did it get us in the past, I ask you? Madmen teem about the countryside, blowin' up army barracks and ambushing soldiers in lonely boreens! We must look to our own Gaelic heritage, study it and cultivate it, so that when the time comes – and mark you, it's coming – we'll be able to hold up our heads proudly and stand beside the best of them!"

Senan O'Looney offered Jonathan the job of sub-editor on the newspaper, and as he hadn't gotten round yet to employing a full-time reporter, he breezily asked him if he wouldn't be too averse to travelling "about a bit" collecting "bits and pieces" from various literary groups. "Something interesting for the masses," as he put it to Jonathan, a mischievous grin on his face. Jonathan accepted the position, his head reeling with the persuasive force of O'Looney's philosophies. He thought he would enjoy working with this unconventional but highly intelligent man.

Jonathan had no contact with Hannah. Apart from his work taking up the most part of his day, he felt the barrier of time had caused the rift between them to have widened irreparably. From time to time, he would see her coming out of her shop in Portobello, a ready smile on her increasingly beautiful face as she spoke with passers-by. Once, he saw her at the theatre in Henry Street where he had been sent by Senan to do a review of Yeats' play, *The Countess Kathleen*. She was sitting near the front of the theatre, the outline of her face illuminated by the spotlight from the small stage. She turned once to speak to Annie, sitting beside her, giving Jonathan a full view of her face. His heart took a wild, bounding leap, for she was still, he felt, an inextricable part of his lonely life.

He enjoyed working with O'Looney, and looked forward to having a few drinks with him after work in Herbert's public house in Ellen Street. By now he had met many of O'Looney's friends, most of them involved with the Literary Movement, one of them a poet who astounded everyone with his spontaneous launches into verse, line after line of humorous anecdote. At home, the atmosphere in the O'Shea household had become relaxed and cheerful once more, thanks to the gurgling presence of baby Mat. Emma's memory was still held dear, treasured in a wooden trunk in Christine's wardrobe: her little dresses, baby vests and knee-high stockings, tiny shoes marked with the faint, poignant bruising of a little girl who did not have enough time to wear them out completely. They would never forget her. But there was Mat, with the roguish smile and the dark wisps of curling hair sprouting on his shapely head. A baby who put out his hand commandingly for what he wanted, and was invariably given it by the adoring Christine.

There was a riot in the theatre the night Jonathan had seen Hannah in the audience. The play had not been well received in Dublin, and a travelling players' group had brought it to Limerick, assuming that the wrath of the Catholic Nationalists would not be as intense in the Limerick audiences. The Countess Kathleen's gesture, in selling her soul to the devil in exchange for food for the starving people of Ireland, brought the audience to its feet. Many booed loudly; some hurtled empty bottles onto the stage, the actors trying to shield themselves from the onslaught.

Jonathan hastened immediately to Hannah's assistance, as she struggled, pushing her way through the angry crowd. "Mrs Sullivan! Hannah." Her name trembled on his lips as he put a protective arm about her, her softness against him causing him to crush her half-angrily to him. Hannah looked up at him, her blue eyes full of reproachful surprise. They shared the same tremor of bittersweet recognition, memories of summer days they had spent on the river, and in the woods at Capanti, coming back forcefully to haunt them.

Hannah had read some of his articles in *The Limerick Lamp* and had been impressed by his way with words, his understanding of the lifestyles of the poor people both in the city and in country towns similar to Glenmore. The night after the mêlée in the theatre, she smiled as she read his comments in the paper.

The Irish Literary Theatre, it seems, has sounded its death knell with William Butler Yeats' new play, The Countess Kathleen. *It is the adamant opinion of those "in the know" that no self-respecting Irish woman would sell her soul for a plateful of salty bacon and potatoes – not even if that bacon came from the notable establishment of O'Mara's Bacon Factory in*

Limerick! I met an old woman outside the theatre who blessed herself reverently, saying that it should be left to the men to bargain with the devil – for they're the proper blaggards – not the poor misfortunate women who have to put up with them!

Hannah read the piece aloud to Molly as she stood in the kitchen, peeling potatoes for the dinner. "Sure what's the world comin' to at all? I'm surprised at a man like that Mr Mayhew, makin' a mockery of the opinion of the good Catholics of Ireland. But sure, what can you expect from a Protestant!"

Nothing more was said of Mr Frederick Bulman in the Deery household. Mrs Deery continued to resume her endless pursuit of a suitable partner for her seemingly unmarriageable daughter. Following her husband's dismissal of Madeline's potential beau, Mrs Deery had cried solidly for seven days, Madeline walking about the house like a silent ghost, her face pale and drawn. Jonathan encountered her in Ellen Street one evening as he left the office of *The Limerick Lamp*. He felt genuinely glad to see her, remembering her kindness to his sister after Emma's death, and her light, gossipy letters to him in the Transvaal.

She looked so forlorn, her eyes dull and with such a hopelessness in them, that he invited her to take some tea with him in Murphy's. She blushed and agreed that that would be very nice. Then looking with interest at the newspaper office she asked hesitantly if it would be possible to go inside, as she had never seen how newspapers came to be printed? He smiled at her eagerness; she was like a little girl anticipating some untoward treat, and so he showed her inside. The place was deserted, for Senan had gone to a meeting at the Gaelic League Hall and the printers were finished for the day. She touched the printing machine respectfully, marvelling at the blocks, blackened with ink, which could be sorted, "Like the pieces of a jigsaw," she said wonderingly, "into whatever word you wanted it to be." Jonathan felt proud. Nobody, not even Christine, had taken so much interest in the newspaper before. He liked the girl's frankness, her small pale face looking up into his as he explained the elementary principles of running a newspaper office.

She brushed a hand across her cheek, a wisp of her hair irritating her, and left a black streak of ink painted diagonally across her face. He reached out impulsively and brushed at the mark with his hand. Madeline blushed self-consciously, and they both looked away, desperately seeking something to make light of the interlude. The office was in semi-darkness, with only the light from the street lamp outside outlining the two figures poised in the room, Jonathan, his hand still on Madeline's cheek, Madeline, her face upturned to his, her mouth half-open in surprised expectancy.

Jonathan moved first. "Come! We'll go to the Tea Rooms before they close, and I'll get you a hand towel from O'Looney's office so that you can make yourself beautiful again!" He spoke patronisingly and Madeline turned away, annoyed with herself for having shown herself to be so vulnerable, flirting with a man who could have no possible interest in her.

Jonathan's hands were shaking as he went into Senan's office and picked up a towel from the desk behind the door. The girl must have bewitched him. There was no other explanation for it. He thought he could never feel the same way about a woman as he had felt for Hannah. There had never been any magic between himself and Madeline, never the exciting stirring of desire that there had been whenever Hannah had held his hand, or brushed against him casually as they walked by the river. But there was no doubt in his mind, there had been something there tonight. As he had looked at Madeline standing silhouetted against the street light, he had wanted to hold her close to him, to protect her from whatever it was that made her look so miserable. Like a sister, he reasoned, surely the feelings of an older brother towards his young sister?

Chapter 12

At the beginning of the year 1905, Hannah Benson was well on the way to achieving her life-long wish, a profitable dressmaking business and a sizeable amount of money in the bank. There was none of the gaucheness of the young girl who had first come to Limerick in the woman who now flitted purposefully between the factory on the dock and her two shops, one in Portobello Street, which was frequented by only the elite of Limerick society, and another on Harry's Mall, where she sold ladies' dresses and suits at cut-down prices, Hannah Benson's "seconds", the shop girls and the factory workers called them enthusiastically. They could dress like the "nobs" in Newtown Perry for a fraction of what the society ladies paid for their finery.

Hannah was also making shirts for the factories in Lancashire. She ordered the material from Belfast and it was transported by steamer to Limerick. The date of delivery to Lancashire was always conscientiously noted by Hannah. The factories paid well if the orders were completed on time, and a generous portion of this bonus was passed on to Hannah's diligent employees. She had earned something of the reputation of her uncle before her, always a stream of hopefuls waiting outside on the dock, looking for work in the sewing factory.

Though Hannah was reluctant to admit it, James McCarthy had done her a favour the night he had dynamited the warehouse. The people of Limerick had rallied round, the girls from the convent working overtime to get the premises back to normal again, the dockers offering her their assistance, "without pay, Miss, for you've seen us right many's the time". Hannah had asked a few of the labour leaders in Dublin to come to Limerick and get the workers organised in a union after she had seen the way they were being treated by the foremen on the quays. The union hadn't been organised yet, as the strength of the labour movement had failed to gather momentum due to outraged opposition from the employers. It had been a warning, though.

Jim Larkin had made a speech in Arthur's Quay, counselling the dockers to take heart, that their time was coming. Meanwhile he had advised them to stay away from the dockside public houses where the whole of their pay was spent on plying the so-called "bountiful" foreman with ill-afforded drink. Hannah Benson had spoken up for them, and they wouldn't forget it in a hurry.

"Mother, I'm going to see May in Dublin." Hannah waited for her mother's reaction. Peggy's face took on a closed look, her mouth firm and uncompromising.

"I can't stop you from visiting your sister, Hannah, but I'll have nothing more to do with her as long as she's married to that scoundrel, James McCarthy." Peggy spoke angrily, her eyes blazing as she looked at her daughter. "Your poor father must be turning in his grave to see her living with that fellow. He had him well sized up, and no mistake!"

"She must be lonely, Mother," Hannah spoke quietly. "She hasn't seen any of us since she got married, just a few letters from Florrie and myself, and Aunt Annie. I feel guilty for not having visited her, but I was that busy with the business, and in the few letters we got from her, she didn't seem keen to have any of us visit her."

Hannah didn't mention that in her last letter, May had told her she was pregnant.

'I'm so frightened, Hannah. How I'd love to have you with me now, to have one of our long chats by the fire. James is so busy, and maybe it's a good thing that he's kept occupied, for he gets fierce contrary when he has nothing to do.'

Hannah had read the desperation in her sister's sprawling handwriting. It had been her first cry for help since her marriage and Hannah could not ignore it.

'He's out most nights at meetings, Hannah, and I get so lonely sometimes, feeling the child kicking inside me, wishing that we could sit together, like we used to when we first got married. God, Hannah, how I miss you all back there in Limerick!'

Hannah felt sorry for May. She was sure James's

business involved nothing but trouble, for the IRB skirmishes in Wicklow had been reported in *The Limerick Lamp*. A consignment of arms had been scuttled off Bray Head and James's name had been mentioned as one of the leaders who had instigated the purchase of the ship's cargo. He must be like a demon, Hannah thought, fearful for May. When things went against him, James McCarthy was a dangerous man. Did May ever know what she was letting herself in for the day she had run away with him to Dublin?

Hannah travelled to Dublin on the eight o'clock morning train from Limerick Railway Station on the following Friday. When she emerged from the station at Heuston, she took May's letter from her pocket and scanned it quickly, noting the address. "121 Clanbrassil Street," she murmured to herself. She didn't know Dublin at all, the maze of streets confusing her as dray horses from Guinness's brewery trundled past, laden with barrels of stout, and young women at street corners shouted hoarsely, "Fresh cockles today, missus – a feast for your oul fella, put him in a good mood!" And the women laughed, a lively banter exchanged between the street vendors and the housewives.

A couple of young men standing outside a public house winked at Hannah and she smiled at them. She had become used to that in Limerick. "Can you direct me to this address?" She went across to them, her smile winning them over, the smart, navy travelling suit impressing them enough to make them doff their caps politely.

"Janey! That's a rough place for a lady to be visitin'," one of them said, a puzzled look on his face. "Are you sure you have the right address, Miss?"

"Yes, my sister lives there, a Mrs McCarthy." They beckoned to her to follow them, leading her through the foul-smelling streets, the stench of boiling fish and cabbage permeating the air.

Hannah put her handkerchief to her nose, trying to block out the horrible smell of decay. If May was living in one of these streets, she must be in a sorry state. She hurried on, the two men leading the way, until they came to a tenement building with the number 121 in black peeling paint on the front door.

"There you are, miss, but I wouldn't hang around here too long, if I was you. 'Tisn't a good place to be for a woman on her own!" She thanked them and handed them a shilling piece each. Their eyes lit up at the sight of the money, and she had to almost beg them to leave her, for they wanted to stay until she was ready to go home again. "I'll be fine now, honest I will, and thank you both for all your trouble!"

They turned reluctantly, and she made her way up the steps and into the dark hallway. She went up the stairs, each step creaking protestingly beneath her. There was the sound of a woman crying in one of the rooms, then the hungry cry of an infant. A man came out onto the landing, lurching sideways, and almost fell against Hannah, the smell of whiskey on his breath.

"Well now, things are lookin' up round here at last, with ladies payin' us visits, and what member of Royalty would you be, missy?"

Hannah sidestepped him, running up the remaining flight of stairs. She could hear his laughter as she knocked on May's door, her heart racing with fright. There was no answer. She couldn't go back down those stairs again, not until he was gone. She knocked again. The door opened and May stood there.

At first, Hannah didn't recognise her. The girl, her pregnancy very much in evidence, looked tired and old. Her dark hair was scraped back in a clumsy knot behind her head, a few stray hairs escaping, and hanging untidily at each side of her flushed face. She wore a dirty apron over a light dress.

"May? Is it you?" Hannah asked uncertainly, horrified at her sister's appearance.

"Hannah! Oh dear mother of Jesus, thank you for sending her!" May flung herself into Hannah's arms, bouts of coughing interrupting her bitter tears. "Oh Hannah, 'tis a miracle to see you here today!"

"We'll go inside, May, out of the cold. The landing is very draughty, and you should dress more warmly. You'll freeze in that dress!"

They went into the room. Hannah looked about her, her fears for May growing as she surveyed the damp, peeling wallpaper, a makeshift partition dividing the room in two, on one side a table and two chairs, on the other side a double bed, a small gas stove in the corner. The only touch of May's handiwork in the room was a loosely-woven lace bedspread, and with a twinge of compassion, Hannah recognised it as the one May had been keeping in her "dowry chest" for the day she would move into her new home with her husband. Her dreams had been well shattered in a dump like this, Hannah thought, a sickening feeling of depression in the pit of her stomach. If James McCarthy had been standing in front of her then, she would have killed him with her bare hands.

"Come, Hannah, we'll sit down by the fire here and have a cup of tea. I still can't believe you're really here, after all this time!" They sat by the frugal fire, May carefully placing two lumps of coal on top of the glowing ashes to keep it alight. It's the sorry day when a Benson has to count the lumps of coal she puts on the fire, Hannah thought angrily. Even in their poorest day back in Glenmore, they always had a good fire to sit down to, and a bite to eat. May made the tea and cut two slices of bread, spreading them skimpily with butter. "I didn't get a chance to go to the shops today," she apologised, handing Hannah a slice of bread. "If I had known you were coming, I'd have had something in!"

Hannah wasn't deceived. She knew May well enough to know that she was lying through her teeth. "Has James work?" she asked, looking through the long window at the smoking chimneys of Guinness's behind the tenements.

"He moves about a lot, never stays too long in the same job. He's working on the trains now. A man called Patterson gave him a job."

Hannah had heard of Patterson. He owned the tram company in Dublin, and several other businesses besides. He was a brute of an employer, sacking his workers for the smallest violation. James McCarthy must be worth something to him to have him employed on the trains.

"Birds of a feather," Hannah said aloud.

"What's that, Hannah?"

"Nothing, May. Just thinking aloud."

"He won't be home until two. That's when his shift ends, so we'll have plenty of time to talk."

"Come on. Get on your coat. We're going into town for a decent meal!" Hannah dragged May up by the arm, looking about the room for her coat.

May's face went red, tears welling up in her tired eyes. "I don't have one, Hannah! I had to pawn it last week – we needed the money. That's why I can't go out to the shops."

Hannah stared at her sister, her face blazing with fury. "Do you mean to tell me that James would leave you without a coat in this weather?"

"He's not too bad, Hannah. He's fine when he's not drinking. It's the drinking that makes him foolish."

Hannah whipped the bedspread from the bed and folded it into a triangle. She tied it loosely about May's shoulders. "That'll have to do until I get you something decent to wear, and God help me but I never want to see you in this state again!"

They had their lunch in the Gresham Hotel, several people looking curiously at the well-dressed young woman with the twist of bright curls on top of her head, and the smaller, pale-faced girl, her magnificent lace shawl not concealing the fact that she was in the final stage of pregnancy. May ate hungrily, her eyes widening with delight as each dish was brought to the table.

"Hannah, this meal is going to be very expensive! Are you sure you can afford it?"

"Eat up, girl," Hannah ordered grimly. The only part of May that looked well-fed was the prominent bump at the front of her dress. Her arms were like two sticks, her face gaunt, with eyes that looked too large for her face. Hannah silently cursed James McCarthy who had brought this misfortune on her sister. She had to get her away from him. She wasn't going back to Limerick without May, she decided firmly, watching some of the colour return to May's cheeks as she sat back in her seat, the warm food relaxing her, her eyes half-closed with tiredness.

"Come on, we have one more thing to do before we go home."

Hannah hurried May along the street, through the crowds shouting and heckling each other as they displayed their wares, and then there were other voices, modified, more refined, ladies holding up their skirts as they tripped daintily along the fashionable Grafton Street.

Hannah knew exactly where she was going now. She had received a letter from a ladies' dress shop in Grafton Street only last week. They had been very interested in Hannah's designs, and would she be willing to run some up at her factory in Limerick for sale in their shop? The amount offered was very enticing, and Hannah had thought about it all week before she made her decision.

They reached Thomas Gardiner's Ladies' Wear and Hannah pushed May inside, the girl nervous and self-conscious of her appearance. "I would like to see Mr Gardiner, please," Hannah asked the girl standing at the shop counter. "My name is Hannah Benson, from Limerick."

The girl was about to protest, when she caught the look in Hannah's eye, a look that demanded obedience. She disappeared into the back room and soon a man appeared. He was small and balding, his movements bird-like as he flitted across the room, greeting Hannah warmly.

"My dear Miss Benson, what a pleasure it is to see you! A woman not only clever but beautiful as well, a splendid bonus to be sure!"

"I have decided to accept your offer, Mr Gardiner. I shall be able to make ten garments each month, with each girl working on different parts of the garment. I shall personally see that every item is finished professionally. You need have no worries."

"Splendid, splendid, Miss Benson!" He beamed at the two of them and May smiled weakly. She would have to sit down soon, for her legs wouldn't hold up her weight much longer. She heard a loud noise in her ears, then a whistling sound, like a train coming into a station. The last thing she noticed was Hannah's alarmed face peering down at her as she lay on the ground, slipping into unconsciousness. Mr Gardiner was very sympathetic. He organised some tea for them, helping Hannah to lift May onto a divan seat in the back of the shop.

"I seem to make a habit of this, Hannah," May said faintly, trying to smile, but the pain in her side made her face contort in agony.

"I'll order a carriage to take you home," Thomas Gardiner said, not liking the look of the younger girl. He looked dubiously at the flimsy shawl about May's shoulders.

Hannah followed his gaze and nodded. "That's what we came here for, besides the business contract, Mr Gardiner, a warm woollen coat for my sister. She has grown too big for her old one."

May smiled in spite of the pain. Hannah would never admit to anyone her situation, no matter how bad.

They picked out a rust-brown coat, loose-fitting from the bodice down, and when May tried it on she felt like a queen, the pleated folds falling gracefully about her ankles. "It's so beautiful, Hannah," she whispered, feeling the softness of the material.

"We'll take this one, Mr Gardiner, and I'll pay for it now, please." He waved aside her money impatiently.

"Nonsense! Consider it a seal on our contract. May it prove to be a profitable one!" He took May's hand, the sincerity in his eyes giving her a warm feeling of well-being. Things didn't look so bad, after all. This morning she was ready to throw herself into the Liffey, baby and all. But now Hannah was here. Hannah would put everything right.

The carriage pulled up outside 121 Clanbrassil Street at three o'clock. Hannah helped May to climb down and assisted her up the stairs, reaching the door just as it opened. James McCarthy was standing there, his face red with too much drink and blatant hostility.

"Well now, if it isn't Miss Bountiful, come to rescue her sister from her life of degradation!" he sneered.

Hannah, outwardly calm, but inwardly her stomach churning with fear, faced his threatening figure clenching her fists resolutely.

"Where's my dinner, May? How's a man supposed to survive after a hard day's work without a bite of food in his stomach?" He turned back into the room, leaving the door open for them to follow. He went to the stove, clattering the pots angrily, then swept a heavy arm across the table, flinging cups and plates onto the floor.

May watched him helplessly. The pain in her side

hadn't eased, and she found it hard to breathe. She was frightened of James when he went on like this.

"May, get your things, just the few items you think you might need – we're going home to Limerick." Hannah spoke calmly, her gaze never leaving James McCarthy's angry face.

"The devil she is, going home to Limerick!" he mimicked Hannah mockingly. She ignored him, going about the room, picking up May's belongings, the tortoiseshell comb Annie had given her for Christmas, the shiny black button boots which she had placed almost reverently on the one small shelf beside the bed.

"And where did the coat come from, I ask you? Were you hoarding away money when I needed it, May?" he demanded, his threatening bulk making May cower in fear in the corner of the room.

"It's a present, from me, and anything else she needs from now on, she'll get it from her family," Hannah said shortly. She wanted to be away from this man with the bulging whiskey eyes and the heavy fists that could throttle a woman to death.

"I always knew 'twas the wrong sister I got," he said, his voice suddenly grown softer. "A complaining oul woman like May would get on any man's nerves. Ever since we were married she's done nothin' but complain. If it isn't the cold, it's the hunger, if it isn't the hunger, it's the loneliness, she says, with me away to the meetings. Jasus woman, are you ever satisfied?" He sidled up to Hannah putting an arm about her shoulders. "'Tis someone like you I should have married, Hannah Benson, someone with a bit of backbone in her."

Hannah stiffened, the touch of his arm like a deadly snake, weaving its way across her back, ready to spit its poisonous venom. "Take your hands off me, James McCarthy," Hannah said quietly.

May looked at her sister and recognised the contempt in her eyes. 'Sweet Mother of God, don't let him hurt her. Please don't let him strike out at her,' she prayed silently, the palms of her hands sweating with fear.

"Maybe 'tis that you're not used to a man's touch, Hannah Benson. From the moment I saw you at your Da's funeral, I knew you were the kind of woman for me, with your haughty ways and a face a man would willingly die for."

Hannah raised her hand and slapped him a stinging blow across the face. An ugly red weal appeared, the impression of her hand full on his surprised face. "Don't you ever lay a hand on me again, James McCarthy! I'm not like May. She might put up with your mauling, but I won't – and she won't have to either from now on. Come on, May, the sooner we're out of this rat hole the better."

May thought for a moment that he was going to strike back. He raised his fist, then dropped it to his side defeatedly. He knew better than to strike Hannah. It was true, she was not like her sister, foolish enough to let herself be taken by a mop of dark curling hair and a teasing smile.

"What will I do without you, May?" His tone was that of a little boy now, pleading with her to stay, his anger evaporated, his expression pitiful.

May hesitated for a moment, allowing memories to stray through her mind, the good times before James had started beating her, the stolen kisses in the darkness of the coachyard back in Limerick. Then she thought of the child kicking inside her. What life would he have with a father like James beating the daylights out of him? She turned and walked towards the door, picking up the brown paper parcel of clothes Hannah had thrown together hurriedly.

"Goodbye, James," she said. She held Hannah's arm, her walk unsteady, as they descended the stairs. They didn't look back. James had already closed the door behind them.

May's child was born on St Patrick's Day 1905, and lived for just three days. The infant was buried in a small wooden casket in Kileen churchyard two miles outside Limerick. May's short-lived marriage to James McCarthy had turned her into a woman overnight, her spontaneous peals of laughter, and her sheer joy in living gone forever with the death of her baby. She followed Molly about the house like a lost lamb, the old woman's comforting words a soothing balm to her grief. She looked for no sympathy from her mother, and Peggy Benson suffered pangs of remorse, thinking of the girl up in Dublin being abused by that madman McCarthy. She should have visited her then, made sure she was being looked after, seen the kind of life she was forced to lead.

All that was in the past now, and it was too late to wish for what should have been. Peggy spoke to Annie about her feelings, and Annie was outspoken in her sensible, rational way.

"Leave the child be, Peggy. She's grieving now for the little baby, the little angel of a girl she should be holding in her arms, instead of watching her being laid to rest in the cold cemetery. Giver her time; she'll soon be her old self again."

So Peggy waited, following her daughter's movements with hungry eyes, wishing that she could hold out her arms to her, just like when she was a little girl and kiss all her hurt away.

Thomas Gardiner wrote to May from Dublin, expressing his sympathy at the loss of her baby. If she needed anything, if there was anything he could do, then she must not hesitate to let him know. May wrote back, thanking him for his concern. She was grieving too much at the moment to notice the tentative interest expressed by the man in his letter. He was haunted by memories of the shy girl with the lace shawl about her slim shoulders standing in his shop. He remembered the frightened look in her beautiful dark eyes, and how he had wanted to gather her in his arms, to protect her from whatever was making her so unhappy. Thomas Gardiner, in his fortieth year, was feeling the first stirrings of romance in his previously untouched heart. The summer of that year was a particularly warm one, temperatures soaring in line with Hannah's profits, which Mr Carstairs at the bank proudly proclaimed at the directors' meeting that August to be "overwhelmingly satisfactory". Hannah was a good client, and a prudent one. The money he had lent her had been ploughed back into her account two-fold, every penny accounted for. At the beginning of September, Hannah paid him a visit, the tellers in the bank looking up appreciatively as she swished past them into Mr Carstairs's office.

"I want to take out a loan for two steamship tickets to New York," she informed him politely.

"New York!" Edwin Carstairs looked at her astounded. "You're not thinking of moving over there permanently, are you?"

Hannah shook her head, her face serious. "No, but it's Annie. She's pining for John this long while, and all summer she hasn't been feeling well, not the same Annie at all." She continued worriedly. "I'm concerned for her, Mr Carstairs. I've discussed it with my mother and we've decided that she should go over to see John. It would be the best tonic for her – and I'll accompany her."

"How long do you intend staying?"

"I don't know. For as long as it takes to get Annie back to her old self again."

She walked restlessly about the office and Edwin Carstairs followed her movements admiringly. He had never met a woman like Hannah before, so independent, and such a sound business head. And when the other side of her character revealed itself, like now, her concern for Annie, leaving her business behind without any hesitation to travel with her to America, then the girl was very exceptional indeed.

"Of course, there's no problem with the money, but who'll run the business while you're away?"

"Martin Manley is an honest and reliable man, and the girls all respect him. I'll leave him in charge; there should be no problems." She knew she could rely on Martin to keep things running smoothly. And May had slowly but surely started to come out of herself again, going back to the shop in Portobello Street, quietly taking up where she had left off when she had gone to Dublin with James. Florrie had become expert at cutting and tailoring, thanks to the guidance of Martin Manley, who found her instruction no great inconvenience, for by this time he was head over heels in love with Florrie Benson.

"Annie, I have a surprise for you." Hannah looked across the breakfast table at her aunt. She thought she had never seen Annie so pale, her dress hanging loosely on her bony frame, for she had lost a great deal of weight over the past few months.

"What is it, Hannah girl? And don't give me a heart attack by telling me that you're thinking of opening another shop in the city, for I don't think I can stand the strain of trying to keep up with your ideas!"

Peggy Benson threw Hannah a questioning look. Hannah nodded, and her mother smiled delightedly.

"We're going over to see Uncle John! I've booked the steamer, and we're leaving from Cobh on Friday!"

Annie put her hand to her mouth, stifling a little cry of amazement. "Hannah! Good God, girl, when was all this decided, and me not hearing a word of it?"

"It will do you good to see John again, Annie," Peggy said firmly. "Hannah has made all the arrangements, so you have nothing to do but pack your things for the journey. All your fretting is only making you sick with worry."

"Does he know?" Annie whispered, her eyes shining with excitement.

"No, we're going to surprise him. I have the address, and as soon as we get to New York I've arranged for a man to meet us there – John's friend, Michael Murphy."

Annie gasped in astonishment. "How did you get that man's address, girl?"

"John has mentioned him in several of his letters, and I know that he lives in a place called Albany, in New York." Hannah looked at Annie, a glint of mischief in her eyes. "I wrote to him, didn't I, explaining the situation to him, and telling him not to breathe a word of our coming to Uncle John. He's meeting us as soon as we get off the steamship in New York harbour!"

"God, but the brazenness of it, I ask you!" Peggy looked a little disapproving. "Writing to a complete stranger, as bold as you like, asking him to meet you off the boat? Hannah, you'll trip over yourself with your antics one of the days!"

"The deed is done anyway, Mother, and he seems a very good-natured man, for he wrote back telling me that his lips were sealed until we were face to face with Uncle John!"

Annie had tears in her eyes. "Imagine, Peggy, after all this time, with only letters to narrow the gap between us, and now I'm going to see John, see his own dear face again!"

Jonathan looked at the clock on his bedside table. Midnight, and he still had a good bit to go before he was finished. He rubbed his eyes wearily, his head bent over the writing desk, sheets of paper stacked high at one side as he scribbled feverishly. If he kept at it solidly for the next couple of days, he'd get it finished. His mind was overflowing with ideas. Each time a flash of inspiration came to him, he would jot it down in a rough writing book, ready to use it at the appropriate time.

It was William Butler Yeats who had given him the idea. He had gone to Dublin in September for a meeting of the Literary Society, and it had been an exciting revelation to him. Yeats had been there, and they had discussed his play, *The Countess Kathleen*.

"It is a most impressive piece of work – but I don't think the audience are ready yet for a critique on their human failings," Jonathan offered, almost apologetically, when asked for his opinion.

"You are quite right, of course, and I appreciate your candour." Yeats had smiled ruefully at Jonathan, and from that moment a unique kind of friendship had blossomed between the two men, an easy rapport established between them that was to last a lifetime.

Cedric Humphries had read some of his poetry, as had Standish O'Grady, a large bull of a man, his physique belying his romantic interpretations of the old legends of Ireland, who had his audience enraptured with Oisin's adventures in Tir na nOg. Jonathan felt grossly inadequate in the midst of such literary talent. At the end of the evening Senan had introduced him to a small man with a large moustache embroidering his top lip, his eyes twinkling with good humour.

"Jonathan, meet the man who's going to help preserve our Gaelic inheritance; meet Douglas Hyde." He was a soft-spoken man, with a vibrancy in his genteel tones as he spoke of the Irish language, of how important it was to see that it didn't go into a decline while the Irish people turned more and more to Britain for its "mock" culture.

"Not only the language, Jonathan, but everything that is truly Irish is in danger of becoming extinct if we don't do something about it."

The man's enthusiasm was infectious. Jonathan had listened, an idea forming in his brain, an idea which seemed a little mad, perhaps, but nonetheless, the possibilities were exciting. Hyde's next sentence was like an echo of his thoughts and Jonathan had stared at him, startled by his perception.

"Do you write at all? I don't mean in Irish, even though that would be all the better – but have you written poetry or short stories? Perhaps you even have a play or two up your sleeve?" Jonathan was silent for a moment, bemused; then he detected the humour in the other man's face.

"My only experience of writing is with the paper, going on whatever guidelines Senan O'Looney has given me," he responded modestly.

"I've read your articles about the slums of Limerick, and the poverty, and the little houses hidden behind the great edifices of the rich – about the people themselves, and the lives they lead." Hyde had looked steadily at Jonathan, his face suddenly serious. "You're a writer, young fellow, whether you know it or not! Senan might have shown you how to put words together in paragraphs, but nobody can teach you how to write. That's up there!" He pointed to his head, and Jonathan knew that never before had he felt so proud. For a scholar like Hyde to have noticed his nondescript articles in *The Limerick Lamp*; that was surely some achievement.

"We've decided to publish a monthly paper, *Guth na nDaoine, Voice of the People*. Everybody in the League will contribute an article, and if you're interested, maybe you'd like to write something yourself? You have imagination, Jonathan, and a good writer needs a powerful imagination!"

He had gone home with Senan that evening walking

on air, his glowing tributes to Hyde making Senan finally shout at him in exasperation.

"All right, all right! So he's won you over, just like he has the rest of us. But have you thought maybe this new paper will take some of our readers away from us? Hyde and myself have the same aims, and nobody will buy a paper that's the copy of another!"

Jonathan smiled and slapped his friend good-naturedly on the back. "Nobody could ever accuse you of being a copy of anything, Senan!"

Senan looked gratified. "Right then, we'll go to Herbert's as soon as we get off the train and drink a toast to Jonathan Mayhew, the new member of the Gaelic League!

The first edition of *Guth na nDaoine* appeared in November 1905. Jonathan's story took up the two centre pages, and after it was published there was a furore in the city, for the article described with honest accuracy the lives of people like the Flannerys in contrast to the lifestyle of the gentry in Newtown Perry. He described the stench of stale urine in the narrow little streets between the rows of tiny hovels, some of them housing families of more than eight children in two airless rooms never touched by the light of day. Then there was the opulent lifestyle of the upper class, the house parties of the merchants in George's Street, the incongruous practice of meticulously draining the cellars beneath the famous hanging gardens, enabling them to stay dry in winter and well-ventilated in summer – a practice that would not go amiss in the dank hovels of the poor.

Christine O'Shea read the article with growing horror. "Jonathan, how could you? What will my friends say? My own brother condemning their lifestyles? The poor will always be with us, brother, and there is nothing anybody can do about it. They are victims of circumstance."

"Then it's about time somebody gave them a little encouragement, made them see that there is somebody who understands them. They, also, need to be allowed some bit of self-respect! This story will open a lot of people's eyes to the privation that exists on their own doorsteps!"

A week after the article appeared, Jonathan received a letter from Sir Cedric Humphries. The Literary Society had by now organised a dramatic company, producing plays written especially for the Irish people. He wondered if Jonathan would be interested in writing a play based on his article, a satire on the injustices which existed between the classes. Jonathan read the letter with mixed feelings. Senan advised him to go ahead. "You have nothing to lose but your head!" he quipped.

Christine, on the other hand, was furious. "Why can't you write something a bit more civilised, Jonathan? You will have very few friends left in Limerick if you continue to hound the upper classes!"

Robert O'Shea waited until Christine had retired for the night before he gave his opinion. They sat together in the parlour, Jonathan working on another article for *The Limerick Lamp*, Robert scanning a medical journal desultorily.

"And what do you think, brother-in-law, of all this business, victimising the gentry for their neglect of the poor?"

Robert O'Shea looked up thoughtfully. He put a finger to his lips, throwing a cautious eye towards the door. "I couldn't admit it in front of Christine, but I think you've said things that should have been said a long time ago. Maybe if they had been said on time there would have been no need for a fever hospital in the city. Keep up the good work, Jonathan. Write what's in your heart!"

Madeline was cautious about giving her opinion. Jonathan's style of writing was new to her, her reading in the past confined to light, trivial novelettes, selected mostly by her mother. His portrayal of the majority of her class was a little disconcerting.

"Don't forget, Madeline, I'm writing about myself also. I'm not excluded from the hypocrisy I see around me each day."

"What happens now? Are you going to write a play and send it to Sir Humphries?" Madeline looked at him with mingled admiration and pride.

Jonathan thought she looked quite pretty tonight, her light-coloured hair dressed in soft waves about her face, the dress from Hannah's Portobello Street shop flatteringly defining her rounded hips. Sensuous was the word that sprang to Jonathan's mind, startling himself with the cursory observation.

He enjoyed Madeline's company, her easy-going manner soothing at times when he needed somebody to talk to, especially now when his career had taken such an exciting turn. They were seen together at music recitals and at parties in Newtown Perry. Mrs Deery kept her fingers tightly crossed that her daughter would not let such a man slip from her grasp. Not the one she would have chosen, with his foolish notions about wealth and poverty, but Madeline wasn't getting any younger, and she and Mr Deery wanted grandchildren. Thank goodness that Hannah Benson was going to America. With her out of the way, Madeline should be able to rein him in easily.

Jonathan's play, *The Inheritance,* was a glorious success from the moment it opened at the Abbey Theatre in Dublin. The audience, most of them from the Dublin working-class, cheered and clapped their hands in approval, calling for Jon Mayhew to come on stage. The play took three rousing curtain calls before Jonathan stepped out into the spotlight. His handsome, muscular figure drew a chorus of appreciative whistles from a group of women standing at the back of the theatre and, when Jonathan waved to them, they blew kisses towards the stage.

Madeline, sitting in the front row, smiled at the commotion. She was lucky to have such a handsome escort as Jonathan. Since she had first met him at his sister's house, her life had changed in so many ways, the boredom she had felt in the past now vanished, a contentment deep inside her that she couldn't fully comprehend. It was as though she was sharing his life, his triumphs, his moments of despondency. She had never been with a man like him before, and in the darkness of the theatre she blushed as she thought of the two of them sharing a bed, away from all the madness of the world outside. Just Jonathan and herself, his arms about her, holding her close, whispering in her ear. But what would he whisper? That he loved her?

Madeline knew that that would be impossible. Jonathan had eyes for only one woman in Limerick. She saw his hungry gaze following Hannah as she walked down Portobello Street. She saw and pretended not to notice. As time went by, she could see a pattern emerging, Jonathan calling to her house each Friday evening after his work in *The Limerick Lamp* was finished.

Then they would stroll into the town, past the bacon factory and the flour mill, as far as the Gaelic League hall. More often than not, Senan O'Looney would be chairing a meeting, and a lively hour would follow, starting with a progress report on the League's activities, and ending with the inevitable benign argument between Senan and Jonathan as to the viability of promoting economic independence in a country like Ireland, which was mostly agricultural and depended on foreign imports for its prosperity. Senan's face would grow purple with agitation as Jonathan denounced his "de-anglicisation theories".

"Stick with the basics, Senan," he would insist. "Put some pride back in our people; organise some classes in the Irish language; get the ordinary people out of the rut they have been forced into. A bit of enjoyment in their lives won't do any harm while they're waiting for this great renaissance in the Irish economy!"

Madeline roused herself from her happy reverie. The curtain had come down for the fourth time on the play, and the three main performers stepped forward to tumultuous applause: the fresh-faced naive young convent girl, the loud and domineering woman whose husband, a rich merchant of the town, had gotten the young girl "into trouble", and lastly, the quietly-spoken beautiful young seamstress who had eamed the respect of her employees by treating them with fairness and sensitivity.

Madeline had no doubt in her mind who had inspired this last character; Hannah Benson was forever cherished in Jonathan's restless heart.

Chapter 13

Hannah read the reviews of Jonathan's play in an old edition of *The Limerick Lamp*, sent to her by Peggy just after they had arrived in New York. She smiled with amusement as she read of the shocked reaction of the gentry to his "satire of the classes".

"No harm to shake them up a bit, with their misplaced notions of what a 'lady' should be like!" Annie said. She reached across to John and he took her hand, their renewed happiness touching Hannah's heart as she observed them, sitting in contented silence. She looked away then, her mind on something that had been troubling her since they had arrived at Maura and Vincent's house.

The journey to New York had been smooth and pleasant, with Annie chatting to everybody who wished her the time of day. Hannah was more reserved as she sat on the ship's deck, plotting out her life as the ship's compass plots its course through the rough seas. She had seen Jonathan at the railway station in Limerick before they had set out for Cobh. He had been with one of his friends who had cast admiring glances in Hannah's direction, but her eyes were fixed on Jonathan. There had been a yearning in his eyes that had unsettled her, as if he still felt some of the magic that had bound them together so long ago. He had raised his hand in polite salute, hesitated for a moment as though he was about to come across to her, then changed his mind as he bade farewell to his companion who had boarded a first-class compartment.

'Now is the time, Jonathan! If you feel anything for me, now is the time to tell me! Don't leave me in a muddle miles across the water in New York!' she had thought wildly.

He had turned then and left the station, his disappearance coinciding with the last, piercing sound of the train's whistle. He would go back to Madeline now, Hannah thought, as the train journeyed onwards to Cobh. Christine O'Shea had indeed succeeded in alienating her brother from an 'unsuitable' relationship. Mrs Deery must be looking forward to the formal announcement in *The Limerick Lamp* for all to see – her daughter Madeline engaged to "that notable playwright", Jonathan Mayhew.

Hannah smiled melancholically at her cynical observations. She was acting like a bitter old maid. She straightened her shoulders determinedly and looked across the carriage at Annie sitting opposite her.

"We're on our way, girl, and it's all thanks to you, for I'd never have the nerve to go on my own!"

"Soon, Annie, you'll be locked in Uncle John's arms, and I doubt if he'll ever let you go!"

The steamship sailed into New York harbour, Annie

worriedly scanning the waiting crowd on the quayside. "What if he doesn't meet us, Hannah? We're all alone in a strange country." Hannah took her hand and gripped it reassuringly.

"Don't worry. The man won't let us down, I'm sure of it!"

Michael Murphy looked intently at the groups of passengers as they disembarked. It wouldn't do to have John's wife traipsing the streets of New York looking for him. If he should miss her . . . His eyes suddenly opened in wonder as he saw the young woman step onto the quay, turning her head sideways to speak with her companion. In all his years in New York, he had never seen a finer specimen of womanhood. From the top of her head, a magnificent head of burnished, shining curls, to the tips of her dainty feet encased in dark-brown shiny button boots, she had the cut of a lady. Her companion was a handsome-looking woman, a look of anxiety on her pleasant face. They were looking around them now, their assorted pieces of luggage lying at their feet.

The young woman's eyes met his for a fraction of a second, great shining pools of blue, and Michael knew, instinctively, that he was gazing upon the face of John Sullivan's niece, Hannah Benson. The girl was everything John had described to him, and more.

He made his way across to them and took his hat off politely. "Mrs Sullivan, Mrs John Sullivan?" Annie nodded, her face lighting up with relief. "I'm Michael Murphy, at your service, ma'am." His eyes never left Hannah as he spoke. He couldn't get over how beautiful the girl was. In spite of the praise John had showered upon her, Michael had expected a dowdy, domineering sort of person, a temperamental old maid who ran her own business and let everybody know who was the boss. This girl standing in front of him with the pink, rosy cheeks and the brilliant blue eyes was an angel sent from heaven itself.

The carriage pulled up outside Vincent Sullivan's fashionable residence in Fifth Avenue. Now that the moment had finally come to see John again, Annie felt a sudden sense of trepidation. What if he should be angry with her for not telling him she was coming? What if maybe he was sick, and hadn't told her for fear of troubling her? What if?

The front door opened suddenly and two young men appeared. They spotted Michael Murphy and immediately ran towards him, one of them whipping the hat from his head, and throwing it into the air playfully.

"Hello, Uncle Mike! Father's inside with Uncle John but I wouldn't go near them if you know what's good for you – another one of their union rows!"

Michael shook his head at them, cautioning them to stay silent, but the damage was done.

Annie turned to him, her eyes wide with bewilderment. "Glory be to God! What are those young fellows talking about, Michael? John and Vincent fighting? Sure there was never a cross word between them in all the time I've known them!"

"Never mind, Annie. There's things between men that women don't understand." He guided them towards the front door, from where they could hear raised, angry voices.

A woman appeared in the hallway, a small thin

woman, her face nervous and frightened. She saw them standing uncertainly in the doorway. She stared for a moment, disbelievingly, then ran towards them embracing Annie with a delighted cry. "Annie, Annie Sullivan! After all this time! Am I dreaming, girl, or is it really you?"

Annie smiled at the warmth of her welcome. Surely the boys had been mistaken? Those angry words they heard could certainly not be Vincent and John quarrelling! "Maura! Isn't it well you're looking, and your beautiful house. Maybe it's the White House we've come to by accident!"

Hannah stood in the background, an uncomfortable feeling niggling at her heart. Maybe she had been wrong in not telling John that they were coming over. The commotion in the parlour was even more heated now than when they had first crossed the threshold.

Maura beckoned them into the drawing-room, shutting the door firmly behind them. "Just a business argument, Annie. Don't worry yourself, like a good woman. John has done very well for himself over here – he has two young Italian boys running his shop for him while he's involved in the lumber yard, so you can rest easy. And will you look at that girl standing beside you, and how rude she must be thinking me for not asking her name!" Maura stood back and observed Hannah admiringly. A girl like that should be in the moving films, a face like an angel she had, Maura thought, suddenly feeling depressed and old.

"This is Hannah, Maura. Hannah Benson, Peggy's eldest girl."

"Ah, the little seamstress! Sure I should have known;

John never stops singing your praises, and sure now that you're in New York maybe you could teach the ladies a thing or two about ladies' fashions, for I declare, they have plenty of money but no dress sense. The outfits some of them dare to show themselves in – they could be mistaken for street girls, God help them!"

Maura talked on and on, a tinge of desperation in her cheerful prattle. What a time for John's wife to visit him, and the girl too. She looked so like the young actress she had seen hanging off Vincent's arm the other night when she had followed him to the East Side, skulking in doorways and behind the corners of narrow streets. Annie and Hannah watched in dismay as Maura's eyes filled up with tears.

"Maura, girl, what's wrong?"

She had followed him to the back entrance of a rooming-house, had seen him bend down and kiss the girl roughly on the mouth, had seen the girl toss back her head, her red lips parted in loud, vulgar laughter.

The parlour door opened suddenly and John came out, slamming it angrily behind him. He closed his eyes for a moment, a picture of Annie, his own darling Annie, appearing in his mind. She was smiling, waving to him from across an ocean of water. "Oh God, what's the use? She's not here with me, and if ever a man needed his woman, I need Annie Sullivan now!" He opened his eyes and blinked incredulously at the vision before him. Annie was standing there beside Maura, holding out her arms to him. The row with Vincent must have gone to his head; he was seeing things! Annie was back home in Ireland; he had written to her only yesterday, telling her that he was thinking of coming home at last, for he had had his fill of New York.

"Annie, is it you, girl? Is it really you?" John saw nobody else besides Annie, as if they were the only two people in the world, coming together after such a long separation. He felt her arms about him, her warm body close to his as she rested her head against his shoulder, heaving a long sigh of contentment.

"Oh John, how I've missed you, man!" He looked about him at last and saw a sophisticated young lady standing behind Annie, her eyes bright with tears.

"And my own darling Hannah! Didn't I know you'd do well, from the first day you came to Limerick! Your father would be proud of you, girl, if he was alive today, and you with your factory on the quay, and your dress shops in the town, and is it over here you've come now to see if you can set up your business across the water?"

"I'm so glad to see you, Uncle John! And my only business in New York is to see yourself!"

John appraised Hannah shrewdly. "I know you, girl. You'll not rest until you've visited every sweat shop on the East Side, trying to find out what the piece-workers earn, and comparing their lot with your workers back home!"

"Maybe, Uncle John. I haven't made any plans yet, but you've put a few ideas into my head!" She went over to him and kissed him, throwing her arms about his neck. He was the same dear John, his face a little thinner than she remembered it, but his smile was the same, an honest, open smile making her feel welcome, part of his family, just as he had when she had come to Limerick all that time ago.

"What's all the commotion? What's going on out here?" Vincent stepped out of the parlour, flushed and irritable.

"It's Annie. She's come with Hannah, and you, Michael Murphy!" John exclaimed, rounding on his friend with mock reproach. "I'll bet you had something to do with this grand surprise. There's been no talking to you this last few weeks, with your fidgeting and smiling to yourself. Sure I thought you were going mad at times, and me with you!" John smiled good-naturedly at his friend.

Vincent grabbed Annie, lifting her off her feet with his powerful arms.

"Vincent Sullivan! Will you let me down, you *amadan* of a man, before you do me some damage!" He placed her down carefully, then turned to Hannah, waiting for an introduction.

"This is Hannah, Vincent," Maura said quietly. She recognised the look on her husband's face and felt frightened for the girl. It was no secret among the immigrants on the East Side that Vincent Sullivan favoured young women fresh off the boats. He was looking at Hannah now with the same look he had given many a young girl who had come to him in search of work. She didn't know how long more she could put up with his philandering ways. Her nerves were so bad lately that the doctor had recommended a double dose of sleeping tablets.

She had to stay with him. What else could she do? A woman alone in New York wouldn't last a week without a man to take care of her. And then there were the boys.

She adored them, all the love she had once felt for Vincent now transferred to Paul and Steven. They were both going to Harvard. What was good enough for the Vanderbilts was good enough for Vincent Sullivan's sons, Vincent had declared proudly. She had to stay; there was no question of her leaving. She had to make sure the boys didn't go the same road as their father. The Tammany Hall politicians could do without her two boys. Her husband had already sacrificed himself to their corrupt ways.

Not long after their arrival in New York, Hannah had discovered a lot of unpleasant facts, one of which filled her with loathing for her Uncle John's brother, Vincent Sullivan. The row in progress when Hannah and Annie had first arrived on Fifth Avenue had been explained by John, simply and reluctantly, as they sat in the drawing-room one evening, just himself and Annie and Hannah.

"There's something up between you and Vincent, John. I want to know about it, for it hurts me to my very heart to see the two of you so cold with each other." Annie waited patiently for his reply.

"It's a terrible thing to speak ill of your own blood, but when the writing is on the wall, then what else can I do?" John ran his hand abstractedly through his thick mop of hair. "Vincent is successful all right, but he's accumulated his fortune by exploiting the poor, ignorant immigrants who come off the boat every day below in the harbour." Hannah and Annie listened in horror to John's account of Vincent's dealings. "It was Michael Murphy who made me see the light, for you know, Annie, I always thought Vincent could do no wrong. An honest and decent man, that's how his friends see him, but sure they're all in it together! The Tammany Hall Corruption Brigade, that's what they're called. Can you believe it, Annie, my brother living off the misfortune of his own kind?"

John got up and paced restlessly about the room, Annie and Hannah sitting silently, trying to digest what he had told them. The character-sketch he had drawn was so abhorrent that they could hardly believe he was talking about his own brother. "I confronted him soon after I went to work in the lumber mills. The workers there were working twelve hours a day for a miserly eight dollars a week. The wages should have been twice that amount for the kind of work those men do. So I went to Vincent and asked him if I could up their wages, give them some incentive to do their work well, for they were that worn out after their shift I thought I'd be burying every one of them before long. And do you know what he said to me?" John turned angrily, banging his fist on the table.

Annie sat motionless, frightened by his outburst. She had never seen John in such a rage before. "He said there was no use pampering them by giving them more money. They either did the job or got out all together! He had plenty more where they came from – and do you know where he got the labour? Scab labour! He brought in more workers to do the misfortunates' jobs if they protested about the wages and conditions in the mill. My own brother, no better than that blaggard Jameson back in Limerick! Did I ever think I'd see the day!"

He sat down again, his face contorted in angry lines. Hannah was not, on reflection, altogether surprised by John's revelations about his brother. There was something she found repulsive about the man. His treatment of Maura was not that of a gentleman. He was rough and boorish with his sons, and Hannah could see the fear in the boys' faces when he asked them how they were progressing in their studies. There was always the hint of a threat in his words. Hannah thought she had never met a more loathsome man in all her life.

Christmas 1905 was a magical time in New York, all the Fifth Avenue houses decorated with multi-coloured streamers, joining together from one elegant portico to the next, Christmas trees lighting every window, each one outdoing the other with elaborate trimmings and tiny wax candles burning brightly on the dark green branches. Hannah received a letter from her mother with news that made her laugh delightedly. Florrie and Martin Manley have set the date for their wedding!

'Sure, didn't I know it was coming for a long time, and I'm that happy for them. It'll be some time during the summer, so make sure you're back home before too long. And that sister of mine and her fortune-seeking husband had better make up their minds to come too, for it will be a great day for all of us!'

Hannah suddenly felt depressed for no particular reason. Maybe it was the thought of Florrie and Martin together, no obstacles barring their way to a happy future. They were so suited to one another. Not like herself and Jonathan.

There was never a night she didn't think of him before falling asleep, sometimes whispering his name softly in the empty darkness. If only Christine O'Shea had left well enough alone, if only she hadn't put doubts in Hannah's head, making her see the hopelessness of such a match. Madeline and he were better suited, the same backgrounds, Madeline a lady of leisure attending tea parties and musical evenings and entertaining ladies in similar circumstances during her 'at home' afternoons.

They would marry, of course. It was inevitable. She could see Mrs Deery's gloating face. She would probably ask Hannah to make Madeline's wedding dress, "something quite exceptional, Miss Benson, for such a happy day!". Hannah panicked at the prospect. She couldn't do it. She couldn't return to Limerick to see Jonathan and Madeline, arm in arm, strolling down George's Street, maybe taking tea in Murphy's Tea Rooms, visiting her at the shop in Portobello Street, Madeline smiling graciously as she held Jonathan's arm. "I want a very special dress, Miss Benson. Only your finest lace will do for my wedding outfit!"

Little beads of sweat formed on Hannah's forehead and she put up her hand to wipe them away. She read the letter from her mother through to the end.

'Mrs O'Shea's brother is a great campaigner for the Gaelic League. He is organising the children in the slums now, bringing them together every Wednesday night in the Gaelic League Hall in Richmond Street, teaching them how to write and telling them stories. Douglas Hyde came down from Dublin and was very impressed with his little band of Gaelgeoiri *as he called them! Mr Mayhew hasn't a word of Irish himself, God help him, but sure that doesn't matter, Mr Hyde said, as long as the children were learning about the Irish ways and the great*

Irish legends. I might even go along to those classes myself, for they'd bring back many's the fond memory, so they would!'

After the New Year, Vincent decided to go away for a short break to his holiday home in Newport. Maura and the boys were going with him and Maura begged Annie to make herself at home in the house in Fifth Avenue. "As if it was your own, Annie, for you're part of the family. So relax and take a few trips into the city, see some shows." Maura's overwhelming show of hospitality was encouraged by the need to compensate for her husband, whose alarming theories on labour unrest in the factories and the mills caused many bouts of dissension between himself and John.

John never argued when the ladies were present, holding his tongue while Vincent spat out his contempt for those "ungrateful immigrants" who sustained his lavish lifestyle. One afternoon, a week after Vincent and Maura had left, John went to Hannah who was sitting in the drawing-room, writing a letter to Edwin Carstairs. "Hannah, I want you to come with me. Not a word to Annie, mind. She's upstairs having a rest so we won't be missed for a while. I want you to see something of what I'm talking about."

They took a carriage into the city, and went first to John's shop on 14th Street on the East Side. Hannah was amazed at the swell of different cultures and nationalities intermingling, working together, the babble of foreign languages spoken almost with one voice as they bargained and traded with each other. The two Italian men behind the counter smiled shyly as John introduced

Hannah, bowed politely, then turned away to get on with their work.

"Good, hard-working lads, Hannah! They're as good as myself for dealing with orders and taking stock assessments. And if their English is a bit slow, then they can make themselves understood in other ways!" He nodded in the direction of the counter, where one of the young Italians was now arguing with a female customer about the price of a bag of flour, he gesticulating wildly, the customer speaking Hungarian, and finally, the two of them satisfied with their confrontation, settling their differences agreeably.

Hannah smiled. There was no difference between these people and those in the market square in Limerick. The faces were the same, a little darker in colour, maybe, but the look in their eyes was the look she had seen on countless faces. They wanted to make a go of their lives, make a decent day's pay to support their families. She sat for a while in the back of the shop listening to the Italians dealing with the customers, John checking on stock, seeing what needed to be ordered. Finally, he announced that everything was in order.

"Where are we going, Uncle John?" Hannah asked him as they left the carriage in the yard behind the shop and walked through the dusty streets.

"To a place called The Bowery," he answered shortly. Hannah remained silent. John had something on his mind, something he wanted her to share with him. She looked sideways at his tense face, his eyes dark and troubled. They didn't speak until they came to a row of tenement houses, similar to those Hannah had encountered in Clanbrassil Street in Dublin. They backed onto the East

River, running parallel to the Brooklyn Bridge. There was a strange silence in the street, unlike the streets and alleyways they had just passed through. This street was like something that had died; not even a curtain stirred in the dirty windows, not even the barking of a dog or the sound of a cat broke the oppressive silence. John led the way up the steps of the house nearest them and pushed in the front door silently. Immediately Hannah recognised the low whirring drone of machines coming from the upstairs landing.

"Sewing-machines, John?" She looked up at him enquiringly. He put a finger to his lips and motioned her to follow him. They went up the stairs, and John knocked loudly on a splintered wooden door. A man answered, opening the door just a fraction to peer out, his eyes wide and frightened. When he saw John he looked relieved, a broad smile suddenly washing over his thin face.

"Mr John, how good it is to see you! We thought you might be one of the inspectors." He opened the door fully and they went inside. The room was small, one narrow window, unopened, letting in sparse light from outside, three rows of sewing-machines, cramped almost one on top of another, a woman or a man sitting behind each one. In the corner there was a small stove with a pot bubbling on top of it, a smell that was strange to Hannah filling the room.

"Spaghetti," John whispered in her ear, "their lunch, which they'll eat sitting at their machines, without a break, until eight o'clock tonight."

Hannah looked around her in disbelief. Four children, no more than eight years old she estimated, sat together on an upturned wooden box, waiting patiently for each garment as it came from the machine. They had tiny scissors in their hands, and they proceeded to trim off any excess threads on seams and buttonholes, their little hands working deftly, tired little faces concentrating on their task.

"Surely that couldn't be permitted, Uncle John?" Hannah asked incredulously.

"They work the same hours as the adults. Sometimes they even sleep here to be sure they get their work out on time. This isn't the only tenement involved in sweat-labour. The whole row of tenements, right up to the Brooklyn precinct, is filled with these immigrants, working like slaves because they're frightened they'll be deported if they object!"

John's face was white with anger. Hannah thought of her own factory back home in Limerick, how happy the girls looked at their work, singing and joking with each other, the bright, spacious premises where one sewing-machine occupied as much space as three in these tenements.

"Who owns such terrible workplaces?" Hannah moved about the room, scanning the row of bent heads, nobody looking up once from their work. They had a job to do, and they wouldn't be paid if the work wasn't finished in time.

She repeated her question, then looked at John's face, a cold feeling suddenly in her heart. "It's Vincent's place, isn't it?" she asked, her voice dwindling to a whisper. John nodded.

"Aye, girl. And the rest of the tenements, the whole row of them! That's how he can afford to leave his lumber business aside and speculate with steel. He's supplying all the steel that's needed for the building of the railroad from New York to the Great Lakes in Canada. Oh, he's doing well, honest Vincent Sullivan," John said sarcastically, waving an expressive hand about the room. "That railroad should bear a plaque dedicated to the workers in the sweat shops on the East Side!"

There was a sudden loud knocking on the door, and the man who had previously answered it beckoned to the children impatiently. They immediately jumped off the long, narrow box and climbed into it, covering their heads with some of the garments they had been completing. The other children climbed into similar boxes, Hannah watching this pantomime bemusedly. When there were no more children to be seen, the man opened the door cautiously.

A small, stout gentleman dressed in a dark pinstripe suit entered the room. For once, the machines were at a standstill, the little group of silent workers looking up at the newcomer fixedly. "Any kids here, Guiseppi? You know the Welfare don't like kids working on the premises. It's against the rules."

"No, no, Mr Marshall, sir, there is no kids here." The man looked about him once more, then went over to the pot and lifted the lid cautiously.

"God, how can you eat such slop? Why can't you people get used to good wholesome American food? Anyone sick, Guiseppi?" He glanced sharply at the woman on the far right of the room. Her worn face had dark circles beneath the eyes, her cheekbones protruding ominously. "Rosa there doesn't look too good. We don't want anything contagious round here, you know. Before you know it, it'll be like a bloomin' plague." The woman tried to smile, straightening her shoulders in an effort to convince him that she was well. He seemed satisfied, and left without further ado, clattering his way down the stairs, breathing a sigh of relief as he emerged once more into the street. Like animals, he thought indifferently. Living like bloody animals.

When the man had gone, the children emerged once more from their hiding places, for the first time smiling at Hannah, as if they had been playing some sort of harmless game with the health inspector.

"Those people earn a dollar a day for their work, Hannah – four shillings a day, and some of them have six children apiece. That woman Rosa has tuberculosis, but they all keep their mouths shut, because they know they'll be fired if the word gets out. The health inspectors come along and fumigate the place and it lies idle for the next unscrupulous politician to take it over and bring in more foreign labour. 'Tis a vicious circle, Hannah, and there's nobody to speak up for the wretches!"

They walked back to 14th Street, both lost in their own thoughts. An occasional wooden trolley, pulled by a barefoot little boy or girl, raced past them, filled with pieces of garments, shirt collars, cuffs, sleeves of suits ready to be attached to the main parts. "Piece-workers are in great demand over here," John explained as Hannah looked at the trolleys curiously. "The young fellows go from door to door with their carts, collecting the pieces from the women, who sit at home stitching all day long, and then delivering them to the factories. The children are made to work for their living from the minute they're able to walk!"

That evening they went to see a show on Broadway, the mecca of light entertainment for New Yorkers who could afford it. John was eager to show off his knowledge of the great city to Annie, and to Hannah. The girl had been thoughtful ever since they had come back from their little excursion this morning. Maybe he had shown her too much too soon, but he had to tell her and he would have to tell Annie soon. How else could he fully explain the terrible friction between himself and Vincent? They sat three rows from the stage, the platform revolving every few seconds to reveal yet another display of colourful dancers dressed in costumes the likes of which Hannah had never seen before. Artificial flakes of snow drifted down on them as they performed a winter snow scene, the dancing and the singing appealingly spontaneous. The lights in the theatre dimmed for a moment, and a girl appeared in the spotlight, tall and handsome, her silky black curls framing a fine-boned porcelain face. A hushed silence fell over the audience as she began to sing, her husky, hypnotic voice filling the theatre. Not a cough or a shuffle could be heard until the song was ended. Then there was an appreciative roar, "Bravo, Helena, your best yet! Bravo, bravo!" The girl smiled graciously, bowing again and again as bouquets of flowers were thrown up onto the stage. The curtain came down to tumultuous clapping and whistling from the crowd.

As they rode home in the carriage, Annie enthused about the evening's entertainment. "John, who was that lovely girl who sang tonight? I declare she has the voice and the face of an angel from heaven!"

"Her name is Helena Curley. She came over from Ireland with her parents ten years ago, came to make their fortune on the streets of New York." John paused, thinking before he went on. "Her parents died a couple of years ago, but the girl has made a name for herself, invited to all the big houses to entertain the elite. She has a house of her own on Nob Hill, a far cry from the tenement building she lived in when she came over first!"

"Well, good luck to her then! There's great credit due to her for getting on so well," Annie said firmly.

Hannah scrutinised John's face, his closed expression preventing her from enquiring further about the singer.

John didn't want to talk about Helena Curley. She was one of those immigrants who made her fortune the easy way. A good figure, a handsome face, and a way with men who were in a position to get her what she wanted. Helena had bartered with all her assets and had won over her benefactors. John remembered the last time he had seen her, strolling along by the East River, "slumming it" as she called going back to her roots, her arm linked through that of the big man walking beside her. She had been smiling up into his face, now and then a peal of laughter breaking through the cry of the seagulls overhead. She had put her face up close to his, expectantly, and then John had seen Vincent stoop down to kiss her.

He couldn't tell Annie all this because she was not the kind of woman who could understand such things. He looked across at Hannah, leaning back against the seat, her eyes closed tiredly. Even in sleep she looked regal, the flawless face composed. John was troubled. He would have to watch his niece with Vincent around. Hannah might have a good business head, but she had no experience of men. The sooner she was back home in Limerick, the better it would be, for her own sake. He had already seen Vincent looking at her with that hungry, wild-eyed look that could only signify one thing. His brother was growing tired of his little actress friend. He was ready for fresh pastures.

Hannah had an idea in her head. It had started as an insignificant notion, burrowing its way into her brain until finally it had become a fully-fledged possibility. Something was driving her, she didn't know what it was, maybe something as simple as ambition, something as complicated as the restlessness she felt inside her. But to set up her business in New York would be the greatest challenge of her lifetime. New York was the gateway to the world, a fashion mecca not just for the upper classes but for the growing number of people who now prospered through their own hard work and who would welcome Hannah Benson's ready-made selection of clothes which would not cost a fortune. She had written to Edwin Carstairs with details of her plans, and within two weeks had received a cablegram from him. "Whatever financing you need, it is available. Don't hesitate to ask my advice." She went to John at the lumber yard and found him in the foreman's office, sorting through mounds of invoices. He jumped up from behind the desk and strode across to welcome her. It was a long time since Hannah had seen him so energetic.

"Hannah, I think the tide is turning at last! I can't stand by any longer seeing those men out there working for a pittance when they're rightly entitled to be earning more."

He told her that he had written to the Industrial Workers of the World organisation in New York, outlining his dilemma. As a representative employer in the lumber yard, would he be in a position to increase workers' wages without consulting the owner? He had received a letter from James Connolly, the Socialist who was presently touring America looking for support for his organisation. Great to hear from a fellow countryman! Will be down to see you within the next few days.

"Do you see that, Hannah?" John showed her the letter eagerly. "From the great man himself, coming down her to organise us! Vincent won't know what hit him!"

Hannah decided to keep her own news for a while longer. She had further plans to make anyway, before everything could be considered in order. From where she stood at the moment, it looked as though she wouldn't be home for Florrie's wedding after all.

The strikers were two-deep outside Vincent Sullivan's lumber yard, rubbing their hands together to keep them warm in the bitter cold of the beginning of 1906. At first, they had been apprehensive about John's plan. Many of them had large families, and if they lost their jobs they had no hope of getting alternative employment. Union agitators were blacklisted in every state in America.

John reassured them. "Look, this man Connolly is a good organiser. He'll not let us down. Now, all you have to do is to stand firm on the pay increase: twelve dollars, and not a dollar less," he winked at them, "to start off with, anyway!"

"And what of your brother, Mr Sullivan? What if he finds out that you're behind all this rebellion in the workers?" A small thin man stepped forward and looked at John with distrustful eyes. John was Vincent Sullivan's brother, and blood was thicker than water. Was there something in it for John Sullivan after all? Connolly was a man they barely knew, only to hear accounts of him by word of mouth. Why would they place their trust in two virtual strangers to fight for their rights?

"My brother is wrong. I have no hesitation in saying it to his face, and I have said it, and it has split us in two," John said concisely. "I am following my own conscience on this issue and Connolly will not let us down in his support!"

After this he'd probably be out of a job himself, but at least he'd have the satisfaction of knowing that he had won some sort of justice for the lumber workers. The strike lasted three weeks. Connolly paid each of the men their wages from the funds of the Industrial Workers of the World. Vincent raged like a mad bull, searching frantically for unwitting scab labour to take up the work in the lumber yard. He had a way of finding out who was behind all the agitation, his sources were thorough, and when he found out, his contempt for his brother only served to widen the split between them. What he failed to realise was that most immigrant workers were in favour of being unionised by now, for the IWW had promised them union protection in their jobs if they remained sympathetic to the strikers. Few responded to the scab recruitment drive of the desperate Vincent Sullivan. It was out of John Sullivan's hands, because the times were changing and the workers were demanding their rights so long denied them.

The workers of New York waited with interest for the outcome of the strike. What happened in Vincent Sullivan's lumber yard was but the rumblings of what would eventually happen all over the country with workers up in arms, demanding fairness and equality at work. At the end of the month, a meeting was called in the lumber yard. Vincent Sullivan, a sullen expression on his face, agreed reluctantly to the increase, twelve dollars a week and the workers were to be allowed to join a union. A cheer went up from the crowd waiting outside the gates of the yard as news of the outcome filtered through to them. John Sullivan's name was like a prayer on the lips of hundreds of women and children that night as their men brought home the promise of extra food on the table.

By the end of March 1906 Annie was getting restless, longing to be back home in Limerick. Hannah didn't seem to be in any great hurry to leave, and this troubled her aunt. Peggy Benson would never forgive her if Hannah had her mind made up to remain in New York. John was being unnaturally secretive with her, something which upset her a little for they had always shared their thoughts with one another. Annie was feeling isolated from the household, with Maura now constantly locked in her room, coming out only for meals or to speak to Paul and Steven. John and Hannah were forever whispering in corners, and one time she saw Hannah show him a large map which she promptly put away as soon as Annie came into the room.

Vincent was a man she avoided, for he was a stranger to her now, and not a very likeable one. The Vincent she had known back in Ireland had been an innocent class of a man, with none of the trickery and ruthlessness this man possessed. From what John had told her, he was a man to be frightened of. He had reduced Maura to a shadow of the woman she had once been, her addiction to the little white pills she kept in a box in her bedroom a source of concern to Annie. Please God, with young Florrie getting married in the summer, they'd be travelling home again, and John would go with them. Such celebrations they'd have when they got home!

Michael Murphy looked at the girl sitting before him in his office. His favourable impression of Hannah when she had first stepped off the boat had not diminished during the time she had spent in New York. If anything, he was now even more taken with her, her luminous eyes looking at him now, so appealing and vulnerable.

"What you have in mind is a big undertaking for a young woman." He scratched the top of his head contemplatively. "Have you gone to Vincent about it?"

"No, not yet. John asked me to talk it over with you first. You'd know what renovations were necessary if my plan was to go ahead."

"The whole row would have to be virtually demolished. Every one of those tenements is a fire hazard, and the sanitation is virtually non-existent."

"But it can be done?" Hannah insisted, her face flushed with eagerness.

"Oh yes, girl, it can be done. But it will set you back a bit."

"I have the money to back me. The business over in Limerick is doing well and we do contract work for the factories in England also. The bank is willing to finance me, at least for the initial costs."

Michael smiled at her, impressed by her enthusiasm. He didn't tell her then that he would finance her whole operation if need be, just to see the sparkle in her blue eyes because he was in love with her.

Hannah sat in the living-room in Vincent Sullivan's house, waiting. The beautiful Italian hand-carved clock, with two love-birds fashioned in solid silver on either side of it, chimed the hour of midnight. The others had long since gone to bed, and she was waiting up for a purpose. Vincent Sullivan was due back any minute now, having attended a Steel Trust dinner in the city. Maura had not accompanied him, pleading that she wasn't feeling well, and that she wanted to go to bed early. Hannah had tried to talk to her, but it was as if a steel barrier had been erected between them, any mention of her dependence on the miracle pills making Maura agitated.

"I know you mean well, my dear, but you don't know what it's like. I need them!" She had pleaded with the younger woman, then turned and went to her room, locking the door behind her. Hannah had given up at that stage, and Annie's overtures to Maura likewise had been given the same response.

Vincent was glad his wife wasn't in the mood for accompanying him to social gatherings. Maura having become an embarrassment to him lately, her eyes glazed, her speech slurred as she spoke to his friends, people who pitied him for having such a fool for a wife.

Hannah lay back on the divan next to the fire, and as she began to succumb to the heat, her eyelids drooped. She woke suddenly, something dark and threatening looming above her. She almost cried out with alarm, but a hand was forced across her mouth and she was roughly shoved back onto the divan.

"Oh, come now, Hannah, like a good girl, a young woman of the world like you! Surely you know when a man is interested? Can't you show some degree of affection in return?" Vincent bent low over her, the smell of alcohol on his breath, his hair hanging rakishly over one eye.

She stiffened as his hands roamed over her body, caressing her, pulling her urgently towards him. She felt sick, her stomach churning with apprehension. She tried to get up but he forced her back down again, his hands on her breasts, the glint in his bloodshot eyes paralysing her.

"Please, Vincent! I need to talk with you. That's why I've stayed up tonight until you came home."

"You wanted to see me?" He looked gratified. "Ah, Hannah, I knew you were something special from the moment I saw you. The finest specimen of womanhood I've ever seen." His eyes travelled over her body, and she flinched uncomfortably beneath his gaze. He wasn't looking at her. He was looking through her. It was as though he saw her naked, her body wide open to him, revealing everything he wished to see with his lecherous intentions. She had heard rumours about Vincent. She was feeling afraid now, afraid of this stranger who towered above her, afraid of the look in his eyes, a look she had never seen in a man's face before.

She closed her eyes and hoped he would go away. She couldn't talk to him when he was in this mood. Then she felt his lips on hers, tentatively at first, but increasing in pressure, so that her breathless cries were drowned by his savage passion. She struggled, but it was useless. He was too strong for her, his bulky, overweight body bearing down upon her, the ticking of the clock on the mantlepiece incongruously soothing. She finally lay back, exhausted, strands of her hair damp with perspiration as Vincent lifted himself off her, a satiated grin on his grotesque, bloated face.

Hannah's blouse had been ripped off her shoulders, her body exposed to his merciless onslaught. Dear God, she had tried to stop it, she thought wildly, tears streaming down her face, her whole body shaking with sobs. He had hurt her, and not only physically, for her whole mind was filled with a mixture of disgust and guilt. She closed her eyes again, feverishly trying to wipe the last half hour from her tormented mind.

"Hannah, we don't have to tell anyone about tonight, do we?" He looked at her pleadingly, now like a little boy.

Hannah looked up at him, her cheeks stained with tears, her eyes dull and lifeless. "No, we don't have to tell anyone," she echoed, then turned away, sinking her face into the velvet cushions. Vincent padded quietly from the room and up the stairs to his bedroom.

What had come over him tonight? It was true that he had been interested in Hannah, had been trying to figure out if she was the sort of girl who wouldn't mind a bit of fun with a rich man like himself. It could have many compensations, as Helena Curley had found out. Hannah wasn't like Helena, though. She was a lady, was the little seamstress. He had enjoyed the struggle, he had to admit, her soft body wrestling beneath him before he finally took control. All things considered, it hadn't been a bac evening. Vincent slept uninterruptedly until morning.

The next morning when Hannah came down to breakfast, her face was unusually pale and listless, her eyes shadowed from lack of sleep. Annie looked at her sharply, but didn't comment. She was a little put out that Hannah hadn't been taking her into her confidence lately, as she had John, but that she supposed was the girl's own business. If Hannah wanted to confide in her, Annie thought, trying to overcome her disappointment, she knew where to come.

After breakfast, Hannah spoke to Vincent, avoiding his eyes. He was equally reluctant to have any contact with her, the night's events suddenly appearing ridiculous to him. To think that he, Vincent Sullivan, should have to go to the trouble of physically taming a woman to make love to him when there were plenty more fish in the sea . . .

"I'd like to speak with you privately, Vincent," Hannah said evenly. She followed him into his study and remained standing just inside the door, while he sat at his desk, drumming his fingertips on its surface, waiting for her to speak.

"Well, what is it? And if it has anything to do with last night, forget it. Nobody would take your word against mine, and you parading yourself about the place with your tight-fitting waists and your airy-fairy ways. Sure, any man would be tempted – there's no blame on my part!"

Hannah regarded him silently. She hated this man with his cold, harsh ways and a tongue like the devil. With all her heart she wished she didn't have to have any dealings with him, but her decision had been made long before last night, and she wasn't a woman who easily reneged on a plan, especially such an exciting one.

"I have been talking with Uncle John and Michael Murphy, and they agree with me that my plan is a good one."

He waited impatiently, looking through the window at the two young men playfully throwing a football to each other. He'd have to see that those two buckled down, did some work for a change. Paul had failed his last term's law exam, and if he failed the next one he'd be kicked out for good. No Sullivan would ever be kicked out of Harvard, he'd see to that.

"I want to buy out your row of tenement houses by the East River," Hannah announced calmly. "I've been to see them with Uncle John, and I think I can sort the place out. I have an idea for a shirt factory on the site, employing all those unfortunates who are presently working for dimes not dollars, stuck in rooms not fit for pigs!"

Vincent stopped his drumming on the table and looked up, his eyes wide with disbelief. "Am I hearing you right, missy? You want to buy out one of my most profitable bits of business this side of the Hudson River and make a feckin' factory out of it, everything unionised and above board, no doubt?"

"Yes, that's correct." Hannah continued to look evenly at him, her decisiveness irritating him.

"I get good money out of that lot."

"And you'd get a good price if you sell it to me. One of these days the tuberculosis will be rampant in your sweat shops and the health authorities will have the place condemned anyway. You'll find it hard to get more immigrants to move in once the authorities have blacklisted the place. At least my way, everything will be legal and you'll have one immigrant ghetto off your hands!" She almost spat the words into his face. To do business with a man like Vincent Sullivan, you had to stoop to his own ways.

Vincent's brain worked rapidly, noting the rationality of her little speech. That side of his business hadn't been doing well for a while. He had, it was true, the health inspectors breathing down his neck, and unions being set up all over the place, campaigning for better conditions for the garment workers. The girl's argument was a sound one. He had another reason for considering Hannah's proposition. Tammany Hall had put forward his name on the Democratic ticket for this year's mayoral election. It would be a bonus to hand over one of the controversial sweat shop tenement blocks to a slip of a girl who wanted to reform the whole garment industry by improving conditions. His face creased in a satisfied grin. By God, the girl had offered him the mayoralty on a silver platter!

Peggy wrote again to Hannah, begging her to make sure she was back home in time for Florrie's wedding.

'They've set the date for June the third, Hannah. If you book your passage now you will be home in time.'

Since the men in the lumber yard had joined a union, relations between John and the workers had never been better, the men treating him like some kind of saviour. The business was going well: the new railway, built mainly from the steel supplied from Vincent's Steel Refinery at Oil Creek, speeded up the process of transporting the lumber from the Great Lakes, thereby eliminating the unreliability of water transport.

Vincent's two sons, Paul and Steven, followed John around like two adoring lap dogs, forever asking him questions about the lumber business. Was there much profit in it? Since the unions took over was the working arrangement more satisfactory between the employer and employee?

At first John had thought that Vincent was behind all the questions, wanting to find out how the business was going without consulting him directly. But then, seeing their reaction to their father at home, the look of hatred in their eyes whenever Vincent started to ridicule Maura, John knew there was no voluntary communication between the boys and their father.

Vincent was a strict parent, and a bully. John had often seen Paul cowering dejectedly before his father as yet another law examination failed to live up to Vincent's expectations. According to Vincent, there was no second chance in life. "It'll do them good to feel the strength of my hand now and again, keep them on their toes!"

From the moment John had arrived in the house, Paul and Steven had adopted him as their father figure, simultaneously relinquishing any ties of affection with their real father. Maura was grateful to John for taking such an interest in the boys.

"Maybe some day, Maura, they might want to take over the running of the lumber yard," John hinted one evening as they sat relaxing after the evening meal.

Vincent had looked up quickly, his eyes suspicious. "The lumber yard? Over my dead body! I'm payin' good money to make first-class lawyers of those two, and they're not going next or near the lumber yard, so they can forget any ideas they might have!"

John could see what Vincent failed to recognise in his sons, a complete lack of interest in the legal profession. Their shoulders were hunched miserably over textbooks as they prepared for exams, while in their heads all they could retain was the exhilarating sight of convoys of freshly-sawn lumber sailing into New York harbour from the Great Lakes. They told John they could almost feel the fresh, salty breeze whipping against their cheeks as they stood waiting for the cargo to dock.

Instead they sat, suffocating beneath mounds of legal terminology that they both knew, beyond a doubt, they would never understand sufficiently to become the great legal men their father determined them to be.

Hannah had to wait impatiently for almost a month for Vincent's answer to her proposition. She had already made up her mind that she wouldn't be going back to Ireland, her life had taken too many twists and turns. There was too much unfinished business in New York for her even to contemplate going home, not even for Florrie's wedding. At her meeting with Vincent, he seemed to derive a kind of pleasure from the tense expression on her young face, reliving the night he had taken her body. There were times when Hannah could almost see the horrible scenario flashing through his mind, and she felt dirty and cheap like one of the dock women waiting for their sailors on the quays back home. Vincent Sullivan had taken away all her self-respect, and she would never forget that. She had worked hard to become a lady, and in one short interlude he had ruined it all for her by defiling her so shamelessly. She would never tell anyone. It was something that she had to keep a close secret, the defilement of her body not something she wanted to dwell on. Hannah shut her mind to the episode, willing herself to believe it had never happened; it had all been a bad dream.

Then something happened that forced Vincent to make his decision. A week before the Easter holiday 1906, a fire broke out in the sweat shops along the East River. Hundreds of employees, some of them children, were inside, trapped by the flames, unable to escape due to the inadequacy of the fire escapes. Some of them tried to jump from four floors up, and were killed as soon as they hit the street below. In all, one hundred and twenty workers lost their lives. An investigation was set up immediately, and Vincent Sullivan's tenements were declared "unsuitable premises for the continuation of their previous activity". The full results of the state's investigations were never revealed, for Vincent had many friends in high places. Nevertheless, he thought he had been more than lucky on this occasion to escape with a mere bureaucratic telling-off. The inspections were becoming a nuisance, and he had no time to be playing games of hide-and-seek with the health department.

He called Hannah into his office shortly after the fire and delivered his ultimatum. "You can have the tenements for your factory. Mind you, I want a good price for them and I want your word that you won't breathe to a soul what happened between us that night." He leaned towards her, and she backed away, recoiling from his ugly leer.

He needn't have any worries that she would reveal the events of that fateful night. It was like a horrible nightmare that refused to go away. She could never tell John, for it would only make more trouble between the two brothers. Poor Annie wouldn't know what to do, thinking of Maura and the heartbreak such a revelation might bring to the poor woman who was suffering so much already. She would never tell Paul and Steven. They were young men, not much younger than herself, but to Hannah they were just little boys, frightened to death of their brute of a father. What happened that night was of no concern to them, or to anybody.

"You have my word. Nobody in this house will ever know what happened that night."

He sat back in his chair, satisfied with the response. "Right then, we'll get the legalities over with as soon as possible and then you can take over the place, lock, stock and barrel. And good riddance to the lot of them!"

After Easter, work commenced on the tenement block. Two of the houses had been completely gutted by the fire, and Michael Murphy, by now a firm and devoted friend of Hannah's, had organised that the whole row be torn down and Hannah's factory started from scratch.

"There'll be no ghosts in your building, Hannah Benson," he said to her affectionately. "Start with a clean slate. 'Twas always my way and I never looked back!"

Edwin Carstairs had forwarded the capital for her New York venture and Michael had organised his own lawyer to oversee the contract agreement between Hannah and Vincent. He didn't trust John's brother. Everything was signed and in order by the time work had started on rebuilding the strip along the East River, and Michael had insisted to Hannah that she leave the rest in his experienced hands.

"You do what you have to do then, Michael," Hannah agreed. "How long will it take, do you think, before everything is ready to begin working?"

"We'll see your shirt factory open at the end of the year, God willing!"

"You can't mean it, Hannah? Not go home for Florrie's wedding? Your poor mother would be devastated!" Annie was incredulous. She had been troubled lately by the girl's appearance, her face suddenly sunken and thin, the slender neck almost too fragile to support her head. "Are you not well, Hannah? Is there something troubling you?"

Hannah shook her head wearily. "No, Annie. Maybe I've taken on more than I can handle, but Michael Murphy is a good, honest man and he's a great help to me, so I need have no worries on that side of things. But I can't go back to Limerick just yet, not even for Florrie's wedding."

She turned her face away from Annie, not wanting her to see the despair in her eyes. More than anything else in the world, she wanted to be at home, especially now, with her mother and Florrie and May there to comfort her. For she needed comfort, more than she had ever needed it. With growing horror she had noticed the changes in herself as she undressed for bed each night, sometimes half-afraid to look in the long mirror in her bedroom, afraid of what she might see. She didn't want anybody to know, not even Annie. She was glad in so many ways that her mother wasn't with her, for she would have been the one to notice it. Annie was less observant, only because she had never had the experience herself.

Hannah had decided, lying in her bed in the early morning light of a fine, blustery spring morning with the bedclothes pulled tightly about her, that she would never go back to Limerick now. She would leave Martin and Florrie in charge of the warehouse on the quay, and May could see to the shops. Edwin Carstairs was always there to give them advice and to consult her if anything unusual needed seeing to. In the meantime, she would lose herself in the bustling mêlée of New York. She felt comforted at the thought that Michael Murphy was by her side, his small, stocky frame like a protective support against any storm clouds that would, she was certain, gather once her secret was out.

"No, Annie, you must go, and Uncle John. I'll write to Mother and explain everything to her in time. Meanwhile, don't be cross with me, and try to understand." She looked at Annie's bewildered face, her heart aching to tell her what was troubling her, to confide in her that her whole world was crashing about her, and she was powerless to do anything to remedy it. She wouldn't tell her, though. Annie would never go back to Limerick if she knew the trouble Hannah was in. She would insist on staying with her, or even worse, taking her back to Ireland with her. No, it was better this way, to cut all ties with the family until it was all over. She would have to move out of Vincent's house, of course. There was no question of remaining there.

"Well, you know best, girl," Annie replied a little huffily. "But Florrie will be disappointed. A great many people will be expecting you there for your sister's wedding. Your mother will never understand why you didn't go."

"I've made up my mind, Annie! I'll be busy here for the next few months, organising workers for the factory when it eventually opens. Mother will understand; she knows what I'm like once I get an idea into my head."

Hannah tried to be flippant, smiling at Annie as if she hadn't a worry in the world. Inside, her heart was full of dark despair. Her meeting with Vincent Sullivan that night, when he had taken her so callously, had such fateful consequences. It had destroyed all her illusions of a tender relationship with a man and, by the end of the year when her factory by the East River would be completed, she would have given birth to Vincent Sullivan's child.

Chapter 14

That same spring Jonathan Mayhew was making a name for himself among literary circles, a series of his short stories printed in *The Limerick Lamp* impressing prominent figures in the publishing world. He already had two offers from publishing companies to publish a book of his short stories, and he threw himself into his work with unbridled enthusiasm. Madeline Deery now always by his side, encouraged him and ignored her mother's repeated pleas to ask "dear Jonathan to tone down the fervour a little in his writing, dear.".

In some ways, Madeline enjoyed seeing her mother's discomfort, for once watching her squirm self-consciously. Jonathan had the lifestyle of his peers trapped beneath a microscope, and Christine O'Shea and the likes of Mrs Deery regarded it as an insult to see their social lives ridiculed so sharply.

He had three more plays shown in the Abbey Theatre in Dublin and then he got an offer from a New York producer to come to America and have *The Darlin' of Erin* performed in a small theatre in Lower Manhattan. The play was about a young girl who had emigrated after the famine and had married a wealthy New York banker, only to find that her ties with the old country were too strong to resist, so she had left him and gone back to Ireland. Her heart was broken because she was torn between love for her husband and love for her darlin' Erin. At the end of the play, the girl died, calling piteously for her husband to come to her, to hold her one more time before she left him forever.

When the play was performed in New York there was not a dry eye among the women, and some of the men blew violently into large handkerchiefs taken discreetly from their pockets. Mrs Deery, reading an account of the play in the letter Jonathan had written to Madeline in Limerick, beamed with satisfaction. This seemed to be a much more agreeable piece of work by Jonathan, Ireland portrayed so romantically, not a mention of upper-class morality to strike a bitter chord. She looked speculatively at Madeline's face as they sat in the parlour. The girl was positively glowing, her eyes bright with happiness as she gazed into the distance, her needlework laid to one side, a dreamy expression on her face.

It wouldn't be long now, Mrs Deery thought, looking forward to the prospect of having a distinguished playwright for a son-in-law. None of her friends could laugh at 'poor Madeline' now, she reflected smugly. She felt sure Jonathan would propose before the year was out. Hannah Benson's beguiling ways were obviously forgotten now. With the little seamstress safely out of harm's way, obstacles to the match between Jonathan and Madeline were obliterated. Anticipating news of an engagement between her daughter and Jonathan Mayhew, Mrs Deery decided to take Madeline to America. They would do some shopping in the fashionable stores in New York; the girl needed all the help she could get to make herself as attractive as possible, Mrs Deery thought wryly.

Hannah Benson's shops were now held in much esteem in Limerick, but she didn't want to have anything to do with that girl's business. Mrs Deery was no fool. She knew a man would find it difficult to get over a girl as attractive as Hannah Benson. She would organise a trousseau for Madeline, but they would stay well clear of the Bensons until the wedding date was firmly fixed.

Hannah couldn't bear to be near Vincent, couldn't bear to see the look in his eyes each time they rested hungrily on her body. She was afraid that he would begin to notice something, even though up until now she had been able to conceal her thickening waistline by lacing her corsets so tightly that she could hardly breathe. This child would have nothing to do with Vincent Sullivan. It would be a Benson, brought up with Hannah's ways.

Hannah felt the tiny thing inside her growing bigger every day, and at the end of the summer, when she felt the insistent kicking of tiny limbs against her ribs, she knew that very soon her secret would be out.

Michael Murphy had found her a small apartment in Albany, two blocks away from where he lived. He hadn't asked her any awkward questions as to why she was leaving the comfort of Vincent's home to go and live on her own in a strange city. He knew there had been words the night Hannah had packed her bags and sat in the hall of the house on Fifth Avenue waiting for him to come and bring her to her new apartment. Michael had stood, hesitating, outside the front door for a few seconds, listening to Maura's bewildered voice.

"But why, Hannah? Are you not happy here?"

"You have been kindness itself, Maura, you and the boys, but I mustn't intrude on your hospitality any further and I'm an independent sort of person." Then he had heard Vincent's voice, half-jeering, and had stiffened with anger at the man's indifference.

"Well now, if she wants to leave, then nobody will stop her. Maybe she has a bit of a *gra* for the builder, eh? Moving out to Albany, a stone's throw away from Murphy's place."

Michael had rung the bell then and the young maid had answered, her eyes wide and frightened-looking. He stepped into the hall and proceeded to take Hannah's bags, ushering her towards the door.

"Come on then, Hannah, time we were going. Good night to you, Mrs Sullivan." He bowed his head politely to Maura, ignoring Vincent. Whatever had forced the girl to move out of the house, he knew Vincent was at the back of it. She was looking pale and sickly lately, not like the girl he had met off the boat the first time he had seen her. There was something wrong with her, he sensed it in his bones, and he was never wrong. He would see to it that she looked after herself from now on. He would protect Hannah with his life.

Work on the factory was progressing nicely, and by the

end of the summer Hannah could see the fruits of Michael's labours as the streamlined factory rose higher each day, the people living in the Lower East Side gathering in little clusters on the work site each evening, like fascinated theatre-goers looking forward to an entertaining performance. Hannah knew most of them by now, for she had made it her business to go through the narrow streets accompanied by Michael.

She had seen women in the tenement sweat shops, had asked them what they earned for piece-work, and was shocked at the paltry amount they received for working a twelve-hour day. The situation was the same everywhere she went, the unhealthy working conditions whole families had to endure for as little as ten cents an hour.

Michael Murphy had had his suspicions for some time about the state of Hannah's health. All the pieces of the jigsaw seemed to fit now, as he thought things over in his mind. Hannah's sudden departure from Vincent Sullivan's house, her refusal to go back to Ireland for her sister's wedding, the pale, tired face and the loose coat she had taken to wearing lately even though the weather had been too hot for anything heavier than a light dress.

They visited an Italian family who lived three storeys up in a tenement house in The Bowery, an area renowned for its dense population of piece-workers for the garment industry all massed together in rooms with hardly any lighting or ventilation. Hannah reached the top flight of stairs, her breath coming in short, panting gasps, little drops of perspiration standing out on her forehead. Her vision began to blur, the door in front of her swaying backwards and forwards. She grabbed hold of Michael's sleeve and he reached out to support her, as she slid to the ground unconscious.

He beat his fists on the door. "Somebody! Help, somebody! There's a lady after having a turn out here!" The door was opened slowly and a woman looked out, her dark eyes puzzled. She saw Hannah lying on the floor, her face pale in the gloom of the landing, took her limp hand and felt for a pulse.

"Her clothing, eet ees too tight, Meester Murphy. She faints because she has not enough air in her lungs." She pointed to Hannah's coat, buttoned up to the neck, the bodice uncomfortably tight about her chest.

"Go on then, woman, loosen the blessed things, for I know nothing about ladies' clothing!" Michael's voice rose with concern.

If anything should happen to her, he would never forgive himself. He should have known better than to go climbing up flights of stairs with her, and she not looking the best. The Italian woman loosened Hannah's coat, unbuttoned the top button of her blouse, and removed the tight belt from about her waist. She paused for a moment to regard Hannah, a thoughtful expression on her olive-skinned face.

Then she turned to Michael, a broad smile on her face. "There is nothing wrong with the lady, Meester Murphy. She ees just with child; she should be wearing theengs which are not so tight for the little one." The woman smiled knowingly at him, and Michael looked alarmed. It was bad enough to have found out for sure what was wrong with Hannah, but this woman thought that he . . . it was too ludicrous for words.

"No, the lady isn't mine, Gina, I mean we are not . . ." He gesticulated with his hands, pointing from himself to Hannah, but the complexity of the situation was beyond him. "It's all right, Gina. I'll manage now. Just look after her for me while I call a carriage to take us home."

The little Italian woman nodded and went back into the room. Presently a small assembly of piece-workers had surrounded Hannah, one man putting a pile of finished shirts beneath her head, another of the women loosening her boots and propping her feet up on a cardboard box.

Hannah opened her eyes and looked around her, bewildered as she saw a sea of faces grinning down at her. "You must rest, Mees Hannah," Gina said authoratively. "Meester Murphy will be back presently with a carriage. He will take good care of you." Then she winked at Hannah conspiratorially and Hannah knew her secret was out.

Michael Murphy probably knew too, and would never speak to her again, not to mind finishing off her factory. Tears spilled down her cheeks and she was still sobbing quietly when Michael returned, his expression as he looked down at her propped up against the pile of garments on the landing, non-committal.

"Michael, before I go, so as not to waste a journey . . ." She turned to the assembly of men and women standing on the landing. "How much do you earn an hour for your work?" she enquired, her voice resuming its business-like tone.

"Ten cents an hour, Mees Hannah," Gina answered, shrugging her shoulders resignedly.

"I'll give each of you three times that amount for an eight-hour day, if you're willing to work hard during that time, and also learn a little bit more about garment making. Back in Ireland I have a lace business, and the work is very specialised, needing good eyesight and an ability for fine stitching." Hannah studied their faces and saw hope light up in their dark eyes. "I want some of my workers to learn the art of lacemaking. I'll have some of my girls brought over from Ireland especially to train you here. Are you interested?"

They exchanged bemused glances, then all their faces broke at once into creases of approval. "We'll be happy to work for you, Mees Hannah," Gina, the spokesperson for the group, said slowly. "Whenever you need us, we'll be here for you."

Michael Murphy helped Hannah down the stairs and into the carriage. The tenacity of the girl never ceased to amaze him. Even in such a predicament, when most women would lament and shed bitter tears about their lot, Hannah Benson picked herself up from the ruins and started afresh. He had no doubt in his mind about what he was going to do next. He was a lonely man, in spite of his respectability in New York. He tapped his foot agitatedly against the floor of the carriage. It was a momentous decision, one that might cost him the girl's friendship if she refused him. Nevertheless, he was never one to let an opportunity pass him by.

"Are you all right yourself, Michael?' Hannah murmured, and his heart did a somersault of wild joy. She was the most perfect woman in the world, the only woman for him.

"Hannah, there are things you haven't told me . . .things I know about you now."

"It couldn't have remained hidden for long, Michael, and I'm grateful to you for not scolding me, for I'm that weary lately." She put her face in her hands and her slim shoulders heaved with sobs. He put out a hand to her and she clutched it tightly, an anchor in a raging storm.

"I want you to marry me, Hannah, *a chroi*. I know I'm old enough to be your father, God knows, but I'll take care of you which is what you need right now. I won't ask you what blaggard got you into these circumstances, and if you won't tell me that's your privilege." He stared at the top of her bent head, watching for some measure of response.

Hannah remained silent, her mind in turmoil. Ever since she had found out she was pregnant there wasn't a night she hadn't lain awake, trying to make plans for the future, once the baby was born. It wouldn't be easy, and she was so tired, bereft of all emotion except that indescribable sense of fear, her constant companion ever since her encounter with Vincent that night in his home. She looked up at Michael suddenly, saw his round, not unhandsome face, the kind eyes, a wisp of grey hair escaping from beneath his hat. She saw a flashing image of her father, standing in the yard of their cottage back in Glenmore and her heart contracted with painful memories. He was so like her father, this gentle builder from New York. With him she would have nothing to fear. Nobody, not even Vincent Sullivan, could ever harm her again.

She smiled at Michael tearfully, then reaching across, planted a light kiss on his forehead. "I'd be honoured to have a good man like you for a husband, Michael Murphy." She closed her eyes and tried to shut out the picture of

Jonathan Mayhew, his arms about her waist, the wonderful stirring of desire that swept through her body when he touched her. She opened them again and saw Michael with a look of boyish delight in his eyes.

The carriage reached Brooklyn Bridge and it was there that Hannah relinquished all ties with the past, mentally casting them into the blue waters of the Shannon flowing through her beloved Limerick. There were times when even Hannah Benson would have to settle for something less than her heart's desire, she thought rationally. "I'll marry you, Michael, as soon as you want me to. And I thank you for your proposal, for you've lightened my heart today!"

They made the trip to New York that summer of 1906 arriving just in time for the production of Jonathan's play being shown in Manhattan in early September. Mrs Deery was worried that Hannah Benson being in the same city as Jonathan might take the opportunity to renew acquaintance with him, but so far he had given Madeline his undivided attention and she relaxed, wishing he would make haste and ask for her daughter's hand in marriage sooner rather than later. The play was to run for a period of six weeks, and on the night before Madeline and Mrs Deery left for home, they accompanied Jonathan to the theatre to see the performance. The audience was a mix of Italian-Americans and Polish-Americans, their accents excited and fused in one loud burst of enthusiastic response to *The Darlin' of Erin*.

It was a play they could all identify with, from their own experience of isolation in a strange country, away from their friends and family in their homelands. For two and a half hours they lived the sorrows of Kate Laffan, the young immigrant girl from Ireland, and as the final curtain was lowered many eyes were filled with nostalgic tears. The applause was thunderous, the fact that many of them couldn't understand the dialogue was no barrier to their appreciation.

The handsome playwright stood on the stage smiling, his long, dark hair falling over one eye as he brushed it back impatiently from his forehead. Then his eyes swept over the audience coming to rest, suddenly, on a figure in the applauding crowd. His heart stood still for a fraction of a second. The crowds seeming to disappear into the background of noise and smoke as he stared at the beautiful woman sitting in the balcony seat, her wide, startled eyes fixed firmly on his face, her face flushed with sudden awareness. Hannah sat, unable to move a muscle as her heart contracted with an almost unbearable longing to be closer to the dark shadow of a man, now bowing and smiling to the audience, now looking up, his gaze fixed upon her, until she felt she could not breathe such was the intensity of the moment. Jonathan. Here in the flesh, how could she bear it? She felt the tears in her eyes and reached out for Michael's hand, thrusting her small hand into his while he took it and squeezed it gently.

Jonathan raised his hand instinctively, then saw the man seated next to her turn and whisper something in her ear. She nodded and they both stood up, the man placing a protective hand beneath her elbow. Jonathan froze. All the fantasies he had kept hidden, his secret dreams that one day he would meet Hannah Benson again and that they would resume their former relationship as though nothing had happened in between, all those coveted aspirations were now lying in pieces at his feet. He saw Hannah turn slowly and walk away from the spotlight through the rear door of the balcony, her companion with one arm about her shoulders, shielding her from the swell of the audience.

Jonathan's raised hand fell limply to his side. He could go back to Limerick now and throw himself even more fervently into his work, for Hannah would no longer intrude on his dreams. She was lost forever to him. The success of his play and the adoring gaze of Madeline as she looked up at him from the audience meant nothing to him in that moment, for he had seen Hannah Benson with another man tonight, her body large with the weight of his child.

The June sun shone brightly on Florrie Benson and Martin Manley as they stood hand-in-hand outside the church after their wedding ceremony, smiling self-consciously at their friends and relations. The factory on the quays had been closed for the day and passers-by looked admiringly at Florrie's beautiful wedding dress, a delicate train of Limerick lace hanging from the silk collar all the way down to the ground, and long lace sleeves tapering at the wrist in little pointed diamond shapes.

Since Hannah had left for New York Martin had been an admirable substitute as an overseer, his kindness to the girls not going unrecognised. They worked just as hard for him as they had for Hannah, seeing the orders were completed on time so that the bonus to the factory would not be jeopardised by any tardiness on their part. They had been told that Hannah was starting up another factory in New York, and there was an air of excitement as the girls sat at their machines, rumours flying among them in urgent whispers.

"Did you hear that she's looking for some of us to go over there to give her a hand – teachin' the Americans how to make the lace! Did you ever hear the like?"

Two girls in particular paid heed to these rumours. Eily Mitchell and Mary Fitzgerald, their babies taken from them, had built up a bond of mutual sympathy, each knowing the heartbreak of the other. They had nothing to keep them in Limerick. Eily Mitchell had heard that James McCarthy was on the run again from the police. His room in Clanbrassil Street in Dublin had been found full of dynamite, ready for another attack on an army barracks in Abbyfeale, south of Limerick. She pitied May Benson, for wasn't she his wife, and what he'd do to her if he ever met up with her again was frightening to think about.

Mary Fitzgerald had been walking back to the convent one warm summer's evening, her foot sore from the constant pressure of the foot pedal of the sewing-machine. She had sat down on one of the wooden benches in Arthur's Quay, stretching her legs out in front of her. A woman had sat near her, and Mary had thought she must be a child's nanny, for she had a little black satin cape about her shoulders with a tiny watch pinned to it in front. Mary had seen them in the convent courtyard, waiting to take the babies from the nun who came to the convent door.

Mary had looked into the baby carriage and seen a

child so much like her own little one, taken away from her because the nuns decided she wouldn't be able to take care of him. She had run back to the convent that night, and had sworn to herself she would get out of that place even if she had to steal to do it. And then Hannah's news came. Martin Manley called them all together in the warehouse. Hannah would pay their passage over, any two girls to start off, then maybe more as soon as the factory on the East River became firmly established. It was the break Mary had been unconsciously waiting for all of her short life.

"I don't understand the girl, Annie, really I don't. Not to come home for her sister's wedding! It's not like her, no matter how busy she is."

"I know, Peggy, but she was that upset when I tried to persuade her, that I just let it be. And Maura has promised to look after her."

Peggy Benson looked down again at the letter she had received from Hannah. It had come three days after the wedding, with a gift for Florrie and Martin, a little French mantle clock in delicate china, exquisitely adorned with raised pink and blue roses. She didn't explain much in her letter, just that she was busy getting ready for the opening of her factory, going from door to door in the tenements on the East Side of New York trying to put together a capable team of shirt-makers.

"Now don't trouble yourself, Peggy. Hannah is a good girl, and she must have her reasons for not coming home. Isn't it a good sign, girl, that she knows the business here is in good hands, so she's not worried on that score?"

Peggy shook her head despondently. "I don't know, Annie. I can feel something in my bones. Maybe I should try and get over there, find out what's wrong."

John came into the room at that moment and Annie's eyes lit up immediately. She hated to think that he would be going back to New York, after such a short time home. She couldn't go back with him. No matter how much she missed him, she had felt like a fish out of water over there, and she couldn't tolerate the tension between Vincent and Maura and their sons. Money definitely didn't buy happiness, she told herself wryly. She had explained all this to John and he had taken her in his arms, promising her that it wouldn't be long before his business affairs would be settled and he would be home for good.

"Will you talk to this sister of mine, John, like a good man, and make her see sense? She wants to go over to see Hannah, but sure wouldn't you only be annoying the girl, Peggy, and she so busy!"

John shook his head emphatically. "You stay here, Peggy. You're not one to be taking yourself off to New York, and you have the girls to look after here. May and Florrie need you for a bit of support, for they're not like Hannah who can stand on her own two feet. Besides, won't I be there soon, so she'll have me to look after her!"

Peggy looked a little more relieved, but her eyes were still troubled as she excused herself and went to bed.

"I have news for you, Annie. Maybe you won't like it though, for you've grown used to being without this old husband of yours for a long time now!" His eyes teased her and she looked up at him, her expression puzzled.

"What in God's name are you going to tell me, John? If

you tell me that you're going back to America for another five years then I'm going with you, for I can't bear the separation, and that's the truth!" Her eyes shone with hopeless tears and he pulled her into his arms, smoothing her hair back from her face with a gentle hand.

"I'm going back, but only for a few months, just enough time to let Vincent know I'm leaving his lumber yard in New York, and setting up my own on the Dock Road, here in Limerick itself!"

Annie saw the excited glint in his eyes, kind eyes, so unlike his brother's which were hard and cold and full of contempt.

"I'm tired of being away from you, Annie, and I miss Limerick, every stone of it. Everywhere I look in New York reminds me of the city I was brought up in – the only difference is the different accents of so many lonely immigrants like myself." He had tears in his eyes now, and they clung together, Annie offering a silent thanksgiving to God for listening to her prayers. John was coming home at last, with money in his pocket. Yet he had no business to come home to.

"But how did this all come about, John? Sure where would you get enough money to establish another business?"

"While I was working in Vincent's lumber business over there, I make a few contacts, Annie. I gave them many a profitable timber load and didn't ask for payment on the nail, when many of them were hard put to pay me." John paused, a faraway look in his eyes. "When they eventually paid me, they added a tidy sum of interest to the amount and I deposited it in the bank over there. Then

I got wind that Tadgh Powell was selling his timber yard here in Limerick, looking for an experienced man to take over. He contacted me a couple of days after Florrie's wedding and he seemed to be impressed with my account of my business in New York. The men, all working away, no strikes, no bitterness between them and the boss. He had heard good accounts of my relations with the men who worked for me – he said he had his sources, and there was a twinkle in his eye, Annie. I knew he was a man I could do business with!"

He smiled, recollecting the tremor of exhilaration he had felt when Tadgh Powell had spat on the palm of his hand and held it out to him. "I've known you a while, John Sullivan, before you ever came into the timber business. You were a good worker then, and you're a good one now, so we'll make a deal and we can sign the necessary papers when you come home to Limerick!"

"Oh, John!" Annie cried, clinging to him, afraid that if she let go he would disappear once more, the thought of him being home for good almost too good to contemplate.

"I'm not looking forward to my meeting with Vincent, though. 'Tis a terrible thing to say, but my own brother is like a stranger to me Annie, and I can't wait for the day when I sever all ties with the man, for he's not the brother I knew all those years ago!"

Hannah wrote to her mother, a long letter full of fulsome descriptions of Michael, of how he had been so kind to her since her arrival in New York.

'The factory is almost finished, and such a wealth of good

workers over here, Mother, grateful to have the chance to earn a decent day's wage.'

It was only at the end of her letter that she broached the explosive news of her impending marriage to Michael.

'He's a good man, Mother, and any woman would be proud to be his wife. It looks as though I'll be putting down roots in New York, as Michael is well established here with many building contracts even as far afield as Montreal in Canada, can you imagine!'

Peggy gave an audible gasp and Annie looked across the room at her, puzzled. She saw her sister's face pale and her hands tremble as she held the letter.

"What is it, girl? Is there something amiss with Hannah?"

"She's getting married, Annie! My brave, stubborn, handsome girl is getting married to a man old enough to be her father. Oh, Annie, where did I go wrong in the rearing of them? First May running off with that that no-good James McCarthy, and now Hannah getting herself married in a country hundreds of miles across the water – and not even her mother there to wish her an ounce of luck!"

She threw the letter on the floor and burst into tears. Annie went to the sideboard and poured her a glass of brandy.

"Take this like a good woman and stop your wailing! What would Peter Benson say, the Lord be good to him, if he heard his wife talking about a decent man in such a cruel way?"

Peggy looked up at her eagerly. "You know Michae Murphy, Annie? You can tell me what class of a man he is Will he be good to my Hannah?"

Annie sat down beside her, taking her hands in hers an earnest expression on her face.

"He's one of the finest men on that side of the Atlantic, honest and good-living, and with a fortune of his own, sc that he has no need to live off any money Hannah might have. So set your mind at rest, Peggy."

"But she's getting married the day after tomorrow, Annie!" Peggy cried. "I should be there with her! She's all alone with no family to speak of."

"John will be there, won't he?" Annie demanded.

She prayed in her heart that this would be so. Hannah had been acting so strangely before they had come home to Limerick, and she thought now that maybe she should have questioned the girl more, tried to find out what was tormenting her. This sudden marriage to Michael Murphy came as a shock to Annie. There had never seemed to be any romantic attachment between the two. There was something Hannah was keeping from them, something so terrible that she couldn't even speak about it to her own family. John would get to the bottom of it. She would write to him without delay and ask him to look after Hannah, discover what it was she was keeping hidden from them. Surely John would be invited to her wedding?

Hannah and Michael were married quietly in September 1906 in the little parish church in Albany. John stood next to Hannah, taking the place of the late Peter Benson, and as the priest solemnly asked, "Who giveth this woman in holy matrimony?" he stepped forward, placing Hannah's trembling hand in Michael's strong, firm grip.

John had been dismayed when he had returned to New York to find that Hannah had moved out of Vincent's and gone to live on her own in an apartment. He had confronted Vincent. "And you let her? A girl not knowing her way about the city yet? Sure anything could happen to her!"

"It was her decision, John," Maura responded quietly.

She had been deeply troubled lately over the circumstances of Hannah's abrupt departure. She recalled how intently Vincent used to watch the girl, and Hannah's uneasiness in his presence. Something else was troubling her. The girl's figure had noticeably increased in size during the last few weeks before she left, her face losing its habitual glow of warm vitality. Maura could remember a similar transformation in her own appearance; it was when she had been carrying Paul and Steven.

The ugly, persistent gnawing in Maura's brain forced her to remember how she had lain awake one night waiting for Vincent to come home from the Steel Trust dinner, wondering if he would spend the night with Helena Curley. She had heaved a sigh of relief when she heard him in the hallway, had waited for his footsteps on the stairs, but he had gone into the parlour first. Maura had tiptoed from her bed and opened the door a fraction. She could hear voices, a soft female voice and Vincent's loud, arrogant tone. Then there was a cry, a sound Maura would not forget for as long as she lived.

Maura had closed her bedroom door and run back to her bed, pulling the bedclothes up above her head to block out the awful sounds, the familiar panting and snorting, punctuated by muffled sobs. She was angry with herself for being a coward, angry that she didn't go down and confront her husband, tear him away from Hannah, but she was so frightened of him. Thoughts of the bruises hidden beneath her petticoat compelled her to remain in her bed – and now Hannah was suffering the consequences. If John knew about it, he would surely kill Vincent. She hated her husband, but she didn't want him dead either. Where would she go? What would she do without his support? So she remained silent, her eyes downcast as John marched angrily through the hallway, banging the door behind him. He was going to find Hannah.

And he did find her. Hannah was sitting in the little rock garden at the back of her apartment in Lincoln Square in Albany, her feet propped up on a little footstool, Michael Murphy sitting by her side. A young maid answered the door to John, and with a welcoming smile, ushered him through to the garden. He stood for a moment on the terrace watching Michael as he placed a rug about her knees, his hand gently brushing back a stray curl from her forehead. John smiled with relief. Whatever trouble Hannah was in, she would be well protected by this man.

He approached them, and they both looked up, startled, Michael's face a mixture of pleasure and uncertainty. John held out his arms to Hannah, and as she struggled to her feet the alarming fact dawned on him that the girl was not far from her time. Hannah Benson was with child and, in all likelihood, the only two people in the world who knew about it were himself and his good friend, Michael Murphy.

"Why didn't you tell us, girl? Why didn't you tell Annie? We would never have gone back to Limerick leaving you in such a state!" He looked into her eyes, and saw the shadow of regret there, as she struggled to speak.

"I was ashamed, Uncle John. So ashamed that I had let you down, even though I swear on my poor father's grave that this . . ." she indicated her swollen body, "wasn't the result of any loving relationship."

"Will you sit down, like a good man!" Michael spoke up. "You've had a bit of a shock – no more than I had, I can tell you. Not a name will the girl give me, for if I knew who he was he'd be one less breathing the air in New York!"

John calculated rapidly. He couldn't tell Peggy for the time being. She'd only be wanting to come over straight away, and maybe make the girl feel worse than she did already. She had enough to cope with besides Peggy lamenting over her misfortunes. "What are you going to do, girl? You can't stay here on your own. You need somebody to look after you."

Hannah darted a shy glance at Michael. Then they both looked sheepishly at John, Michael's face turning a bright red colour. "I'm going to look after her, John. I've asked Hannah to marry me and she's kindly consented."

John addressed Hannah sternly, his eyes never leaving her face. "Is this what you want, girl? For if it's only for the child's sake, then speak up now, for Michael is a good man and he deserves better than a quick compromise."

Hannah took Michael's hand in hers and replied

evenly. "I like and respect this man, Uncle John, but Michael knows I don't love him. I have never led him to believe otherwise, but he's willing just the same to take a chance and I'm grateful to him for that. I'll make a good wife for him, never fear! You'll give me away, Uncle John? And not a word to the family back home?" Seeing him hesitate, she pleaded with him. "What good would it do to tell them now? I haven't long more, and soon it will be all over. I'll tell my mother then."

John nodded resignedly. He would let it be for the present. But he wouldn't rest until he had found out what scoundrel had shattered Hannah's life. He'd find him, no matter how long it took.

"They're not happy, Vincent, and all the money you spend on them at Harvard will not make them good lawyers. Sure, can't you see they're big, brawny young men, eager for the outdoor life, not cooped up in a lawyer's office all day long?" Maura argued with her husband, watching with some alarm as he stood up, towering above her, his face threatening.

"And whose fault is it, I ask you, woman? Two milk sops you've made of them, two mammy's boys cryin' on your shoulder when the schooling gets too tough for them! Call them in here. I want to talk to them!" Vincent roared, the blood vessels on his temples standing out with rage.

Maura left the room quietly and returned with Paul and Steven, their ungainly strides more pronounced as they faced their father fearfully.

"Your mother tells me you both want to leave

Harvard, go out into the world and make your fortunes." Vincent sneered at them, and Paul spoke up, his voice unsteady as his eyes met his father's.

"Uncle John has told us about his timber yard on the docks in Limerick. He wants us to go back with him, that is, if you give us permission. We'll be able to work with him, for there's plenty of it over there now – lumber contracts for nearly every state in America, so Uncle John says. They're even transporting it to South Africa. It's what we want to do, father." Paul pleaded, backing away from the dangerous glint in his Father's eyes.

"You ungrateful pup, you and your brother. I've slaved to get the money to send you to college, and this is the thanks I get!"

"Vincent don't, please!" Maura grabbed his arm as he went to strike Paul.

Steven stepped in front of his brother, his face a solid mass of hatred. "We're going back to Limerick with Uncle John, whether you like it or not. We've had enough of your bullying, making a laughing stock of our mother by taking up with every two-bit actress this side of the Hudson river."

The room echoed with the resounding blow, as Vincent struck out. Steven stumbled, falling against the mantelpiece, and Paul moved quickly, his body shielding his brother from another angry blow. Vincent raised his fist once more, then saw the look on his son's face, a look that no man had ever dared give big Vincent Sullivan in all his years in Tammany. Steven lay on the ground, blood streaming from his nose. Maura was crying helplessly, and the young servant girl in the hallway trembled with fright at the sounds coming from the parlour. The doorbell rang, and she went to answer it, her face lighting up with relief when she saw who the visitor was.

"Oh, Mister John, I'm that glad to see you, for there's terrible trouble in the house this night." She pointed shakily to the door of the parlour and John swung it open, his eyes rapidly taking in the terrible scene.

Maura swivelled around and John was shocked by her appearance. Her hair, always so elegantly piled at the back of her neck, now hung loosely about her face, which was puffy and blotched from crying.

"What's going on, man? Are you mad, frightening the daylights out of your family?"

"Oh, now here we have the real 'Honest Sullivan'," Vincent jeered, swaying towards him, for the row with his sons had been partly provoked by the effects of a half-bottle of poteen he had consumed earlier that evening. "It's *your* fault. Ever since you stepped inside my door, you were out to cause trouble for me; getting the workers in the lumber yard to organise a union, undermining my authority, even in my own house! Trying to get my boys to go back with you to Limerick . . . Your own lumber business, no less. My, hasn't the little shopkeeper mighty notions?" He moved towards John, his whole body shaking with fury.

Maura, bending over Steven, helped him to his feet, her handkerchief pressed to his face to stem the flow of blood.

"Paul, help your brother to his room. Everything will be fine. Uncle John is here now."

They hesitated, looking at John, and he nodded

reassuringly. His face was white and tense with anger. When the door had closed behind the two young men, Maura turned to her husband. She had no more tears left. It was time to stand up to him and say her piece, before she lost her nerve completely. She had nothing to lose now. Her boys would be going back to Limerick with John. He would make good, honest men of them, and she was glad they could depend on him. It was one worry off her mind.

"Vincent, the boys will go with John when he sails next week and I shall take up permanent residence at the immigrant welfare centre. All I needed was one final push to help me see things straight, and you've given me that, tonight."

"What are you talking about, woman? Where'll you be without your fine house, and your grand carriage?"

Maura looked at him steadily. "I did without them before, remember, Vincent? And I'll do without them, again. I'll be paid for my work at the centre; I don't want a penny from you. I'll have two comfortable rooms, and a roof over my head. So you can bring Helena Curley in to share the house with you for all I care, for I won't be here."

John stood back, admiring her for her courage. He didn't think she had it in her. From a mouse tiptoeing about the house, afraid of her husband, this crisis had turned her into a decisive, capable woman, her future mapped out independently, a future without Vincent.

"*You* can go to hell, for all I care. But there's no way those boys are going with my boyo here. They'll return to Harvard, and they'll finish their studies, or they'll feel the back of my hand." Vincent sat down triumphantly. He had won. That had knocked the spirit out of her.

Maura hesitated, then, straightening her shoulders. She looked her husband squarely in the eyes. "I didn't want to speak about this in front of John, but you leave me no choice. I know what happened in this house that night with Hannah, I was listening in my bedroom, and it's to my own discredit that I didn't come down and throw you out of the house. For you to take advantage of an innocent young girl . . . I don't know how you sleep at night, Vincent. Didn't your actress friend make herself available to you that night, Vincent? Were you so desperate for sport that you insulted a guest in our house by molesting her?" She was shouting at him, calling him names, years of frustration now released.

John came forward, pushing Maura gently to one side while he faced his brother. So that was what had happened. Poor Hannah, and she afraid to open her mouth, afraid that she wouldn't be believed no doubt. He lunged forward, seizing Vincent, squeezing his throat between his hands. He saw Vincent's face turn purple, his mouth open, a gurgling sound coming from his throat.

"John, for God's sake, the man's not worth it. Leave him go, there's a good man." Maura' s words reached him through the mist of rage. He released his hold, then backed away towards the door.

"I'm sorry, Maura, for all you've endured with my brother. I think I can say I'd be doing those sons of yours a favour by taking them back to Limerick with me. They're not suited to the corruption and immorality this fellow has been weaned on since he set foot in America."

He smiled suddenly. "I'm grateful to you, Maura, for telling me what happened with Hannah, for now I can repay you by taking care of your sons. They'll get a fifty per cent share in the timber business in Limerick; enough to set them up for life." He walked then, down the front steps and the long driveway, out the front gate and into the carriage. He would never set foot in the house again. Vincent was no brother of his.

Rebecca tried to force back the tears, but finally gave up the effort, her eyes filled with misery as she walked beside Paul into Central Park where they sat without speaking on one of the park benches.

"I'll be going to Ireland with Uncle John in a couple of weeks, as soon as I'm finished my exams. I can kiss Harvard goodbye and it doesn't matter what results I get because I'm going into the lumber business with John." His eyes lit up with enthusiasm, then he saw the look on Rebecca's face and became serious, his face filled with concern. "You can write to me and I'll write to you and as soon as I have enough money earned to be my own man, then I'll send for you and we can get married and live in Limerick for the rest of our lives." He looked at her earnestly. "We'll be happy, I promise you." He grasped her hand firmly in his own, looking deep into her eyes as though searching for some form of consent to his dreams.

She didn't answer him. Paul was a dreamer, refusing to see what was so obvious to her. Mama and Papa would never approve a marriage between them, especially now with Paul giving up his studies to follow his uncle to Ireland. They would never understand, and she didn't expect them to. And Paul was not Jewish. There was no question of her marrying outside her religion. All these thoughts flashed through Rebecca's mind as she saw the enthusiastic glint in Paul's eyes, such beautiful eyes, and such a handsome face, she thought, as she put out her hand to touch it.

"Mama and Papa, they are gone into the city shopping and the house is empty. If you like, we could go there and I'll make us some coffee?" Rebecca stopped short, embarrassed by her boldness. Maybe he would think she was 'flighty'. Her palms felt sweaty as she clenched them tightly together, afraid to look up into his face.

"I would love to come home with you and have some coffee," Paul said, gently.

She looked up then, saw the urgency in his face, desire naked in his eyes. She nodded slowly. They stood up, walking side by side through the park gates, oblivious to the knowing winks of passers-by until they came to the front gate of the Goldman home, where Paul paused for a moment until Rebecca gently pushed him in. He remembered the young prostitute in Little Italy, the way she had tried to coax him to come home with her to make a man of him. He could never compare Rebecca's shy invitation with hers. Instinctively, he knew that there would never be anyone else for him, and he felt sure it would be the same for Rebecca Goldman.

They sat on the bed and Paul took her gently in his arms, stroking her trembling body soothingly until she lifted her face to his and he bent and kissed her. Any inhibitions she might have felt previously were now gone completely in the sheer joy of their lovemaking.

The room was beginning to darken when Paul stirred drowsily, gently taking his arm from about her naked shoulders. She looked so beautiful, he thought suddenly. That such a beauty should love him so much, knowing the disapproval of her parents . . . It frightened him a little, too. This afternoon they had made love, the first time for both of them, and it had been all, and much more, than Paul had ever imagined. He had been to Heaven and back with Rebecca. She stirred in his arms, and he bent down and kissed her.

"I must go, Becca. It's getting late, and I don't want to be here when your parents walk through the door. Can you just imagine what they'd say?" They both exchanged looks. They weren't children any more. That afternoon they had become lovers and with it came the responsibility of adults.

She watched him as he dressed, her eyes caressing every movement of his body. "You're not ashamed, Paul? You don't think less of me because we did such a thing?" she asked, her voice no more than a whisper.

He pulled her close to him, not saying a word and she knew then. It had been special for Paul, also. There would be no regrets, only happiness that she had given him something beautiful to take with him to Ireland. She had loved him for so long, and she had given him the only thing she knew would prove that she loved him and would continue doing so, until the day she died.

Jonathan had worked constantly since coming back from America, his involvement with the Gaelic League now taking on a new impetus as he organised competitions in both Irish and English verse-speaking, singing and dancing competitions, rounding up teachers from all parts of the country. Young Sean Flannery he had taken a special interest in, struck by the boy's enthusiasm in getting little groups of boys and girls together in the Gaelic League Hall every Wednesday night. He was an intelligent boy, and Jonathan determined to see that he got a good education. If the boy's father had his way, he'd have been waiting on the docks, looking for a few days' work carting goods to and from the ships.

Jonathan made an agreement with Sean's father that if he allowed the boy to finish his schooling, Sean would be paid a wage with the Gaelic League. Sean's father had reluctantly agreed, and Ellen Flannery had told her neighbours proudly that Sean was one of Mr Mayhew's "right-hand men".

Jonathan's engagement to Madeline had come as no surprise to anybody, for Christine O'Shea and Celine Deery had waited with bated breath for the announcement for some time. Jonathan's proposal to Madeline had not been a passionate declaration of undying love, nor had she expected it to be so. She was a wise girl, and was grateful that he had finally laid the ghost of his past relationship with Hannah Benson to rest. Madeline had no illusions about herself. She was matronly in her ways. She was not a good conversationalist, was shy and awkward when meeting strangers, and only felt really relaxed when she and Jonathan were alone.

Jonathan had been sitting in the Deerys' parlour one evening after their return from New York, contemplating his purpose in coming to see Madeline. He had seen

Hannah with another man, a man who was obviously her husband, for her condition signified that she had been married for some time. He had been hurt and angry, but then he thought realistically, they had been separated for a long time. Hannah had made a new life for herself in America – why should she continue to hold any affection for him, no matter how strong he felt their bond was at the time? Madeline had been following him about like a comforting little shadow for weeks, aware that something was upsetting him, soothing him as only she could. Perhaps the time had come.

"Madeline, there is something I've been meaning to ask you for some time now." She sat by the window, her needlework in her lap, the needle poised expectantly in her raised hand.

"Yes, Jonathan?" Her composed face belied the nervous fluttering of her heart as she waited for him to speak, her needle once more moving back and forth across the flowered tapestry.

He crossed the room to where she sat, the lengthening shadow of the evening sunlight outlining her body against the casement window. She would never take the place of Hannah; there was no electrifying force drawing them close together, but Madeline had been his comfort, the gentle shadow by his side when he needed an antidote to his depression. They would make each other happy.

He gently removed the needlework from her lap and sat next to her, pulling her close to him. Her cheeks were flushed, her eyes bright with anticipation. "I want you to be my wife, Madeline," he murmured, brushing her lips with his. "Perhaps there is no great passion between us, and maybe there will never be, but I do love you and if you even have the remotest fondness for me, then I think we shall have a good marriage. Will you marry me, Madeline?" He waited for her reply, the silence in the room unnerving.

Finally Madeline held out her arms to him, her voice no more than a whisper. "I know you still have a soft spot in your heart for Hannah Benson, Jonathan. I'd be a fool to think otherwise." She stroked his cheek gently with her hand. "But I'm gone beyond the age to care about things that happened in the past. I want to be your wife, Jonathan, and I'll make you forget Hannah Benson, for I'll smother you with so much love you won't have the time or the inclination to think about what might have been!"

She smiled then, tears in her eyes, and he held her, tenderly at first, then as Madeline's kisses became more urgent, he pressed closer to her, his desire for her soft yielding body quickly aroused. He felt her breasts heaving against him, and uttered a low moan of desire. He closed his eyes and despite all efforts to rid his mind of the torment, he wished with all his heart the woman in his arms was his own beautiful Hannah.

The November edition of The Gaelic League monthly magazine, *Guth na nDaoine*, carried the notice on the front page.

'Miss Madeline Deery, daughter of Eamonn and Celine Deery, and Mr Jonathan Mayhew, ex-His Majesty's regiment, formally announce their engagement to be married.'

Peggy Benson sat and cried for poor Hannah when she

read it. She cried for her daughter's lost dreams, for the broken heart she must be nursing, for all Peggy's instincts told her that Jonathan Mayhew was the only man who ever mattered to Hannah.

John sent them news of Hannah's wedding, and praised Michael Murphy, saying what a good man he was. Peggy remembered her courtship with Peter – the excitement, the tenderness, the feeling of desire growing between them, and lamented that Hannah hadn't experienced the same youthful kindling of love. She knew her daughter could never love this older man, and her reasons for marrying him she would never understand. John was non-committal, simply saying that Hannah would write and explain everything in her own good time.

And Hannah did write, a letter that sent Peggy running to Annie, her face white with alarm. She handed the letter to her sister, unable to speak.

Annie read the first lines, holding her sister's hand tightly.

'Dear Mother, I can now tell you what I've been longing to tell you for so long. This morning, with my poor devoted Michael hovering outside the door of my bedroom, my baby was born, a beautiful blue-eyed golden-haired girl. I have written to John, telling him to explain everything to you, and I hope you'll forgive me for shutting you out for so long – but I had my reasons, darling Mother, and now that everything is over, I am so happy!'

Chapter 15

Christmas Eve 1910. The siren in the factory sounded at six o'clock sharp, indicating the end of the shift. The gates of Benson's Shirt Factory in Washington Place were opened and a steady stream of workers flooded through, laughing and heckling each other as they waved their pay packets in the air. "This will be a good Christmas, Isaac, even better than the others!" a small dark-haired man shouted to another, his face aglow with seasonal good cheer as he thought of the presents he could buy for the family with Hannah Benson's Christmas bonus.

"Don't spend it all at once, Boris!" Eily Mitchell laughed loudly as she passed him, her fashionable suit provoking whistles of admiration from the male workers. She loved every minute of her life in New York. Hannah had arranged for herself and Mary to stay in her old apartment in Albany on her own removal to Michael's house. They were "doing lines" with two Italian brothers, Joseph and Tony Guardino, who worked at the Singer sewing-machine factory in New

Jersey. Mary and Eily were both supervisors in Hannah's factories, Eily in Washington Place and Mary in the 14th Street block, Hannah's first New York venture. She was teaching the piece-workers lacemaking, and they had already established themselves by supplying the big stores on Madison Avenue with substantial orders.

Hannah had two dress shops in Manhattan as well as the factories, and Mary Fitzgerald, as dependable as a cornerstone, divided her time between the shops, seeing that they were always well-stocked, keeping a sharp eye on price variations in other dress shops, and reporting back to Hannah if they were selling items at lower prices than their own. Hannah would respond by advertising exclusive designs at sale prices, and the ladies of New York would flock to Hannah Benson's establishments, for a bargain was a bargain, no matter how much money you spent on it.

Hannah now lived in the exclusive area of Burough Park in Albany with Michael Murphy and her little girl, Peig, called after her own mother. Michael's business had made him one of the wealthiest men in New York, his building contracts taking him to almost every state in America. The railroads had opened the gates to new towns, with increasing populations and hotels and apartment buildings were in constant demand. Michael Murphy's name was synonymous with honesty and quality workmanship, and his chain of hotels were renowned for their exclusivity.

Hannah sat in the conservatory behind the house, surrounded by exotic plants, deep purple gardenias filling the air with their sultry perfume. The door opened and Michael appeared, a little girl clutching his hand obstinately.

"Mummy, I don't want Daddy to go away for Christmas.

Please tell him to stay with us! We can go to the ice show on Broadway and eat toasted popcorn, and maybe a ride on the carnival coaster on the way home."

"Here now, hold your horses, young madam!" Michael smiled down at her, protesting at her demands, but knowing that whatever she wanted he'd find himself hard-put to refuse her. He marvelled at her resemblance to her mother, the proud tilt to her chin, the golden mane of curls reaching below her waist. And then there were the eyes – his own dear Hannah's eyes repeated in the young lass.

Michael looked across to his wife for support, his heart missing a beat, for even now, after all the years they had been together, she still had the power to make him feel like a young lad walking out with a desirable lady. "There's nothing I can do about it, Hannah, my love. The weather is unusually mild for the time of year, and I have to be in Detroit to see to it that there's no slackening on the job. If the rains come then I'll have to lay them off for maybe a couple of months, and the contract won't be worth the paper it's written on!" He threw up his hands in resignation. "The perils of the building trade, I'm afraid. The weather is our worst enemy! I can just about manage to stay here for Christmas, but I must be in Detroit on St Stephen's Day and I'm that sorry to disappoint you both!" He put his arms about the two of them, Peig looking up at him tearfully. "Look, if I can manage to organise the men before the end of the week, I'll be high-tailin' it back here, and then we'll all go to the ice show at the end of the week. Is that a deal?" He winked at Peig, then lifted her up on his lap, hugging her close to him.

She twined her arms about his neck, whispering in his

ear, "I'll be waiting. You have until the end of the week to finish your business, and then you'll come back to New York, promise?"

Michael Murphy inclined his head solemnly, putting his hand on his heart. "You have the word of a true Irishman, my girl!"

Hannah laughed at the antics of the two of them, and Michael blessed the day he set eyes on the little seamstress from Limerick, for she had changed his life so completely that his happiness was frightening at times. He didn't know what he would do if anything ever happened to change their lives.

Christmas Day they spent alone, sitting in front of a blazing log fire in the parlour. Peig sat in a corner, playing with her little china doll dressed in pink satin with a little miniature apron tied about the waist. She sang and spoke to the doll in her own childish language, scolding and comforting at the same time as she cradled the doll to her, her antics lovingly watched over by Michael and Hannah.

Michael glanced at Hannah, his eyes twinkling good-humouredly. "She's the image of you, my love, and I'm that happy, sometimes I feel guilty for having so much good fortune in my life!"

Hannah looked at him, her eyes mirroring his love for her. There was no finer man in the whole world for her than this man who had so willingly committed himself to both her and little Peig.

They sat together, Hannah resting against Michael's shoulder on the divan by the fire, Peig's childish laughter echoing through the peaceful scenario – a scene Hannah was to remember with poignant clarity the rest of her life.

She had received a letter from her mother just before Christmas. She and Peggy had not seen each other since just after Peig had been born, when Peggy had come to New York, determined not to like Michael Murphy, the "cradle-snatcher" who had married her daughter, trapping her at a time when she was most vulnerable.

But the moment she had laid eyes on the rotund little man with the twinkling eyes, who looked as though he had never had a dishonest thought in his life, Peggy Benson had fallen under his spell. She had begged Hannah to tell her who Peig's father was, but Hannah had refused adamantly. She had put Vincent Sullivan out of her head forever, an unpleasant part of her life in New York best left in the past. Her mother need never know what had happened between them, and she had made Michael Murphy promise that he would keep her secret. Michael was only too happy to comply with Hannah's wishes. Vincent Sullivan was a bad lot, his appointment as Mayor of New York the result of a good many underhand deals with gambling houses and prostitution rackets.

Hannah took her mother's letter from her pocket now, reading it through once more while Michael nodded off beside her, his head slipping sideways as he snored gently. Florrie's second baby would be born in January. The first one, a little boy, was just one year old and a "holy terror" according to Peggy. Hannah's face became suddenly serious at her mother's next lines.

'Things are looking serious between May and Tom Gardiner, Hannah. He visits Limerick every month, by the by to see Martin Manley about orders, but I know there's been something going on

between them two for a long time now, and she still married to that McCarthy, and he into it up to his eyeballs with the IRB! If he should come looking for her, I don't know what I'd do! Dear God, Hannah, 'tis at times like this I need your sound advice. Taking after your poor father you are for the common sense!'

Hannah folded the letter thoughtfully. Maybe it was time to go home for a visit, if only to see how the shops and the factory were doing. She had made Martin a partner in the business, getting Edwin Carstairs to draw up the necessary papers. Even then she didn't have the nerve to go back to Limerick, couldn't bear the thought of seeing Jonathan Mayhew and his new bride riding through the city on their way to their new home in Southland House. So she had remained in New York, her business growing profitably each year, workers clamouring to be employed in her factories. She had insisted that they all join the International Garment Workers' Union, in that way lessening the risk of any worker's grievance resulting in a strike. There were no strikes in Hannah Benson's factories, because there was no reason for any. Large, well-built spacious premises, an eight-hour day, and a dollar an hour pay.

Yes, Hannah thought with pride, she had done well for herself in New York. But no matter how successful she was, there was always the longing to go back to Limerick, to walk through the narrow cobbled streets past the market place with the vendors shouting each other down. "Fresh chickens! Potatoes like balls of flour, miss! Herrings straight from the boat this morning." So different from the babble of foreign dialects in the Lower East Side, and yet so much the same.

Michael stirred and opened his eyes slowly. The clock in the hallway struck the hour of ten and he nodded in Peig's direction, the little girl sleeping comfortably on a cushion next to the fire.

"Tired out, the little *cailin*," he whispered, taking Hannah's hand in his, and pressing it close to his cheek. "Do you ever regret it, *a chroi*? Do you ever think maybe you'd have made a better life for yourself if you hadn't taken up with an old man like myself?" But the sight of Hannah's face glowing in the firelight was sufficient to quell his doubts.

She remembered the night, several months after Peig had been born, when Michael had come hesitantly to her room. He had stood in the doorway, his eyes wide with wonder as he watched her brush her hair loose from its pins, and she had turned to him, her arms held out, her eyes telling him it was time for them to be together as man and wife.

She had been apprehensive as he held her in his arms, whispering loving words in her ear, her body tense and unyielding beneath him. The memory of Vincent's violent lovemaking had still been fresh in her memory then, her failure to blot it out only adding to the tension of the moment. Michael had reassured her with tenderness and understanding and, when their lovemaking was over, she had lain back on the pillows, her body relaxed and filled with a warm feeling of contentment. He had shown her the other side of love, a side where anger and lust were replaced by tenderness and respect.

Hannah looked at Michael sitting beside her, the pungent smell of tobacco on his jacket. "I have been a lucky woman,

Michael Murphy. What a fool I'd be to have any regrets."

Michael left for Detroit the following day. Hannah stood at the front door, little Peig waving sadly as the shiny black Ford motor car drove slowly down the driveway and out the front gate. Hannah stood there for a long time, even after the car had disappeared from sight. She felt a strange sense of foreboding, as though something fateful was about to happen. She gripped Peig's hand tightly until she felt the little girl wince.

"Mummy, you're hurting me."

She relaxed her grip, and led her daughter back into the house.

Hannah whispered a quiet prayer that Michael wouldn't have to stay so long in Detroit. She hated it when he was away from home. She had come to depend on him so much, his faithful presence always there, to give advice about factories, to boost her morale at times when she felt despondent, missing her mother and sisters and dear Annie and John back home in Limerick. She closed the door firmly behind Peig. It wouldn't be long, please God, before Michael would be home again. They'd have a special New Year's Eve party, just the three of them.

Tony Guardino was frightened. He wouldn't have admitted it to anybody, not even to his own brother Joseph, but right now, he would gladly have gone back to Sicily, to work in the fields once more for a few miserly liras. Anything, rather than face El Padrone.

He knew they were looking for him. He had seen dark shadows following him from the factory after his night shift, had felt the dryness in his mouth as he gasped for breath, running, always running, away from the someone or something which threatened his very existence in the America.

El Padrone had got him the job in the Singer factory. He was earning enough money now to send a sizeable amount home to his mother in Palermo, and to put some aside for the day when he could move out of the disease-ridden Italian ghetto. That would be the day, he thought proudly, when Tony Guardino's name would be spoken with respect.

The neon light from the drug store across the street flashed ominously across his face as he crouched in the corner of the room. It was past eight o'clock. Eily would have finished her shift since six o'clock at the factory in Washington Place. It would take her an hour to cross through town to the tenement block where he and Joseph had rooms. Maybe they'd see her coming in. They'd notice that she called on Thursday every week, at exactly the same time, and then they would follow her, just as they were following him, and maybe they'd do something terrible to her. He couldn't bear to think about it, his beautiful Eily, her face disfigured with the mark of the 'Mafiosi', lying in some derelect shed by the harbour.

"Let the prayers of my mother be heard now," he whispered desperately. "Keep Eily safe. Please let nothing happen to her until I get things sorted out!" He looked down into the street, hiding behind the heavy brown faded curtains. Then he saw her. She was rounding the corner of the street, her face upturned to his, her hand half-raised in salute.

"Mother of Jesus!" he prayed silently. "Let her get into the house safely. Let nothing happen to her."

The man moved quickly, crossing the street to Eily. Tony watched as he said something to her, saw Eily's face, puzzled, then shake her head as if she didn't understand. Tony ran from the room, taking the stairs two at a time, pulling the hall door open just as Eily appeared before him, startled, as he pulled her inside quickly.

"Eily, Jesus get in, please! That man – what was he saying to you? You didn't tell him your name; please tell me you didn't tell him your name!" He spoke continuously as he pushed her ahead of him, up the stairs and into the room. He locked the door behind him, then leaned against it, his face pale with anxiety. Eily sat in the chair, frightened. She had never seen Tony so agitated, his hands trembling, his eyes darting about the room like a trapped animal.

"Tony, tell me – what's wrong? I know you're involved in something."

"How do you know?" he asked sharply. "Has Joseph been opening his big mouth? I wish to God he'd learn to keep silent about such things!"

Eily stood in front of him, silently asking herself what could she say to a man like this, a man whose past life in Sicily had been something similar to the terrorist activities James McCarthy was involved in back in Ireland? Only there was no comparison between the two men, Tony had a heart, and genuine feelings for Eily. That was why she must try to help him now.

They sat and talked until the early hours of the morning. Tony spoke of the Mafiosi, their activities in New Jersey, half of the Italian immigrants involved in some form of crime.

"El Padroni wanted me to do some running for them. The drugs they were importing, they wanted me to be their distributor, handing out little packets of white powder to vagrant fools who hadn't enough money for food, but lived for the white powder at five dollars a shot!" he shouted angrily until the whole room reverberated with his emotions, Eily moving closer to him, stroking his neck soothingly. She had heard of El Padrone and his drug smuggling, had seen the frightened looks on the faces of some of the girls in the factory. Bella, one of the Italian girls, had a brother who had disappeared mysteriously one night and later the police had found his mutilated body wrapped in sackcloth in an open barge down on the river.

"We could go away, Tony! We could get married and you could find a job away from the city." Eily's eyes were bright with hope, her hand held tightly in his. "We could go to Louisiana! I've heard some of the women saying that their men have gone there for the sugar harvest and maybe you could get a job there, where none of these men will find you."

Tony shook his head despondently. The idea had occurred to him, but they would follow him there.

"The man on the street, what did he say to you, Eily?" Tony asked, half-afraid of her answer. He knew the man to be a lackey for El Padrone, a spy who roamed the alleys and narrow streets of Little Italy, looking for new recruits for the organisation.

"He just asked me my name, and who I was visiting," Eily replied.

Tony looked at her keenly, puzzled at the blush spreading from the neck of her ruffled lace blouse to her forehead. "Did you –"

"No! If you must know, Tony Guardino, I told him it

was none of his business who I was, or who I was visiting, and then he told me to watch my lip or he'd have the tongue cut out of me."

"What did you say to him Eily?" Tony waited, anxious for her reply. Nobody spoke to the Mafiosi the way Eily had spoken tonight. He was surely a dead man after her outburst. Eily looked up at him obstinately.

"I told him there was many the one who would thank him for ridding them of the tongue of Eily Mitchell!"

Tony laughed aloud. He laughed until the sound reached the landing, floating down the stairs and into the hallway where Joseph Guardino, his foot poised on the first step, looked up in surprise. It couldn't be Tony. Tony who had been so morose these past few days, his head filled with dark thoughts, filled with nightmares each night as he woke drenched in a cold sweat. He opened the door of the room and saw Eily, a satisfied look on her flushed face as she watched Tony, his face streaming with tears of laughter.

"Joseph, come here and listen to what my brave, beautiful woman has said to Augusto. Never will he be the same man again after the sting from her wicked tongue!"

Joseph smiled. It was good to see Tony like this. Tonight he would cook some spaghetti for the three of them, and they would open a bottle of wine, and laugh and forget the shadows lurking outside, and the threats of the Mafiosi.

"Ah, Antonio, there's a good boy. Come, sit here, where I can see you." The hoarse voice called to him from the depths of the leather-backed chair behind the oak desk.

Tony hesitated, then felt himself being shoved roughly forward. His eyes were sore from the restrictive blindfold that had been tied tightly about them. He blinked several times, trying to focus on the face of the man sitting there, only the swirl of foul-smelling smoke from his cigar intimating his presence.

They had finally caught up with him. Their tentacles were at the ready once more to draw him into the organisation, and he could see no way clear to escape.

"Antonio – you know what we want of you and what's the use in being difficult? What would your Mama think of you, back home in Sicily, to turn away from your birthright? The Mafiosi legacy is a worthy one, not to be discarded lightly." The subtle threat in the voice was not lost on Tony. He shivered as he stood before the man, and knew that he would do as he was told, because there were too many other people connected with him who would be hurt if he did otherwise.

As though reading his thoughts, the man's voice wheezed breathlessly at him, his words wrapping a cold band of ice about Tony's heart. "Your girl, she is so nice, Antonio, a bit too forward maybe, not like a good, obedient, Italian girl, but she can be taught our ways, you understand Antonio? And your brother, Joseph, he is a good boy, but a little stubborn. Maybe if you were to have a word with him now that I have made things clear to you . . ."

Tony nodded. "What do you want me to do?" The man stood up from behind the desk, grasping Tony's hand in his. It felt cold and clammy, like the skin of a snake against his palm.

"That's a good boy! I only want you to do what you have

always done for the organisation. Deliver a few parcels, keep your eyes and ears open. An apprentice to Augusto, eh?"

The men standing behind Tony laughed nervously at the man's attempt at wit. "You will keep on your job at the factory by day, but by night you will work for me, Antonio, and I will get you a good tailor, so that you can dress respectable, eh?" He smiled then, a slow, gratified smile. "You will be treated well, Antonio, with more money in your pocket than you have ever dreamed of. The promise of the New World, yes?" He laughed then, the other men laughing with him out of fear rather than amusement.

Tony was blindfolded again before he was led down some stairs, through what seemed to be a narrow hallway, and out into the street. Then he was bundled into the same car that had driven him to the meeting with the Mafiosi and when it eventually came to a halt, he was thrown unceremoniously out on to the pavement.

"We'll be seeing you, Tony!" He heard them laughing as the car sped away, then slowly he pulled the dirty blindfold from his eyes. He was lying in the gutter outside his lodgings, Joseph's concerned face peering down at him from the window. He picked himself up slowly, then went up the steps to the front door. He hesitated for a moment, trying to unravel the churned-up thoughts in his head.

He wouldn't say anything to Joseph or Eily. It would only mean trouble for them if they knew too much. He knew his new-found wealth would come under the keen scrutiny of Eily, but he could always tell her he had been promoted at the factory. It was better this way. If he did what he was told, maybe in a few years when he had enough money put together he could cut all ties with the organisation. For the moment, he was just a little fish in a large pond. His time would come. All he had to do was to wait.

Raised voices could be heard coming from Senan O'Looney's office in Limerick. The early days of the New Year 1911 had been volatile ones in the newspaper office. Young Sean Flannery averted his eyes from the door, embarrassed, for he respected both Senan and Jonathan and hated to hear them at odds with one another.

Jonathan wanted to go home to Madeline. He shouldn't even be here, but he had to get it off his chest, the anger he felt inside had to be voiced to Senan. He was fed up trying to make him see that the Gaelic League was becoming a front for the Republicans. Two articles had already appeared in last month's edition of *The Limerick Lamp*, praising the bravery of the IRB 'our lads who scuttled a consignment of arms off Kinsale Head to avoid handing them over to the authorities'.

"Who was it who printed those pieces of Republican propaganda? Can you answer me, Senan?" Jonathan had raged on and on. "Are we becoming a propaganda machine for revolutionaries?" He thumped his fist on Senan's desk angrily and Senan looked at him with raised eyebrows.

"Impartiality is the key word, Jonathan. We print it as we see it. The truth cannot be hidden no matter where our loyalties lie." He gazed at him directly. "Maybe your friend Hyde has had a change of heart. Maybe he's given up the struggle to keep politics out of the League," Senan had returned, equally annoyed. "Sure everybody knows them

Republicans are mad for a bit of notice. They won't get it anywhere else only in the newspapers, if the League are fool enough to print it."

"Hyde would never agree to turning the League into a political machine, and if the IRB are trying to get in by the back door, then I'm getting out! They're a dangerous bunch, and I have Madeline and the child to consider. I will never allow the name of Mayhew to be associated with any subversive force!"

Jonathan frowned impatiently at Sean Flannery, who was shifting from foot to foot at the door, then he went home to Southland House, to Madeline who was expecting their child any minute, a miracle according to the specialist they had gone to see in Dublin after Madeline had complained with pain in her left side shortly after they were married. A blocked ovary had been diagnosed and her chances of ever conceiving a child were not very favourable.

As he entered the house, Robert O'Shea met him in the hallway, his face troubled. "Jonathan, Madeline has just started and I must warn you, this is going to be a difficult birth – she is not so strong."

"What's the matter? Can I see her?" He went towards the staircase, but Robert stopped him, reaching out to him with a persuasive touch on the arm. Jonathan looked at his brother-in-law fearfully. If anything should happen to Madeline, or to the child – he couldn't even bear to think about it. Madeline would be fine, and they would have a healthy child, boy or girl, it didn't matter just as long as Madeline and the baby would come through safely.

"The baby is a breach, Jonathan. I'm doing my best to turn it into the birth position, but Madeline is a small woman, and she is already so worn out trying to cope with the birth contractions."

Robert O'Shea had seen many such births before. He had seen them in the slums in the back streets of Limerick, mothers roaring with pain, their faces contorted in agony as they tried to give birth to babies, some already dead because they were in the breach position. He prayed that this wouldn't be the case with Madeline. The contractions were becoming stronger, and unless he could turn the baby soon, her heart wouldn't stand much more of it.

"Wait here – I'll call you if I need you."

Christine O'Shea sat next to Madeline's bed, her brow furrowed as she looked down at her sister-in-law's drawn face. It was a difficult labour, even worse than her own all those years ago when she panted and moaned in agony to give birth to little Emma. Madeline's face was bloated, her cheeks chalk-coloured, her lips almost purple. She grasped Christine's hand tightly, staring up at her with eyes full of pain.

"If anything should happen to me, Christine, promise me you'll look after Jonathan and the little one."

"Hush, Madeline! What nonsense! You'd swear you were the only woman in the world having a baby!" Christine spoke angrily, trying to hide her apprehension. She knew, from the look on Robert's face, that things weren't going well. Almost two days in labour was not a healthy sign.

Madeline persisted, ignoring her protests. "Maybe we shouldn't have interfered, Christine. Oh, I know you were anxious to break the bond between Jonathan and Hannah, but in all the years I've been married to him, there was still that ghost in our lives. I never really believed that he belonged to me completely." She lay back on her pillow, exhausted, tears streaming down her pale cheeks. "He loved her, you know. I think he will never love another woman the way he loved Hannah Benson!"

Christine O'Shea remained silent, knowing that all Madeline said was true. Jonathan's writing was his antidote to the yearning in his heart for Hannah. His work with the Gaelic League had been another blessed encumbrance, keeping him from delving too deeply into the past and what might have been. If Christine was to be honest with herself, she would have to admit that she had done more harm than good. Hannah's name was on the lips of all the titled ladies who travelled regularly to New York to purchase from her elegant shops in Madison Avenue. There had been a photograph of her in *The Irish Times*, opening her new shirt-making factory in Brooklyn, a tall handsome lady with the proud air of a successful businesswoman.

She had been wrong in thinking they were never suited for each other. Hannah had tried to escape her misery by remaining in America, isolated from people and places reminding her of her lost love. Jonathan had married Madeline on the rebound, hoping in some way to find a little of the magic he had enjoyed with Hannah, and in the end settling for second-best. Madeline knew this; Christine O'Shea knew it. The guilt she now felt was an almost unbearable burden in her heart.

Robert O'Shea went to the door of the bedroom. He called wearily to Jonathan, his brother-in-law bounding up the stairs two at a time, his face grey with worry.

"Come, Jonathan. You should be with your wife at this time. She needs you."

Jonathan entered the room quietly, going across to Madeline's bed, and lifting her head gently against his shoulder. "Well, my love, will our baby be born soon? Or does the little one insist we wait still further before it condescends to enter into this mad world of ours?" Jonathan smiled down at his wife, seeing the look of hopelessness in her eyes. He couldn't bear it if anything happened to her. Madeline was his life now.

Christine left them alone, her eyes moist with tears. Madeline's strength had weakened, her pulse faint as she pressed her hand into Christine's before she left the room. Her expression frightened Christine, as though she was trying to say goodbye.

Jonathan remained in the room throughout the night, Robert O'Shea working feverishly to save Madeline and her unborn child. As the first light broke through the half-drawn curtains, the baby finally made its sad journey into the world, a little girl with dark curly hair, a tiny smile on her lifeless face. Two hours later, Jonathan held Madeline in his arms for the last time, tears coursing down his cheeks onto her damp hair. He remained in that position until Robert finally dragged him away, the taller man leaning against him for support, his body heaving in spasms of grief.

Madeline and the baby were buried side by side in Kileen churchyard and after the funeral Jonathan locked himself away in Southland House, refusing to see visitors, the curtains drawn in his bedroom as he consumed bottle after bottle of whiskey. He remained in the house for two weeks, after which Senan O'Looney decided to take matters into his own hands. He called to see him one evening after he had closed the newspaper offices and delivered an ultimatum to a slovenly, bearded Jonathan, his eyes bloodshot from lack of sleep and the effects of the whiskey. Senan was shocked by his appearance.

"Now listen to me, man. I'll not have you sittin' in this big house feelin' sorry for yourself. Madeline wouldn't have wanted it; indeed she'd have been repulsed to see you in this condition."

"And what would you know about it, Senan," Jonathan cried out in anger, "an old bachelor like you who never had the good fortune to have a woman like Madeline by your side!" The words of anger tumbled out, while Senan just stood there calmly waiting for the tirade to cease.

When Jonathan had finally exhausted himself, he sat down wearily, his head resting in his trembling hands.

"Well now, that you've got that out of your system, I want to propose something to you. A partnership in the newspaper – fifty-fifty, on one condition, that you pull your weight alongside myself and give over your self-pity, for I won't stand for it. Do you hear me?" Senan bellowed at Jonathan, his fiery red hair standing up wildly as he paced up and down the room. Jonathan thought of Madeline and his dead child. Madeline had been his solace when Hannah had left him.

Now Senan was offering him a ray of hope in his present despair. The newspaper was all that was left to him. From now on, the newspaper would be his life. Nothing else would matter.

Jonathan wrote another play, and Douglas Hyde accepted

it for the Abbey, calling to see him at Southland House after Madeline's death. Jonathan had worked constantly on the play after his day at *The Limerick Lamp* was finished, sometimes falling asleep over his writing.

"This is a good one, Jonathan," Douglas Hyde enthused. "One from the heart, and there's no need to ask where the inspiration came from." He looked sharply at Jonathan, saw the dark hair so recently sprinkled with grey, the hollow cheeks, the jacket hanging loosely on shrunken shoulders. The man had put his whole soul into this play, and by God, he was going to get acclaim for it. "We should be ready in two weeks' time. We'll get a cast together, and advertise it in *Guth na nDaoine*."

"Have you made up your mind about the League? Is it still apolitical, or will you allow the Republicans to join?" Jonathan asked him, his expression ponderous. He had made up his mind that he would resign from the League if it became a propaganda ploy for the IRB. He had no wish to belong to an organisation promoting the violence of republicanism.

"As long as I'm in charge of the Gaelic League, there'll be no politics involved, I give you my word," Hyde affirmed. Jonathan nodded, satisfied.

Michael Murphy wasn't feeling well. He had remained in bed all day in his hotel room overlooking the building site. He had a good foreman in charge, one who kept the lads on their toes, so he had no worries there. The weather seemed to be holding too, so there would be no profit lost on 'wet time'. He lay back on his pillows, the pain across his chest intensifying. As he reached out to the glass of water by his bedside, the pain shot like a scorching blade through his heart. He cried out in alarm, then took a few deep breaths, in and out, slowly, more slowly still, until gradually the pain subsided and his breathing became easier.

There was a knock on the bedroom door and the foreman appeared, his face concerned. "Are you all right, Mr Murphy? You don't seem so well. Maybe I could call a doctor?"

"No, no, Pat. Leave it be. I'm just tired after the journey from New York. Damn motor cars, they're a nuisance! They take twice as long to get from A to B. Next time I'll take the train!" He smiled weakly at the man. No use alarming people over a simple pain in the chest. He swung his legs off the bed and straightened his clothes. "Come on! I'm like an oul' woman lolling in the bed all day. We'll go over and see how things are progressing. There'll be no fat bonus for any to us if Clayton Heston's hotel isn't finished on time!"

The lift cranked its way up the side of the scaffolding, two floors, three floors, four floors, up to the eighth floor where they got out onto the rickety timber catwalk supported by cement blocks and wooden beams. Michael looked about him with satisfaction. He never got tired of viewing the sights from the lofty perches of his half-finished 'skeletons'. He could feel the breeze ruffling his hair, blowing softly against his skin as he stood, his face turned upwards, gazing at the patches of white and blue sky penetrating the maze of scaffolding.

He closed his eyes for a moment, and a picture of Hannah and Peig came into his head, just as they had been on Christmas Day. The shout startled him. He wheeled around quickly, saw Pat stagger backwards towards the edge of the catwalk, the nightmare drop below him. Michael grabbed him by the hands, summoning all his strength to hold him, while the men below shouted excitedly, each holding a corner of a tarpaulin sheet, waiting to catch them.

Michael felt his grip relax and Pat's eyes widened in fear. "Mr Murphy!" he shouted hoarsely.

"I can't hold on, Pat! The pain, oh God, the pain!"

Pat slipped from his grasp to the safety blanket below. Clambering out of it, he pointed upwards. "It's Mr Murphy. He's had some kind of attack! Look!" The men watched, horrified, as Michael swayed high above them on the wooden platform, then keeled sideways, banging his head against the scaffolding. He stumbled backwards, falling as though in slow motion, not a sound from his lips, his body hitting the ground with a sickening thud. They ran then, across the rubble and debris of the building site to where Michael Murphy lay, blood oozing from his mouth and the side of his head. His black hat lay incongruously unharmed beside him. One of the men bent down to check Michael's pulse, then looked up at his companions, his face grey with fear. He shook his head slowly, while they blessed themselves over the body and covered it carefully with the sheet of tarpaulin that had saved Pat's life. Michael Murphy, one of New York's most colourful businessmen, was going home by train after all.

Hannah and Peig stood side by side at the graveside. Peig buried her face in the folds of her mother's coat, her little face puzzled, not understanding the grief of the moment. Hannah held her close, her own face hidden beneath the black veil of mourning. The whole of New York seemed to have turned out for the funeral, all Michael's good friends and business associates, people who had come to know and respect him since he had emigrated from Ireland so long ago. John came for the funeral, and he stood by Hannah now, his presence comforting as the final prayers were said over the coffin, and she watched it being lowered into the earth.

She couldn't cry. She had felt the same at her father's funeral, unable to unleash the pent-up grief eating away inside her, feeling only anger and betrayal at the injustice of a God who could be so cruel.

"Will you be coming back with me now, Hannah girl? Sure wouldn't it be better for you to be at home with your mother at such a time?"

"No, Uncle John," Hannah replied, sighing resignedly. "I'll stay here in New York. Sure I'd have nothing to do at home in Limerick, with Martin and Florrie managing the business now. My life is here with little Peig."

John said no more. It wasn't the time to argue with her, he knew she had her mind made up, and it would be a hard task to try to change it.

Hannah saw a man approaching, his figure vaguely familiar, his bloated cheeks almost hiding the narrow, cold eyes. She shook involuntarily, holding on to John for support. John waited as Vincent came nearer, his head bowed solicitously. Maura Sullivan stood beside Hannah, staring into the deep hole in the ground in front of her. The cold breeze whipped her face into a raw, red colour. She wished with all her heart that it was Vincent and not Michael Murphy who lay inside the coffin. Michael Murphy had been a good man, a man who had done much for the city of New York, his fine skyscraper buildings enhancing the industrial climate of a city forging its way successfully into the twentieth century.

"Hello, Hannah, you've been keeping well by all accounts, a right little businesswoman, eh?" Vincent put out his hand to her as she stood at Michael's graveside, and Hannah backed away, while Peig stared up at the big man with childish awe.

"You should have stayed away, Vincent. You have no place here today," John hissed angrily. He was ashamed of his brother. There had been no contact between them since their last confrontation, and that was the way John wanted things to stay.

"If there's anything you need, Hannah . . ." Vincent went on, ignoring his brother, "or the child?" He looked at Peig. There was something about her, a look that reminded him of Paul and Steven when they were children. Hannah wanted to shield the child from him, from his gaze that might suddenly turn into one of unbearable comprehension. He must never find out. She was Michael's child, for he had showered enough love on her to put any father to shame. He had adored her, and Hannah would never see that right taken from him, even in death.

"We want nothing from you, Vincent Sullivan," she said coldly. "Michael has seen that myself and Peig are taken care of, and I am a businesswoman in my own right, don't forget. I'll want for nothing!"

She turned away then, John walking beside her, Peig holding a hand of each of them.

Vincent stood staring after them thoughtfully. Hannah

had spoilt him for other women. Even bold, brassy ones the likes of Helena Curley could no longer satisfy him after he had had a taste of Hannah's soft, struggling body. And the child, there was something about her. He turned away, his brow furrowed with bemusement.

Jonathan's play ran for almost six weeks at the Abbey in Dublin, the theatre packed to full capacity each night, upper-class and working-class patrons mingling together in full-blooded enjoyment of the show. *Tinker's Curse* had been written during the long nights of loneliness spent in his room, a photograph of Madeline in front of him on his writing desk. The story opened with a young travelling peddlar 'with raven hair and beguiling tongue' coming to a village, selling his pots and pans, coloured hair ribbons and a medley of items that would take a woman's fancy. The young daughter in the manor house on the edge of the town came under his spell, and he made love to her under the stars on the banks of the river flowing through her father's lands. She begged him to take her with him, for she would surely find no other man as warm and true as her gipsy lover.

The audience sat enraptured as the story unfolded, the girl's father riding out in pursuit of his daughter and the vagabond gipsy. For almost a year he searched for her and eventually found her in a damp, cold cave on a hillside, her baby about to be born. She begged her father to forgive her and, when the child was born, to take him back to the fine house which she had left behind, for her gipsy had absconded, leaving her alone in her plight. Tears of compassion were shed all over the theatre as the young girl died giving birth, and the grief-stricken father buried his daughter with her infant son, still-born, on the cold hillside.

The girl looked so like Madeline that tears came to Jonathan's eyes as he sat in the wings listening to the thunderous applause, everybody standing now and calling for him to present himself. He stood in the spotlight, a lump in his throat, and suddenly, from deep inside him, he could feel the gentle touch of a healing process which had tentatively begun. An overwhelming sense of relief washed over him, the vision of Madeline's gentle, smiling face less painful as he bowed to the audience, the waves of applause rousing his dulled senses.

He would bring the play to New York. He felt a passion for the New World, for the excitement generated by the melting pot of different nationalities who frequented New York theatre, an audience so different from home, and whose different cultures put a new interpretation on the theme of his plays.

Once more he found himself booked on a passage to New York, in the spring of 1911, his play to run for four weeks at the Tivoli Theatre in Manhattan. Jonathan's last play in New York, *The Darlin' of Erin*, was still remembered there, and the theatre was heavily booked for *Tinker's Curse*.

The Irish element in the audience clapped and stamped their feet appreciatively, the Italians shouting *"Bella! Bella!"* as the final curtain fell. It was the last night and Jonathan felt drained. He had sat through every performance, each night for four weeks, afraid to stay alone in his hotel room, old memories revisiting him with haunting clarity. Madeline had been with him the last time, had smiled up at him encouragingly, her eyes glowing with pride.

"Author! Author!" came the cry from the audience. He stepped out into the spotlight, the applause deafening. Flowers were showered onto the stage, Jonathan's name on every woman's lips as he appeared, tall and distinguished, the slight limp as he walked across the stage endearing him to each one of them. The Irishmen in the audience slapped each other heartily on the back, proudly proclaiming, "He's one of our own, you know, an Irishman through and through!"

Jonathan's eyes wandered to the theatre box in the balcony where he had last seen Hannah, and he raised a hand to his eyes, wondering if perhaps he was dreaming. He would wake up soon and find himself at home in Southland House, his half-finished play by his side. But no, it wasn't an illusion.

She was there, in the same box, and as he stared up at her she half stood, her smile uncertain. Then slowly, she raised a gloved hand, and for a moment they were alone in the theatre. Then, as quickly as she had appeared before his eyes, she was gone, swallowed up in the surging crowds as they made their way to the exit.

He would have allowed Hannah to walk away now, become lost in the crowd and return to her husband, a man who must surely be the happiest man in New York tonight, but for one single object he had seen fastened about her white neck. It was the little silver locket he had given her that last Christmas they had been together. She was wearing it tonight, and had made a special point of showing it to him as she stood there, her eyes holding his in a mutual bond of hope. He had to speak with her. He couldn't go back to Ireland without seeing her once more.

"Uncle John, it was the most wonderful evening, and such an enjoyable play!" Hannah had gone to the theatre this evening, one part of her heart wanting to stay away, the other part longing to catch a glimpse of him, if only to satisfy her belief that Jonathan Mayhew no longer meant anything to her. Michael had been like a father to her, always there when she needed him, and when he died she thought the stability of her life would surely be shattered forever. But she had to guiltily acknowledge that almost two months after his death her life, far from being shattered, had taken on a new meaning.

She had once more entered into the pulsing life of the Lower East Side, going from factory to factory, meeting with her employees, solving any working dilemmas. Michael had frowned on these outings and had always insisted that she should be accompanied. Now she was free once more to do as she pleased, even enjoying the raucous humour of a few unsavoury street vendors, and loving every minute of it. She had almost forgotten what it was like to be her own woman. No matter how amiable and good-natured Michael had been, or how much she had respected him, he had still been her husband, the man whose hands held the bridle on her impulsive nature. Now she was free as a bird, missing Michael, but relieved at her newfound independence.

"Will you not come back with me this time, girl, and bring little Peig with you? It would do your mother good to see you; she hasn't been well this long time."

Hannah turned to John sharply. "Is that why you've come over, Uncle John? What's wrong with Mother? Is it serious?"

John looked doubtful. Peggy Benson was a shadow of the woman she had been when she had first come to Limerick. Annie thought it was the worry of Hannah being so far away.

"She worries about May. She goes to Dublin now every few weeks to see Tom Gardiner, even though she won't admit it. And your mother can't sleep at night thinking of James McCarthy and what he'd do to her if he ever met up with her again."

Hannah sank slowly into an armchair. She had been a selfish fool, thinking only of her own problems when her mother needed her so badly. "What's happening over there, Uncle John? We hear such rumours about the war. Will Redmond involve us, do you think?"

"I don't know what will happen, girl. That speech he made at Woodenbridge calling on the Volunteers to join the British army and fight in Europe, that was the biggest mistake he ever made. Sure the IRB made a great show of solidarity, saying that they'd fight for no other country but their own, calling themselves the National Volunteers now. There's trouble brewing, and no mistake!"

And James McCarthy will be in the thick of it, Hannah thought grimly. Fighting for his country, and beating up women as a sideline. She made a quick decision. "When are you leaving for home, Uncle John?"

"I've booked the steamer for next weekend, and two bookings in reserve!" He smiled at her, a mischievous twinkle in his eyes. "Sure didn't I know the kind of woman you are, soft behind that fierce independent coat you wear all the time!"

She laughed softly. It would be good to be back home again, if only for a little while. She would see Florrie and the children, and May, see what was happening between herself and Tom Gardiner. She was so much older now, and wiser. Sometimes when she looked in the mirror, she could see the beginning of little thread lines etching her clear blue eyes, and grimaced resignedly. None of them was getting any younger. And she would show off little Peig to everyone, maybe even see a smile cross the face of Mother Mary of the Angels as Peig entertained her with her infectious humour. And there was Jonathan. Her heart missed a beat whenever she thought of him, for he was a torment to her soul, the locket she had kept hidden until this very night a constant reminder of his gentle hands as they fastened the chain about her neck. She had to speak with him, had to find out if he returned her feelings. Her mother had written to her, telling her about Madeline and the child, and her heart bled for his sadness, a sadness she had experienced on the death of her dear Michael.

Jonathan had searched the sea of faces outside the theatre in vain. Hannah was not among them. He had made enquiries at the box office, asking the wide-eyed girl behind the ticket desk if she had seen a beautiful woman dressed in black silk with a silver locket about her throat. The girl had shaken her head firmly. There had been too many people in the theatre tonight, and many women wore black silk, especially the wealthy women who sat on the balcony. He felt defeated. New York was a big city, and Hannah could be living in any one of the business areas stretching from Manhattan to Flatbush. It was hopeless.

He was about to turn away, despondent, when he saw a woman looking at him, an uncertain smile on her face. She was a handsome-looking woman, silvery hair piled high on top of her head. A woman in her late fifties, Jonathan surmised. She hesitated for a moment, obviously wanting to talk to him, but unsure how to start.

"Mr Mayhew? I believe you were enquiring about a woman? Forgive me, but I couldn't help but overhear, and the name you gave is known to me. You see, Hannah Benson, but she isn't Hannah Benson, you see. She is recently widowed – her name is Mrs Murphy." She came nearer to him, saw his eyes light up with hope.

"You are?"

"My name is Maura, Maura Sullivan. My brother-in-law John is Hannah's uncle."

Jonathan felt that some marvellous twist of fate had brought this woman here tonight. He took her hand, looking intently into her face. "People say it's a small world, and if it is, it has been to my advantage tonight, for I know John Sullivan well and his good wife Annie." Maura studied the man's expression, the intensity of his feelings written all over his face. He was in love with Hannah. Maura knew the time had come at last to right the wrong Vincent had done to the girl.

Hannah and John sat on the verandah of the house in Burough Park watching Peig as she danced about the front lawn, trying to catch butterflies, laughing delightedly as they escaped her grasp. Everything was arranged for their trip home, the steamship leaving at ten o'clock the following morning.

"I'm a little bit frightened, you know, Uncle John," Hannah confided, hoping for some reassurance that she was doing the right thing in going back to Limerick.

He grasped her hands in his warmly. "It's time you

brought little Peig home to see her own people, Hannah, and sure you'll have no problems here while you're away. You made a good choice when you brought over Mary and Eily to work in the factories. My God, look how much you've achieved since Peter Benson first brought you to Limerick in the horse and cart!" He looked at her in admiration, and for all her sophistication, saw beneath the cool exterior, the little Hannah Benson who had stood before him that first night in Limerick, dressed so plainly in her simple Sunday dress, her young face full of ambition.

"I do miss them all at home. I thought I could stay over here forever, cut all ties with the past. I have another life in New York, a good life, secure in the knowledge that May and Florrie are capable of taking charge back home. So what's come over me all of a sudden, Uncle John? Besides my mother wanting to see me, there's something else inside me, always, tearing at my heart. Michael used to say to me, 'You'll never be happy, Hannah, for you've a yearning inside you that can't be satisfied.' What if he's right, Uncle John? Will the rest of my life be one long struggle to accomplish even more?" She was on the verge of tears, leaning her head against his shoulder, trying to take comfort from his strength.

"You're feeling down, girl. It isn't so long since Michael died, and you're still trying to get over it."

"But that's the trouble, John! I am over it! Sometimes I feel so guilty for not grieving more for him, for he was a good, honest man who loved me and Peig with all his heart." She shook her head sadly, her eyes veiled with tears. "Sometimes I think my marriage to Michael was all a dream. The years I spent with him seemed to pass so quickly, and now there's nothing left. I can't even recall his face clearly. Is that not a terrible thing for a wife to say of her dead husband?"

John felt helpless, unable to offer any words of comfort. Annie had been his one true love for as long as he remembered. If anything should happen to her, he knew he would keep the memory of her dear face fixed firmly in his mind for an eternity.

A shadow fell across the lawn, the tall figure of a man standing still, watching Peig as she played, her hair falling like a cloak of brilliant gold about her shoulders. Hannah shielded her eyes from the sunlight, trying to identify the visitor's face.

"Are you expecting someone today, Hannah?" John asked, looking curiously at the man as he approached.

"No, all my business affairs are in order," Hannah began, "and Mary and Eily will see to things." She stopped. The sun felt hot on her head, the sound of bees humming, the scent of the flowers so hypnotically pungent that she felt almost light-headed. She was dreaming. She was sitting by the Shannon river, watching the boats cross the finishing line, the rousing cheer as the winners of the regatta held their trophy aloft. Suddenly there was no New York, no Vincent Sullivan, not even her own dear Michael – just Hannah and Jonathan sitting on the grassy bank, his hand stroking her cheek so tantalisingly.

"Hannah, are you all right, girl?" John's voice seemed to come from a great distance. The man came slowly up the steps of the verandah and stood in front of Hannah. The years melted away.

"I wanted to speak with you at the theatre that night but I couldn't find you." Jonathan spoke in a broken whisper, his lips trembling as he held out his arms to Hannah.

She couldn't move. She had wanted him for so long, and now that he was finally here, she was afraid to touch him for fear that it was only a dream.

John gazed from one to the other, realisation dawning on him. He was intruding. This was a moment when lovers should be together, a private moment for two people who had found each other again. He called to Peig on the lawn.

"Come, my love, we'll go into the house and have some cool lemonade. Your mother will be busy, I think, for a long time!" He smiled slyly at Hannah and she nodded gratefully.

Jonathan's eyes never left Peig as she followed John into the house. "So like you, Hannah, it's uncanny! I thought I was seeing things when I saw the two of you together."

They sat together, and when he took her hand and pulled her close she didn't move away. She wanted the moment to last forever. If he should go away again she would surely die, for there was no other man in the world who could make her feel so complete, so utterly contented.

"There are so many things to explain, Hannah, so many things I didn't understand."

She put a finger to his lips, her eyes filled with such tenderness that he reached out and pulled her body closer, his mouth suddenly on hers. Impulsively, he reached for the pins holding her hair, loosening them one by one, watching, fascinated, as the burnished gold mane came tumbling down her back. "The most beautiful hair in the world," he whispered and Hannah smiled through her tears.

Chapter 16

At the end of September Peggy had received a cable from Hannah. "She's coming home at last, thanks be to God!" Peggy breathed softly.

Annie watched her sister covertly, a worried frown on her brow. There was a change in Peggy these last few months, sitting in her room most of the day staring vacantly through the window, her needlework untouched. It would do her good to see Hannah once more. Maybe that was all she needed, the reassurance that Hannah was well, after all she had been through. Please God, she'd stay at home this time.

Florrie heard the child cry aloud in her sleep. She turned in the bed, reluctant to leave her cosy position tucked in beside Martin. Martin muttered sleepily, "The little one, Florrie, she needs seeing to," then turned once more on his side, snoring loudly. Florrie sighed. There was no getting away from it. She got up wearily and crossed the room to the cradle. The baby, just about to unleash another yell, stopped as soon as Florrie's face appeared, a big toothless smile on her face. "Well now, *alannah,* is it restless you are to see your famous Aunt Hannah? And she coming home to us tomorrow, please God!"

She picked the baby up in her arms and sat in the chair by the bedroom window, the silvery light of dawn breaking through the night sky. She'd be glad to see Hannah again. It seemed so long ago since she had left Limerick. They'd surely be like strangers to each other. Hannah was so used to the sophisticated ways of New York. Maybe she'd look down her nose at them, or find fault with the way Martin was running the business. Though God knows, there was no need to, for he had trebled the profits in the last couple of years. She had married a good man, Florrie thought with satisfaction, watching the baby's eyes close tiredly, the little head of curls lolling against her breast.

May found it difficult to sleep. She had been up to see Tom Gardiner in Dublin at the weekend and he had brought her out to lunch and then a walk in Stephen's Green. They had seen the National Volunteers drilling, parading up and down as brazen as you please, and she had cowered behind Tom's back, afraid that maybe James McCarthy might be among them. But he was a big fellow now on the Supreme Council. He wouldn't be wasting his time drilling when he was probably giving orders to the wretches to conceal their weapons in a safe place until they got the word. Tom was convinced that there would be a rising soon. The arms were coming into the country from America and Germany, and nobody stopping them.

She shivered beneath the sheets as she remembered James's face the day she had left with Hannah, the hatred and the cold gleam of fanaticism in his eyes. Tom Gardiner wanted to marry her. But how could she with James still there, and she married to him? He could come and get her any time he wanted, and she'd have to go with him, for wasn't it against her faith to do otherwise? She relaxed a little when she thought of Hannah coming home. This time tomorrow night she'd be back in Annie's house, sleeping in her old room and her little girl, Peig, with her. Perhaps she could confide in Hannah, ask her what she should do. May closed her eyes, thinking that it was a pity she hadn't met Tom before James McCarthy had bewitched her. But then maybe she wouldn't have given poor Tom a second glance. God, but life was so complicated!

Christine O'Shea received word from Jonathan. The play had gone down very well, the critics all giving it good reviews in the New York papers. He was coming home, and she was to prepare herself for a surprise. He had met Hannah Benson and she was travelling with him and her uncle John Sullivan. They would be home for Christmas.

'I must first go to Dublin on my return home – but rest assured, I shall be home with you to tell you all my news as soon as my business in Dublin is completed!'

Christine handed the telegram to her husband. He scanned it quickly, then peered at her, a questioning look in his eyes.

"Well, my love? Do you believe in destiny now? Will you not interfere this time and let them get on with their lives? Do they not deserve it, after all they've both been through?"

Christine nodded sadly. "Fate has brought Jonathan and Hannah together again, and if it's meant to be, then who am I to say otherwise? I want them both to be happy." Robert O'Shea smiled lovingly at his wife. Christine was growing up at last.

Hannah and Jonathan stood on the deck of the *Elizabeth* bound for Cobh. John was in his cabin with little Peig, who was suffering the ill-effects of the sea and, after staying awake with her all night, Hannah now drank in the fresh sea air blowing across the Atlantic. The sun's heat was intense, beating down upon them as they stood close together, Hannah's head resting on Jonathan's shoulder.

"There is something I must ask you, Jonathan. Do you love me? The word had never passed between us before, and I must know, for there's so much hope in my heart."

His face was so close to hers, she could feel his warm breath, see a look of such passion in his eyes that she had to turn away, the naked longing between them overwhelming.

"I love you now Hannah Benson, have always loved you, and will love you until the day I die!" he murmured, pulling her closer to him. He put his hand over hers as they stood there, watching the bow of the ship splice the foaming waves.

Hannah's eyes rested on the signet ring on his finger, her present to him, the initials JM glistening in the sunshine. The ring she gave him? Should say so. "In return for the locket of friendship you gave me all those years ago – it's been a long time coming, Jonathan – and it's no longer just a friendship token". . . She knew it held the promise of a bright, new future together, just the two of them, and little Peig, with no obstacles marring their happiness.

"My mother and Annie will be meeting us off the ship at Cobh. Will you travel to Limerick with us?" Hannah clutched him possessively. Now that they had found each other agaln, she didn't want to leave him out of her sight. The wind had whipped a faint, pink blush to her cheeks, her lips parted enticingly.

Jonathan fingered the silver locket about her neck, his caress sending a surge of long dormant emotions through her body.

"No, my love. I must go on to Dublin. Hyde has organised a meeting of the Gaelic League." His voice grew tense. "The IRB are trying to take over, making it a political machine, and if that happens Hyde will resign. Damned revolutionaries! They taint everything with their one-sided bigotry!"

Hannah saw his face darken with anger, and felt a touch of apprehension. The country was on the brink of some great upheaval, something that would change the course of their lives, perhaps forever. Jonathan read her troubled thoughts and smiled reassuringly.

"Nothing will ever change my feelings for you. Our fortunes are linked together, for good or bad. A lady of destiny, and a man eager to do her bidding – a match made in heaven, don't you think, Miss Benson?" He looked at her teasingly.

"Oh, Jonathan, it will be so good to be home again, to

see how much things have changed!" She gazed towards the horizon, absorbed in her own plans.

This woman would never belong to him, he thought. She would never belong to any man. He wouldn't wish to change her. He was content to know that she loved him, that whatever happened in the future, they would never be separated again. He caught his breath as her beautiful face turned upwards to his.

"Don't ever leave me again, Jonathan, my love, for I'd surely die if anything were to separate us now."

He bent towards her, pressing his lips against hers, sealing their fortunes with a long, lingering kiss.

They were all waiting inside the harbour wall as the ship docked in Cobh. Hannah spotted her mother first, looking so much older than the woman she had left behind, the thin, anxious face scanning the travellers as they disembarked.

"Mother, Mother, we're here!" Hannah cried, clutching Peig's hand, the little girl bewildered as Hannah dragged her through the crowds. "Oh, Mother!" She flung herself into Peggy's arms and everybody waited, standing to one side, not daring any word or movement that would intrude on this moment when the love between mother and daughter was so touchingly on view.

Annie watched as they embraced, the old jealousy stirring in her heart. It would have been nice to have had a daughter like Hannah, to have partaken in such a tender reunion.

Suddenly John was by her side, his arm about her waist, his hand tilting her chin up to his face as he bent to kiss her. She smiled at him, her own darling man, and wasn't she the fool to be looking for things that could never be when she had the cream of men, the handsome, stalwart figure of her dear John? The cloud of despondency evaporated as suddenly as it had come.

"Is there nobody else going to get a hug from her ladyship? And her new brother-in-law standing here like a gombeen, waiting for her to take notice of him?" Martin Manley demanded, winking at Florrie.

The tension was broken. Soon they were all laughing and crying with happiness, tears running down May's cheeks as she hugged her sister, standing back in amazement when she was introduced to Peig.

"Well, if this one isn't going to be the spitting image of yourself, Hannah! Will you look at the hair, like an angel's, and those eyes!"

Peggy Benson held out her arms to her granddaughter a little hesitantly, for she didn't know this grandchild of hers. Maybe she was different to Florrie's young ones who loved to sit on their Nana's knee while she told them stories.

Peig looked at her grandmother uncertainly, her head to one side as she made a wary inspection of her.

"Will you look at the little angel!" Peggy said softly, stroking the little girl's cheek with a gentle hand. Peig reached up and took her hand, a slow smile spreading across the baby features. Peggy sighed with relief. There would be no barriers between her and her very own little granddaughter.

"You have travelled with Mr Mayhew, then?" Annie asked mildly.

Jonathan was just getting into a coach beside the quay

wall, and Hannah turned quickly, her heart thumping as she watched him leave for Dublin. They had decided on the ship that there would be no fuss made of their plans until a more suitable opportunity arose. It was too soon after Madeline's and Michael's deaths. Even though they knew they wanted to be together now and for always, it was only fitting that some time should elapse before they took any positive steps towards marriage. John had understood. She would explain everything to her mother and Annie as soon as they got to Limerick.

"Yes. His play was a great success in New York; all the critics are talking about him. He's a famous man now, and all the women falling over themselves trying to catch a glimpse of him, bowing and smiling at everybody in the theatre. Isn't that right, Uncle John?" Hannah darted a conspiratorial glance at him.

"Sure, he's the toast of New York, that fellow – and going places too. His name is mentioned in all the New York newspapers. Jonathan Mayhew, co-owner of *The Limerick Lamp* newspaper in Ireland, a prominent member of the Gaelic League, a man to be proud of, that's what I say!"

Annie raised her eyebrows. It wasn't like John to be so forceful in his praise of anyone, unless he was a person particularly close to him, or to the family – or maybe to Hannah? Annie turned an appraising eye on her niece. She was a picture of loveliness in her cream travelling suit, a white lace blouse ruffled becomingly at her throat, a little silver locket nestling between the folds. A mature woman now, lifelines etched on her face which added only to her sophisticated appearance. The years had been kind to

Hannah Benson, Annie thought intuitively.The locket, surely it was the one she had received from Jonathan Mayhew that Christmas before he had left for Africa? The Christmas when Hannah had nursed a broken heart because she thought there was no future for them together? After all these years, she still displayed it proudly about her neck.

"Have you something to tell us, girl?" Annie asked abruptly, an excited sparkle in her eyes.

"Maybe, Annie, maybe. As soon as we get home, I'll tell you everything!"

"Come in, then, little missy!" Annie put an arm about Peig as she helped her up into the carriage, Sean Og beaming down at them, now a broad-shouldered, strapping young man, doffing his cap politely at Hannah, while a self-conscious blush arose from his throat.

"Sean Og, I didn't know you there! Sure you're a man now, and I feel so old! A century seens to have passed since I saw you all!"

May's eyes were glued to Hannah, her face flushed with excitement, Peig leaning comfortably against her shoulder as the carriage moved off, beginning their journey home to Limerick. "You'll never grow old, Hannah," she said quietly. "You're one of the few who seems to have tasted Biddy Early's youth potion!"

The others laughed, but May remained serious. They had all aged in the years since Hannah's departure for New York. Maybe outwardly the changes were not noticeable, but inside, May thought regretfully, inside she at least had become a different woman. She lived in constant dread that James McCarthy would find her, drag her away from her family and friends and make her go with him to Dublin. She couldn't bear it if she ever had to go back to him again. She had told the priest in the confessional that she was living away from her husband because he had treated her badly. The whole church had heard him shouting at her, telling her that she was a disgrace to the married state and that she should go back to him. She'd sooner go to bed with the devil. That was why she didn't take the sacraments any more. That was why she wished with all her heart that something would happen to James McCarthy to free her from this terrible burden that was weighing her down every day of her life.

Hannah noticed the change in May. The spark of fun had disappeared, and in its place was an impenetrable wall of veiled silences and furtive glances. Florrie was the only one who remained unchanged, Martin Manley dancing adoring attention on her, their little boy laughing up at them, and the baby gurgling contentedly in Florrie's arms. Hannah smiled. Florrie seemed to be the only one on whom fortune had smiled favourably, at least where love was concerned. But things were changing for the better for her also. Jonathan would be back in Limerick within the week. She would once more walk down George's Street, his tall handsome figure by her side, as far as Arthur's Quay to hear the bands play on warm summer evenings with only the breeze from the river to cool her blushes. Hannah's eyes shone expectantly as the carriage reached the outskirts of the city, the boats in the harbour sounding their muffled sirens as though to welcome her home.

"Anyone can join the League, Jonathan. Irishmen, Englishmen, Nationalists and Unionists. It's not for me to tell them, 'Sorry, we don't want your kind in this organisation!'" Douglas Hyde looked helplessly at the angry face of his companion. Jonathan felt irritated. He was doing no good here, his arguments unheeded. More than anything he longed to be back home in Limerick, with Hannah, away from this aggravation. They were sitting in Tandy's Bar on Stephen's Green after a particularly heated discussion at the Gaelic League's headquarters. The Republican element had almost completely taken over the running of the group, Tom Clarke shaking his fist at the committee members, shouting that a "free" Ireland should be a Gaelic Ireland.

"There should be no room in the Gaelic League for outsiders," he had proclaimed pointedly.

Douglas Hyde had argued, saying that anyone who had a love for the Irish language and culture should not be prohibited from joining, whether they be Irish or otherwise.

"It's getting to be like another Republican outfit, a front for recruiting young men into the IRB," Jonathan said flatly. "Maybe I should get out now. How can I justify my involvement with the League to the Literary Society, who are mostly Anglo-Irish, and who now see me as becoming yet one more anti-British Republican? I never wanted to get involved in the politics of the country."

"None of us did, Jonathan," Hyde said reprovingly. "But whether we like it or not, we have a responsibility. The truth is there for all to see: the Gaelic League is being taken over, its members proselytised by fanaticism of the most dangerous kind!"

The atmosphere in the parlour reminded Hannah of the

long evenings spent in the cottage in Glenmore. John was sitting in the armchair by the window, his feet stretched out in front of him, the smoke from his pipe curling languidly into the air. From a distance, he looked almost like her father sitting there, and she wished fleetingly that the clock could be turned back to a time when life had seemed uncomplicated. But she had achieved all that she had set out to do, and now her future had never looked so promising, for Jonathan was finally hers.

Peig sat on the large circular mat on the floor, Florrie's two children staring at her wide-eyed as she pretended to feed her doll with a miniature feeding bottle, all the while talking and scolding. Florrie touched Hannah's arm and pointed in the children's direction.

"'Tis the first time I've ever seen them so quiet together. Little Peig has a way with her, for they haven't taken their eyes off her since she arrived!"

"It's good to see her so happy. I was afraid she'd find it hard to settle down here after New York."

"And you, Hannah, are you happy?" Florrie looked at her sister enviously. No matter how she tried, she could never hope to be even half as beautiful as her sister. Even her figure had started to develop a matronly plumpness after the birth of little Catherine. She was lucky that Martin still thought her the most wonderful woman in the world. It had its drawbacks, of course. If she didn't mind herself she'd be having babies every year – and two was plenty for the time being, at least.

"I have something to tell you, all of you," Hannah said quietly, looking about the room.

May raised her head from her book, and Annie and

Peggy stopped sewing, their needles poised over a complicated piece of lace altar cloth. John was the only one who didn't seem particularly curious to hear what Hannah had to say. He sat there, a half-smile on his lips as he tapped his pipe against the brass fender of the fireplace.

"Maybe I'm looking for your blessing, because I'm that nervous, and I don't know how to say it."

Peggy looked at her daughter, and recognised the message written on the girl's blushing face. She was in love. Peggy glanced uncertainly at Annie, unsure of her feelings. Annie's eyes told her to keep quiet until Hannah had said her piece.

"I met Jonathan Mayhew in New York when he was over there with his new play, and we found we still love each other, more than we ever did, and we want to be married as soon as possible!" She sat back in her chair, her heart thumping wildly. What would they think of her, Michael not twelve months dead, and already her heart was given to another man?

"Does he make you happy, girl?" Annie asked, searching Hannah's face intently. Both of them had had their share of heartbreak. It was time that they had the happiness they deserved, without anyone telling them whether it was fitting or not.

"He makes me happier than I have ever been in my whole life, Annie," Hannah responded quietly. "I loved Michael, but in a different way. He reminded me of my father, so kind and gentle, and so good to little Peig." She went to her mother and knelt before her. "Do you understand, Mother? Please say I'm not cold-hearted and indifferent! I've tried to be practical, tried to put him ou of my mind – even when I was married to Michael. It's sin, I know, but I couldn't stop thinking of him, wonderin what he was doing, if he ever thought of me the same wa I thought of him!"

She stopped then, unable to say more, but for a silen prayer to her father to let things be all right for them, le her mother not condemn her for thinking so much o another man so soon after Michael's death. Peggy drew Hannah to her and held her close to her chest, as she would a child.

"It isn't up to me to tell you what to do, Hannah, and if you decide to marry this man, then I'll be the first to give you both my blessing. I only want you to be happy and to care for each other, like myself and your poor father, God be good to him. We didn't have much in the line of wealth, but we were happy together, and that's what matters in the end. Aren't I right, Annie?" She looked across the room to her sister, who nodded approvingly.

There was a silence for a moment and then there was a miraculous release of tension. Everybody started talking together, Florrie putting her arms about Hannah and hugging her, May taking hold of little Peig, dancing her about the room, the little one bemused by the sudden commotion.

"And when are we to have the pleasure of meeting this fine man who has swept our Hannah off her feet?" Annie asked as John poured a glass of sherry for each of them, toasting Hannah's future.

"He'll be back from Dublin at the end of the week. I was thinking maybe I could invite him to dinner here, and Dr and Mrs O'Shea, if that's all right with you, Annie?"

"Splendid! Molly will prepare one of her extra special meals, and I'll get a bottle of the finest port, for Dr O'Shea I know is partial to a nice glass of port after his meal!" Annie continued making plans, Peggy interrupting her now and then as they made arrangements for the celebration dinner.

Hannah regarded May and Florrie, wondering what they really thought of all the excitement. She felt sorry for May, and the way James McCarthy had ruined her life. Florrie seemed to be happy and contented, her plump face full of motherly concern for little Peter and baby Catherine.

May and Florrie returned her gaze and all three smiled simultaneously, a smile from their childhood days, bringing back happy memories of all the plans they had once made, all the handsome young men who would be running after them, begging them to marry. They raised their glasses, May whispering in Hannah's ear, "Maybe this time Peig will have a real baby sister or brother to play with, instead of the doll!" Hannah blushed self-consciously. The thought of Jonathan's warm, eager body so close to her in the darkness of their bedroom, his hands touching every part of her body, making her come alive to his yearnings, gave her a feeling of such anticipation that her whole body tingled with desire.

The house was ablaze with light as the carriage pulled up outside the front door, and Jonathan stepped down. He turned to help his sister alight and Robert followed. Annie and John stood at the foot of the steps leading up to the hall door and welcomed them warmly.

"There's a chill in the air this evening, Mrs O'Shea! Come in and warm yourself by the fire and Molly will bring us some hot punch!"

"Thank you, Annie. It was so nice of you to ask us here tonight, and for such a happy celebration!"

Hannah and her mother waited in the parlour, Hannah nervously patting her already perfectly-groomed hair. On entering the room, Christine O'Shea had to stifle a sudden gasp of admiration. Hannah stood with her back to the window, the pale evening light silhouetting her dignified figure. Christine was looking at a woman equal to her own sophisticated awareness of what constituted a lady.

There was some initial awkwardness between the two women, Peggy Benson hovering in the background, knowing instinctively that this reunion between the two would lay the foundation for their future relationship. Then Jonathan came to Hannah's side, taking her hand and pulling her gently forward until she stood directly in front of his sister.

"Christine, I want you to meet my future wife, and your sister-in-law."

Christine smiled then, a slow, satisfied smile lighting up her face so that Hannah relaxed, returning her smile without inhibition. The tension that had marred their last meeting, when Christine had subtly pointed out that Jonathan was not the man for her, evaporated in the warm, friendly ambience.

"Hannah, a lot of things have happened that perhaps,

in my own foolishness, I was mainly responsible for, and for that, I'm sorry."

Hannah held out her hand and clasped the other woman's hand firmly. "All that is in the past now, and Jonathan and I have been lucky."

Christine looked at her, puzzled.

"Yes, lucky," Hannah went on, motioning Christine to sit. "We've both had good marriages, not ideal ones perhaps, but Madeline was there when Jonathan needed somebody to comfort him, and Michael stood by me when I needed his support. We will never forget their love, given without reservation, even when they knew their feelings could never be returned fully."

Jonathan put his arm about Hannah, and Peggy Benson felt all her previous misgivings fade away. He was a good man, just the kind of man who would make her daughter happy, in as much as a man could make such an ambitious woman happy. She went to him, kissing him playfully on the cheek. "I think it's about time these two were settled once and for all, don't you agree, Mrs O'Shea?"

"Without a doubt," Christine replied. "Next weekend, Hannah, we will have a party at our house to celebrate your homecoming. The whole of Limerick will come to view the happy couple, whether out of curiosity or otherwise, but who cares? It will be your night, yours and Jonathan's!"

Hannah could imagine what some of the ladies would say, whispering between themselves, commenting sagely on her distastefully short period of mourning. But Michael would understand. He had been that sort of man. "Take your happiness while you can, Hannah, for there won't be a second chance!"

She was taking it now. A miracle had brought Jonathan back to her. Damn the ladies with their begrudging tongues. She smiled to herself. She had finally earned her place at Christine O'Shea's dinner table.

On Easter Monday 1912 Jonathan Mayhew and Hannah Benson were married in the cathedral in Limerick. Hannah had asked May to stand with her, and little Peig, held tightly in her grandmother's arms, carried a posy of daffodils and lilies. Peggy wept openly as Jonathan placed the ring on Hannah's finger, the look of love that passed between the couple reminding her poignantly of her own wedding day. Florrie sat next to Martin Manley, a child on either side of them, sighing resignedly as she felt the stirrings of a third inside her. May held the long, delicate veil of Hannah's headdress, marvelling at her sister's radiance. That was the way it should have been for herself and James McCarthy.

Hannah and Jonathan went to Dublin for their honeymoon, leaving little Peig in the adoring care of Peggy and Annie back in Limerick. They were staying with a friend of Senan O'Looney's in Rathmines. Christy Rourke was a bachelor whose whole life was devoted to reading the volumes of books lining the walls of almost every room in the house.

"Feel free to come and go as ye wish," he told them. "Treat the place as your own!"

He may have been a bachelor, but he knew the significance of a honeymoon, and for the whole fortnight they spent in Dublin they rarely saw the man, just a brief glimpse of him in the morning as he banged the hall door on his way to his bookshop in Eccles Street, and again in the evening when he disappeared up the stairs and into his bedroom, closing the door firmly behind him.

His eccentric habits did not worry them. Their newfound happiness was so precious that Jonathan and Hannah kept it jealously guarded against any outside intrusion. They were happy just to be together, the blissful hours spent in each other's arms in the big double-bed in the front bedroom making them wish that their interlude in Dublin would never end. Hannah thought she had been blessed to deserve such happiness twice over, once with her own beloved Michael, who had taken such care of her and little Peig – and now with her sweetheart Jonathan, the man who had captured her heart before even she knew it, so long ago now.

Martin Manley sat in the small office at the back of the warehouse and looked thoughtfully at his visitor. It was late November 1913 and Europe was stirring with the rumblings of war, the world on the verge of a precipice which would catapult it into a whole new way of life from which there would never be a return. The man seated in front of him was a small, insignificant figure with heavy, bushy eyebrows.

"Well, Mr Manley, and what's your answer to be? I needn't tell you this order will be the makings of your business for as long as the war lasts!"

Martin looked doubtful. The workers in the factory would have no reservations about making army uniforms, but there was a fairly substantial Republican element in the city just waiting for an Irishman like himself to make the mistake of taking on the job of manufacturing British army uniforms. The offer was an enticing one, the money offered for the first batch way beyond his expectations. He'd have to discuss it with Hannah. She had a good business head on her shoulders. She wouldn't let a band of troublemakers get in her way if she had a mind to do something.

"I'll let you know by the end of the week," he told the man decisively. "I'll discuss the deal with my partner, and we'll not keep you waiting. You'll have our answer by Friday at the latest."

"The girls have no objections to making the uniforms, Martin?" Hannah asked him when she came to see him at the warehouse the following day.

"None at all, Hannah. Most of them have fathers and brothers, even sweethearts, fighting in France. They're delighted to think they could be doing something to help them."

Hannah thought for a moment, then slapped her hand decisively against the cutting-table. "That's that then. Tell the man you'll take the order. If we don't take it, then somebody else will. It will mean more money for yourself, and don't tell me you don't need it with Florrie expecting another child."

Martin's face broke into a delighted grin. "That's just what I thought you'd say, Hannah. I'll get on to him straight away."

A look of uncertainty crossed his face. "But what about any intimidation? If the Republicans find out we're making uniforms for the British?"

"We're making uniforms for our own, Martin. There's more Irishmen over there in France than there are here in Ireland at the present." She thought of James McCarthy and imagined what he was doing now in Dublin, getting ready probably for the fight of his life, organising gun-running brigades, hiding the arms in safe houses around Howth. And she thought of men like Mrs Flannery's husband, who had taken the King's shilling and gone to fight for the freedom of small nations he knew little about because he couldn't get enough work to feed his family and keep them out of the poorhouse. At least while he was away his family were well looked after on his earnings from the army.

"Tell the man we'll take the order, Martin," she repeated firmly.

May had gone to Dublin to spend the weekend with Tom Gardiner. The weather was unseasonably mild for springtime, with just a chill breeze blowing to remind them that it wasn't yet time to discard their heavy outdoor clothing. May, her cheeks rosy red from the breeze and a sparkle in her eyes, wore her grey fur collar pulled close to her face as they sat on top of the tram to Dollymount Strand, the fresh sea breeze tossing her hair about her face as she looked up into Tom's eyes as he held her hand in his. They got off the tram and ran along the Strand, May's bonnet caught with the wind, dancing across the wet sand, Tom running after it as it skimmed dangerously close to the foaming waves.

"Oh, Tom! Catch hold of it like a good man! I haven't another as presentable as that one. Oh Tom, will you look at the spray of lilies on it, drenched to the last petal!" May burst out laughing, and Tom stopped for a moment to admire her, her dark hair tossed wildly about her smiling face. She was the woman for him, the only woman he would ever love until the day he died. At times he would lie in his bed at night, and curse James McCarthy, wishing him dead, saying a prayer afterwards for his wicked thoughts.

"Oh, May," he whispered now in her ear as she rested her head on his shoulder, "is there ever a chance that some day soon we can be together, without McCarthy's shadow looming over us like a cursed torment?"

May looked at the normally quiet-spoken man in surprise. She had thought the same thing many a time, each parting from Tom becoming more and more difficult as he begged her to stay.

He might be years older than she, but as they lay together in the bedroom of the little flat over his shop in Grafton Street, his demands were those of a young man newly initiated into the exciting ritual of lovemaking. He never made her feel frightened, as James had when he had fumbled for her in the damp tenement room in Clanbrassil Street, the smell of stale whiskey making her stomach heave with revulsion. Tom's lovemaking was gentle, making her feel that she was the most precious creature on earth. She loved him with every breath in her body. If only James could vanish from their lives forever, she could start off on a clean slate with a good man to take care of her.

They sat on the warm sand, May's face turned up towards the sun, her eyes closed against the warm rays. A shadow fell across her face and she opened her eyes, thinking it was Tom. "Will you move out of the sunlight like a good man, and let me make the most of it before I catch the train home." There was a glint of brass buttons in the dazzling light, the green uniform covering the broad bulk of the man standing over her. A lock of dark, curling hair fell across his forehead, and as the sun went in behind a cloud, she saw James McCarthy's mocking face looking down at her.

Tom stood up, putting himself in front of May protectively, sensing the tension between them.

"Is there something you want, soldier? That's my girl you're looking at!" Tom didn't like the look of the man, his brazen stare as he eyed May from head to toe as if she was some hussy off the streets.

"'Tis all right, Tom," May said faintly. What possessed them to come to the Strand this day of all days? Sure didn't the whole of Dublin know that the Volunteers did their drilling on the Strand, and wasn't James the head bottle-washer of the outfit?

She had been so happy this weekend, last night one of the happiest nights she had spent with Tom. When he had suggested they go to the Strand for a picnic, she never thought that James might be there, might actually come up to her, as brazen as you please. Even with Tom by her side, she still didn't feel safe.

"Well now, she's your girl, is she?" James drawled lazily, catching a strand of May's windblown hair between his fingers, and caressing it slowly. Tom put out his hand to stop him, but James shoved him away angrily. "And did she tell you that she had a husband she walked out on? And a child? What about the child, May? My child? Where is he today, and you flirtin' with a man old enough to call your Da?"

May watched in horror as Tom swung for him, surprising James with a blow to the left side of his face. He staggered back, then regained his balance quickly. He was about to retaliate when they heard the sound of running feet, steady, rhythmic steps in unison, and a group of Volunteers approached, each dressed like James. He straightened his uniform quickly when they spotted him, and they held back, waiting for him at the water's edge.

"There'll be another time, old man. I'm not done with you yet, nor you, May. You're still my wife, and don't you forget it!"

"There's something you should know, James, before you go." She caught hold of his arm as he was about to move away, her voice shaking with nervousness. She wanted to see the look on his face when she told him, wanted him to feel something of the pain she had felt after the baby had died, the little white bundle in her arms. "The child – it was a little girl. She died a few days after the birth." She waited for him to show some sign of emotion, a sadness of some kind. Surely even a man as hard as James would grieve for the loss of his own flesh and blood?

His eyes were cold as ice. Not a flicker of emotion crossed his hard, unyielding face. "Maybe 'twas for the best. And a girl, at that. Sure what would I be needin' a girl for? Isn't it a fine strappin' young lad would suit me, somebody I could train to carry a gun and who'd be proud to call himself an Irishman!"

May's face turned pale. Her head began to throb painfully and in a moment she knew she would faint if he didn't go away, far away where she would never have to set eyes on him again.

"Come on, May. 'Tis getting cold, there's a good girl!" Tom put his arm about her shivering body and she drew close to him, thankful for his firm support as he held her until the tall figure of James McCarthy moved off along the Strand, leading the group of Volunteers. "So that's the bold James, is it?" Tom looked down at May and was filled with compassion for her. The face that an hour ago had been so happy, so alive, now looked the picture of death.

"I'll never be rid of him, Tom. Every time I think that things are beginning to get better, just when I feel I'm over the worst part of my life, he'll come along, just like he did today, and ruin everything!" She started to cry hopelessly, her thin body shaking as Tom held her, murmuring words of comfort into her ear.

"There now, my love, hush there. I'll always be here for you, never fear. He won't bother you any more as long as Tom Gardiner is around, I give you my word!" He closed his eyes, clenching his fists angrily. The fellow would get what was coming to him, one way or the other, even if he had to do it himself. He was surprised at himself for thinking such things. He could no more kill a man than he could leave May to the mercy of such a monster. But love plays strange tricks on people, making them do things they wouldn't have dreamt of doing before.

May didn't tell anyone about the meeting with James McCarthy in Dublin. As soon as she got back to Limerick she tried to put the whole incident out of her mind, concentrating on the work at the warehouse. The order for the uniforms had gone through, and the girls were working well into the late evening to get the first batch finished. The factory had come a long way since Hannah had first employed the three girls from the convent.

The years had been good to Hannah, her marriage to Jonathan seeming to bring out the best in her, her beauty not diminished by the years, her yearning to make a success of her business only intensifying as the restlessness inside her took hold periodically. She sat across from Jonathan at the breakfast table, her eyes shining as she told him her good news.

"Two more orders for uniforms, Jonathan! If things go on like this, we'll be looking for bigger premises, with extra machines," said Hannah. They would be celebrating their third wedding anniversary in a week's time and Jonathan, looking at her now, thought she had never looked more lovely, her beautiful eyes sparkling as she outlined her plans to him.

Jonathan halted her tirade with a finger to her lips. "And what about your promise to take things easy, Mrs Mayhew? Our quest for a baby brother or sister for little Peig – have you forgotten that that is a most enjoyable priority at the moment?"

Hannah blushed, and he reached for her hand, holding it in his firmly. "I know your work means a lot to you, my love, so we won't rush things, not until you think the right time has come.

Hannah smiled. Time enough to start a family. After

all, they had little Peig who was fast becoming attached to Jonathan in the most endearing way, her shy smiles completely winning him over.

In the meantime she'd have to go and see Martin in the morning. There had been some trouble at the warehouse over the last few days. Some of the girls had been showered with stones and called "British lackeys" on their way home from work in the evenings. They were frightened, and justifiably so. Most of the people in the city had relatives fighting abroad, and were proud of the fact that the factory was manufacturing uniforms for the soldiers. There were always the few, though, who thought that any connection with the war was a slight on Ireland's fight for freedom. They'd have to be careful. She didn't want a repeat of James McCarthy's dynamite escapade.

Florrie's baby girl was born on the stroke of midnight on Christmas Day 1915. Martin Manley looked down at his wife and his new baby daughter in the bed, wondering what had he done to deserve such happiness. Florrie sighed, cuddling the infant close to her breast, her eyes shadowed with tiredness after the lengthy labour.

"I think this much should do us now, Martin, don't you think? Or else we'll have enough of our own to run the whole warehouse without ever employing another soul. I'm not getting any younger, you know!" She added ruefully.

Ah well, she thought resignedly, lying back contentedly against the pillows, things could be worse. At least she had married a good man who thought the sun, moon and stars shone out of her! She wondered how long it would be before Hannah produced an offspring of hers and Jonathan's. Maybe that would put a stop to her gallop, she thought, smiling tiredly as she turned uncomfortably in the bed. Was there ever a woman like her? She didn't know where she got her energy from. Florrie closed her eyes, the infant nodding sleepily against her breast. She felt so tired, and now another little one to look after. Still, she wouldn't change places with Hannah for all the gold in the world.

Martin looked in several minutes later and found her sleeping peacefully, the infant turned safely on her side in the crook of Florrie's arm. He picked up the baby and placed her in the crib by the bed.

Midnight Mass was nearly over. They'd all be back soon to see the new arrival. He'd make a pot of tea and get out the bottle of whiskey for the men. It was a night for celebrating.

Hannah received a letter from Eily Mitchell in New York. She had married Tony Guardino, she was very happy over there and the business was going from strength to strength.

'The only thing I regret, Hannah, is that we have no family, not yet anyway. Tony is disappointed too, but he never says anything, for fear of upsetting me. Lately I've been plagued with guilt about little Matthew, and how I let the convent take him away from me. I should have put up more of a fight. After all, he was my *son!*

Hannah became troubled as she read the jumble of

sentences, the anger jumping out at her from every page. She was the only one who knew the truth about young Mat. He was Mrs O'Shea's pride and joy and already the makings of a gentleman with his refined, gentle ways.

This letter from Eily was unsettling. She read on.

'I am thinking of coming home for a short visit, just to keep you up to date with what's happening in New York, my new ideas for expanding the business, and to see can I trace my son, Hannah. The pain is just eating away inside me. Every day I wake up thinking, what's he doing today? Does he ever think of his real mother? Has anyone even told him about me?'

Hannah wrote back, her words almost frantic as they raced over the page, her thoughts in a whirl as she thought of the consequences of any visit from Eily.

"Think hard, Eily, of what you are thinking of doing. Don't rush into anything you might regret later. Your life is going so well now – what would be the point in raking up the past?"

Eily replied, and Hannah could almost sense the anguish in her words as they leaped at her from the pages.

She would save hard, because it would not be fair on Tony to pay her fare and her keep while she was in Ireland. All things going well, she was hoping to be home for Easter of next year.

Hannah was worried. Eily could make a lot of trouble for several people, most of all for Christine O'Shea and young Mat. She would keep the news to herself for the time being. There was no sense in upsetting people before it was necessary. Not even Jonathan would know the real reason for Eily coming home. Maybe Eily would change her mind in the meantime . . .

Jonathan had thought it would be impossible to be happy again after Madeline's death, and their little child's. Sometimes he felt guilty at the love he felt for Hannah, a love that had never really been extinguished even during their separation, rekindled again with such passion on their wedding day. Hannah had worked hard for her business, and it was now showing the fruits of her labours, her warehouses lining the docklands buzzing with the laughter and the whirring of machines as the orders came in even from as far away as France and Germany, her reputation passing by word of mouth from the most fashion-conscious ladies in Europe.

Peig was the apple of her grandmother's eye, and every chance Peggy could get she took her to the People's Park, proudly showing her off to all those who stopped to admire the little girl, who unaware of their admiration, sat on the grass making daisy chains, singing softly to herself.

On one of Hannah's infrequent afternoons off, while she and Jonathan sat on the grassy bank by George's Quay watching the first relay of boats of the summer regatta head off over the Curragower Falls, Peig in animated conversation with an elderly couple who were obviously entranced with the childish chatter, Hannah reached up to Jonathan, putting a restraining hand on his mouth while he looked down at her, smiling with contentment.

"You remember your wish Jonathan – that great wish of yours that we have a little companion for our darling

Peig" She looked at him coyly, nodding her head while he gazed at her disbelievingly.

"Your wish is my command, husband – our next wedding anniversary should see the advent of such a miracle . . ." He reached out to her, putting his arm about her, and the elderly man and woman smiled understandingly, remembering how it used to be in the first flush of such wonderful togetherness.

Jonathan had been working very hard during the early months of 1916, travelling up to Dublin and back, the atmosphere of unrest among the Volunteers the main news item in *The Limerick Lamp*. There had been another arms consignment in from Germany, and now they were openly distributing the arms among themselves, the army and the police looking on, as if they knew they couldn't stop the inevitable. "There's going to be a rising, Hannah," Jonathan had said to her only a few days previously. "Connolly and the Citizen Army have joined ranks with the Volunteers. There's talk of a big shipment of arms around Easter time. They'll not wait any longer than that. The atmosphere in Dublin is one of impatience. They're only waiting for somebody to give them the word and they're ready to fight!"

Eily Mitchell arrived back in Limerick in the springtime and Jonathan drove her from the station to Southland House where Hannah greeted her with cries of delight, marvelling at her appearance.

"Don't you look the elegant one with your check suit and the hair! It's so –"

"Chic?" Eily suggested, pleased at the look of admiration in Hannah's eyes. She patted the dark, gleaming braids of her hair affectedly. "Mrs Mayhew, don't you know that this is the latest style from New York? The sooner you get back there the better, madam, for I fear you're falling behind in your knowledge of what's in in the fashion world!"

She looked at Hannah's slightly rounded body, envying her neat figure in spite of her pregnancy. Her baby due in only a few weeks, Eily marvelled, and still her breasts were high and firm, not loose and ugly like hers had been when she had been expecting Matthew. Matthew. That was her main reason for coming.

She had tried to explain everything to Tony, and he had said he understood, his dark Italian eyes looking at her sorrowfully, making her feel guilty for wanting to see a child that wasn't part of him.

"I just want to see him, Tony, just to see that he's all right, that he's well looked after. I won't rest easy until I see him!" She had pleaded, and in the end he had given her his consent to go back to Limerick to put her mind at rest. "Maybe I should go to the convent. They'll know who has him. Maybe they'll give me an address where I might find him."

"You are so kind, Hannah, to allow me to stay with you – especially when I know you're not exactly pleased with my reasons for being here."

Jonathan had gone to the newspaper office and they were sitting alone at the breakfast table, Eily's breakfast untouched in front of her, her hands fidgeting restlessly with the hem of the tablecloth. "I am grateful to you,

Hannah, for offering me your hospitality in this lovely house of yours – and I'm sorry that I'm troubling you at this time about – well you know . . ."

Hannah looked at her, her expression sympathetic. "Eily, you are always welcome in my house – and you may stay as long as you wish – but I think maybe you should leave well enough alone. Mat is happy now. He has a good home and two of the best parents you could wish for him."

"Mat? His name is Matthew. How do you know so much about him?" Eily demanded, and Hannah could see before her the same girl who had confronted her all those years ago back in the warehouse, the sullen, angry girl who had come to her looking for a job. She hesitated. The Reverend Mother had sworn her to secrecy, and until now there had been no question of her breaking that oath. Christine O'Shea was her sister-in-law, and a dear friend. She couldn't cause her any unhappiness, not after what she had been through after Emma's death. Eily was staring at her now, her dark eyes suspicious.

"You know who has my son, Hannah, don't you? You know the woman he calls his mother, the woman who has looked after him since I foolishly gave him up that day at the convent. Tell me who she is, Hannah, because if you don't, I swear I'll find him. I'll search the whole of Limerick until I find my son!" Her eyes blazed with anger, and she stood up, her head tilted back aggressively.

"You'll make so many people unhappy, Eily," Hannah said quietly. "I'll arrange for you to see him, somehow, but promise me you won't do anything to take him away from this woman he thinks is his mother." Hannah pleaded with her, holding Eily's clenched hands between her own beseechingly. "She's a good woman, and she loves him so much!"

"And I suppose I don't love him at all! Is that what you're sayin' to me, Hannah Benson?" Eily cried wildly, tears running down her cheeks. "I've cried oceans of tears ever since that day they took him from me at the convent! I must have been out of my senses to give him up, and I'm not going to make the same mistake again!"

"I'll arrange for you to see him, and then you must make up your own mind about what you should do," Hannah said firmly.

It was the only thing to do. Eily would be persistent until she got her way. If she went looking for Mat herself, she might upset too many people, intent on finding her son with no thought for the consequences.

"Very well, but I'm making no promises, mind," Eily said sullenly.

The strained atmosphere between them was noticeable when Peggy Benson came calling at lunch-time, and after a few polite exchanges of chat, Eily said she was going into town to see how much it had changed since her departure for America.

"What's up with her, Hannah? Is it the business? It's not going so well?" Peggy enquired curiously. She didn't want Hannah to be worrying unnecessarily until after the baby was born. If Eily Mitchell had said anything to upset her, then she'd have Peggy Benson to contend with.

"It's nothing, Mother. The business is fine. She even wants me to think about going back there again."

"Glory be to God! Doesn't she have two eyes in her head? Can't she see you have a fine husband and a grand house, and little Peig just settling in nicely, not to mind that young one only waiting to be born!" Peggy pointed at Hannah's stomach angrily.

Stirring up things, that one was. The quicker she went back to her husband in America the better it would be for Hannah.

"Now, Mother, take it easy. I'd never leave Jonathan and the children. They'd have to come with me if I ever decided to go, and I can't see any likelihood of that in the near future. Jonathan is so taken up with what's going on in Dublin at the moment."

Peggy sighed with relief. Thanks be to God her daughter had sense. When the baby came along she'd have enough to occupy herself without thinking about going across to America again.

"Christine, I was thinking of having a little tea party here in the house on Tuesday afternoon. I'd like all the children to be there. Eily has never seen them and I'm very proud of my nieces and nephews, no matter how wicked they can be sometimes!" Hannah smiled at her sister-in-law, hoping she wouldn't read any more into her invitation other than a harmless invitation to tea. She felt so guilty that she feared Christine would surely see through her, would know that Eily was there only to try to take her darling Mat away from her. But Christine nodded approvingly.

"Of course, Hannah. It will be such a treat for the children, and the weather is so hot they can play in the gardens while we have our tea in peace inside. What a lovely idea!"

Hannah prayed silently that her plan would succeed. When Eily saw how happy Mat was, what a fine young man he had turned out to be, surely she would give up her foolish notion of taking him away from his home and family, the only family he had known since he was born? "Blood is thicker than water," she could hear Eily argue stubbornly. In this case, Hannah believed that the love between the O'Sheas and Mat overruled that argument. In body and soul, he was now part of the O'Sheas, and nothing Eily would say could alter the fact.

"What about you and I going to Dublin for the Easter weekend? An anniversary celebration? We could stay with Rourke again." Jonathan looked at her shamefacedly. "I must confess, I've already arranged everything, because I knew if it was up to you, you'd be down at the warehouse organising work orders on the first big holiday of the year!"

"But what about Peig? Will we take her with us?" Hannah asked.

Jonathan shook his head firmly. "Your mother and Annie will look after her while we're away. There are too many things happening up there at the minute, the Volunteers drilling at every street corner. It's no place for a little one, and I'll have my hands full trying to look after my darling wife!"

He looked in wonder at Hannah, for if he had thought her beautiful in the past, he was now convinced that no other woman could compete with her, even at this stage in her pregnancy. Her face glowed with a healthy sheen, the magnificent golden hair curled luxuriantly at the top of her head, her body more desirable than ever as it carried their child.

"Mat, will you pass around the plates, please? There are

some sugar biscuits and jellies for the small ones. See that they don't make a mess of their best clothes." Hannah looked about the lawn of Southland House, wondering what had happened to Eily. She had gone into town earlier, just before lunch, and had promised to be back in time for the tea party. Maybe she had changed her mind about seeing Mat, she speculated, a little relieved. She was just about to pour the tea for the adults in the house when Eily arrived, breathless, her cheeks flushed with excitement.

"Did you hear? The news is on the front page of *The Limerick Lamp*. Another arms ship arrived in Tralee yesterday. None of the Volunteers were expecting it, so the British scuttled it in Queenstown. I'm tellin' you, we're on the verge of a rising."

"Hannah, don't you think it's best to stay clear of Dublin this weekend, in your condition? Sure anything could happen!" Peggy looked at Annie for confirmation of her fears, and Annie nodded vehemently.

"Your mother is right, Hannah. It would be safer for you to stay in Limerick. We can have an anniversary dinner at my house, and Peig won't lose out on her weekend either. She can stay with us while you and Jonathan spend the weekend alone here." She winked at Hannah. "A second honeymoon is as good as a tonic, girl."

Hannah looked doubtful. She had her reasons for going to Dublin, besides her anniversary celebration. She wanted to see Tom Gardiner, ask him what were his intentions with regard to May. Since her last trip to Dublin, May had cut herself off from everyone, working from morning until late evening in the warehouse, speaking only when spoken to, and then only to murmur yes or no, much to Hannah's frustration. James McCarthy was troubling the girl. She would never be happy as long as he was in the background, his possible return to Limerick a threat to her peace of mind.

"I'll wait and see what Jonathan says when he gets home tonight," she replied, dismissing the conversation. She had other things on her mind just now. Mat had shyly offered Eily a plate of sweet cake, and she had stared at him for such a long time that he began to look uncomfortable. Hannah went across the room quickly, and put a hand on Mat's shoulder.

"Eily, I want you to meet this handsome nephew of mine, Mat. Mat O'Shea, Mrs O'Shea's son."

Eily looked incredulously from Mat to Christine O'Shea, sitting on the verandah, laughing and talking with Annie and Peggy Benson.

"Mrs O'Shea," she said faintly. She remembered now. The little girl Emma dying of the diptheria, Christine O'Shea locking herself away for weeks after the funeral. Eily studied her now, saw the way she turned her graceful neck several times during her conversation to look at Mat, the smile that passed between them so natural and full of unspoken love.

Eily's heart cried out hopelessly. She had lost her baby forever. This young man standing before her would never regard her in the same way he did his mother. She knew now that Christine O'Shea was his mother, the woman who had looked after him since he was a baby, her baby, whom she had given away because at the time there had been no other alternative.

"Would you like another piece of cake, Mrs Guardino?"

Mat asked politely. He had such lovely eyes, eyes as dark as sloes, a mop of coal-black curls falling casually over his forehead. Her eyes filled with tears and she shook her head, wanting to be away from this house, away from the memories, back with Tony again and his strong arms holding her comfortingly.

Hannah took her gently by the arm, asking Mat to see to the young ones on the lawn, and guided her through the hall and up the stairs to her bedroom. The bedroom door safely closed behind them, Eily flung herself on the bed and sobbed until she thought her heart would break. Hannah stroked her hair comfortingly, waiting until the sobbing finally ceased.

"Wasn't I the fool of a woman to think I could start up where I left off all that time ago. Sure the boy is a stranger to me, Hannah! And I can see from his breeding that he fared out better with the O'Sheas than he would ever have done with me!"

"They adore him, Eily. That's what I couldn't explain to you. You had to see it for yourself," Hannah said, full of pity for her.

"I'm going back to New York, Hannah. I can't stay here now. There's a steamer leaving the North Wall in Dublin on Easter Monday. I can get the morning train up from Limerick Station."

"Jonathan and I will be spending the weekend in Dublin," Hannah decided suddenly. She couldn't let Eily leave in the state she was in. "You can travel with us in the coach, and maybe we can do a bit of sightseeing while we're there. We had such a lovely time on our honeymoon."

"You must be out of your mind to think that I'd

intrude on the pair of you like that!" Eily looked up, wiping her tears away angrily with the back of her hand, her unhappiness momentarily forgotten in the absurdity of Hannah's suggestion. "I'll take the ride to Dublin with you, and grateful for it – but I'll stay in the Shelboume, not in some lovers' hideaway where I'd be demented lookin' at the pair of you making sheep's eyes at each other all day long!"

Hannah laughed aloud, and Eily jumped up from the bed, hugging her close. "I'll have my own Tony to make me forget my troubles back home – back home, do you hear me, now. I'm thinking already that New York is where my heart is – and maybe 'tis true, Hannah. I have a different life now, and I should be thankful I had the good fortune to meet a man like Tony!" Her face looked softer now, more relaxed, the eyes bright and mischievous, just like the old Eily.

They would have a great weekend in Dublin, Hannah thought cheerily. She was looking forward to it. The days seemed to drag now, her increased weight making it impossible to rest comfortably in any position. The weekend would perk her up and give her something to look forward to.

James McCarthy lay smiling in the darkness. It was a good time to be alive, this period of time would be forever etched in people's memories and in the history books, he told himself. There was going to be a rising at last, and Redmond had fallen into their trap, urging Irishmen to fight in France side by side with a country that had milked Ireland of its life's blood. No self-respecting Irishman would stand for talk like that. Now was the time for Ireland's glory, while England was taken up with fighting her battles on foreign soil. He felt the rising thrust of excitement within him as he anticipated the fighting that was to come. He looked at the empty space on the pillow beside him. He had missed May all these years. He had thought she meant nothing to him, but she had burrowed her way into his heart and, like it or not, he couldn't forget her. Maybe when all this was over, he'd start again with her. If James McCarthy wanted his woman back, he'd defy any man to try to stop him.

On a warm April evening James McCarthy sat in the back room of Dobson's public house. Three men were seated in front of him, their faces taut as they felt the current of anger directed against them.

"Jesus, what a mess!" McCarthy exploded savagely. "If it had been left to me, I'd have the rising over and done with by now, and none of this shilly-shallying that's goin' on! Orders given, orders retracted, like a crowd of feckin' schoolboys!" He pointed to one of the men, who looked away uncomfortably. "Didn't I give you the order to attack the Limerick barracks? What in the blazes are ye doin' down there at all?"

"Weren't we ready for it, and then we got orders from MacNeill that everything was called off after *The Aud* was scuttled. Sure, we're not the brains behind this outfit! How are we to know what goes on in your minds up here?"

The man looked sullenly at James. He had spoken impulsively, forgetting his habitual fear of this dark giant of a man. They were fed up with the carryings-on of the

Military Council. Orders were confused, men waiting in vain at railway crossings to unload arms that never arrived. It wasn't their fault that things weren't going according to plan.

"Now you listen to me, Sean Dalton," James McCarthy towered over him threateningly, his dark, brooding face filled with contempt. "You take the next train back to Limerick and you tell them down there that they're to be ready for an assault on the barracks, and this time it'll be my orders they'll be following, nobody else's!"

When they reached Dublin, Eily Mitchell booked in to the Shelbourne Hotel for two nights. "As soon as you're settled in at Rourke's place, come back into town and I'll treat you both to dinner. 'Tis the least I can do for puttin' up with me this past few days!" Eily grinned at Jonathan. "Did I ever think I'd see the day when I'd be hobnobbin' with the playwright and newspaper owner, his eminence Jonathan Mayhew – little Eily Mitchell from the slums of Limerick!" Jonathan laughed at her self-mockery.

"And did I ever think I'd see the day when I'd be entertained to dinner by one of the most impertinent women I ever had the misfortune to meet!"

After dinner, they strolled along by the canal, the heat of the day not in keeping with the usual spring weather of cool breezes and blustery showers. The weather had become more like summer in the last few days, and they sat on one of the benches, watching the barges for Guinness's Brewery being pulled along slowly by the dray horses.

The scene was a peaceful contrast to what they had just witnessed an hour ago outside the hotel, where Volunteers had scuffled with passers-by on the street, ridiculed by occasional shouts of derision. "Hooligans! Have ye nothin' better to do with yerselves than to be frightenin' the lives out of innocent women and childer?" The police had dispersed the angry mob, but Jonathan had felt uneasy.

He had been to the *Independent* newspaper office shortly after their arrival, looking for information about the unrest in the city. The editor had told him there was nothing planned for that weekend anyway, because Eoin MacNeill had placed a notice in the paper for the following day, notifying all the Irish Volunteers that manoeuvres had been called off. Later, as they sat by the bay window looking out into the sleepy cul-de-sac in Rathmines, Christy Rourke shook his head in bewilderment.

"It's like as if we're all sitting on a powder keg, just waiting for it to explode. No matter what MacNeill says, there's something stirring, and we'd all be better off in our homes until it's over!"

They spent a quiet day on Easter Sunday, Hannah feeling unwell because of the heat. They had their lunch in the back garden, admiring Christy's display of daffodil and crocus beds. The air was quite still, not a rustle of a breeze to cool Hannah's perspiring forehead. She didn't want to trouble Jonathan. It was probably just the heat and the travelling that were giving her such terrible pains across her back. Eily noticed her though. She watched her anxiously as they lounged in the shade beneath the elder tree, Hannah's pale face grimacing in pain.

"Hannah, is there something the matter? Will I call Jonathan?"

"No, Eily. Leave him be. He likes a chat with Christy,

away from the wagging tongues of us women. I'll be fine once I've had a good night's sleep."

"I'll take a carriage back to town and make arrangements for travelling in the morning."

Hannah began to protest, but Eily silenced her firmly. "Now, no buts. You and Jonathan need time together this weekend. I've been in the way, and sorry I am for the nuisance I've made of myself."

"Don't be ridiculous, Eily! Sure didn't we have a grand time together, and Jonathan enjoyed the break as much as myself!"

"I'll not argue with you any further. You look as though you could use a rest right now, so I won't be troublin' that husband of yours to drive me into the city. I'll order a carriage now, and I'll be back at the hotel before he knows I'm gone!"

She got up to go into the house, and impulsively bent down to kiss Hannah on the cheek. "I'll see you both in the morning, please God, and we'll have a drop of port and lemon to speed my journey!" She disappeared into the house, and Hannah remained in her seat, feeling so weary, a tiredness she never remembered having with Peig. This child was taking a lot out of her. Maybe it was the time of year. If only the weather was a little cooler. She laid her head back against the armchair, closing her eyes gratefully. Tomorrow she would go and see Tom Gardiner. She only hoped she was up to going back into the city again. The air was so oppressive in the dusty, busy streets. Her head fell sideways, and she slept.

Eily Mitchell woke suddenly to the sound of insistent

hammering on her bedroom door. "Come out quickly, whoever is in there. His Majesty's forces have taken over the hotel. You must evacuate immediately."

"Glory be to God, what's happening?" Eily whimpered, frightened by the peremptory tone of the man's voice. "I'm comin'," she called, her voice trembling. She dressed quickly, stuffing her clothes into the travelling bag, making sure her steamship ticket was secure in her purse. When she got downstairs to the foyer of the hotel, a group of confused residents was already there, some still in their nightclothes. She looked through the glass door and saw policemen lining the street outside.

"What's wrong out there?" she enquired of an elderly man sitting just inside the main door.

"It's the Volunteers. They're staging a rising. Nobody had any warning of it." He scratched his forehead, bewildered. "It seems the hotel is a good vantage point over one group of them holed up in the College across the way there."

He pointed towards the building opposite, and Eily could see the gleam of steel rifles in the morning sunshine, aimed in their direction. She shivered and crossed her forehead with the sign of the cross. Dear God, would she ever get out of this alive? Would she ever see her Tony again? And what about Hannah and Jonathan? It was a dangerous place for a woman to be in Hannah's condition. She was near her time, Eily could tell. The baby had dropped a good bit, and whether Hannah realised it or not, the child would be born well before her due date.

"You'll have to leave now, missus." A soldier came up to her. He was no more than sixteen, Eily thought.

"All right, just let me get my bag." She left with the rest of the people waiting in the foyer, stumbling nervously as she hurried past the row of hidden faces behind the guns in the College of Surgeons. She went straight to the steamship office, where she enquired about the noon sailing to New York. She was told it was cancelled until further notice.

"The Volunteers are all over the place! The GPO is taken over by Pearse and Connolly. There'll be no travelling in or out of the city until this thing is all over!"

The man inside the steamship office prattled on, his eyes blazing with excitement. "By God, but here's a bit of excitement, what?" Eily turned and walked away slowly. A carriage pulled up close to the kerb and Jonathan got out, his eyes lighting on her with relief.

"Are you all right? I couldn't get into the hotel, and the shooting has started without any warning to anybody. I must ring Senan in Limerick and see what's happening down there." He took her bag and helped her into the carriage. As they rode through the city, Eily could see the changes that had occurred since the peaceful calm of the day before. The Volunteers were occupying most of the important locations.

"Hannah isn't too well, Eily. I'd be grateful if you could stay with her for a little while."

"I have all the time in the world, Jonathan," Eily told him. "There's to be no sailing today. So I'm stuck here until either the British or the Volunteers surrender, if they'll ever do that, for God knows, one crowd is as stubborn as the other!"

The house in Rathmines was silent, only the sound of distant gunfire could be heard in the bedroom at the front of the house where Hannah lay in bed, the pains across her stomach growing more intense by the minute. Jonathan had gone back into the city, hearing rumours of unrest, Volunteers parading up and down the streets of Dublin. He was accompanied by Christy Rourke.

"I got in touch with Senan and he said there's nothing happening down there. It seems no orders got through to the Volunteers in Limerick, so they're on their own up here, and God help the lot of them. They haven't a chance!"

He had no time for the IRB's military campaign, but he had seen some of the Volunteers today, old men and young boys, their faces alive with resolve, their heads held proudly as they trained their guns on the target points. It was a pity it had come to this. What chance had they got against an army that was experienced in warfare, that had penetrated enemy lines in the muddy fields of France?

"You'll be all right, my love, until I get back?" he looked at Hannah anxiously. The pains had ceased momentarily. "There's no getting back to Limerick for the time being, so we'll have to stay put." He looked worriedly at her tired face, saw the lines of strain about her eyes. A picture of Madeline came into his mind, and he felt a shiver of apprehension going through him. If only they were at home in Limerick, Robert would be there to look after her. Surely it was too soon to be having the birth pains, unless there was something terribly wrong?

"Eily will stay with you, and I've contacted a midwife for the area – nurses are like gold dust at the moment with all the happenings in the city – and I promise you I'll only be gone an hour. I want to send a message to Senan before the Volunteers cut us off completely. Tomorrow's edition of *The Limerick Lamp* should carry news of today's happenings."

Hannah nodded, trying to force a smile, while Eily sat by her side, moistening her parched lips with drops of water. Jonathan left, still with the uneasy feeling inside him, determined to be back within the hour as soon as he had made the dispatch to Limerick.

"I think the baby is coming, Eily. I can't hold on much longer . . . the pain." She turned restlessly in the bed, her golden hair darkened with sweat. The woman at the end of the bed smiled at her encouragingly, her crisp white linen apron denoting her profession, her expert hands manoeuvring Hannah gently into a prone position in the bed.

"There you are, my love. Let's get you nice and comfy for the birth of this baby. Just one more push, there you are my love, good girl!"

Eily stood back to allow the woman to do her job. A vision of the nun in the convent who had attended her at the birth of little Matthew came into her head. This woman was so different, so kind, so gentle. The nun who had attended her had been so cold, so disapproving, not a word of comfort from her as she writhed with pain on the hard, uncomfortable mattress. The midwife turned Hannah over on her side gently, her hand going in circles, round and round on Hannah's back, trying to ease some of the hurt away.

"My only wish now is for Jonathan to come back safely, and the baby to be born soon," Hannah whispered faintly. "Please God, let him be born soon, for I don't think I can stand much more of the pain!"

At ten o'clock that evening, a small infant cry penetrated the silence of the avenue in Rathmines. Eily Mitchell, her face beaming with excitement, looked down at Hannah in the bed, and stroked her damp forehead gently.

"'Tis a little boy, Hannah, a little brother for Peig, and the face of an angel with those blue eyes and golden wisps of hair on his head!"

Hannah nodded, too tired to speak. A little boy. Jonathan would be so pleased. He already had his name picked out for him. John Peter Mayhew. If only he would come back from the city! She could see through the window as the gunfire lit up the sky, the sound of ricocheting bullets making her tremble for his safety.

"Can I hold him, Eily? I need to hold him. I want a part of Jonathan to be close to me."

Eily wrapped the infant carefully in the white cotton blanket at the end of the bed. She placed him in Hannah's arms, watching as he curled his tiny fingers about Hannah's, his grip firm and determined.

"There's a fist for you! The strongest and the most handsome of babies born this side of the Liffey tonight!"

"I wish he'd come, Eily. I'm so frightened! Suppose he got hit by a stray bullet?"

"Now don't you be thinking them things, *a chroí*!" The midwife sponged her down gently, taking off her sweat-soaked nightdress, putting a fresh one over her head and tucking the blankets firmly about her. "He'll be walking in that door in no time, and we want you looking fresh and lovely for him, and that little babby as well!" Hannah closed her eyes with exhaustion.

The baby in her arms started to cry fretfully as he

sensed her fear. Eily made a decision. She would go into the city, look for Jonathan, and bring him home safely to Hannah. The woman had been good to her since the moment she had walked into the warehouse all those years ago, looking for work. She would do this for her in return.

There was no point in looking for a carriage at that hour of night. Eily slipped soundlessly from the room while the midwife took up her position in the chair at the end of the bed. She had placed the baby in the little drawer of the dressing-table that Eily with her intuitive enterprise had prepared especially for him as soon as they knew the birth was near. Eily slipped quietly from the house, walking briskly to the end of the avenue. There was nobody about, all the windows shuttered, the doors closed firmly on any intruders. The trouble in the city had everyone in a state of apprehension, talk of looting and rioting mobs roaming the streets keeping them safely inside their houses.

She reached Grafton Street, her heart thumping wildly as she heard the sound of gunfire from the College of Surgeons, the Shelbourne Hotel looking battle-scarred after the day's fighting. It was quite dark now, and Eily was frightened. A bullet whizzed past her cheek, and she heard somebody cry out, "Get that woman off the street unless she wants to be killed!"

There was the sound of excited cries and cheers and as she turned, wild-eyed, a rowdy mob made their way from Patrick Street, armfuls of men's suits and other pieces of clothing, foodstuffs and washbasins clasped possessively to their chests. Some were drinking from bottles of whiskey, smashing the empty bottles against the ground as they converged on Eily, knocking her to the ground. She was going to die. She was never going to see Tony Guardino again, never lie beside him in the big feather bed in their apartment in New Jersey. They would have no children, because she would be dead, murdered by the angry bunch walking over her body as she lay still on the pavement. Even a bullet would be a more merciful way to go than this way.

James McCarthy tied a dirty rag about his leg where the bullet had pierced his flesh. The blood was coming in quick, hot spurts, leaving a bright red stain on the bullet-strewn floor. They were running out of ammunition fast. Damn the inefficiency of the whole feckin' lot of them! They hadn't a tinker's hope of pulling this one off successfully. He lit a cigarette, striking the match against the heel of his boot. He dragged at it slowly, savouring the moment, inhaling the smoke gratefully in his parched throat. He went to the window, cleaning a space in it to peer through to the street outside, and was about to turn away when he saw a bundle of clothes lying on the ground. Then it started to move, rising slowly from the ground. It was a woman, standing up now and brushing down her skirts, her hand shaking with terror.

As he stood there, she looked up into his face, a pleading look in her dark eyes. Eily Mitchell, after all these years! He was back in Mitchell's house once more, in the dirty back street with the open channel of filth running past the front door. Eily Mitchell was lying with him in the bed behind the partition that sealed off her bedroom from her Da's. He could feel her hot kisses on his body, could smell the scent of the carbolic soap she used to wash her hair every Friday night, long fat curls of dark hair brushing his face as he made love to her. She had carried his child. A feeling of remorse came over him. She looked so pathetic standing there, her face streaked with the dirt from the street, her skirts crumpled and stained with dregs from the whiskey bottles he had seen smashed beside her on the street. What he would give now for an hour with the woman who had excited and infuriated him like no other had since.

From the corner of his eye he spotted a quick movement from the top floor of the hotel, then a rifle held steadily, aimed at the street below where two Volunteers were making their way towards the College, one supporting the other, their faces caked with dried blood. Eily Mitchell was standing between them and the pointed rifle. James felt angry with himself, and angry with Eily Mitchell for putting him in this position. He couldn't let her die out there on the street. The past had a way of creeping up on you, hitting you in the face when you least expected it. He ran from the room, calling to the men under his command to cover him as he limped out onto the street.

"Get out of it, woman! For Christ's sake, make a run for it!" He moved towards her, all the time keeping an eye on the window above, the barrel of the gun aimed dangerously close to his head. He threw himself on top of her, and Eily barely made a sound, her whole body frozen in shock. She heard a loud, explosive sound in her brain, and closed her eyes.

"Oh, my God, I am heartily sorry for all my sins," she

murmured. She had been shot, she knew she was dying, the blood trickling down the side of her neck, something heavy lying across her body, pinning her to the ground. She opened her eyes, saw the dark curling hair against her breast, the blood flowing onto her white lace blouse. She screamed then, an animal-like cry of terror, as she realised it was the man who had come running out into the street to warn her who had been shot. She eased herself out from beneath the body, and only then noticed the bodies of the other two men, lying side by side, their arms still about one another as they tried to reach safety. She turned the man over onto his back and looked down, stupefied, at the lifeless face of Jem McCarthy. There was a muffled, rushing sound in her ears, then blackness, and she fell to the ground, unconscious.

"Eily, Eily, like a good girl, wake up now. I'm taking you home."

Jonathan bent over the prone figure, then looked up at Christy, perplexed.

"What is she doing here, of all places, at this hour of night? And what about Hannah? Maybe there's something wrong back at the house! My God, Christy, if anything has happened while I've been away from her . . ."

They both helped Eily to her feet, supporting her between them as they dragged her to the carriage. By the time they reached Christy's house Eily had come round, trying to explain what had happened.

"Never mind that now, Eily. I just want to see that Hannah is all right."

Jonathan ran up the stairs, and threw open the

bedroom door where a scene met his eyes that would remain in his memory for as long as he lived. Hannah was sitting up in the bed, her hair loose about her shoulders, a smile on her pale face. Close to her, sleeping peacefully, was his infant son.

"Jonathan!" Hannah held out the baby to him and he stepped quietly across the room, taking the baby from her. "Our son, Jonathan. Say hello to Master John Peter Mayhew!"

"I'm sorry, my love, for being away from you for so long. I should have been here, but there were cordons all around the city. Impossible to get through." He bent down and kissed her forehead, while she extended her arms, winding them about his neck. "So many things have been happening – all over the country not just in Dublin. Such terrible times, my love." She had closed her eyes and was now lying back on her pillow.

Jonathan remained silent. This was no time to tell a woman of the happenings in the city that Easter weekend. He had the baby's birth to celebrate. New life amidst such death and destruction. He stroked his baby son's cheek, and said a silent prayer of thanksgiving. The woman sitting by the bedside rose silently, giving Jonathan an encouraging smile.

"She's fine, Mr Mayhew. Everything went well and the baby is a healthy little fellow!" She left the room quietly, beckoning to Christy Rourke, who was standing gazing at the miracle of the little bundle lying sleeping in the makeshift crib, to close the bedroom door as Jonathan bent down to kiss his wife.

"Thanks be to God some good has come out of the troubles this night!" he said philosophically.

Eily thought swiftly. As soon as the cordon around the city was lifted, she could make her way back to Limerick and book a passage from Cobh to New York. Her close encounter with death tonight had told her how lucky she was. And Jem McCarthy had sacrificed his life so that she could go back to live with Tony Guardino and have his children. Maybe the man wasn't a devil after all. She'd say a prayer for his soul tonight. She wondered what May Benson would feel when she heard that Jem was dead.

Hannah and Jonathan returned to Limerick with baby John after the turmoil of the Easter Rising. Eily Mitchell had gone back to America, with a promise from Hannah that she would be over to see how things were doing in the factories as soon as the baby was old enough to be left with her mother.

"There'll be no travelling for you, madam, at least for another twelve months," Jonathan warned her severely. "I think you've had enough excitement to last you quite a while. Peig and baby John, and myself, of course, need your undivided attention now and we're going to make sure that we get it!"

They were sitting outside on the patio at the back of the house, baby John sleeping in his crib, a light mesh covering shielding him from the flies. Peig was rocking him gently to and fro, singing a lullaby, her likeness to her mother never ceasing to amaze Jonathan.

"What do you think will happen to the rebels, Jonathan? They'll surely not be executed?"

"I don't know. Maxwell is adamant. They're holding secret court martials, and the public are outraged. They want everything out in the open. If they are executed, then it will be the biggest mistake the British have made so far in this terrible struggle. They'll make martyrs out of the rebels. People are very sympathetic to the cause of men who have died so tragically for their country."

Jonathan's words were prophetic. As soon as the court martials were completed, the leaders of the uprising were executed. The bishop of Limerick sent a letter to General Maxwell, condemning him for his harsh treatment of the rebels, and Senan O'Looney published it in *The Limerick Lamp*.

"What did I tell you, my love?" Jonathan said to Hannah. "Yeats's words were never more fitting, 'a terrible beauty is born'. The rebel cause has turned into a glorifying requiem for the executed."

Hannah was becoming restless, her days spent at home with Peig and the baby tediously long and unfulfilling. She longed for the excitement of the business world again, getting orders out on time, organising the workers as she had done in New York, the frenzied competition between her shops and their rivals. Now that the order for army uniforms was well established, Martin didn't seem to have any further ambitions for the business, her suggestion that perhaps he might expand further into the country towns meeting with a gentle refusal.

"I'm happy enough as I am, Hannah, unless of course you want to change things." And she hadn't the heart to push him, because she knew he wasn't that sort of man.

She was just about to feel that the four walls of Southland House were closing in on her, when something happened that brought Jonathan home one evening, his face bright with enthusiasm.

"The Americans, they've joined in the war, Hannah! Senan has just got a cable from New York. President Wilson has called on the American troops to mobilise! What a time it is to be over there, in the thick of the excitement! What headlines could be written for *The Limerick Lamp*." She ran to him, his enthusiasm infectious.

"I think you're telling me something, my love." Hannah put her arms about his neck, drawing him close to her, the smell of orange-blossom in her hair like a heady opiate to his senses. "You want to be over there, talking to the troops, maybe even following them to the front, for you'll never get the feel of the army out of your bones." She traced the line of his cheek with a gentle finger. "And what about me, Jonathan? What would I be doing over here while my husband was dodging in and out of enemy lines, trying to get stories for Senan O'Looney to print in *The Limerick Lamp*?"

She shook her head solemnly. "No, no, my darling. I could never allow it, for a good and loving wife must always remain close to her husband, whatever the circumstances."

Jonathan looked puzzled. Surely she wasn't thinking of going with him, not so soon after the baby, not a year old yet, and there was Peig. This was her home, not wandering like a nomad from one country to another, on the whim of her incorrigible, beautiful, restless mother?

"Peig will remain here with Mother and Annie," Hannah announced. "She already spends more time with Annie than she does here, anyway, and I'll take baby John with me. He's too young to be left without his unpredictable mother and father!" She saw the look of uncertainty on Jonathan's face and her eyes grew serious. "I miss the buzz of New York city life, my love. I miss the thrill of bargaining with suppliers, heckling them for the last shilling, 'the thrill of the chase' I think you called it one time, more important than the ultimate reward!" She looked at him pleadingly. "Eily is determined to try for a baby with Tony. She wants to put the past behind her, and she says the only thing that will take the restlessness from her is a baby – a little baby she can love without any fear of it being taken from her. She has kept the business going for me over there – and now it's my turn to help her." The thought of throwing herself into the mêlée of New York business again excited her, and she already felt a tingle of anticipation race through her body as she looked at her husband expectantly.

Jonathan felt as though his life was suddenly out of control, this temptress of a woman was bewitching him with her wily coaxing. Senan had suggested he go over there to relay back to him accounts of the American mobilisation. The idea was very tempting, but he hadn't bargained on Hannah's insistence on coming also. He would never know where he stood with this woman.

"Life will never be dull with a wife like you by my side, my darling, darling seamstress," he whispered, kissing her urgently on the lips as she raised her head, a challenging look in her eyes.

"Does that mean you give your consent for me to travel with you, husband?" she asked innocently.

"What else can I do? You're a headstrong, determined

woman, and I love you for it!" He went to the table in the corner of the room and poured two glasses of brandy, handing one to her. "Let us drink a toast, my love. May our fortunes never be separated."

Hannah raised her glass to his, the glow of the setting sun behind *Knock Fierna* reflected in the sparking crystal as their hands joined in a loving, bright promise for the future.

THE END